CELEBRATE THE MOST ROMANTIC
TIME OF THE YEAR

Celebrate Christmas with six best-selling Zebra authors as they spin tales of holiday love and passion at this most romantic time of the year.

In these heartwarming yuletide tales, passion ignites — sometimes unexpectedly — against a backdrop of festive carol singing, stolen kisses under the mistletoe, and presents under the tree. As the handsome heroes and winsome heroines enjoy skating parties, sleigh rides, and starlit walks in the crisp, cold air, you will almost be able to smell the piney Christmas tree and hear the voices raised in holiday song.

So as the snow gently falls outside and the fire crackles in the hearth, warm your heart with the stories of Janelle Taylor, Carol Finch, Emma Merritt, Georgina Gentry, Jo Goodman, and Evelyn Rogers, and revel in the season of love.

Christmas Rendezvous

JANELLE TAYLOR
EMMA MERRITT
JO GOODMAN

CAROL FINCH
GEORGINA GENTRY
EVELYN ROGERS

ZEBRA BOOKS
KENSINGTON PUBLISHING CORP.

ZEBRA BOOKS

are published by

Kensington Publishing Corp.
475 Park Avenue South
New York, NY 10016

Second printing: November, 1991

Printed in the United States of America

"Kiss of the Christmas Wind" Copyright © 1991 by Janelle Taylor

"Circle of Love" Copyright © 1991 by Connie Feddersen

"Texas Magic" Copyright © 1991 by Emma Merritt

"Cheyenne Mistletoe" Copyright © 1991 by Lynne Murphy

"Tidewater Promise" Copyright © 1991 by Joanne Dobrzanski

"Cactus and Thistle" Copyright © 1991 by Evelyn Rogers

CONTENTS

Kiss of the Christmas Wind
by Janelle Taylor

1

"I'm sorry, Carrie Sue, but I have to leave at dawn, just as soon as it's light enough to see their tracks. It's my job; I'm the marshal of Gates." Thad Jamison stroked his wife's flaming red hair, mussed from the cover she'd worn while doing evening chores in the near-freezing weather. He gazed into her violet blue eyes as he continued, "The little Adams girl was shot during that bank holdup; I hope she'll be all right. And I hope you'll be all right, too. Lordy, I hate leaving you alone again so soon, but I have to bring those two robbers to justice and get that money back. Folk here depend on me."

An array of conflicting emotions came and went in her gaze. Carrie Sue's voice was strained as she replied, "I know, T.J., but it isn't fair. You've hardly shaken the trail dust off your boots since your return. It's almost Christmas, our first Christmas." Carrie Sue hung up the thick coat she had removed and draped her wool scarf atop it on the large peg. Her cold fingers tried to straighten her hair, but her husband grasped them between his larger ones to warm them. She looked into his smoky gray eyes. "This is the first holiday season I've looked forward to in years. It's my first home since I was a young girl and my parents were . . ."

Thad lightly pressed his forefinger against her wind-dried lips. "Don't think about the past again, love; it's over."

9

Carrie Sue moved his finger aside to refute, "Over? How can it be over when we're still controlled by it? My pardon was based on you taking this lawman's job and risking your life every day. It that weren't true, we could be ranching, like we half-do now. I'm sorry I got you into this trap. I'm ashamed of all those years I rode with Darby's gang of outlaws."

Thad didn't want to bring up her dark past again, but he saw how much it was on her mind tonight; her mood had been troubled ever since the rider delivered his shocking news just before dusk. Thad's first duty was serving as the marshal of Gates and the surrounding area; he'd been appointed by President Grant himself. If he'd been in town at his small office, he could have stopped the holdup and prevented a little girl from getting shot. But, having just returned from helping the law out in Fort Collins—north of Gates—he'd been helping his wife with chores she had done alone for over two weeks. He had been home less than three days, and now this . . .

But he couldn't let Carrie Sue blame herself for this predicament. He smiled gently and said, "I prefer to think of you as a daring desperado who had no choice in what she did if she wanted to survive. The Texas Flame is dead, love; you're Mrs. Thaddeus Jerome Jamison now and forever. You were trapped in that miserable life, with no one to help you break free."

She returned his smile and caressed his chilled cheek. "Until you came along, Mr. Texas Ranger, and saved me from myself and the law. There's so much I wish I could change about the past. It sounds crazy, but Darby tried to protect our victims from harm. Darby worked hard to hire only men who wouldn't kill except in self-defense. But he made mistakes where a few were concerned."

Carrie Sue snuggled into her husband's arms as she murmured, "I wish I'd never gotten involved with my brother's wickedness even if we did start off seeking justice. After the Hardings killed my parents and stole our ranch, I was just too stricken with grief and anger to think clearly."

Thad rested his cheek atop her head, his ebony hair a striking contrast to her fiery locks. "You were young and confused, love. Darby should have known better than to drag you into his bloody schemes, but I guess he was also hurting and too riled to think clearly. It just got out of control, and then it was too late, or almost too late. At least I got you out of that mess alive."

Carrie Sue Stover Jamison had never imagined she could love and desire any man as she did her husband. He had entered her life and changed it, had changed her, both for the better and for the best. *Almost,* her mind challenged. If only they could live where they wanted and how they wanted, they would be blissfully happy and safe.

Her present fatigue, the cold and snow outside, and her love's impending departure pressed down on her as a heavy weight. They brought back memories of the miseries that had ended this past July. "I was so tired of running and hiding, tired of being scared, tired of being shot at, tired of being pursued until I was exhausted or forced into committing violence in self-defense. I was tired of the loneliness and anguish. I hated to see innocent people get hurt. That's no way for a seventeen-year-old girl to be living, and I never wanted that kind of life. The Good Lord knows I tried to go straight many times, and so did Darby and the boys."

Thad stayed quiet and still as she went on, "We all wanted normal lives, peace, and safety. I wanted a home, a family, a loving husband. I wanted to ranch again. I wanted to be the Carrie Sue Stover I was before the Hardings destroyed my whole world. Those seven years on the outlaw trail were awful—the hot summers, blinding rains, cold winters, dust, and hunger. Finally I couldn't pretend to be hard and tough any longer. I wanted real meaning in my life. I wanted friends, not just other bandits. I hated what people thought and said about me."

She lifted her head to meet his consoling gaze. "Blazing stars, T.J., I was twenty-four and I'd never been in love, never been married, never had a child! I was galloping down the wrong road into a box canyon with the posse on my tail. Surely the Good Lord and fate sent you into my life, even if you did only want to hunt down the Stover Gang and destroy us."

"I never counted on the Texas Flame being so irresistible," he teased with hopes of lightening the somber mood in their home. He kissed the tip of her nose, then her forehead. He comforted, "I know how you feel, love, about us having to be apart at a time like this. I haven't had a home either since my parents died. It's been strange hotel rooms, or rowdy bunkhouses, or crumbling shacks, or sleeping on the trail. We were on different sides of the law, but we existed in pretty much the same way. I didn't have anyone special in my life. I was about to kiss thirty without a home, wife, and children. I didn't think much about them until I met you. Mercy, woman, you showed me how miserable and empty my life was."

He cupped her face between his hands and said, "It didn't take long to get to know the real Carrie Sue and to love her too much to see her destroyed. I hate to keep riding off and leaving you with all the chores around here. I hate leaving you alone for days and weeks at a time. Now that I've found you and have you, I can't stand being parted more than a day."

Carrie Sue read the anxiety in her husband's eyes. "If there's one thing you know about me, Thad Jamison, it's I'm a hard worker and expert shot. I'll be fine. Don't worry about me so much that you're distracted on the trail; that's dangerous, my love."

"I know you are, but I can't help worrying about you when I'm gone. Accidents happen. Outlaws roam the country. The weather gets crazy."

She stroked his jawline, which had darkened with stubble since his shave early this morning. He was so handsome and his gaze so enticing that it always stole her breath when she watched and touched him. How lucky she was to have this special man. As her fingers teased over his parted lips, she said, "I wish a blizzard would lock you in with me. A

12

fresh snow would leave you without a trail to follow."

Thad captured the mischievous fingers and pressed kisses to their tips. He wanted to lift her in his arms, carry her into their bedroom, and make love to her forever. But he had grave responsibilities staring him in the face and preparations to be made. "You don't want those outlaws to get away any more than I do. They were smart to hit the bank at dusk; they knew it would be morning before anyone could ride after them. They won't be traveling hard and fast, and they may doubt anyone will pursue them in this weather and under these conditions. I'll overtake them and capture them quick and easy. I'll make it back before Christmas."

Carrie Sue knew he might not be able to keep his promise, despite his impressive skills. The weather was unpredictable, outlaws were desperate men, and travel over snow-covered landscape was hazardous and slow. "Can't you take someone with you this time?" she urged.

Thad shook his head. He couldn't tell her that he didn't want to drag men away from their families during the holidays or out into the harsh weather. She would only respond that if he could risk his life and endure the hardships to protect their lives, they could do the same to assist him to end the matter swiftly and safely. So he simply said, "I can move faster without anyone to slow me down. I can handle two men alone."

Carrie Sue knew he wasn't boasting, just stating a proven fact. "I don't understand why President Grant insisted you come to Gates as the town marshal. There are plenty of towns and lawmen nearby to handle trouble."

"Too many of them have conflicts of interest, love. Most of them are battling over mining sites, railway locations, and ranch lands. Me, I'm unbiased, and well-trained with problem situations. With so much gold and silver and timber around, this territory is growing fast. Where riches can be made quick and easy, there'll always be trouble. Besides, no one knows us here; we've made a fresh start far from Texas."

13

"You mean, no one here knows me or about my villainous past."

"You're still being too hard on yourself, Carrie Sue. You're free, pardoned. Your past is over, done with, gone."

"As long as we do as we're told. My pardon was based on you marrying me, keeping me out of trouble, and resigning from the Rangers and as a Special Agent for the President *and*," she stressed, "on you becoming marshal of this town."

"I'll admit Grant gave me a way out of a nasty situation. I'm grateful to him. And I'm glad I'd saved enough money to buy this ranch outside of town. A man surely doesn't spend much of his earnings when he's on the trail alone. We have twenty beautiful acres in this valley, love, and forty more in the adjoining one. We're sheltered on nearly all sides by mountains from the worst weather winter could throw at us. We've got plenty of water, a cozy home, a big barn, sturdy fencing, winter feed, a few cattle and horses, food to last for months, and each other. It's more than either of us has had since childhood."

She reasoned in a gentle tone, "But how can we enjoy it, make it succeed and grow, if you're called away half the time to put yourself into danger? I'm grateful for all we have, but maybe I'm selfish in wanting my husband safe and at my side more. Some of those claims disputes get out of hand and bullets fly wildly. I don't like you riding into a den of greedy wolves alone. Gold and silver crazed prospectors could rip you to pieces just to frame their enemies. I feel like we're still paying for my wicked past, and we'll keep on paying for my mistakes until we're too old to ranch or you're killed tracking down countless outlaws. How many do you have to bring to justice before you've paid for freeing one?"

Thad ignored that question; to answer it would give away a special surprise in the making. "I'll be fine, love. You worry about me too much."

"Because I love you and I want you around forever. I have confidence in your prowess, T.J., but—"

14

"No buts, Mrs. Jamison. I won't be marshal forever; I promise. My belly's rumbling and our supper will be burning soon. Let's eat and talk about more pleasant things on my last night home. For a while," he added to remove the lines of fear that crept in around her eyes.

But his innocent statement shot through her body like a rifle bullet, wounding her deeply. What if it was his last night at home? In her arms? In her life? Every time he rode off with a badge pinned to his shirt in the names of Law and Order, it could be the last time she ever saw him. No, she commanded, she must not think that awful way! God and fate had brought them together. She reminded herself that they had more than most folk, so she must be appreciative and optimistic.

"You're right, my love. Now, get those wet boots off before you mess up my clean floor," she teased, playfully yanking on a midnight lock. "I'll put the biscuits in the oven and set the table. You can add wood to the fires. It's going to be mighty cold tonight, and you'll be up early."

Thad halted her departure. "What I need first is a hug and kiss from my wife to settle me down." He embraced her with mixed feelings—love that stirred his body and consumed his heart, and the misery of knowing how much he would miss and worry about her soon. He closed his eyes to savor the way she felt in his arms. She was a strong woman, a proud and loyal one. He couldn't imagine his existence without her, if anything ever happened to her. He wanted to be with her every day—working side by side, expanding, learning, enriching their relationship, and having their children. He no longer felt the urge to roam the countryside and to test his prowess against that of criminals. His heart was here with her, and his spirit at peace.

Thad's lips journeyed over her face, a soft terrain he had learned well since their meeting in April. Had it really only been seven and a half months since they'd encountered each other in that stage stop on her way to Tucson—with her making one more attempt to go straight as a schoolmarm and with him tracking an outlaw before concentrating on hunting down the Stover Gang? She had sent crazy stirrings throughout his mind and body, sitting at the table and looking so prim and proper while her heart raced with panic over his bold stares. He had only been overwhelmed by her beauty and appeal; he hadn't seen through her disguise as she'd feared. Thank God he had followed her and saved her life when her stage was attacked. Thank God they had both been heading for Tucson. She had led him on a merry and sometimes perilous chase, but he had captured her for himself, for all time. He had put his life, his job, his honor on the line to win her. Miraculously, he had succeeded; she had been pardoned by the President. Now, he would let nothing and no one harm her again.

Carrie Sue sensed the tension in her husband's body. She knew part of it was the result of her digging up the past tonight. She wished she could forget it, but things sometimes triggered memories she couldn't suppress. But it was wrong to send her husband away on a dangerous mission with a troubled mind. Christmas was approaching, as was the new year of 1877. It was time to bury her dark past for good. It was time to look to their bright future.

"I love you, T.J.," she murmured, then sought his lips with hers. Her hands caressed his strong back and she nestled closer against him. He always made her feel safe and happy in his arms. She adored him. She would give her life to save his. She could hardly wait until Christmas to give him her special gift . . .

"I love you, Carrie Sue," he responded when their lips parted. "I'll return soon. Don't worry, love."

"You know I will, just like you'll worry about me. If we ever stop worrying about each other, that's when we both should worry most."

They shared laughter at her jesting tone. Both relaxed, hugged again, then separated. Carrie Sue went into the kitchen to complete their evening meal. Thad removed his damp boots and slipped on the thick woolen socks she'd bought him in Denver, south of Gates and their ranch.

While Carrie Sue worked, Thad added wood to the fires

in the kitchen, parlor, and bedroom to keep the house warm for earlier than usual rising. He liked this house as much as she did, and they were lucky to find it and be able to afford the ranch. The home was cozy, but not too small. It was well-built to keep in heat and to keep out the Colorado cold.

When Mr. Carnes had sold it to them before returning East, the widower had left all his furniture behind, wanting no reminders of the beloved wife who had shared it with him for only a year. Carnes had been so taken with them that he had given Thad a wonderful deal on the ranch.

The house was set in a group of hardwoods that sheltered it from brisk winds. A large barn was nearby to ease chores during the worst of winter. There was a well close to the house, and a stream ran from one end of the mountain-protected valley to the other, supplying plenty of water for man and beast, when Thad was ready to buy their small herd.

Upon their arrival in late July, the meadow had been adorned with colorful wildflowers and verdant grass. The valley, foothills, and mountains had been green with pine, spruce, birch, oak, elder, cottonwood, willow, and aspen. During autumn, they had watched the leaves of hardwoods turn to blazing shades, then fall to leave the branches bare in ghostly freedom and ready for their cloaks of white. Now only the green of pine, spruce, and a few others could be seen through blankets of snow and ice which often over-burdened and broke their limbs.

It was cold this time of year and this far north—in the thirties most days and dipping into the teens at night—but the coldest and worst weather would come in January and February. He dreaded walking his horse in the snow and over frozen ground, then trying not to freeze at night in a bedroll alone near a camp fire that would almost refuse to burn. He wondered how he had ever learned to ignore such hardships during his years on the trail, only to lose that ability after a five-month marriage. With luck and prayers, he would catch those outlaws fast and get back into his cozy home and into his wife's warming arms.

Careful, he warned himself, *you have to be careful; these two men are dangerous. Jake Sawyer and Slim Reeves enjoy killing.*

Thad glanced into the kitchen at his busy and humming wife. He hadn't told her he knew from descriptions who had robbed the Gates Bank. Sawyer and his friend were well-known in the nearest states. Carrie Sue had heard of them, and it would frighten her to learn who he was pursuing. Maybe it was wrong to keep a secret from her, but he felt it was best. Maybe she sensed he was withholding something or perceived his unusual tension and that's what triggered her bad memories tonight. He wanted to keep his lawman's work separate from his ranch life and family; he never wanted her drawn into those kinds of situations again. He wanted to protect her from perils and from unhappi—

The redhead called out, "Supper's ready, Marshal Jamison. Let's eat, so I can help you pack. I want to make sure you leave with a full belly and warm body. Then you'll work harder to get back fast to all you have here."

Marshal Thad Jamison joined his wife at the kitchen table. He eyed the venison she had sprinkled with spices and roasted slowly for hours; its aroma caused his mouth to water in anticipation of each tender bite. Fragrant coffee gave off rising steam to say it was too hot to drink swiftly or carelessly. Green beans and corn from canning jars did the same, and catshead biscuits released wispy white warnings to grasp them carefully.

Thad served his plate. Following a few bites of each, he remarked, "You're a great cook, woman. I'm gonna miss this fare while I'm gone."

"Not at first. I'll wrap leftovers for you to take on your journey. Even in your saddlebag, they'll freeze and stay good for days on the trail. I just hope you can get a fire going hot enough to thaw and warm them. You have to make certain you stay nourished and strong."

18

"What would I do if I didn't have you to take care of me?"

"Thanks, Marshal, but you did fine before you met me. You can tend yourself better than most men I know. I'm glad, because you help me around the house as much as I help you around the ranch."

"We make good partners, love. But you do more than your share around here. It won't always be this one-sided, Carrie Sue."

She didn't bite her biscuit until she said, "I don't mind. In fact, I love having a home and ranch to tend. I can hardly wait until we get our cattle next summer. We can't do much with the three head we have."

Thad stopped cutting his meat and looked at her. "I hate to buy cattle until I'm around more to help you. Maybe we should wait a while longer."

"A small herd isn't much trouble, and we need to get started raising them; they take years to mature for selling. All they'll do next summer is graze in the pasture and drink water from the stream. I can tend our chickens and milk our cow without any help. I can take care of the garden, too, after I get it planted in the spring. Don't forget, my love, I lived and worked on a ranch before I became an out-law. I remember all my parents taught me. I'll put it to good use on our land and in our home."

"Our land and our home," he echoed. "I love the sound of those words. You are a hard worker, woman, and a smart one. With my job keeping me away so much, we were lucky that Carnes left us in good shape. There were no re-pairs to be done, and no heavy work until we expand."

Carrie Sue glanced around the kitchen. "It is a beautiful and strong home, T.J. We'll have a good life here." She didn't want to think about why Carnes had sold out and left—the death of his mate. She didn't want to think it could be the same for her one dark day. "We cut plenty of firewood to last until spring. We have enough supplies and feed for the stock and chickens. There's not much work in the winter, so I'll be fine alone. All I have to do while you're

19

gone is tend the animals and sew."

"You be careful going out on icy ground. And make sure you're bundled up in case you take a fall. You could freeze out there before I returned."

Carrie Sue vowed to be extra cautious during her husband's absence, as she had more than the animals and herself to protect. She was chomping at the bit to reveal her pregnancy, but she wanted it to be a surprise at Christmas, especially with him leaving on a dangerous mission that required his full attention. Too, she remembered how disappointed they were to discover she wasn't carrying their child when they left Waco in July, as they'd believed. She had waited this time until she was positive it was true. *A baby, our baby . . . A real family. It will be wonderful, perfect.*

After they finished eating, Thad helped his wife clear the table. While Carrie Sue washed the dishes, he dried them. He enjoyed being around her and helping her any time he could. She was good company. She made him laugh, smile, and feel wonderful. That was something else he missed whenever he was away from her and home. He liked hearing her talk about their future with such excitement and joy. She was right; they needed to get their herd going next spring. If things worked out as he hoped, he'd be around more after next summer to be a real partner in their marriage and ranch. Once children started coming along, and he dearly wanted them, he couldn't leave all the work and responsibilities in her lap, as he'd been forced to do since their arrival here. He was a damn lucky man to have a wife like Carrie Sue, and he would not let her work herself into exhaustion or an early grave while he chased criminals all over Colorado and farther!

She pulled the damp cloth from his tight grasp. "That's all, T.J. You best start packing while I put away the food. I'll be in to help you soon."

Thad kissed her cheek and left before he was tempted to risk all they had by refusing to chase Sawyer and Reeves, and by telling the authorities what they could do with their demanding and dangerous job! He couldn't, because he was a man of honor, and he'd given his word to be marshal here. What he hadn't thought to ask was how long it would take to satisfy his debt?

He'd taken this job with good intentions, even thought he'd enjoy it and need it; but he didn't. Not once after he'd moved here and gotten a taste of what he'd been missing all his life. He'd worked ranches on undercover assignments, but he'd never owned one. He'd never been married, never been in love. He hadn't known he would want only his wife, home, and ranch in such a short time. He hadn't known he would resent every time he was compelled to leave them behind. He had believed it would take longer to settle down, to change his life-style completely.

Carrie Sue had made the difference. Together they had made this ranch theirs, down to the rocking *J* on the wooden arch that spanned the road onto their land. They had their future brand on a post; now, he wanted it on cattle and horses. The few they owned still carried Carnes's boxed *C* mark. He wanted to do the heavy chores while she tended the house and children. He wanted to be at her side every night. He wanted to be with her on holidays, not miss them as he had Thanksgiving because miners were squabbling over claims and killing off each other on the Big Thompson River, which wasn't even his territory, but he'd been called in to assist the authorities there. He wanted his feet firmly planted on his land, their land, where his heart now belonged.

Carrie Sue entered the room. "How's it coming, T.J.?"

His smokey gray eyes looked up from the task his hands were doing. "I'm about finished," he replied in a somber tone.

"You get everything you'll need? She glanced at the things he'd laid out to make certain he'd be warm in the freezing weather.

"Yep," he responded, then stuffed the items into saddlebags. "I cleaned my weapons after my return, so they're ready for use again. The rest of my gear is in the barn. I'll get it in the morning."

21

"I have your supplies prepared. The food from supper's on the back porch to prevent spoiling. Your two canteens are filled and on the table." As usual, she'd send him off with a full stomach of scrambled eggs, hot biscuits, invigorating coffee, and fried meat. Accustomed to cooking and tending himself on the trail, he wouldn't have any trouble with meals, unless wood was too wet to burn.

"Thanks, love." Thad walked into the parlor and sat his possessions beside the door. He put his gun belt of double holsters with two Frontier Colts, his '73 lever-action Winchester rifle, and knife-in-sheath atop them. His bedroll, slicker, and extra blanket were in the barn with his saddle. It wouldn't take him long at first light to finish his tasks to leave. *Leave,* Lordy how he had come to resent that word and action. Deep inside, maybe he was hoping for a blizzard to strike so he wouldn't have to go. It wouldn't, and he would. But the sooner he did, the sooner he could return.

"We'd best turn in, love. It's getting late. I feel like I'm heading for prison instead of —" He halted when he saw the effect of that rash word on his wife. "I'm sorry, love."

"Don't be, T.J. You don't have to watch every word you say to me. I wonder how Darby's doing," she murmured. "Sometimes I feel guilty about him being in prison and me being free."

"I'm responsible, love, but it had to be done."

"I don't blame you, T.J. If you hadn't captured my brother, some other lawman would have, and he could have been killed. Or worse, a bounty hunter could have gotten to him, to us, first. They have no mercy. The Stover Gang had to be stopped, and you were assigned to do it."

Thad reminded, "His trial went well. He had a good lawyer and a strong defense. It was proven many of the charges against him and the gang weren't true. Few people had been hurt during his crimes, especially by him. He was lucky on that count, considering he was an outlaw for seven years. That trait went strong in his favor. Besides, all the money from his last job was recovered. If you'll remember, the newspapers and public almost made a hero

22

of him, a gentleman bandit, a real western legend."

"Those interviews and stories your friend Bill ran helped a lot. So did those telegrams from the Texas Governor and President to remind the court those violent deeds were frames by the Hardings."

"I think everyone realized there were mitigating circumstances for all of you becoming and staying outlaws. The way his lawyer presented his case, he had the court and public on Darby's side. The crowd was screaming for a pardon, but the judge knew that was impossible; Darby will have to serve those fifteen years. Nearly six months is gone already. Before you know it, he'll be out and starting fresh somewhere."

"That was kind of you to tell him he could come here when he's freed. He'll need help. Besides, the judge did say there was a possibility of an early parole if the right things happened, whatever that means. East Texas just seems so far away. I wish I could visit him."

"He wouldn't want you to see him in a place like that, no man would."

"I wonder if Sally is still waiting for his release."

Both reflected on the saloon girl that Darby loved and who loved Darby Stover and had sworn she would wait for him, even though Darby had told her not to do so.

"I sent his letter to her in San Angelo, but I doubt she'll take heed to it. From what I've learned since meeting you, woman, love is too powerful to be destroyed or denied. She'll wait for him."

"I'm glad. I'm also glad she quit the saloon and is working for that seamstress. That tells how much Darby changed her."

"Love changed her, Carrie Sue, just like it changed us. How else would a Texas Ranger and Special Agent wind up with the Texas Flame? Or a beautiful and daring desperado yield to a persistent lawman on her tail?"

She jested, "Because we're both irresistible, of course."

Thad swept her into his arms and carried her into the other room. He placed her feet on the floor near the bed. "I love you, Carrie Sue Stover Jamison, and I need you," he said in a husky voice.

"I love you and need you, Marshal Thaddeus Jerome Jamison." She unbuttoned his shirt and peeled it off his broad shoulders. She spread kisses on the bronzed surface. She removed her dress and undergarments, then pressed her silky flesh against his. She gazed into his eyes and challenged, "Why don't you capture me again tonight, Mister Lawman?"

He discarded the rest of his clothes and accepted the heady inducement. He covered their naked bodies with the quilt and her lips with his. This was one trail he would never tire of riding . . .

On December eighteenth, one week before Christmas, the couple rose while it was still dark outside to send Marshal Jamison on his way.

With a delicious breakfast under his belt, Thad saddled his horse, a black stallion named Nighthawk. He and the animal sent bursts of white, hot breath into the frigid air from their mouths and nostrils. The frozen ground crunched beneath boots and hooves during their movements and tried to imprison them in the depressions made. A dense bluish haze concealed the ridges that nearly surrounded his ranch. He hoped the lighter one on his level would lift as the day continued, as he needed good visibility for his pursuit. The ground was white, as were many ice-encased limbs. Most evergreens attempted to expose as much color as they could beneath their tattered cloaks of ivory. It was a wild and rugged land, but beautiful and challenging.

Carrie Sue watched her husband tie bedroll, blankets, and slicker into place near the hand-tooled bags that held his garments. Two canteens and supply sacks hung from his pommel. His Winchester was in a leather holder on his saddle, and his Colts were strapped around his waist. The knife-in-sheath was secured near his calf, in easy and quick reach when needed.

She knew her cheeks were as red and her nose as numb as Thad's were. Both were bundled up, but the Colorado cold and wind still seemed to find little places to sneak up on her body. Beneath gloves, her hands felt stiff and frozen, and she was certain his were too. The redhead shuddered and blinked as northern gusts dipped into the valley, tugging at her clothes and lashes. She glanced at the narrow scarf around Thad's head and beneath his hat to make sure his ears and neck were protected.

"Don't push yourself, T.J., trying to return fast. Keep a sharp eye on the weather; you don't want it as an enemy too. Guard your back, my love."

Thad pulled her against him. Their misty respirations blended as they gazed into each other's eyes. Their mouths meshed and they shared a soulwrenching and body-stirring kiss. They embraced tightly.

"I'll be careful, love. Get back inside and get warm. I'll see you soon."

They parted for Thad to mount. Their gazes locked once more for a brief moment, gazes that revealed their love and concern for the other.

"Goodbye, Carrie Sue. Stay safe, woman."

"Goodbye, T.J. I love you."

"I love you, too. Now get inside. I'm gone."

But the redhead watched her husband ride toward the opening between two ridges to begin his journey away from their home. She knew she would spend her days watching for him to reappear and praying for his survival, and spend her nights missing him beside her.

Carrie Sue knew she was skilled and tough enough to ride with him, and if she weren't pregnant, she would have insisted on helping him. He had told her he wouldn't stay gone more than two weeks. If he did, she would risk going to search for him. But two weeks meant missing . . .

Christmas was a time for lovers and families to be together. It was a time for loving and sharing, and for being grateful. Yet the only gift she wanted this year was her love back with her. She didn't want him to feel the kiss of the dark and dangerous night wind alone. She wanted them to be kissed by the joyous Christmas wind together, this year and for countless ones to come.

Would he make it home in a week? Alive and unharmed?

2

Carrie Sue gathered the eggs, but left their chickens penned up because of cold weather. She tossed feed on the coop floor and gave them fresh water. She fastened the gate, used cleansing snow to scrape chicken-do from her boots, and trudged back to the house. She placed the basket on the table and lifted a milk pail, not wanting to risk carrying too much while she traversed the frozen and often slippery ground.

The redhead went to the barn. She opened the stall doors to let the three steers and other horses roam the snow-covered ground if they needed or wanted exercise today. Cautiously she climbed the ladder into the loft, opened a small door, and tossed down hay for the stock to eat. She closed and bolted the door, then laid aside the pitchfork. With care again, she descended the ladder to the wooden section of the floor.

Carrie Sue went outside to break up an impenetrable surface in the water trough so the animals could drink. As she did so, the heavy iron tool sent echoes across the quiet landscape of breaking ice. As each blow landed, white shards shot in many directions in protest of being disturbed. She was glad the thick trough didn't allow the entire contents to freeze solid from top to bottom. Later in the winter, it would. Then, she'd have to draw fresh water for the animals from the nearby well each day.

Strong and lithe, she was able to manage the task. She returned the tool to its place, shivering as cold attacked her body through her garments. She closed the barn door to keep as much frigid wind out as possible while she milked the cow. She talked softly to the animal as she placed a short stool near its back legs. She hated to remove her gloves, but she had to do so to get a grip on the cow's teats. She kept speaking in a mellow tone as she worked as fast as her stiff fingers allowed.

When she finished, Carrie Sue moved the pail so the cow wouldn't knock it over if she changed positions. She put away the stool, replaced her gloves, and fed the animal. It would be left inside for its own safety. In a day or two, she would need to shovel its stall to prevent a foul stench from building up in the barn.

Carrie Sue lifted the full pail and left the barn, making her way to the house with great care. She didn't want a fall to injure her or the baby. With doors locked and safely back inside her home, the pail joined the egg basket on the kitchen table.

She removed her coat and scarf, then hung them on their peg. She pulled off her gloves and stuffed them into her coat pocket. She changed from work boots into house shoes. She went to the parlor fire to warm and loosen her fingers. As the heat worked on her hands and body, Carrie Sue relaxed and savored the luxury her husband was missing. She knew Thad wouldn't be warm and comfortable until he entered this house again.

At least for a while, she would have chores to distract her from constant worry about her love. There was milk to be churned into butter. There were animals and chickens to be tended. There were fires to be fed. There was cleaning to be done. Warming water to wash clothes and doing that task would require many hours, especially when she included ironing. She also had some mending and sewing to take up more time.

Yet there were other important things to do. She needed to visit the Adams, perhaps take little Lucy some cookies and a handmade doll. If the weather was good tomorrow, she would do just that without putting herself or their child into danger.

She would have privacy to finish the shirt she was making for Thad for Christmas. As the special day neared, she could get special food and treats prepared, ornaments ready for the tree she might have to fetch alone, and make the tiny candles she wanted to use on the tree. Yes, she had plenty to keep her hands busy and her mind occupied.

"You shouldn't be so scared, woman. T.J. can take care of himself." She stroked her lower abdomen and murmured, "Don't you worry, little one; your father will be home soon and learn about you. He'll be so happy. We don't care if you're a boy or a girl, just be born healthy. You'll add so much to our lives. You'll grow up safe and happy on our ranch. You won't experience the heartaches and hardships we did. We'll be good parents, little one, just wait and see. Next June when you come into the world, we'll be on the trail to a great life."

Carrie Sue was glad she wasn't having trouble with illness in the mornings as she'd been warned about when she'd believed herself pregnant in July. Her monthly flow had come in August to tell her she was wrong. But September had passed after many glorious nights in her husband's arms and without the flow she'd expected. Then October and November had passed without any signs of its return. Now December was passing, and she knew she was right this time about carrying Thad's child. She was ecstatic.

If her husband had noticed the absence of her woman's flow, he hadn't mentioned it. Either he assumed it had occurred when he was gone or he was reluctant to start hoping prematurely.

"One week, can I wait that long to tell him? If he doesn't return before Christmas, I'll have to. Maybe I should have said something before he left. No, I don't want him thinking about me and the baby instead of keeping his mind on his business. Please protect him, God," she prayed.

"Get busy, woman. That milk isn't going to churn itself. Better get that out of the way before you start that doll and

29

cookies for Lucy."

Carrie Sue took the butter and milk to the cabinet on the back porch to keep them fresh. She returned to the kitchen to mix dough for cookies. She hummed as she worked, and thought of how lucky she was.

The fire in the parlor gave off a steady and comforting blaze. Carrie Sue was snuggled under a quilt before it as she worked on the doll for Lucy. She halted to pat her tummy and say, "If you're a little girl, I'll make lots of dolls for you. I wonder if you'll favor me or your father."

She envisioned a small replica of Thad Jamison with black hair and gray eyes. Her heart leapt with joy and anticipation. "What shall we name you, little one?" Many choices raced through her dreamy mind.

As her wandering gaze touched on one window, she straightened and shrieked, "It's almost dark, Carrie Sue! Get that stock into the barn."

In a hurry, she put aside the doll and quilt over her lower body. She changed into her work boots. She donned her coat, scarf, and gloves. As she stepped out the door, she cautioned herself not to rush.

The redhead trudged across the frozen yard to the corral. She opened the gate, entered, and refastened it. "Let's go, boys; time for bed," she called out, but the stock knew the schedule by now and were waiting near the barn door. "I see I have you well-trained already." She smiled.

The steers ambled into a large stall they shared. The horses were placed in separate ones. Doors were closed and bolted. Carrie Sue made certain they had water and feed, just in case the weather prevented her from coming to tend them tomorrow morning.

Ice crunched under her boots as she returned to the house. At the porch, she grasped the rail to steady herself as she mounted the slippery steps. She glanced back before going inside to see the familiar blue haze settling over the white landscape.

Somewhere miles away, her husband was preparing to camp for the night. It was too dangerous to continue riding after dark. Soon, he would be working to get a camp fire going and his meal warmed. She knew he must be chilled to the bone and miserable, and missing her. One day of separation was gone, leaving only six until Christmas.

Carrie Sue locked the door and discarded the unneeded items. She went to the hearth to chase the cold from her flesh. When she was warmed, she went back to work on the doll and on Thad's shirt.

With the house secure and fires tended, Carrie Sue climbed into bed alone. She curled into a ball until the chill of the covers left. Everything was set for her visit to the Adams tomorrow. Thad's shirt was finished. She had eaten canned vegetable soup for dinner, a gift from one of their neighbors. She was tired, even sore, from the ice-breaking and churning. She relaxed her body and closed her eyes.

"Go to sleep, Carrie Sue," she commanded herself, but feared she was in for a long night alone and anxious. "I love you, T.J., and miss you. If anything happens to you, I'll hunt down those men and kill them."

Her weary mind added, *You can bust Darby out of prison to help you!*

Darby . . . She was free, pardoned for her crimes, thanks to her husband. As soon as her beloved brother served his sentence, he would be free, too. Maybe he would go to San Angelo, fetch and marry Sally, and bring her here for their fresh start. How wonderful it would be to live in the same area, to both be ranchers, to have their children grow up together.

Yes, she wanted her brother nearby. She also wouldn't mind if Kale Rushton, their half-Apache friend, moved to this area after his release. The doctor from San Angelo, who had treated her after her gunshot and who had been impressed with Kale's natural medical skills, wanted Kale to train as a doctor and to teach him the ancestral arts Kale had learned from his Indian people. Kale had promised to study the doctor's books while in prison, then to become the man's apprentice when he was released. She hoped he kept that vow.

Of course, the doctor could be dead in fifteen years. Or prison could change dear Kale for the worse. She prayed that wouldn't happen; she and Kale, and Darby and Kale, had been close since meeting years ago. Kale had been the reason why they had stayed alive, as he'd taught them skills his Apache people had taught him. Basically Kale Rushton was a good man, but a troubled one who'd endured a hard life.

Despite the hardships and perils of outlaw life, she had enjoyed many good times with Kale and Darby. If it had been only the three of them and if Quade Harding, the old man's son, hadn't been determined to have her or destroy her — they wouldn't have remained outlaws very long. As Thad had said, they had been caught in a trap with no way out until it was too late.

But she didn't want the other gang members to come near her or her home. She had a new life now, a loving husband, and a family on the way. She didn't want her dark past to damage this bright dream. Perhaps — and hopefully — in fifteen years, the others would forget about her or would leave her in peace. She had been special to them, so surely they would.

If not, Thad Jamison would deal with them in his own way! Thad would not mind Darby and Kale living nearby and being parts of their life, but he wouldn't allow the others to do so. She couldn't blame him.

Carrie Sue ordered her rambling mind to settle down, as it was fretting over events that couldn't happen for fifteen years. She had written to her brother earlier this month and had sent Darby a Christmas present. She could only hope he received it in that East Texas prison so far away.

Her mind returned to her husband, home, and baby. Slowly she drifted off to sleep while making beautiful plans for them.

* * *

32

With morning chores out of the way, Carrie Sue saddled her horse and left the ranch. The gifts she was taking to Lucy Adams were suspended in a cloth sack over her saddle horn. She was bundled up in her thick coat, wool scarf beneath a hat, and leather riding gloves. She was clad in denim breeches, a wool shirt, boots, wool socks, and long johns. She noticed how snug the pants were because of the long johns and her expanding waistline, and she smiled.

The sun was out today, and the bluish haze had lifted. It was above the freezing mark, so the ice and snow was attempting to melt. Still, when she exhaled, it came forth in smoky pants. For safety, she walked her horse, a surefooted pinto. She heard the suction his hooves made with each step taken. She saw the trail her husband had taken, his tracks beginning to become holes of slush as the white covering softened and slid into them. At least he would have a better day and conditions under which to travel. She prayed once more for his safety and swift return.

When she reached the location where Thad had continued southward and she was to turn eastward, she gazed in that direction. She saw nothing of man or beast, nothing but the sun sparkling off the white ground.

Carrie Sue pulled on her reins to guide her mount toward the Adams ranch. Slowly they trudged for over an hour, their cautious pace making the journey longer. At last, she arrived at her destination.

Tom Adams came out to greet her and to assist her down. "Howdy, Mrs. Jamison. Good to see you, but you shouldn't be out in conditions like these and with those villains roaming the area."

Carrie Sue smiled at the genial man and ignored his gentle reprimand. "I brought little Lucy some treats. How is she today?"

"Doc's been to see her. Got her bandaged good. Says she'll be fine in a week or so. Bullet passed clean through her arm. No broken bone."

"Tom, don't keep Carrie Sue standing out in the cold while you jaw," the man's wife admonished him. "Come on in, Carrie Sue. You'll take a death chill out there."

The redhead followed the kind and jolly woman into the house. It was a warm and inviting place. She thanked Tom for assisting her off with her coat, which Mrs. Adams took to hang up during her visit. Carrie Sue doffed her hat, scarf, and gloves. The older woman put them aside, too.

"What brings you out in weather like this?" Martha inquired.

Carrie Sue knew the tone of the woman's voice didn't carry a trace of unwelcome, only concern. She repeated the reason for her visit, then held up the cloth sack she was holding.

"Lucy will be happier than a hog wallowing in mud. You best go right in though. I just gave her the doc's medicine, so she'll be asleep soon."

"I won't stay long. I know she needs her rest." Carrie Sue was familiar with the demands of a gunshot from her past, so she knew what the little girl was enduring. She liked the Adams, and they were good neighbors. She enjoyed having friends and doing nice things for them.

"While you chat with her, I'll make some hot coffee to thaw you before you go out in that freezing cold again."

"That sounds wonderful, Martha. It's still cold out, even with the sun shining at last. Tom said Lucy's doing good. I'm glad. T.J. was so worried about her. He's gone after those two bank robbers; he left at dawn."

"Oh my, how awful in this sorry weather, and so near Christmas. I suppose that's the bad side of being a marshal."

"It is, but it's his job. I just wish he didn't have to track them alone."

The woman looked shocked. "Marshal Jamison went after them two cutthroats alone?"

"Yes. He figured he could move faster and easier by himself."

"I suppose he knows best, but it worries me. I guess he's been a lawman long enough to know about such things."

"Yes, but it's still dangerous. I hope he gets back soon."

"With Christmas and worse weather coming, me, too."

Martha guided her to the child's room. The little girl looked pale and small beneath the covers which outlined her size. A cheery blaze burned in a small fireplace, and the room was lovely.

"Mrs. Jamison is here to see you, Lucy. She brought you a surprise."

Carrie Sue approached the bed, bent over, and kissed the girl's cheek, and asked, "How are you feeling today?"

In a whispery voice, the child replied, "My arm hurts bad. Papa says it'll be better in a week. Doc put me a big bandage on it."

"I see he did, a very nice one, too. You stay in bed and take care of yourself; and you'll be up running around soon."

The eight-year-old muffled a yawn and her eyes drooped, but she battled to stay awake. Carrie Sue took the doll from the sack and handed it to her. "I hope she'll keep you company while you're in bed. I made her yesterday. You'll have to think up a good name for her."

Lucy's small hands clasped the doll. Made from a sock, with button eyes and stitched features, it was clad in a cotton dress from old material Carrie Sue found in a trunk which had belonged to Mrs. Carnes. Strips of yellow yarn were sewn to the doll's head to give it blond hair.

Lucy's eyes glowed with joy. She hugged the doll to her chest and squeezed it. "Thank you, Mrs. Jamison. I'll name her Carrie Sue. She'll stay in bed with me."

The redhead was delighted by the child's happiness. She withdrew her other gift and said, "I also made you some cookies, but you and your doll have to take a nap before you can have some. Agreed?"

"Yes, ma'am." Lucy yawned again and her eyes drooped even more.

"I'm leaving now so you two can sleep. I'll see you again soon."

"Why don't you have a little girl, Mrs. Jamison?"

"I've only been married since this past summer, Lucy.

But Marshal Jamison and I want a baby next summer." Carrie Sue realized the words had leapt from her joyous heart before she could stop them.

"Can I come over and play with her?" the child asked excitedly.

"Of course, you can." Carrie Sue didn't lengthen the subject by saying it might be a boy. "You rest now and get well real soon."

"Goodbye, Mrs. Jamison. Thank you."

"Thank you, Lucy, for being such a polite and special little girl."

The child was almost asleep before the two women could leave the room. Martha quickly asked, "You're expecting a baby?"

"Yes," Carrie Sue whispered in the hallway. "But don't tell anyone. I haven't even told T.J. yet. I just realized it was true, and I didn't want to worry him while he was gone."

"I understand. Men can be funny creatures about such things. You be real careful riding home, and don't be doing too much hard work. Take care of yourself over there alone. If you need anything, you can count on me and Tom. I'll get him to check on you every few days while Thad's away."

"Thank you, Martha. That's very kind of you two."

"I like having you as a neighbor, Carrie Sue. Horace and Dorothy Carnes were allright, but she wasn't too friendly. Frail thing, too. Shame she died in childbirth like that." Recalling the news she had just learned and thinking she had made a careless and cruel slip, Martha flushed. "You don't have to worry about nothing like that. You're a strong woman."

Carrie Sue embraced the woman and smiled. "I know."

Martha left her to prepare the coffee. Tom asked Carrie Sue to have a seat in their parlor. He sat in a chair, his chores done for a while.

Carrie Sue remarked, "That's a fine daughter, Tom. T.J. and I were so glad she wasn't injured badly. T.J. felt terrible about not being around to stop that trouble, but a lawman can't work all the time." She had to question one point that troubled her. In fact, the curious matter hadn't struck her until this morning. "Tom, what was the bank doing open on Sunday evening? Why were you and little Lucy there?"

Tom looked surprised. "Didn't John tell you when he came to your ranch?" After she shook her head, he added, "Thad didn't tell you either?"

Carrie Sue shook her head again. "What happened?"

"Lord have mercy, Carrie Sue, it was terrible. We were over to the Maxwells for Sunday supper. Those two outlaws rode in and took us all prisoner. They took Max, me, and Lucy to the bank. They used her to force Max to open the safe. One of those bastards, excuse my language, saw a pistol inside the safe and jumped at Max. His gun went off and he got Lucy in the arm. They grabbed the money and rode off. I feared they were gonna kill us all. I never seen anybody as mean as Sawyer and Reeves. I hope Thad guns them down!" he nearly shouted, his rage renewed.

"Sawyer and Reeves?" she repeated, her voice shaky, her eyes wide, and her face ashen. Tremors swept over her body.

"I see you've heard of them. John said the marshal recognized their names and descriptions. I'm a law-abiding man, Carrie Sue, but I hope he kills them instead of bringing them in for trial. Outlaws don't deserve to live. They go around robbing and terrorizing innocent folk. We all worked hard for that money; Thad has to get it back."

"I'm sure he will, Tom." Carrie Sue rose and said, "I best be going."

Martha entered the room during their conversation. "What about your coffee, Carrie Sue? It'll be perked soon."

The redhead winked at the woman and said, "I don't think my tummy is set on coffee right now, but thank you." As she donned her outdoor garments, she continued, "I should head back before the weather turns and it gets late. I'll visit again soon. Take care of Lucy."

Martha didn't know if it was truly morning sickness or if

the news she'd just learned had her young neighbor upset. But she understood when a woman needed to be alone. "You ride slow and careful. Tom will be coming to check on you in a few days. If you need anything, he'll get it."

"Thanks. Goodbye." Carrie Sue mounted, waved, and departed.

Martha turned to her husband and chided, "Tom Adams, you rag-eared mongrel, you shouldn't have told her about those outlaws. Carrie Sue don't need to be worrying about her husband living or dying out there while she's alone, not in her condition."

"I didn't know she didn't know about everything. What do you mean, in her condition?"

Martha scolded herself, "Aw, husband, I done spilled a secret. She's expecting a baby, but nobody knows it but me. Don't you be spilling it, too. She ain't told Thad yet. Didn't want him crazy with fretting on the trail after them outlaws. We'll keep watch over her for him. She's a good woman. I like her."

"I like them both," Tom concurred. "We'll see to her. Don't worry."

Carrie Sue reached the location where Thad had headed southward yesterday morning and reined in her horse. She stared in that direction again. *Jake Sawyer and Slim Reeves.* The last she had heard, the two cold-blooded killers, were riding in the Arizona and New Mexico territories. She'd never met them, but Darby had. Two years ago, they had tried to get her brother and the Stover Gang to pull off some big jobs with them. As usual, Darby had refused to get connected with vicious men like them.

Now they were cutting a path through this area, and her beloved husband was on their trail. Why hadn't Thad told her who he was pursuing? For the same reason she hadn't told him about the baby she was carrying, she decided, to keep her from being afraid.

Thad was an ex-Texas Ranger and Special Agent for the

President, so he knew how to handle men like Sawyer and Reeves. He knew how dangerous and evil they are. He would be extra careful tracking them.

But, she fretted, Sawyer and Reeves were smart. That's how they had eluded the law so long. They had gunned down a Ranger shortly after trying to join up with her brother's gang, which wasn't an easy feat. Probably few men were wanted as badly as those two!

Knowing who had robbed the bank and how, Carrie Sue could not understand why those bastards had let Max, Tom, and Lucy live. Those two usually murdered all witnesses. It was strange . . .

Carrie Sue's mind filled with crazy ideas. She dismissed the one about Max and Tom taking the money and blaming innocent men. Both were good men, and little Lucy had been shot. Besides, no man in his right mind would frame dangerous outlaws like Sawyer and Reeves! Of course, men like those two cutthroats were crazy, so their actions didn't always make sense. Perhaps little Lucy had been what stayed their deadly hands.

The redhead shivered and her teeth chattered. The sun had vanished behind ominous clouds. The temperature was dropping rapidly. She had to get home, get her chores done, and get out of this frigid and damp air.

Carrie Sue guided her pinto toward the Rocking *J* Ranch. The ground was freezing again and she heard the crunch of warnings beneath her mount's hooves. It took her longer to return, but she finally made it.

She dismounted, unsaddled her horse, and put away her gear. While she was out, she put up the stock and tended them for the night. Her footsteps were loud in the almost eerie silence in the sheltered valley. She sighed with relief when she was inside with the doors locked. She leaned against the wall, closed her eyes, and was thankful to be home safe. She only wished her husband was here with her.

Sawyer, Reeves, and a possible blizzard in the area . . . Thad out there in the midst of all three . . . "God, protect my love."

39

Carrie Sue discarded her outerwear. She fueled the fires with new wood. Her appetite was lagging, but she made hot coffee to warm her. She had to do something to busy her hands and mind.

As she sipped steaming coffee, she stitched cloth ornaments for their first Christmas tree. On one, she put her name and the date. On another, she put Thad's name and the date. On a third, she put BABY and 1876. She sewed the tiny bells, stars, and assorted shapes she had cut out in secret from material from Dorothy Carnes's trunk.

Tomorrow, she would dip the pine cones she'd collected into red and white paint she'd found in the barn. They could dry by the fire while Thad was gone. She could melt wax and make the tiny candles to use to light up the momentous tree. She could cut long strips of colorful ribbons found in the trunk. She could place everything in a wooden box when finished. Then when Christmas neared, she and Thad could fetch their first tree and decorate it together. What fun that would be!

If Christmas Eve came and he hadn't returned, she would decorate the tree alone to have it ready for his arrival. She wanted this first Christmas to be special, all of them to be special. She wanted to begin the traditions that would follow them through their marriage. How could she, if he didn't make it home in time?

Was sharing such tasks and such days together all-important? Not as important, she decided, as Thad making it home alive whenever he could.

On Friday morning, December twenty-second, Thad had been gone for four days and nights. Carrie Sue could not imagine what was taking place on the trail, and she fought hard to keep up her faith and optimism. Never had she worried about him more than during this absence.

In the last few days, she had completed the ornaments for their first Christmas tree—the tiny candles, the handmade assortment, the ribbons, the pine cones, and a star for the top painted white. Thad's shirt was wrapped in a square of green material. Her menu was decided, and food would be cooked on the twenty-fourth. Garments in need of repairs had been mended. Washing and ironing were done. Every room in their home was clean, including the porches.

As she was about to head back to the barn to shovel out the milk cow's stall, Tom Adams arrived on horseback. She went to greet him.

He swept off his hat, nodded, then replaced it. "Howdy, Carrie Sue. You doing all right?" he inquired with concern.

She overlapped her arms and cupped her elbows in her palms. "Everything's been fine, Tom; thanks. How is Lucy?"

Tom beamed with joy and relief. "Stronger and talkier every day. Doc says she don't have to stay in bed all the time now. Should be healed in another week, he says."

"That's wonderful news. Thad will be happy to hear it."

Tom shifted nervously. "Heard from him yet?"

Carrie Sue read the caution and worry in Tom's eyes and voice. She figured he felt partly responsible for her husband being gone and in danger. Too, the four had become good friends and neighbors since their arrival in Gates. Despite her growing fears, she tried to lessen Tom's. "No, but that's expected. T.J. doesn't send word unless he gets near a town. I'd imagine those robbers are staying clear of them for a while. I guess they know by now they're being pursued." From past experience on the outlaw trail and from hearing about those two criminals, she knew that was a fact, not a guess. She prayed again her love didn't fall into an ambush.

"Me and the wife are praying for him. We want that money back bad, but Thad's safety is more important. I hope he don't take no chances."

With confidence, she assured him, "He won't, Tom, but he'll keep going until his mission's over, no matter how long it takes."

"I sure hope that isn't much longer, Carrie Sue." He realized he might be frightening her, so he changed the subject.

"Here I stand jawing when I came to see if you need any chores done and to bring you these things from Martha. She made you two one of her special cakes, and sent over more of her canned soup. I grew most of these vegetables myself." He passed the bundle to the redhead with a smile.

Carrie Sue accepted it. "Thanks, Tom, and thank Martha. She makes the best soup I've put in my mouth. It's even better on a cold day. When our first garden comes in next year, Martha will have to teach me how to make soup. It's been a long time since I've done canning and such."

"You miss teaching school?"

Tom didn't know much about her past; he knew she had once worked in a Tucson school, but not that she'd only been using the identity of Carolyn Starns, schoolmarm, as a cover while she fled her outlaw existence. "I haven't had time since I quit, married, and moved here. With getting the ranch started next spring, I doubt I will."

"You're sure good with children. My little Lucy loves you. That was mighty kind of you to make those cookies and that doll. She finished them off in a few days and never lets that doll go for more than a minute or two."

Carrie Sue assumed Martha had let her secret slip to her husband, but she didn't comment on her pregnancy. "I'm happy she likes it. She's a fine girl, Tom. So sweet, polite, and smart. Be proud of her."

The man beamed again. "We are. It scared years off my life when she got shot. You never think about things like that happening to you."

No innocent victim of a crime did, she thought, ashamed again of her past that could have had little Lucys in it if Thad hadn't stepped into her life. "At least she'll be well soon; that's a lot to be thankful for."

"Me and Martha got plenty to be thankful for, more this year than most. Sure is nice to have good neighbors like you and the marshal. Now, tell me what I can do to help out whilst he's gone."

She could ask Tom to shovel out the cow's stall, but she needed work to distract her and she wanted to be alone in

42

case Thad returned home soon. Yet Tom had ridden over and needed to do something for her. "I appreciate the offer, Tom, but my daily chores are few and easy. The only thing I can think of is help with the water trough. It froze too deep last night for me to bust through. I was about to work on it again."

He was delighted to do a good deed for her. "Just show me your breaker and I'll get rid of it. That's hard and heavy work for a female."

Carrie Sue led him to the barn and handed him the tool which looked similar to a large hammer. They went into the corral. She watched Tom slam it into the hard surface several times, sending chips of ice flying in all directions. He labored until the frozen barrier yielded to his superior strength and efforts. He flipped large hunks to the white ground, then filled it halfway with water from the nearby well.

"It'll probably freeze again at night, so just pour two buckets of water atop it every morning. That'll give you enough room to add what the stock needs for a few days. Least we haven't gotten that blizzard yet, but it's been threatening to come for a week. Getting colder ever' day." Tom glanced around at the lovely valley and cloudy sky as he checked the weather and talked. "Course Wednesday's snow is soft and pretty. Might be best if the sun don't come out and warm it. Minute it gets cold, it'll freeze into ice; that's what's dangerous. After you been here a winter or two, you'll learn the signs and get used to it. What else can I do for you?"

"That's it. Thank you. Would you like some coffee?"

Tom studied the gloomy sky once more. "I best get back home. Weather's as sly as a fox this time of year. You stay close to the house. I'll be over again Sunday or Monday to see if you need anything."

Carrie Sue expressed her gratitude again. She waved goodbye to her nearest neighbor and watched his departure. She stared at the ominous sky. "Hurry home, my love; this weather doesn't look good. I don't want you and

Nighthawk stuck somewhere during a violent blizzard."

She went to the barn, shoveled out the waste-stained straw, then spread fresh straw in the stall. She checked those of the horses and steers, and decided those could wait another few days, as they were not penned up day and night as the milk cow was.

The redhead returned to the house and took a bath. She also scrubbed her flaming tresses, then sat before a hot fire to dry them. While she waited, she devoured the vegetable soup Martha had sent to her. As she brushed her hair and tested its dampness, she talked to the child she was carrying and prayed for her husband, for all of them.

By mid-morning Saturday, Carrie Sue realized it was going to snow and get colder that night. She had experienced enough winters and learned enough from Kale Rushton to recognize the signs. If they were going to have a tree to decorate, she needed to fetch it today. She had already picked out the one she wanted and it was six feet high and growing on a low hill west of the house.

She bundled up good, saddled her pinto, took an axe and a rope, and headed in that direction. It wasn't far, so she'd be safe, and the chore wouldn't take long. She rode to the site and dismounted. It was almost deathly quiet. Not even snow or ice softened to drop to the ground and make noise. She didn't hear any birds or animals, not even sounds from their stock, or any rushing of water in the stream far away or in rivulets created when the white covering melted. The world around her was white, with splotches of green, especially from pines that towered above the other trees. Even the haze settling closer and closer to the earth didn't have its bluish cast today. There was a dampness in the air that chilled to the bone. Knowing she needed to hurry back inside before she took sick, she eyed her target.

A smile crossed her face. The tree was perfect. She only wished Thad were there to share the fun task. She chopped into the bark on the trunk, hardened by the weather.

Finally, it fell to the ground. She let out a whoop of joy and success, and heard it echo across the silent landscape. Her pinto's head jerked upward, his eyes found her, and he neighed as if answering a question. She secured the rope around the trunk and lower branches, then tied it to the pommel. She mounted. They trudged toward the barn, the tree leaving a furrow behind them in the snow.

Carrie Sue unsaddled her pinto, praised him for his assistance, and gave him some sweet-feed. She replaced the axe, took the saw, and dragged the tree to the back porch. After a straight cut was made at the base, she stood it in a bucket of water to prevent drying. Pleased with herself, she cleaned up the mess she'd made and put away the tool.

Later, she boiled water, killed their fattest hen, and plucked its feathers. She wrapped it in a clean cloth and placed it in the cooling cabinet on the back porch until it was time to roast it tomorrow. She baked cornbread for her dressing and put it aside. She looked around and decided there were no more preparations to be made until Sunday, Christmas Eve.

As expected, fresh snow began to fall as she finished her outside chores. The wind carried a frigid edge and urged her to hurry, which she did. Snug inside her home, she remembered there would be no church service tomorrow to attempt to reach. It was not the Sunday for the minister who served four towns to visit theirs.

"One more day, my love, and no sign of your return." She caressed the area where her unborn child lived and whispered, "Don't worry, little one; he'll make it back soon. I know he will." Yet, hope was fading fast.

Christmas Eve arrived, and no Thad Jamison appeared. The hen was baked. The dressing was done. The egg, rice, and raisin pudding was cooked. Jars of canned vegetables stood ready to be warmed when the other food was reheated. Martha's cake was on a lovely platter. The house smelled wonderful with the mingling of delicious aromas.

Carrie Sue looked at the mantel in the parlor where she had placed small branches of pine and candles to be lit for a romantic setting. She gazed at the tree in one corner. It looked so barren, so beckoning, so lonely. She wanted Thad here to help decorate it, but that could be wishful thinking. Maybe it was best to do it herself tonight, to have it look beautiful when he first glimpsed it. But that would ruin the tradition she wanted to begin of decorating together, as her family had done each Christmas Eve.

Carrie Sue went to a window and stared outside. Snow was still falling, getting thicker on the ground by the hour. She heard wind howling through the valley and in the trees near the house. The conditions allowed very little moonlight to brighten the outdoors, so she couldn't see far.

She felt lonely, beckoning, and miserable—like the naked tree. Perhaps working on it would lift her spirits. It would certainly occupy her time, hands, and mind. She fetched the decorations.

The redhead took great caution as she mounted the wooden stool to tie the white star to the top branch. She lit a large candle. She dripped pools of soft wax onto forks of the largest branches, then placed one of the tiny candles she'd made there and blew on the area until it set and held. She hung the handmade ornaments with yarn loops, giving prominence to those with their names and dates. She smiled with delight as she suspended the one marked, BABY, 1876. She could hardly wait to point it out to her husband. She draped the colorful lengths of ribbon around the tree. She filled in empty spots with the small red and white pine cones.

Carrie Sue Jamison stepped back to admire her handiwork. She envisioned it with the tiny candles aglow, with only the fire giving other light in the room. She fetched a length of red material and concealed the base and stand. She placed Thad's gift underneath, and took another look.

"Beautiful," she murmured. "It's been so long since I've enjoyed a Christmas tree and this holiday. Hurry home, T.J., I don't want to miss sharing another moment of this

46

special time with you."

It was nearing midnight, and she was exhausted from all her work and worry today. It was obvious her husband couldn't make it home tonight; traveling this late and under the harsh conditions outside was hazardous. Thad was too smart to take such risks even to reach her side. All she could do was go to bed, and pray again for him to arrive tomorrow.

Christmas Day was gradually ending. It was almost five and dark, but no Thad. The outside and inside chores were done. The food was waiting to be warmed and devoured. The tree candles were ready to be lit. Cheery fires glowed in every room for heat and beauty. She was clad in her prettiest dress. Her fiery locks were brushed and hanging free as Thad preferred. Everything was ready to be enjoyed together, but she was alone.

The snow and wind had ceased, but it was cold beyond the house. She knew travel would be difficult, if not almost impossible. It was late. Surely Thad couldn't make it home tonight, or risk trying. If he was alive and uninjured, that would more than make up for their first Christmas being spoiled. She would wait up until midnight. If he didn't arrive, she'd put everything away, then hope to celebrate with him tomorrow.

Carrie Sue was dozing in a chair before the fire when a loud knock at the door awakened her. She glanced at the mantel clock, temporarily sitting on a side table: Twenty minutes to eleven. She went to the door and—without unlocking it—asked, "Who's there?"

A voice replied, "Mrs. Jamison, I have news about your husband."

47

3

Carrie Sue unlocked the door with quivering fingers and flung it open. Cold air blasted her in the face, but she didn't mind. She gaped at the man standing there, grinning, snow on his clothes, and his cheeks red.

He laughed merrily as he said, "Part of the good news is that your husband's home before Christmas is over. Just barely."

She went into his arms as she squealed, "T.J., thank God!"

Thad hugged her tightly and joyfully. He eagerly responded to the heady kiss she placed on his chapped lips. All else was forgotten for a time. When they shivered from the cold outside and the fiery passions within their bodies had parted, he said, "Let's get inside; we're freezing."

Carrie Sue stepped back for Thad to enter the house, her love-filled gaze glued to him. Her heart sang, *he's home!* As she started closing the door, she was saying, "I've been so wor—"

Thad grasped the edge of the door, halted it, and interrupted. "Aren't you going to let in your Christmas present?" He grinned.

"My pres—" She halted and stared at the second man whose presence had been blocked from view by her husband's size and the darkness. He, too, was grinning broadly and absorbing the lovely redhead. "Darby! How?"

Darby Stover grabbed the startled young woman and

hugged her. "Mercy, you're a beautiful sight for these sore eyes. It's been too long, Sis."

They embraced as both sets of eyes dampened with emotional moisture. For a time, they held each other in silence and in gratitude. Thad closed the door and observed the event with a happy heart.

Carrie Sue leaned back and asked, "But how? You didn't escape?"

Thad responded, "Nope, you're looking at the new Special Agent, D.S. Rogue, who replaced me."

Her eyes widened even more. She stammered, "You're f-f-free? You're out of prison? You're a . . . lawman?"

At her reaction, Darby chuckled. "Shocked me, too, Sis. Seems they wanted and needed me more out of prison than inside one."

"But why you?" she asked in astonishment.

Thad explained, "Partly a gift from Governor Hubbard and President Grant for all my good deeds in Texas and elsewhere. They also needed somebody to replace me to chase down outlaws. Who better than a man who'd been one, who could think like they do, who can get close enough to capture them? Darby really made a good impression on the authorities, so they figured he'd go straight if given the chance. He agreed with their idea, a good suggestion I made. He's been paroled, as long as he doesn't commit any more crimes and until he's served as a Special Agent for seven years, one for each year he was an outlaw. A fair trade if you ask me."

Carrie Sue was stunned and thrilled with this news. "When did you get out? Why didn't you write and tell us? I can't believe this."

"Like Thad said, I'm a Special Agent, so I work undercover. They changed my name to D.S. Rogue. Darby Stover was reported killed after he escaped from prison. When I meet up with outlaws I know, I just tell them how I tricked the law into thinking I'm dead with a burned body. So far, nobody's caught on to me. Of course, I haven't handled but three cases to date. I see why Thad loved this job so much; it's exciting and challenging."

"But what if I'd heard you'd been killed?" Carrie persisted.

"You'll be getting a letter from me soon. I've only been out a month, so I guess it hasn't reached you yet. Or maybe some outlaw robbed the stage or train carrying it. I was chasing Jake Sawyer and Slim Reeves when Thad and I ran into each other. They're sitting in a Denver jail right now, and Thad has that bank money in his saddlebags. They gave us a good chase, but they couldn't outsmart the two of us together. I can only stay until tomorrow. I can't risk spoiling what you and Thad have here."

"Leave tomorrow? But we have to visit, talk. So much has happened."

"It's not wise, Sis. We don't want anyone recognizing me around here and endangering your new cover. I only agreed to come here with Thad to let you see I'm all right. No matter what you hear, you'll know the truth. So will Sally soon; my next assignment is in San Angelo."

Carrie Sue brightened. He was right. "That's wonderful. I'm so happy you're free. We'll have to celebrate. We can stay up all night having fun, eating, and talking. You two get out of those damp clothes while I warm the food and brew the coffee. This will be a glorious Christmas."

Darby and Thad exchanged mischievous looks. They were exhausted, but happy to see her so overjoyed.

"Better do as she says, Darby; she's a headstrong woman."

"I remember. She always wanted things her way, the right way."

The two men laughed, and Carrie Sue joined in. She left for the kitchen while they entered the bedroom to change garments.

Thad finished first and walked up behind his wife at the stove. He wrapped his arms around her and nestled his cheek against hers when she leaned back against him. "How do you like your Christmas present?"

"It's wonderful, T.J. Isn't it strange how miracles happen

51

when you least expect them? You and Darby home for Christmas."

He murmured into her ear. "I have some other good news for you: Kale Rushton is studying medicine and working with the prison doctor. If he impresses them as Darby did, he might get an early parole."

She turned in his embrace and hugged him. "So much good news on one day. My heart feels like it'll burst."

He met her gaze and asked, "Can it hold a little bit more good news?"

Curiosity filled her periwinkle eyes. "What more could there be?"

"I'll only be town marshal until the new one arrives, then I'll be a full-time rancher. No more galloping after outlaws and being gone for weeks."

"They're letting you resign? This soon?"

He tickled her nose with a flaming red curl. "Yep! Another gift from Grant before he goes out of office. He'll be yielding his job to Hayes soon, so he handled my case and Darby's fast. We'll buy those cattle come spring, then be real ranchers. One day, we'll be expanding enough we'll have to hire hands to help us. A few sons would be nice to help out their old man."

"We'll have to work hard to grow one every year," she teased, holding her surprise for later. "Everything's ready. Call Darby to join us."

The three sat down at the table. They exchanged smiles.

Darby followed suit when Thad and Carrie Sue bowed their heads.

Thad prayed, "Lord, bless this food to the nourishment of our bodies and make them strong to serve Your will. We're grateful for all the blessings You've bestowed on us this year and for those in the years to come. Thank You for giving us this special Christmas together, as a real family. Amen."

"Amen," Carrie Sue and Darby added.

"I carved the hen so it would be easier and quicker to

handle. I know you two must be starved and tired. Serve yourself," she invited.

The men took helpings of roasted chicken, baked dressing, canned beans, potatoes blended with milk and butter to make up for the moisture they had lost with age, hot biscuits, and steaming coffee.

After a few bites, Darby glanced at his sister and said, "Delicious."

"I haven't forgotten all Mother taught me."

"I can see you haven't. I wish you could have met our parents, Thad. You'd have liked them, and they'd have liked you."

"I'm sure we would have gotten along good, Darby."

"At least their deaths found justice," the man said, instead of using the word *revenge,* which pleased the couple. "I wish I could have kept the ranch after the law took it back from the Hardings. It was sold, and the money was used to repay some of the people I'd robbed over the years. I guess that was justice, too. I'm not bitter about it. I'm glad I'm getting my life turned around in a new direction."

Thad stopped eating to say, "When your seven years of service are up, you can always come here and start a new ranch. We'd be glad to have you as a neighbor. There's good folk here, Darby."

"I'm sure Sally would like being a rancher's wife," Carrie Sue hinted.

Darby nodded and grinned, then put a bite of chicken into his mouth.

They ate and chatted with leisure and delight. Hungry and appreciative of the good meal, the men almost cleaned the platters and bowls, and nearly finished the entire pot of coffee.

When they were done, Carrie Sue suggested, "Why don't we have our cake, pudding, and milk in the parlor by the fire? We can light the candles on the tree and enjoy it with our dessert."

"That's a pretty tree, love. I'm sorry you had to do everything by yourself this year. I promise from now on, Christmas is together."

As Carrie Sue rose from her chair, the two men did so, too.

"We'll help you clear the table and prepare dessert."

"Thanks, T.J., but I can manage. You might need to add more wood to the fire. Darby can help me bring in the milk and plates."

Thad left to check the fires in the parlor and bedroom. Darby helped his sister fill glasses with milk from the cooling cabinet on the back porch. She sliced the cake from Martha Adams, then spooned pudding beside it. She and Darby carried the laden dishes into the parlor. It felt wonderful to be together again, sharing and talking.

Carrie Sue lit the candles on the tree, grinning as her gaze touched on one special ornament. She doused the lanterns. In the glow of the candles and fire, they ate their dessert and drank their milk.

"You can bed down in here tonight, Darby. No cold trail for a while."

"Thanks, Thad. You two have done a good job with this ranch. I can see how happy you are. Carrie Sue said you were a special man; I can see you are. I'm glad you came along to free us, brother."

The last word touched Thad deeply, as he'd been the one to plan and execute the trap to capture Darby Stover and his gang. During the last few days with her brother, he'd learned that Darby held no resentment against him. The ex-outlaw realized he'd only done his job and what was best for everyone. The man also knew he was partly responsible for his fresh start. "So am I, Darby. Carrie Sue is making me the happiest man alive."

Carrie Sue rose, went to the tree, and called to her husband, "T.J., come look at this ornament. I made it especially for this Christmas."

Thad stood and went to join his wife. He read the one she pointed to, then looked confused. Was it wishful thinking, he wondered, or was she telling him something?

"It will have a name on it next time," she hinted.

"You mean, you're expecting our baby?" She nodded and grinned. "You're sure?" he pressed.

"Positive, over three months. You'll be a father early next June."

"A baby?" Darby said in wonder and pleasure.

Carrie Sue glanced past her husband to tell her brother, "Yes, you'll be an uncle in June."

"That's great news, Sis! Congratulations, you two."

Thad hugged his wife and teased, "That was a sneaky way to tell me, love. Seems I came home at the right moment. It's the best gift you could give me." He hugged her again, then kissed her, unmindful of Darby.

"You two have really got a bright future before you."

"You do, too, now, Darby."

"Thanks to a man we met as T.J. Rogue last summer," she jested. "I sent your gift to the prison, Darby, but I have another one for you, T.J."

As she retrieved it, Darby said, "The man in charge will keep any mail and send it to my superior. Mercy, that's a strange word to be saying."

They all laughed as Thad unwrapped the shirt.

The marshal examined it, smiled, and thanked his skilled wife. "I do have another present for you, something to keep you warm when I'm not around, which won't be much as soon as the new marshal arrives." He fetched the gift and handed it to her. It wasn't wrapped.

Carrie Sue tossed the wool shawl around her shoulders. "It's beautiful and warm. Thank you, T.J." She kissed him.

Yet both knew the best gifts they had received this year were the baby, his safe return, and Darby's new life.

"It's time to get you into bed, woman; you need your rest. It's late."

Carrie Sue was more than ready to curl up with her husband. While Thad and Darby carried the dishes into the kitchen, she fetched blankets and a pillow for her brother to use on the parlor sofa.

"I'll clean up everything tomorrow. Let's all turn in. I'll cook you a big breakfast before you have to leave, Darby."

She wouldn't argue about his departure, because she knew it was the best thing for all concerned.

"Thanks, Sis. I'll see you two in the morning."

"I'm glad you're here with us tonight, Darby. I love you."

"I love you, too, Sis, and it's great sharing this Christmas with you."

"Good night, Darby."

"Good night, Sis, Thad. See you in the morning."

"Good night, Darby," Thad said to his brother-in-law.

The couple went into their bedroom and closed the door. Darby stretched out on the sofa and gazed into the smoldering fire. He closed his eyes to dream of his first Christmas, in his first home, with Sally . . .

Carrie Sue and Thad Jamison snuggled in their bed. They kissed and embraced, and sent forth prayers of thanks for being together and safe.

"I love you, Carrie Sue," Thad murmured against her lips.

"I love you, T.J. Merry Christmas."

"Merry Christmas to you, love," he responded, then kissed her mouth again.

Soon, they were making passionate love, their future as bright as the candles on the tree before them . . .

Circle of Love
by Carol Finch

Grayson Hart leaned leisurely against the wall, watching dozens of fashionably dressed couples whirl around the dance floor at Jonathan Stiles's spacious home. The grand ball marked the beginning of the holiday season, and it seemed as if everyone in the community was trying their best to resurrect the fallen South, to reestablish the life-style they'd known before the war. Parties and celebrations had been scheduled even earlier than usual this year. Grayson was thankful for the distraction. Since his return from battle he'd spent endless hours putting his life back in order and gathering his herd of horses and mules, which had become all too accustomed to running wild on the sprawling pastures of his plantation north of town.

Although this joyous celebration — attended by the crème-de-la-crème of Alexandria — provided plenty of refreshments, activities and companionship, Grayson felt like a bystander — an observer of life. He was alone in every crowd and he had no family with which to share the profits he'd made selling his livestock. Even the servants who'd once worked for him had wandered away from Hart Plantation during his extended absence. Now he was forced to hire occasional help when he encountered a task he couldn't tend himself.

Grayson shoved his disjointed thoughts aside and pushed away from the wall. He'd come to this party to amuse himself and forget the emptiness that surrounded him. For the past hour he'd been standing on the perimeter, watching other members of his social set enjoy themselves. It was time he mixed and mingled. Determined of purpose, Grayson threaded through the crowd to select a dance partner. He'd only taken five steps before an eager redhead latched onto his arm. Grayson went through the paces of dancing with the chattering female in his arms, but he found one woman to be pretty much the same as another. They were nothing but bundles of elegant ruffles and lace, murmuring well-rehearsed lines of conversation, flashing artificial smiles.

Odd, wasn't it, Grayson mused as he glanced at the young widow's pale complexion and revealing gown. The women in his social circle reminded him of china dolls; they held no particular lure for him. His mind kept wandering to the sassy imp who lived down the road from his plantation. Pilar Maguire was never seen at these festive gatherings, but Grayson had noticed her plenty of times in the past few months on his travels to and from Alexandria, when he would stop occasionally to enlist the services of her grandfather.

Of course, the spirited chit didn't give him the time of day. Maybe that was why she fascinated him. Grayson was the kind of man who preferred to do the chasing. Most of the females who attended these social functions seemed to be husband-hunting—like this over-eager widow in his arms for instance. She was like a bird of prey, pursuing him for her dinner . . .

On that unnerving thought, Grayson detached himself from the clinging redhead and propelled himself toward the study where several men had gathered to indulge their passion for fine brandy. Before he made it to the door, a female barricaded his path. Grayson swore the poor girl's eyelashes were going to beat her to death. Indeed, she was batting them so rapidly at him that he could feel the draft.

Employing the excuse that he had to lubricate his vocal chords with drink before he returned to the dance floor, Grayson sidestepped around the waterfall of lacy ruffles and made a beeline for the study. He was bored to tears and he just couldn't get into the swing of the holiday festivities, or the pursuit of amorous women. During this particular season of the year, the thoughts of eligible young women focused on social events, romance, and marriage. A man had to be swift of foot to avoid standing under the mistletoe and kissing boughs that were draped over every doorway. Not that Grayson had an aversion to kissing, but he preferred to be the one to decide whom he kissed and when. Simply standing in a doorway didn't seem reason enough. He was lonely but he wasn't *that* lonely! True, there was something crucial missing from his life and he couldn't find satisfaction, but . . .

"Grayson, I've been meaning to speak with you," Jonathan Stiles declared as he ambled across the room with drink in hand. "I'm in need of more of your horses and mules to equip my wagons. You've already provided me with plenty of prime stock, but I still don't have enough animals to meet the demands."

From his towering height, Grayson peered down at the merchantman who'd been doing a thriving business since the end of the war. Jonathan had been swamped with orders for lumber and supplies to rebuild in areas where the Yankees had wrought destruction.

"How many head of stock do you need?" Grayson asked as he poured himself a glass of peach brandy.

"At least a dozen, equipped with harnesses," Jonathan informed him. "With so much construction underway, my fleet of wagons and stable of livestock aren't large enough for all the deliveries."

Grayson nodded agreeably. "First thing in the morning, I'll see what I can do about selecting dependable animals and having harnesses made to equip them."

"I appreciate that. I'm already a week behind schedule. But rest assured that you'll be well paid for your efforts, Grayson."

What difference did it make how well paid he was, Grayson thought to himself as he wandered off, only to be approached with another request for livestock. All the wealth he'd acquired couldn't buy happiness. He could afford to

61

garb himself in the fancy trappings of a gentleman and attend these gay affairs, but he still felt like an extra person in the world. There had to be more to life than going through the paces and counting one's stack of money. If he didn't discover what was missing and quickly . . .

"You promised me a dance, Grayson." The reminder was followed by another flurry of batting eyelashes and a noticeable draft. "And don't forget about Emily Foster's wedding this weekend. You'll be there, won't you?"

Grayson glanced around the corner of the doorway to survey Jonathan's daughter—the same female whom he'd encountered earlier. Artfully dodging the kissing bough above the door, he allowed Melissa to shepherd him back to the ballroom. One last dance, Grayson told himself. Then he was going to make a discreet exit and quit pretending he was teeming with holiday spirit and good tidings of joy. He was tired of playing coy games with women who were obvious in their intentions. He might never find his special niche in life but he knew beyond all doubt that he wasn't going to find it here—exposed to the cold draft of batting eyelashes!

"How come cows have tails?" Rory asked his older sister.

Pilar Maguire paused from milking the cow to glance at her eight-year-old brother, wondering when he'd emerge from this phase in which *how* and *come* were the first two words out of his mouth. Sometimes Pilar swore Rory posed a hundred questions a day just to hear the sound of his own voice. He was at the age where he couldn't formulate a thought without sharing it with the rest of the world. He talked nonstop. And why he felt compelled to follow on her heels like a puppy, Pilar would never know! Couldn't a woman have a few minutes of peace and quiet just once during the course of a day . . . ?

"How come, Pilar?" Rory persisted when he didn't receive a prompt reply. Patience wasn't one of Rory's virtues.

"The length of a cow's tail determines her age and she uses her tail to swat away pesky flies," Pilar replied in the most tolerant tone she could muster. When the milk cow's tail slapped Rory across his freckled face, Pilar stifled a grin. "She can also use her tail to silence boys who ask too many questions."

Rory brushed his hand over his cheek and glared at the offending cow — Bertha was her name. "How come Bertha don't like me?"

"Doesn't like you."

"How come—" His voice evaporated when he heard approaching footsteps and glanced over to see the silhouette of a man framed by the barn door.

Pilar followed her youngest brother's gaze and then froze like a block of ice when she recognized the muscular figure of the man she'd come to envy and resent over the past few months. It was bad enough that she was caught in men's clothes, straddling a stool, and milking a cow like a common farm hand. But it was far worse to have *this* particular man see her doing it!

"How come you're here, Mr. Hart?" Rory questioned with his customary candor.

The faintest hint of a smile pursed Grayson's lips as his assessing gaze slid from the young boy to his improperly dressed sister. Pilar looked as if she'd prefer to crawl under Bertha to avoid him rather than offer a morning greeting.

"I came to speak with your grandfather. Is Virgil here?" Grayson inquired politely.

There were many things Pilar resented about Grayson Hart, such as his rugged good looks, polished boots, tailored clothes, and his grand house on the hill which had been spared the ravages of war. But that deep, resonant baritone voice of his — which could send goose bumps cruising across her skin — was positively the worst! Or maybe she resented even more the way he stood there dominating everything around him. Pilar had never actually taken the time to rank her resentments by degree, so she couldn't say for sure.

"I'll go fetch my grandpa for you," Rory volunteered as he raced out of the barn, leaving the words streaming behind him.

Rory had only one speed, Pilar noted as her brother kicked

up dust which mingled with the splinters of sunbeams that sprayed through the cracks in the roof and walls of the barn. The boy was a bundle of potential energy who couldn't sit still for more than five minutes. He was like a locomotive with an inexhaustible supply of fuel.

To avoid meeting Grayson Hart's direct stare, Pilar studied the sparkling sun rays that lanced through the dilapidated barn. Ah, just once she'd like to find herself alone in the stables at sunrise, enjoying solitude. But such was fate. She'd been granted little privacy since the war had taken its toll on the South. She had responsibilities galore and chores aplenty, unlike Grayson who could come and go as he pleased from his elegant mansion without answering to anyone, especially a young boy who asked how come *this* and how come *that* at regular intervals.

"It's a fine day, isn't it?" Grayson murmured for lack of much else to say since Pilar was doing such a superb job of ignoring him.

"I wouldn't know," Pilar muttered crabbily. "The view from under a cow isn't all that spectacular, Mr. Hart."

"Grayson," he corrected.

His lips quirked in a wry smile as he surveyed her shapely derriere and the rigid set of her back. A sassier female Grayson had never met. She was the anchoring rock of the Maguire family, surrounded by two brothers, a sister, and a delightful old man whose dry sense of humor never failed to amuse Grayson. He envied the simple pleasures of Pilar's life *and* found himself illogically attracted to her at the same time. She possessed a natural, wholesome appearance that an artist couldn't begin to capture on canvas. Even her tattered men's clothes couldn't detract from her arresting beauty. Too bad she had the same overstocked supply of sass as good looks, Grayson mused. She, with her distant aloof airs, that haughty toss of her long golden hair, that defiant glint in those sky-blue eyes, the inviting curve of her lips . . .

"Why are you staring at me?" Pilar snapped when she found herself the object of his intense scrutiny.

"I was just wondering if your kisses were as fiery

as your tongue," he replied with a taunting grin.

"You'll never know, Grayson Hart!" She released an unladylike snort to dispel any romantic fantasies he might be having.

Pilar wondered why she was being so rude to the tall, raven-haired ex-soldier who sauntered deeper into the interior of the barn. Honestly, she couldn't fathom why Grayson Hart brought out the worst in her. She couldn't seem to keep a civil tongue in her head when he was around. The shameful fact was that she would've exchanged places with him, if wishing could've made it so. He had it all and she had damned little—besides a bucket half-full of fresh milk. That counted for nothing in Pilar's book.

"Do you mind if I ask you something?" Grayson questioned as he came to tower over Pilar who was setting a new speed record in cow milking.

"I suppose not," Pilar said without paying him the courtesy of glancing at him. "It's a free country . . . or at least it was before the Yankees bypassed your house and left ours in shambles on their way to victory."

Curse it, there she went again. Smarting off had become one of her worst faults, especially when this green-eyed rake was within snapping distance. She shouldn't have behaved as if it were his fault that his house on the hill had suffered little damage from marauding Yankees, when her family's quaint home on the south end of their property had been ransacked and burned. Her family had taken up residence in the original homestead while Grayson wasn't the least bit inconvenienced by cramped spaces.

Grayson squatted down on his haunches to pose his question to Pilar—face to face. "Do you dislike me in particular or just all men in general?"

Pilar responded by squirting milk on his polished boot. There, that should answer Mister Spit and Polish's question. And if he provoked her, she'd squirt milk on his other boot so he could back away with a matched pair.

With admirable restraint, Grayson unfolded his six-feet-two-inch frame to glare holes in the back of Pilar's well-worn shirt. "I can certainly see why you aren't married," he muttered through gritted teeth. "There isn't much demand for short-tempered shrews."

"Nor for swaggering rakehells who flaunt their elegant clothes in front of the poor and deprived," Pilar shot back, even more snidely than she intended.

"God, you're an impudent little snip," Grayson scowled, resisting the urge kick her in the seat of the pants and send her cartwheeling across the straw. "I pity your grandfather, brothers, and sister. You're likely to curdle their bucket of milk before you can tote it back to the house!"

Childish impulse tempted Pilar to squirt the sarcastic rascal in the face, and watch milk dribble down his clean-shaven chin to stain the store-bought shirt and tailored black jacket which accentuated his broad chest and lean waist to best advantage. She relented by squirting milk on his other boot instead of his face. To her satisfaction he glowered at her. Not to be outdone, she glared right back while her pet tomcat trotted over to lap up the squiggles of milk that streamed over Grayson's boots.

"Perhaps you have nothing better to do than dawdle about while the rest of us live our hand-to-mouth existence, but I have work to do and I need no distractions," Pilar said tartly.

Grayson toyed with the options of either loosening Bertha's restraining kickers to let her have a go at this saucy sprite or simply boxing her ears himself. Unfortunately, he wasn't granted the time to pursue his spiteful inclinations. Virgil Maguire arrived on the scene, wearing a pleasant smile of greeting — a custom Pilar truly should adapt if she knew what was good for her!

"Good morning, Grayson. What can I do for you?" Virgil asked as he ambled into the barn, his youngest grandson at his side.

Now here was an individual who didn't raise Grayson's blood pressure a quick ten degrees at first sight — thank goodness! "I was hoping you could spare the time to make some more halters and harnesses for my horses and mules," Grayson requested, forcing his irritation with Pilar aside.

"Your workmanship is the finest in the area and I want the best."

Of course he did, Pilar thought sourly. He was accustomed to having everything he wanted.

"I'd be more than happy to take your order. Times have been hard in Louisiana, after so much destruction of personal property and casualties of war. I'm delighted to have the chance to make extra money." Virgil pivoted toward the barn door. "We'll discuss the arrangements over breakfast. Pilar will be glad to fix you a bite to eat."

Pilar would be nothing of the kind! It was bad enough that she shouldered the responsibility of raising and caring for her younger brothers and sister after her parents' tragic death in an overturned buggy accident five years past. But to feed this annoying rascal who could easily afford a succulent meal at the city's finest restaurant? She'd rather ingest poison! Or better yet, she'd rather poison Grayson—I've-got-everything-going-my-way-Hart!

"How come you have milk all over your boots?" Rory inquired.

Virgil glanced down to note what his grandson's keen eyes hadn't overlooked. When Virgil's gaze bounced back and forth between Grayson and Pilar, he detected the tension that crackled between them. A faint smile hovered on his lips as he steered Rory toward the cottage. Having already forgotten his question, Rory took off in his customary fashion of running full speed ahead. When Rory was out of earshot, Virgil glanced meaningfully at his granddaughter.

"Mind your manners, Pilar. Grayson is a guest in our house."

No, he was a *pest* in the house, she silently amended as she struggled with the brimming bucket of milk.

"I'll carry that for you," Grayson insisted as he reached for the pail.

Their hands met on the metal handle. Pilar felt a jolt of awareness that left her quivering like a tuning fork. Although she possessed mule-quality stubbornness which bade her to defy this handsome, self-confident rascal for pure spite, she released the handle as if she were holding live coals. The last thing Pilar wanted was to be reminded of this unwanted physical attraction she felt for Grayson—God Almighty—Hart. His close proximity had a peculiar effect on her pulse, making it pound like a carpenter driving nails. Pilar had her heart set on disliking this man who owned the spacious house on the hill. So why did her traitorous body respond when he came within five feet of her? Darned if she could figure it out!

If Pilar was baffled by the warm tingles that danced on her nerve endings, Grayson was doubly confused by the sizzling sensations that speared through the most sensitive parts of his male anatomy. True, he found his eyes settling on this curvaceous sprite each time they chanced to meet. But she was a feisty little tart who had a chip on her shoulder the size of the Rock of Gibraltar. She always looked unapproachable, and yet the lure of her feminine body left his thoughts detouring down the most arousing avenues imaginable.

"The Foster family is holding a wedding for their daughter and her fiancé who has finally recovered from his battle wounds. Would you like to accompany me to the festivities tomorrow afternoon?" Grayson heard himself ask out of the blue, and then wondered why the devil he had.

Wide blue eyes, surrounded by thick curly lashes, swept up to rivet on him. Pilar's bewildered stare caused Grayson to shift awkwardly as he toted the bucket of milk toward the cottage beside a grove of cypress trees.

Of all the things Pilar expected Grayson to say to her after she'd lambasted him with her tongue and squirted milk on his boots, *that* wasn't even on the list! Why would he invite her to a wedding party when he could have his pick of dozens of women who'd kill for the chance to have him for an escort? Was he making the offer just because her grandfather had agreed to craft his harnesses? Or did he simply feel sorry for her because she looked like a ragamuffin in her dowdy clothes and wanted to give her the excuse to socialize for the first time in years? Most likely it was a combination of both, Pilar decided. But she didn't need this man's charity. She'd wallow in self-pity and resentment and plow through the hard times, just as she'd done the past five years.

"No thank you," she said in a voice that didn't sound the least bit appreciative of the invitation.

"How come?" Grayson's full lips curved into a sly smile when he posed the question Pilar had heard at least a zillion times.

"Because I don't like weddings," she declared with an aloof tilt of her chin.

A deep skirl of laughter reverberated in Grayson's chest as he lengthened his stride to match Pilar's quick pace. "I wasn't asking you to be *in* one, only to accompany me *to* one," he clarified.

Pilar sliced him a sharp glare. "As if I'd marry the likes of you," she sniffed distastefully. *"You,* with your uppity manners and your fancy house that stands empty on the hill. Why would I want to rattle around in that lonely house when I've got a passel of family surrounding me?"

"And why would I want to marry myself to this family and bear the responsibilities of a shrewish wife when I can come and go as I please without answering to anybody?" Grayson countered, willfully resisting the urge to dump the bucket of milk on her lovely blond head. Damn that tongue of hers! This blue-eyed terror could spring the trap on his temper faster than any woman alive!

"The answer is still no," Pilar muttered. "I've no intention of flouncing around the Foster's house on Sunday afternoon."

"Fine. Just forget I even asked," Grayson scowled at her.

"Forget what?" she scowled back.

Pilar scurried up the steps to the cottage, wondering why envy and resentment could make a woman say such hateful things. Nothing would've pleased her more than to shed her responsibilities for one afternoon and breeze off to socialize with people her own age. But the embarrassing fact was her Sunday-best gown had seen its better days and she'd have been too self-conscious of her appearance to enjoy herself in the company of an aristocrat who could well afford to garb himself in the latest fashion. She'd be the *laugh* of the party instead of the *life* of it. Grayson's offer only served to remind Pilar that she was doomed to spend the prime years of her life caring for her family and scrimping on modest funds. This was as good as things were going to get. If she had any sense, she'd never let herself forget that . . .

Pilar pulled up short when she stepped inside the house to find disaster awaiting her. Since she had been detained in the barn longer than usual, her ten-year-old sister Amity, under the supervision of her thirteen-year-old brother Clay, had made an attempt to prepare breakfast. That spelled disaster! The eggs Pilar had gathered from the henhouse at the break of day now lay scrambled on the planked floor. The ham she'd smoked and left to cure during the hot muggy days of summer was burned into an unrecognizable black slab in the overheated skillet. Virgil was waving a towel to clear the smoke from the air while Rory demanded to know *how come* eggs had shells. Pilar was ready to throw her hands up in resignation and dash back outside for a cherished moment of peace and quiet which never came often enough in this chaotic household.

In a flash, Grayson left the milk pail by the door and sped over to retrieve the smoking skillet before Clay unthinkingly removed the hot utensil with his bare hand. Setting the skillet aside, Grayson squatted down to scoop the weeping eggs into the upturned bowl that lay beside them. Having taken command of the situation and setting the catastrophe aright, he ambled back to fetch the pail of milk.

"I can see why you wouldn't want to venture out into the world and leave your family behind. I stand corrected. Your life is to be envied," he smirked as he brushed past Pilar.

Pilar glared hot pokers at him. She supposed she deserved his ridicule after all her snide remarks. But the painful truth was that she wanted what he had, even if she was too proud and stubborn to admit it. If not for the war and her parents' death, Pilar would've enjoyed a coming-out party. But she'd come of age during the most difficult times. The time for her introduction into society, and to eligible young bachelors, had passed unnoticed.

Now she was twenty going on fifty, carrying a yoke of obligation that would probably weigh her down all the days of her life. By the time the last of her family was married and out of the nest, she'd be a shriveled up old spinster with callused hands, leathery skin, and hunched shoulders. And who was the fool who said life was grand? Probably one of Grayson Hart's rich relatives, that's who!

After Virgil had cleared the air — literally — he gestured for Grayson to take a seat at the table. "Pilar and the children can see to the meal while I take your order."

Pilar can do *this* and Pilar can do *that,* she thought crabbily. Even her grandfather, whom she loved dearly, depended on her to such extremes that it was infuriating. Pilar spitefully wondered what would happen if she walked away without looking back. Too bad her conscience would give her hell if she ever dared to leave her family on their own.

While Pilar spouted orders, left and right, putting her younger brothers and sister to work preparing the meal, Virgil set a cup of coffee in front of Grayson and plunked into his chair. "I'm anxious to make all the halters and harnesses you need," he murmured confidentially while he watched the bustling breakfast brigade. "I'd like to purchase some special gifts for my grandchildren to celebrate the season and the end of the war. They've been forced to do without so many things because prices have escalated beyond my means." Virgil shook his head in dismay. "Four years ago I paid forty cents for five pounds of sugar and now it costs almost six dollars. Fifty cents worth of coffee now costs twenty dollars. At my age, I can't seek outside employment to provide luxuries. But for one time during this year, I'd like to see delighted smiles on my grandchildren's faces. Especially, Pilar's. I ask and expect a lot of her."

Grayson surveyed the crew of four who hovered around the cupboards and stove. His gaze transfixed on the glowing mane of blond hair that rippled down Pilar's back. Although he could easily afford the kind of luxuries Virgil desired to give his grandchildren, Grayson had never known the feeling of belonging to such a close-knit family. He was the only son of an only son and he'd been orphaned at the tender age of ten. Although he'd inherited money, he'd come up through the ranks of life the lonely way. But he'd been fortunate to be spared serious wounds of battle and to return to the home he'd constructed before the war.

Although the crops in his fields had been burned and part of his livestock had been confiscated for food and mounts, he'd managed to overcome his setbacks. Problem was, he envied sassy Pilar Maguire's position in her family—a family who cared, needed, and depended on her. Pilar would laugh herself sick if he admitted the truth, especially after he'd poked fun at her. But she was right on the mark. His home was indeed an empty house of echoing footsteps—his own. Feisty Pilar Maguire had it all—the love of family, the warmth of companionship, and the fulfillment of the need to be needed.

Even the meager but tasty home-cooked meal that Pilar placed before him served to remind him of the simple pleasures which had escaped him. He could afford the juiciest steak in town, but it was served by a stranger on a plate that hadn't been chipped by young helping hands that were eager to assist and emulate the efficient talents of their blue-eyed spitfire sister.

Grayson savored his meal, surrounded by giggling voices and *how come* questions which he volunteered to answer. The smiles on the young faces touched him deep down in his soul, making him realize how much he was missing and what riches lay at Pilar's fingertips. He'd have exchanged places with her if only for one day to soak up the warmth of family like a sponge.

When Grayson ambled outside an hour later, the loss he felt was as palpable as the brisk November wind. He glanced up at the gigantic house on the hill, seeing a monument to loneliness encircled by tall oaks whose outstretched limbs seemed to reach out to grasp something they couldn't hold. Heaving a heavy sigh, Grayson swung onto his bay gelding to begin his half-mile journey home. There'd be no inquisitive

72

young faces to greet him, not even a sassy, shapely little blonde who seemed to be in his thoughts more than she should be, considering her nasty temperament.

Each time Grayson found himself in Pilar's company her image lingered longer than the time before. She was totally unlike the shallow, selfish females who'd come and gone for twenty-eight years of his life. Pilar didn't cater to him, flirt with him, or flatter him with effusive compliments. No, not that gorgeous firebrand with sun-gold hair and luminous blue eyes. She simply squirted milk on his boots and forced him away when he was feeling all the arousing male responses that made him yearn for female companionship. Honest to God, Pilar always left him debating which he wanted most — to take those lush pink lips under his and kiss the breath out of her, or strangle her swan-like neck for mocking him. If Virgil Maguire was searching for a means to make extra cash, he should consider selling Pilar's oversupply of sass. With the cash the family collected they could purchase the entire state of Louisiana and still have funds left over to stock the defunct treasury!

"How come you always stand out here every night and stare at the house on the hill?" Rory inquired as he hoisted himself up on the corral fence to peer at his sister.

"How come you ask so many questions?" Pilar tossed back as she watched the setting sun cast a crimson glow on the grand home that symbolized everything she wanted and knew she'd never have.

Ah, wouldn't it be wonderful to have that nice big house all to herself; to rise from bed when she was so inclined and trot off to town on a well-bred steed to take her meal at a restaurant and purchase store-bought clothes whenever it met her whim? Grayson Hart never had to squat under a contrary cow that would kick Pilar senseless if not restrained, or mop floors after her brothers and sister created calamity. He didn't have to darn old socks or stitch up the seat of pants which had been ripped during a playful tussle. He never had to bandage injured fingers that poked into the wrong places, or fetch a glass of water for a young boy who grasped at every excuse not to be left alone at bedtime . . .

"How come you don't marry Mr. Hart? Then you could move into that house instead of staring at it all the time," Rory chattered like a magpie.

"How come you don't go to bed?" Pilar grumbled tiredly.

"Will you tuck me in?" he asked in a hopeful voice.

"Grandpa can do it this one time. I have a few more chores to attend."

"No, you don't," Rory said with perfect certainty. "You just want to stand here and stare at that house like you always do. As for me, I don't want the house. But I'd like for my head to grow as big as Mr. Hart's so I could borrow his black felt hat with the shiny silver band to keep the sun out of my eyes."

"Get to bed, Rory. Black felt hats indeed!"

Pilar playfully lunged at her youngest brother, provoking him to giggle and bound off like a jackrabbit. As usual, Rory took off in a dead run.

The sound of plodding hooves caught Pilar's attention. She glanced toward the lights of town to see a shadowed rider on horseback. That would be Grayson — I-can-come-and-go-as-I-please-Hart returning home after dining out at his leisure — again. Pilar wondered how her taste buds would react to such fine cuisine, which she didn't have to prepare and serve herself. The shock would probably turn her against home cooking for life.

Grayson reined his steed to a halt when he spied the curvaceous silhouette in the moonlight. Out of sheer boredom, he'd made an unnecessary trip into Alexandria, hoping to find a warm willing female to accommodate him. Trouble was, he took one look at the smiling tavern maid, only to find her eyes and hair were the wrong color. Why was it that the snippy, five-foot-two-inch hellion who lived down the road kept boring into his mind like a termite into wood? She disliked him and all he represented. That was glaringly apparent. She flung saucy rejoinders at him like a porcupine casting quills. And yet, he was magnetically drawn to her strength of character, her irrepressible spunk, and her enchanting beauty — drawn like a moth to the proverbial flame. He knew full well that she'd singe his wings — fire-breathing dragon that she was. But he simply couldn't resist.

When Grayson peered up at the dark house on the hill, he cringed at the silence and empty corridors which awaited him. He'd prefer a heated debate with Pilar to solitude. The nights were always the worst, with only the flickering fingers of lantern light dancing on the walls to keep him company. On impulse, Grayson swung from the saddle to lead his steed toward the corral fence upon which Pilar had propped herself.

"I thought perhaps you'd like to accompany me to dinner in town tomorrow night," he said as he paused directly in front of her.

"Why would you think a thing like that?" Pilar's chin tilted to that belligerent angle that was only too well spotlighted in moonlight. "I'm quite capable of cooking my own meal."

"Did I say you were incapable?"

"You implied it."

"I did no such thing!" Grayson erupted in frustration. "Damnit woman, must you always be so contrary? I swear, if you don't have good cause to instigate an argument, you simply invent one! I have mules who possess better dispositions."

"And I've known roosters who didn't crow as loudly as you do, Grayson Hart, and with far more reason to do so!" she hurled back at him.

Here they came again, those conflicting urges to kiss her silent or wring her lovely neck — or maybe both simultaneously. "It costs no more to be nice than it does to be nasty," Grayson gritted out.

"I wouldn't know," she flashed as she retreated back into her own space, out of range of his titillating male scent. "I can't afford either one —"

A startled gasp broke from her throat when Grayson yielded to the former of his impulses. Without warning, he molded Pilar into his masculine contours. When his head moved deliberately toward hers, Pilar felt herself holding her breath until his sensuous lips descended on hers in gentle possession. It was as if he were testing his reaction and allowing her to test hers as well. His mouth courted hers with such tender expertise that Pilar immediately lost the will to resist. Grayson seemed content to accept only what she offered without demanding more than she knew how to give.

Pilar was ashamed to admit this was the first time she'd ever been kissed and she never dreamed it possible for the meeting of two pairs of lips to cause such a riot of sensations within her. And for that wondrous moment, Pilar couldn't imagine why she'd ever want to be free of the scintillating pleasure that claimed her. Instead of pushing a respectable distance away — as she should've done when Grayson took uninvited liberties — she discovered, to her shame, that her arms had involuntarily glided over his powerful shoulders to anchor herself to him. Good Lord! Where was her pride? Drowning in a whirlpool of unprecedented sensations, that's where it was!

Yet, this may be as close to romance as she'd ever come, considering the mountain of responsibilities which towered over her. If this was the only time she was ever going to be kissed before she became a dried-up spinster, then she was going to savor every splendorous moment.

A shudder of unappeased desire riveted Grayson's sensitized body when Pilar responded to his unexpected embrace. Inexperienced though she obviously was, he sensed the untapped passion that bubbled beneath that self-imposed shell she wore like a turtle. Grayson groaned in delicious torment when her petal-soft lips opened like a fragile blossom, offering him an invitation he couldn't refuse. His darting tongue explored the moist recesses of her mouth, imitating intimate pleasures that he was more than willing to unveil to her.

Her natural fragrance reminded him of the whole outdoors, combined with the lingering scent of freshly baked bread. She had that unique compelling quality and wholesomeness that lured him ever closer to the flame she'd unknowingly ignited inside him. His hands began to move on their own accord, investigating the gentle curve of her hips, the trim indentation of her waist and the ladder of her ribs. When his thumbs brushed over the taut peaks of her breasts he felt Pilar tremble in his arms, felt the unprecedented sensations echo out of her naive body and reverberate through the very core of his being . . .

"Good night, Pilar . . . Mr. Hart . . ."

The chorus of three young voices wafted from the cottage porch, shattering the moment like broken crystal. Pilar launched herself away from temptation so quickly that her spine slammed against the fence, knocking out what little breath she had left — which wasn't much. Pilar blinked twice to orient herself before she spied the stair-step figures on the stoop. Beside her siblings stood her grandfather, puffing on his corncob pipe as he did every evening. The golden glow from the bowl of his pipe revealed a wry smile.

Pilar had never been so embarrassed in all her born days. Wouldn't you know that her first, and probably her last, kiss would be witnessed by a rapt audience — an audience which would never allow her to live the incident down! Her grandfather might spare her the mortification of her predicament but her siblings wouldn't, not in a million years! She could already hear Rory asking *how come* she was outside kissing Grayson and melting all over him like wax dripping off a flaming candle. Pilar wished the ground would open and swallow her alive. No such luck. She was doomed to face the snickers, giggles, and teasing remarks invited by her own foolishness.

After the snickers and giggles erupted, Clay grabbed his younger sister to pantomime the romantic scene. Grayson felt an amused grin spread across his lips — ones that still tingled with the taste of kisses sweeter than peach brandy. Well, this sassy little imp had gotten exactly what she deserved. She, with her cool aloof demeanor that had melted like ice at first kiss! If that was the kiss of a woman who hated everything about him, he'd eat his hat, brim and all. Let her convince her sniggering brothers and sister that she hadn't

77

enjoyed kissing him, especially after she'd given him the cold shoulder routine in the barn and at the breakfast table two days ago. Served little miss distant-and-remote right, it did!

"How come you're kissing Mr. Hart?" Rory had the gall to ask, there and then. "I didn't think you liked him."

If Pilar could've reached across the distance that separated them, she'd have punched Rory in the mouth so his lips would swell shut and he could never pose such humiliating questions again. God, was a simple hole in the ground to climb into asking so much? It wasn't as if she'd asked for the moon or an elegant wardrobe or anything as frivolous as that.

Herein lay the problem of living in a household of inquiring minds and watchful eyes, Pilar thought dispiritedly. A woman had no privacy whatsoever, no solitude. She couldn't even kiss the man she had her heart set on hating without being put on display and forced to explain her illogical actions.

With an expansive wave of his hand Virgil silenced the giggles and laughter. "Off to bed with the lot of you. We have chores to tend bright and early tomorrow."

When the still-snickering threesome trooped back into the house, and Virgil followed in their wake, Pilar half-collapsed against the fence and cursed herself but good. She'd made a complete ass of herself in front of her family. She might as well request Virgil to make a harness for *her* while he was fashioning halters for Grayson's mules.

"There's no need for you to be embarrassed," Grayson murmured as he peered down at the shapely bundle who was still chewing herself up one side and down the other. "Kissing is as natural as breathing."

"That's easy for you to say," Pilar sniffed disgustedly. "You don't have to explain the whys and what-fors to those three clowns when you climb upstairs to bed down beside them. You can bet they'll be wide awake when I get there, ready to give me the dickens!"

"Don't you think it was worth it?" he teased her.

The audacity of this rapscallion! He had the nerve to imply he'd done her some stupendous favor. Well, he wasn't God's gift to womankind and she wasn't his charity case either!

"I'd have sooner kissed a pig, if you want to know," she spewed in bad temper. "Now kindly take yourself off!"

"I kissed you and you liked it!" he contradicted her.

"I did *not* like your kiss, you arrogant lout!" Pilar spouted in offended dignity.

"I was getting an entirely different message from your body. You were as involved in that kiss as I was and don't you dare deny it," Grayson muttered, nearing the end of his patience.

Pilar would've stormed into the house but she hadn't composed herself enough to endure the ridicule she knew awaited her. Better that Grayson mount his prized steed and gallop off to grant her time to prepare for the unavoidable encounter. "Will you please leave. You've done enough damage for one night."

Her terse command didn't earn her the slightest obedience. Out of pure orneriness — and he could be as ornery as Pilar when he felt like it — Grayson leaned down to brush his lips over hers, reacquainting her with the tantalizing sensations he'd evoked from her minutes before. "The invitation to dinner still stands," he assured her in a low caressing voice that had melted the heart of one or two stubborn women in his time. Alas, none of them could hold a candle to this fiery female.

"Thank you, but no." Besides, what would she wear? This worn calico gown or another one just like it? "Instead, why don't you join us for supper. Then we'll see how well you can field straightforward questions. Rory will be the worst. He knows no shame."

Grayson was game. In fact, he would've invited himself to dinner the first time Pilar rejected his offer. But he predicted she'd take offense. He'd enjoyed watching the youthful antics of her siblings the morning he'd joined them at breakfast. He rather liked being one of the crowd rather than an outsider.

Grayson had endured his share of pain. Now he longed for the simplicity of life. Unfortunately, Pilar was determined to shut him out of her world and she declared she had no desire to enter into his. Not that he blamed her, so who was he to complain about her standoffishness? Who'd want to rattle around — as Pilar so aptly put it — in his empty house that didn't possess the ingredients of a true home? His mansion had become a soundless prison — a symbol of the vacuum of his life. Why would a woman who was accustomed to laughter and activity ever settle for monotonous solitude? Pilar had everything the heart desired right now. To Pilar, he was probably a nuisance, an unwanted intruder who upset her scheme of things, even though she'd enjoyed kissing him more than her stubborn pride allowed her to admit . . .

"Well? Do you wish to join us for supper tomorrow or not?" Pilar prompted when he lingered so long in thought. "I can certainly understand your hesitation. After all, who'd enjoy watching Clay plug boiled potatoes into his eye sockets just to get attention, or dodge a spill when Rory reaches for his glass of milk and sends it streaming through the cracks in the table. And then, of course, there's prissy Amity who tries to set the silverware on the wrong side of the plates and swears she's done it right — again."

"I'll be there promptly at seven o'clock," Grayson informed her before he wheeled around to untie his steed.

In stunned amazement, Pilar watched Grayson disappear into the canopy of oaks that lined the path to his sprawling home on the hill. No doubt, he'd only accepted the invitation to check her grandfather's progress on the harnesses. Otherwise, he'd have preferred to trot into town to order whatever he pleased on the menu and dine with folks his own age and from his social class.

Grayson would undoubtedly cringe when Rory wiped the milk mustache off his upper lip with his shirt sleeve, as he'd been told not to do a thousand times. Grayson would lose his appetite completely when Clay put on one of his outrageous displays at the table while he had a captive audience. The boy belonged on a stage, to be sure. Clay delighted in entertaining the family with his outlandish shenanigans. Pilar supposed it was his way of drawing attention to himself. Being the second oldest child did have its drawbacks. Clay wasn't the only boy, or the baby, so he felt compelled to make his own unique mark on the family as its resident comedian. Perhaps Pilar could bribe Clay into behaving for the duration of dinner. For some unexplainable reason it had become important to her that Grayson didn't perceive her family as a passel of ill-mannered bumpkins.

A reluctant smile cut dimples in Pilar's cheeks as she propelled herself toward the house to face the music. Of course, she'd shoot herself in the foot rather than admit those stimulating kisses were worth the embarrassment that awaited her. But she'd enjoyed their rendezvous in the moonlight. Grayson's seductive expertise had left her throbbing with sensations that lingered long after they'd been interrupted by that choir of impish little devils. The feel of Grayson's sensuous lips moving skillfully over hers had awakened her slumbering passions and left her craving a dozen more arousing kisses. The feel of his hands mapping her body set her to wondering where those magical sensations might lead if she dared to follow the whispers of her heart . . .

My, what a dangerous spell that green-eyed wizard cast! She could feel this ill-fated attraction tugging on her like a kite battling a fierce wind. Pilar reminded herself that a man like Grayson Hart was only toying with her to appease his basic needs. She'd heard men were prone to do that sort of thing when lust overcame them. She was convenient now that her grandfather was providing a service for that devastatingly attractive rake. Pilar had to watch her step to ensure *she* didn't provide services for him too. Now *that* would be humiliating degradation at its worst!

A lopsided smile appeared on Grayson's handsome face when his hand slid ineffectively over the greased doorknob at the Maguire cottage. He should've known something was amiss when his rap at the door was met with Clay's loud call to "come in." The ornery prankster was up to his old tricks. Grayson retrieved his handkerchief with his clean hand and

81

wrapped it around the slippery knob to gain entrance. Sure enough, the flare-up of mischief in the culprit's eyes gave him away. But Grayson bore no hard feelings, especially when his gaze wandered, as it had so often of late, to the shapely blonde who peeked up at him from beneath a fringe of thick curly lashes.

Grayson was quick to note the change in attitude of the youngest members of the Maguire clan after they'd witnessed their sister's kiss the previous night. Amity directed Grayson to the opposite end of the dinner table, placing him as far away from Pilar as he could get without seating him outside on the stoop. It was as if Pilar's brothers and sister were leery of his intrusion into her life. But Grayson understood their reservation. Pilar was the only mother figure they had!

"How come you like kissing my sister so much?" Rory inquired as he passed Grayson the bowl of peas.

The blunt question caused Grayson's hand to stall in mid-air. That wasn't a good thing. The exchange between hurried young hands to immobilized fingers brewed disaster. A yelp of surprise erupted from Grayson's lips when the bowl somersaulted over his wrist to plop upside down in his lap. The accidental spill was proceeded by bursts of snickers and the scrambling of pint-sized bodies to see how much damage had been done. Small hands clawed at Grayson's lap, making him wince when groping fingers gouged the private parts of his anatomy.

Pilar sighed in dismay as she bounded from her chair to shoulder her way to Grayson's side. No doubt, Grayson was cursing himself for accepting this dinner invitation-turned-catastrophe. His expensive black breeches were soaked with vegetable juice and butter. Amity and Rory were scooping handfuls of peas from Grayson's lap, unaware of the discomfort they were causing him.

"You can borrow a pair of my trousers," Virgil offered as he heaved himself out of his chair. "They may be a mite tattered and worn but at least they're clean and dry."

Grayson leaped at the chance to vacate his chair and escape Amity and Rory's groping hands. When he unfolded himself, he found his gaze locking with Pilar's. Suddenly his discomfort came from a different source.

"I did warn you that there'd be embarrassing questions and accidental spills," she murmured as her eyes fell to the buttery stains on the crotch of his breeches. An impish grin hovered on her lips as her long lashes swept up to meet his intense stare. "Even *you* may not be able to afford the expense of replacing clothes if you accept future invitations."

"I can handle the questions and the accidents," Grayson assured her as he brushed past her, savoring the only close contact the Maguire clan had permitted him.

The disarming smile Grayson awarded Pilar before he moved away had the most remarkable effect on her heartbeat, not to mention the instantaneous reaction of her body. There was no doubt about it. Although she envied this striking figure of a man and the blessings of his life, she was also attracted to him. Or was she attracted to him *because* of all those blessings she envied? Pilar wasn't sure, but lately she'd found herself thinking about Grayson a hundred times a day and fussing over her appearance, as well as the evening meal. Pilar scolded herself for all these hopeless romantic notions, but she still liked him far more than she preferred to admit, even to herself. To Grayson, she was just a convenient distraction. To her, he'd become . . .

"You like him more than you like us, don't you?" Amity pouted as she plunked into her chair.

"Of course not," Pilar reassured her little sister.

"Then why've you been acting so *different* since you kissed the stuffing out of him last night?" Clay snorted.

"Yeah, how come?" Rory demanded as he dropped the last of the spilled peas back into the bowl. "I asked you a bunch of questions this afternoon and you didn't hear any of them."

"Sit down and finish your supper," Pilar snapped.

"Good idea," Clay said with a snort. "If we don't, Mr. Hart will gobble it all up and we won't get any."

Pilar rolled her eyes at Clay's remark and stuffed Rory back in his chair. "Just eat."

Still grumbling about Grayson's presence in their house,

83

the children did as they were told. Pilar studied them, realizing how foolish they looked while they were puffed up with resentment. No doubt, she'd looked and sounded just as ridiculous while she'd been flinging caustic rejoinders at Grayson. But envy was a human flaw which was difficult to overcome. As for herself, Pilar was going to quit behaving so childishly, or at least she'd try. With each passing day it was becoming more difficult not to like that green-eyed rake whose charismatic smiles could melt the ice around her heart. She'd enjoyed the way he made her feel when he took her in his sinewy arms and taught her the delicious pleasures that had escaped her for twenty years. She liked the scent of him, the sight of him—probably way too much for her own good, if the truth be known!

"I've completed your order for the harnesses and halters," Virgil announced as he handed Grayson a spare pair of breeches.

Grayson paused from unfastening his stained trousers to gape at the stoop-shouldered old man. "Already?"

Virgil nodded his gray head. "I put Pilar in command of her brothers and sister to tend the chores so I could devote all my time to the task." When Grayson reached into his pocket to pay the price agreed upon, Virgil flung up his hand in a deterring gesture. "I'd like to ask a favor, Grayson. Save back enough money to purchase a fancy bonnet for Pilar. You know more about women's fashions than I. Although I wanted to get Pilar a fine, store-bought dress for Christmas, I can't afford it. A stylish hat is the best I can do. But at least she'll have something new that she didn't have to make with her own hands. Would you see to that matter for me, son?"

Grayson stepped out of his breeches and grasped the tattered pair Virgil offered him. "I'll make the purchase for you," he promised. "I also spoke with the blacksmith yesterday and he's anxious for you to make some bridles and harnesses for him as well."

Virgil beamed in delight as Grayson dropped the remainder of coins in his hand. "I appreciate that. That extra money will mean enough gifts to go around, come Christmas."

"I could lend you . . ."

Grayson's offer trailed off when Virgil gave his head a negative shake. "I appreciate your generosity. But all I want is your promise that you won't hurt Pilar." When Grayson stuffed the wrong leg into the borrowed breeches and shifted awkwardly, Virgil's face crinkled in a smile. "I've noticed the way Pilar looks at you when she thinks no one's watching. I've also seen the way your eyes follow her. She's pretty, but she's also very inexperienced when it comes to men. I'm pleased to see a new light in her eyes. I don't want her hurt."

The conversation was making Grayson decidedly uncomfortable. It was the first of its kind that he recalled having. "If you prefer I don't come around—"

Virgil's hand clamped down on Grayson's massive shoulder and his wry grin displayed the missing tooth at the corner of his mouth. "Would *you* enjoy being somewhere else just as much?"

Grayson met the old man's direct stare. "I could've been elsewhere. This is where I chose to spend the evening."

"That's all I wanted to know." Virgil snickered when Grayson pivoted toward the closed door, anxious to avoid more probing questions. "I suggest you button those breeches before you confront my grandchildren. Rory's powers of observation border on phenomenal. You can expect him to point out your lack of attention to your gaping clothes."

Grayson turned as red as a suntanned man could get while he hurriedly buttoned himself into the skintight trousers. He'd partially exposed his feelings about Pilar to Virgil, and that had made him self-conscious. Better that he didn't expose even more of himself to the rest of the rambunctious clan. They seemed to be having difficulty accepting his intrusion as it was. Perhaps it would be best if he backed off . . .

Grayson moseyed back to the dining room to take his seat, but not without discreetly checking his chair for booby traps. Knowing Clay's penchant for pranks, Grayson wouldn't have been surprised to find a tack in his seat. But the instant Grayson sank down, his gaze focused on Pilar's enchanting face and thoughts of Clay evaporated. The same hunger that had gnawed at him for days came back in full force, and it didn't go away after he'd taken his meal either. He had but to look at those soft luscious lips and he could taste her innocent and yet tantalizing kiss. God, was he so lonely for affection and companionship that he'd become obsessed? Had Virgil perceived that vulnerability? Was that what their private conversation was all about? Virgil had seventy years of experience to his credit. He could probably see through Grayson like a window pane. Was it truly this curvaceous little imp who attracted him in particular or was it desire for sexual pleasure in general? Was it the bustling activity of family and this modest but homey cottage that lured him? Or was it a combination of both . . . ?

"How come you're so quiet?" Rory questioned in his usual forthright manner.

"I was just thinking," Grayson replied as he focused on the inquisitive face and intelligent eyes that reminded him so much of Pilar's.

"How come you don't think out loud like I do?"

"Rory, stop giving him the third degree and eat your vegetables," Pilar demanded. "You should follow Grayson's example and keep a few of your thoughts and questions to yourself."

Having been taken to task, Rory shoveled a fork full of potatoes into his mouth and chewed vigorously. But the rebuke slid off as fast as water down a duck's back. "Are you going to marry Pilar and move her up to your house on the hill? She stares at it all the time, you know. And how come — ?"

"Rory!" Pilar railed in humiliation. "I'll stitch your mouth shut if you don't learn to hobble your runaway tongue."

A sly smile twitched Grayson's lips as he watched Pilar turn all the colors of the rainbow. *Stared at his house,* did she? Now why do you suppose that was?

"Excuse me. I better wash the stains from Grayson's trousers before they set," Pilar mumbled.

She couldn't clamber out of her chair fast enough to escape the twinkle of amusement in Grayson's emerald eyes. Curse that little brother of hers! It was bad enough that she was forced to deal with the unprecedented sensations this midnight-haired rogue aroused in her without Rory blabbing her preoccupations all over creation! Sweet mercy, wasn't a woman allowed any solitude or privacy of thoughts around here?

Only when Pilar stomped onto the back porch with soiled breeches in hand did she expel the exasperated breath she'd been holding. Her tormented gaze reached toward the silhouette of the sprawling mansion on the hill, wishing she were there, surrounded by the finer things in life and the peacefulness she yearned to experience.

Ah, lucky Grayson Hart with his grand home and his expensive store-bought clothes! Her gaze dropped to the soiled breeches that she'd plunged into soapy water. On closer inspection of the garment, Pilar frowned thoughtfully. Her critical gaze drifted over the fabric, buttonholes, and seams. Although she didn't fancy herself a renowned dressmaker, she decided her skills with needle and thread were comparable to the efforts on this garment.

For weeks, Pilar had been fretting over how she could earn the money to purchase Christmas gifts for her family. During the war, she'd made alterations for Laraine Barton who owned and operated the town's fashionable shop. If Pilar could make arrangements to design entire dresses, she could afford a few gifts. By wisely allotting her time, she could complete the garments before the holidays. With money in hand, she could make her store-bought purchases for her family and they could enjoy a real Christmas for the first time in five years. Pilar decided she'd ride into town and approach Laraine the first chance she got. And if there was any money left over, she might even buy a gift for Grayson, though what she could buy a man who had everything she couldn't imagine!

By the time Pilar had hung the breeches up to dry and returned to the dining room, the table had been cleared. Virgil was puffing on his corncob pipe and Clay had challenged Grayson to a game of checkers. To Pilar's surprise, Amity and Rory had taken a seat on Grayson's knees. The wariness they'd displayed earlier had evaporated. Amity had even looped her arm over his broad shoulder, as if they were dear friends. When Rory demanded to know *how come* Grayson had moved one of his checkers to a new location, Grayson employed the kind of patience Pilar had exhausted months ago. In fact, if this handsome rake was bothered by the affection and attention he was receiving from the younger members of the family, he disguised his irritation well. Of course, Grayson would probably expel an enormous sigh when he finally bid the clan good night to seek refuge in the peaceful halls of his home.

When Grayson's gaze lifted over Clay's sandy-blond head, where he sat poised in profound concentration, Pilar felt as if those intense green eyes bored through flesh to touch her soul. The jolt of instant awareness paralyzed her, leaving a flood of longing to channel through every fiber of her being. When she stared at the sensuous curve of Grayson's lips she remembered, with vivid clarity, the kiss they'd shared the night before. Pilar clutched at the back of a nearby chair to steady herself, marveling at the dramatic effect of his eyes on her and the wayward direction of her thoughts. My God, the man had ruined her for life! He'd taken one look at her and she wanted his mind-boggling kiss, his pulse-jarring caress. Had she no shame, no willpower? If she didn't get a grip on herself she'd soon be the consistency of the plum pudding which was fermenting for five weeks in preparation for Christmas dinner!

The thump of Clay's hand pounded the game board, shattering Pilar's pensive musings. She glanced down to see that Clay had bested Grayson, leaving him not one checker.

"I won!" Clay erupted in triumph, and then his eyes narrowed suspiciously. "You didn't *let* me win, did you?"

Let him? Let him! Grayson had been so damned preoccupied with visualizing how Pilar would look lying naked in his arms on the homemade quilt which covered her grandfather's bed, that checkers had been the farthest thing from his mind. Egad, this saucy female was really getting to him! He looked at her and he wanted her beyond reason. When they were apart he wondered what she was doing, wondered if she'd mentally relived their kiss as often as he had. Was it truly *this* woman he ached for? Or was it only *a* woman to appease needs he'd allowed to lie dormant for more weeks than he cared to count?

With tremendous effort, Grayson tore his hungry gaze away from gorgeous temptation to glance at Virgil who was lounging in his favorite rocking chair beside the hearth. Through the white fog of smoke, Grayson saw the knowing smile that curved around the stem of the pipe Virgil clamped between his teeth.

"Maybe you should come down to the barn with me to fetch the harnesses and halters," Virgil advised with a wink. "Maybe you could use some cool fresh air too, Grayson."

Cold bath was nearer the mark, Grayson decided. He was steaming like a clam with lusty thoughts that would've shocked the starch out of Pilar. Damned good thing *she* couldn't read his mind. It was bad enough that Virgil could!

"I'll go with you," Pilar volunteered.

"We'll all come," Clay announced as he bolted from his chair to stand possessively beside Pilar.

Grayson resigned himself to the fact that he wasn't to be granted time alone with Pilar. Her pint-sized guard dragons were back on alert, providing a human shield which prevented him from caressing what his itching fingers yearned to touch. Maybe he didn't like this close-knit circle of family and constant activity as much as he thought he did. These ornery little brats were standing between him and this curvaceous blonde, practically daring him to make one move toward her and see where it got him.

Feeling as frustrated as one man could get, Grayson gathered his harnesses and bid the family good night. The sound of distant thunder rumbled to the south, forewarning of the rainy night ahead. All too clearly Grayson could picture himself lying abed with Pilar, letting his heartbeat match the pat-ter of falling rain, whirling in a storm of unleashed passion . . .

His gaze drifted up the hill to the lonely house. The wealth he'd amassed couldn't buy what his heart desired. In fact, all the money in the federal treasury couldn't compensate for this lust attack he was having! Lord, he had to get himself under control! He was behaving like a love-starved school-boy.

When thunder rumbled overhead, Virgil glanced sky-ward. "Better set a quick pace, Grayson," he suggested with another perceptive grin. "You might get a cold shower before you arrive home. But then, I've taken a few myself when certain circumstances prevailed."

With a quick but longing glance in Pilar's direction, Grayson nudged his bay gelding toward the path. *When certain circumstances prevailed,* he thought as he trotted off, wincing as the saddle horn stabbed at him in taunting reminder of his uncomfortable state of arousal. The Civil War had raged for four years, he recalled. He wondered if his obsessive need for that saucy nymph would last just as long. Perhaps he should take up smoking a pipe as a substitute for the pleasures he was doing without. Damnation, he needed some kind of relief!

When the clouds opened to drench him with buckets of rain, Grayson found minimal relief. It was not, however, the kind he preferred. He had the depressing feeling the cold shower had only temporarily relieved his symptoms. Unfortunately, there was only one cure for what ailed him and he was doomed to be hounded by erotic dreams which would interrupt his sleep.

Sure enough, Grayson didn't sleep well that night . . . or the night after . . . or the night after that . . .

Pilar couldn't honestly say she was pleased with the restrictions Laraine Barton placed on their business arrangement, but she settled for it nonetheless—out of desperation for Christmas funds. The plump, red-haired matron refused to pay cash until the garments Pilar offered to create had actually sold.

"You must understand my position," Laraine blared in her typical loud voice. The older woman was slightly hard of hearing and she presumed that if she couldn't hear herself, then no one else could either. "I've already been extremely generous in covering the cost of the fabric and thread. And if, by chance, your creations aren't acceptable or saleable, I have to incur the loss of my investment. The only way I can possibly agree to this proposition, and be a conscientious businesswoman, is to pay you the portion of your profit *after* the gowns sell to my clientele."

Laraine was getting into the Christmas spirit, wasn't she? Her motto was—don't give unless you're sure you'll receive. It was no sweat off her brow that the Maguires were in dire straits. Laraine looked out after *hers truly* and let her neighbors and customers struggle as best they could. The widow counted her blessings in cash and saw the Christmas holidays in monetary value. It was a spiteful thought, Pilar knew, but she hoped the only gift crabby ole Laraine received was the one she gave herself!

"I can understand your position, Laraine, but I was hoping to make sure I had cash before Christmas—"

Laraine flung up her hand to demand silence. "That's my first and last offer. Take it or leave it."

Swallowing pride and irritation, Pilar consented. "I'll take it."

Gathering the fabric she'd decided upon, Pilar wheeled toward the door, trying not to notice the fashionable bonnets, frilly petticoats, and stylish gowns that surrounded her. Besides, where would she wear such elegant garments? To the barn to milk Bertha? Or in the kitchen to boil molasses for taffy and prepare mincemeat pies for the holidays? No, calico was practical and comfortable and it suited Pilar's domestic activities. Let cranky ole Laraine sashay around her shop in her costly ensembles. The stylish clothes were truly all Laraine had going for her. Pilar wouldn't have exchanged places with the woman on a bet. If they did trade roles, Clay would give Laraine fits and she wouldn't last a day.

Dissatisfied but resigned to the arrangement, Pilar breezed outside and glanced every which way at once before propelling herself toward the swaybacked plow horse she'd been forced to ride into town. Of course, Grayson Hart wouldn't be caught dead on such a pathetic creature. But this was Pilar's only mode of transportation. One did what one had to do if one wanted to travel, even if it wasn't in style.

Pilar strapped the package to the saddle and piled onto the horse. Although she nudged the plodding beast, the animal refused to set a swifter pace. Like Rory who had only one speed—fast—this nag's one and only pace was slow. Pilar had ridden two miles before she heard the pounding of hooves behind her. When she swiveled around, her heart sank at the sight of Grayson Hart moving like a centaur, gobbling up the distance like poetry in motion. Damn, he would have to come along right about now. Here she was, practically begging this broken-down nag to run and Grayson's fine animal was cantering in graceful strides, making Pilar all the more aware of the differences between her life-style and his.

Despite her reluctance at being caught riding such a pitiful creature, Pilar felt a smile of greeting surfacing on her lips. Her eyes absorbed the muscular length of him, his masculine, confident posture, that dynamic quality which commanded her attention.

Grayson reined his laboring steed to a halt when he reached Pilar and her pathetic plow horse. It had been a week since he'd seen this bewitching sprite—a week of wanting and doing without. Well, noble reserve be damned, Grayson decided. He'd been battling this intense craving for seven days and enough was enough! If he didn't get a taste of those honey-eyed lips that had haunted him for an eternity, he was going to die of starvation!

Without preamble, Grayson snaked out his arm to scoop Pilar off her saddle and plant her in his lap. His lips came down hard and faintly forceful. He savored and devoured the addicting taste of her. Grayson knew he was lost and gone forever when he felt her voluptuous body molded familiarly to his. It was like coming home again after an extended sojourn in purgatory. His body came to life, throbbing in rhythm with his accelerated heartbeat. Suddenly, he was a burning flame that fed upon itself until the fire threatened to consume him.

His hand glided over her thighs, burrowing beneath her skirt to make stimulating contact with her silky flesh. When his fingertips splayed over the velvety plane of her belly, her sharp intake of breath assured him that each shuddering sensation he aroused in her was like nothing she'd known before. That pleased him immensely for some reason. The other women who'd come into his arms had known where fervent desire could lead. But Pilar's responses to the newness of a man's hands and lips on her body were instinctive and unrehearsed, provoking pleasures Grayson couldn't begin to describe. He had the confident feeling that he and this blond hellion would be like wildfire if they ever wound up in the throes of unbridled passion. She was the kind of woman who could make a man ever so glad she'd chosen *him* to introduce her to splendrous desire.

Pilar couldn't begin to count or even explain the kaleidoscope of ever-changing sensations that burgeoned inside her. Grayson's masterful caresses and kisses sent her senses reeling. This powerfully built giant was so close and yet so unbearably far away. She couldn't seem to get enough of the taste, scent, or feel of him. He made her want things that were forbidden and yet wickedly alluring . . . And if she didn't pry herself loose from these intoxicating kisses she'd be so drunk on the taste of him that common sense would float away! Halfheartedly, Pilar pressed her palms against his chest, feeling the heat of his masculine body, the thunder of his heartbeat which matched her racing pulse.

"I can't think straight, much less breathe," she gulped.

"When I'm kissing you I don't care if I do. You're all the air I need. You absorb all thought," Grayson rasped, his voice husky with the effects of their ardent embrace.

"Just because you're accustomed to having whatever you

want doesn't mean you can take what you please," Pilar snapped, thoroughly ashamed of herself for responding to the fiery burst of pleasure that still radiated through her. She squirmed in his lap, making matters worse. Innocent though she was, she could feel the abrupt changes in his male anatomy. "I'm not some tainted rose you can uproot and replant in your lap when the mood suits. You could've at least had the decency to *ask* if I wanted to be snatched off my horse."

Pilar was objecting because he was being *demanding?* A lot she knew! He'd shown admirable restraint! He'd stolen a kiss when what he really wanted was the whole woman and the satisfying rapture he sensed awaited him. He ached to make wild sweet love to her, here and now, to turn his erotic dreams into passionate reality.

His hands gently framed her oval face, tilting her petal-soft lips to his awaiting mouth. "Would you mind very much if I kissed you again?" Grayson questioned huskily.

All she'd wanted was the chance to accept or reject his embrace. And since he'd been polite enough to ask, all was forgiven. Pilar's arms glided over the padded muscles of his chest, drawing him ever closer, longing to feel herself come back to life after a week of monotonous existence . . .

"Well, damn, one would think we're right smack-dab in the middle of a busy intersection in town," Grayson grumbled when the clatter of hooves and the rumble of a wagon shattered the breathless silence.

Hurriedly, he fastened the buttons on the front of her gown to conceal the ripe swells of her breasts that he'd kissed and caressed until he was so on fire with wanting all of her that he'd completely forgotten where they were — on the back of his horse, for pity's sake! In frustrated disgust, he scooped Pilar up and deposited her on her nag. Nudging his steed in the flanks he led the way past the approaching wagon and waved to the single occupant who sat on the seat. Grayson didn't fail to notice how the young lad's eyes zeroed in on Pilar's enchanting face and then dipped to her full bosom. A stab of possessiveness knifed through him. Confound it, what had this feisty female done to him? All he'd done was kiss her a couple of times and explore her tempting curves and swells, and poof! He was behaving as if she bore his stamp of ownership.

Grayson was still wrestling with the silent question Virgil Maguire had forced him to consider the previous week: Was it this particular woman who aroused his hunger, or could it have been any woman with an alluring face, figure, and delightful spunk? It was so difficult to know his own mind when he was with Pilar because his wants and needs became impossible to separate. His respect for Virgil and Pilar demanded that he be certain of his intentions. He and Pilar were both playing with a white-hot fire that could burn out of control. For her sake, as well as his own, he needed to sort out the truth of his emotions before his passions took him past the point of no return.

He was a lonely man reaching out for affection and companionship. Was that what motivated him and attracted him? Was it because Pilar lived conveniently close and he enjoyed the circle of family which surrounded her? Or was his need for affection the result of this growing attraction? Damned if Grayson knew. But Virgil Maguire's wrinkled face kept popping to mind and his words echoed in Grayson's ears. Southern pride may have been broken by defeat, but Southern honor was still as strong as ever. If a man was without decency, then he was truly alone in the world — even more alone than Grayson was now.

"Um, I forgot something in town," Grayson mumbled as he reversed direction and took off like a house afire.

Pilar misinterpreted his noble restraint for temporary satisfaction. Why that lusty rogue! He'd only followed her to steal a kiss and tease her with his seductive caresses. Having appeased his needs, he trotted on his way. *Fool,* she berated herself. If she had any visions of a lasting relationship with that rogue, she was kidding herself. Grayson was only interested in her body, or that of any other woman. He wasn't concerned about the personality and difficulties attached to that feminine body. Women were like toys he pulled from the shelf to amuse him at his leisure — nothing more. Well, what had she expected from a rich man? Devotion? Loyalty? Love? Pilar scoffed at such absurdity. Grayson Hart didn't need her for the right reasons. He had everything he wanted in life. She was going straight home to wash away the masculine scent that clung to her and guzzle a glass of water to drown the taste of his kisses, once and for all. So there!

Although thirty days had November, it seemed an incredibly long month for Grayson — one of the longest in living memory. December was also turning out to be every bit as long and lonely. He'd hoped for an invitation to Thanksgiving dinner in the Maguire home, especially after he'd presented Virgil with a dressed turkey to show his appreciation for completing the order for halters so quickly. Grayson had even advertised Virgil's skilled workmanship by word of mouth to all his business acquaintances to secure several more cash orders. But each time Grayson employed an excuse to stop by the Maguire cottage, Pilar took a wide berth around him or refused to show herself at all. It was damned frustrating to feel his gaze searching for her, his body aching for the feel of her shapely flesh molded intimately to his, and to receive not one smidgen of satisfaction . . .

"How come you're always staring off in the distance when you stop by?" Rory queried as he peered up at the muscular mountain of the man who eclipsed the sun. "Pilar does that all the time too. She hardly ever hears my questions while she's doing that."

Grayson gave himself a mental shake and glanced down at Rory who stood beside his grandfather.

"Grayson has a great deal on his mind, I suspect," Virgil responded for his distracted guest. "Why don't you go toss some hay to Bertha for me, Rory. I have a private matter to discuss with Grayson."

After Rory bounded off like a jackrabbit, Virgil turned his sly smile on Grayson. "Pilar has made a spectacular display of avoiding you lately. Should you be telling me the reason why?"

Grayson's breath came out in a frustrated rush. "I was hoping *you* could tell *me*."

"Probably because she's a woman," Virgil said, as if that explained everything. "Or maybe she doesn't even know herself. If that's the case, it explains a lot."

Grayson didn't have a chance to quiz Virgil about his enigmatic remark because the old man jumped to another topic of conversation like a grasshopper. "Have you found time to purchase that bonnet for Pilar yet?"

"I browsed through Mrs. Barton's selections and found nothing to my liking," Grayson replied as his gaze automatically drifted back to the house, longing for the sight of that saucy blue-eyed siren who haunted his days and tormented his nights. "A new shipment of merchandise was due to arrive this week. I'll check with Laraine this afternoon."

"I've purchased all my other gifts," Virgil declared with immense satisfaction. "Thanks to the extra orders you've brought me, it's going to be a grand holiday season. There'll be gifts and peace on earth at long last."

For the Maguires maybe, but not for Grayson Hart. The silence that met him at home these days was deafening. He'd even tried to seek appeasement elsewhere and then turned away at the last second. That tormenting female who'd been avoiding him was ruining his love life and damaging his sanity, When the front door of the cottage flew open and shouts burst in the crisp morning air, Grayson felt a rueful smile tug at his downturned mouth. He'd missed this family more than they'd ever know.

Clay leaped off the porch and raced toward the barn while Amity, brandishing a wooden spoon, chased after him. Behind her, Pilar appeared in the doorway, ordering her young sister not to pound her brother over the head, though the ornery prankster probably deserved it. But the instant Grayson's gaze locked with Pilar's she stepped back to slam the door, locking him out of her life — again.

"Kids . . ." Virgil shook his head and chuckled. "They love to squabble." His perceptive gaze darted between Grayson and the closed door behind which Pilar had conveniently disappeared. "But then, petty disagreements aren't confined to youth, are they? Sometimes a man just has to decide what he wants. And if he wants it bad enough, he's got to make a few concessions and compromises."

Grayson snapped his head up to focus his unblinking gaze on Virgil's wry smile and stubbled chin that awaited the attention of a sharp razor. "Yes . . . er . . . well, I'd better be on my way. I have business to conduct in town."

Executing a perfect about-face that would've done the Southern army proud, Grayson marched toward his steed. Damn that Pilar Maguire and her tortuous memories! She was driving him crazy with wanting and refusing to let him near her. Only God knew why she was being so distant and remote. Grayson certainly couldn't figure it out. And curse that old coot Virgil for seeing through him so easily. Maybe he ought to consider selling his plantation and moving away. Or better yet, he'd give that lonely house to the Maguires. At least there would be something besides emptiness inside those brick and timber walls. But if he had his druthers . . .

Grayson clamped down on the half-formulated thought which ricocheted around his brain. As Virgil had said, a man had to decide what he really wanted before he could pursue his options. Grayson needed to analyze his motives before he acted. At the moment, the lure of that unattainable female was too fresh on his mind and too hard on his male body for him to think straight. She made his blood run hot for all the normal reasons. But Pilar Maguire wasn't a woman to be taken for granted, nor would Virgil allow Grayson to do so. Virgil wasn't giving Grayson a standing invitation to rejoin the circle of his family or enjoy Pilar's company until he knew the younger man's true intentions. Hell, Grayson wasn't certain of those intentions himself. He was just frustrated to no end!

Maybe he should gallop into town and snatch up any old hat for Pilar's gift and deliver it to Virgil. Afterwards, he'd find himself an accommodating female to appease his needs. Let little Miss Maguire spend her life raising her siblings and avoiding him. What did he care? He didn't care at all! He could snap his fingers and there'd be plenty of women to satisfy him. And if he wanted to be surrounded by laughter and conversation he could park himself in a chair at the tavern. He didn't need Pilar or that passel of children who lived down the hill. Grayson had been a loner for years on end. He should be accustomed to it by now. To hell with the Maguires, and especially Pilar! If she wanted nothing to do with him then maybe he didn't want anything to do with her either!

Still harboring spiteful thoughts, Grayson burst into the shop to select a bonnet for Pilar. He truly should buy that termagant the most old-fashioned headgear in the shop. Virgil wouldn't know the difference since he was out of touch with fashion. What did Grayson care about the special emotions of the holidays anyway? For him, Christmas would be as empty and uneventful as Thanksgiving . . .

"May I help you, Mr. Hart?" Laraine Barton blared in her customary loud voice.

Grayson's resentful musings evaporated when his gaze sped past the buxom proprietor to settle on the bonnet on the rack beside her. Obviously the new shipment had arrived from the East. With determined purpose, Grayson strode toward the rack to pluck up the dainty ostrich-plumed hat with its long blue silk veil that streamed behind it. The vivid color of the bonnet matched the deep blue shade of Pilar's eyes when they darkened with the passion he'd evoked in her. This hat had Pilar's name written all over it.

"We also have some lovely new gowns that copy the latest European styles," Laraine declared as she gestured a pudgy hand to the left. "Or if you prefer a less expensive garment, one of the young ladies in the community made some dresses on consignment for extra cash at Christmas, provided they sell. Of course, they aren't as exquisite as these gowns created by the renowned dressmakers from the East. But Pilar Maguire does sew a fine seam, even if her family doesn't come from proper breeding—"

Grayson spun around so quickly that he could've stirred up a dust devil. And who was this snobbish old bat to look down her nose at the Maguires, he'd like to know! And who was she to say that Pilar's workmanship didn't compare to eastern dressmakers? Grayson doubted if any of those dressmakers had been forced to schedule their sewing around a bustling family and extensive chores. The fact that Pilar had found time to design gowns, while she was so busy meeting herself coming and going that she didn't have time to tell herself hello, amazed Grayson. She needed no outside projects with the mound of responsibility which had been heaped on her. When did she find time to sew? At night when she needed to be sleeping to regenerate energy? Or did she race through her chores at record speed to work on her projects while the children were in school, and then collapsed from exhaustion into bed? Whatever the case, Pilar had made time to earn cash for her precious family and shut him out of her world. That certainly signified *his* importance in her life, now didn't it?

Although the thought stung like a wasp, Grayson couldn't help but admire the sacrifices Pilar had made for her family. If Pilar had killed herself making the gowns, which Laraine labeled as sub-quality, then he'd ensure she received payment to purchase the gifts for her family. Maybe he did have a bit of the Christmas spirit in him after all. Despite his exasperation with Pilar, he was touched by her unselfish deeds and personal sacrifices.

"I'd like to see the gowns Miss Maguire made," he requested, resisting the urge to shake Laraine for her irritating remark.

"Just don't expect perfection, Mr. Hart," Laraine advised as she waddled toward the back of the shop. "The price may be right, but the styles are of her own design. Considering her simple background, Pilar chose to combine practicality with modest fashion. Of course, these gowns aren't meant to be worn to a grand ball, but . . ."

Grayson stopped listening to Laraine's clanging voice. His fingers were curling into a choke necklace which would've fit perfectly around the old crone's fleshy throat. It was one thing for him to criticize Pilar and quite another for Laraine to do it!

When Laraine held the gowns up for his inspection, Grayson felt like strangling her all over again. Pilar's efforts were absolutely stunning, if he was any judge of fashion. She had the knack of capturing feminine beauty and subtle style. The garments weren't cascading with layers of ruffles and lace, it was true, but they were elegant without being flamboyant. Pilar was every bit as talented with needles and thread as her grandfather was with leather and silver. While Grayson ran an inspecting hand over the satin and velvet gowns, he visualized how Pilar would look in all these garments. Breathtaking, he speculated.

"I'll take them all," he announced on impulse. When Laraine blinked in disbelief, Grayson smiled a tight smile. "I happen to disagree with you, madam. These gowns have a quality that European styles lack. They are tastefully exquisite and also exemplary of our Southern legacy. Their workmanship is excellent. Indeed, if I were you, I would request that Miss Maguire design a dozen more of similar style. They appeal to the masculine eye in a quiet, alluring way which scads of ruffles and piles of lace do not."

"Are you suggesting I have no taste for what is fashionable?" Laraine demanded, highly affronted by the implication.

There was menace in his glittering green eyes and the thinning of his lips. "I'm saying that a man knows what he likes to see a woman wearing. I find Miss Maguire's innovative style intriguing. In fact, I think her designs warrant the same price as your other inventory and I intend to pay it. I also expect that Miss Maguire be compensated with the extra profit, despite whatever arrangement the two of you agreed upon."

Laraine gasped at the very idea of Grayson telling her to give Pilar the extra money she could've kept for herself. But Grayson's imposing stance, and the expression that was carved in his chiseled features, warned her not to slight Pilar. He had the look of a man who intended to see his wishes carried out to the letter — or else.

"Very well, Mr. Hart," she conceded in a begrudging tone. "The girl will receive the extra cash as her profit, but only because I'm being generous during the holiday season."

What a crock, thought Grayson. Laraine was complying because he'd refused to let her be greedy. Given the chance, she would've hoarded the money for herself. Laraine—Mrs. Ebenezer Scrooge—wasn't fooling him for a minute!

"I'll also take that bonnet over there." He directed her attention to the hat he'd selected earlier. "And—"

His critical gaze flooded over the rack of gowns. Grayson was feeling generous. He remembered what Virgil had said about Pilar wanting a dress she didn't have to make with her own hands. Grayson intended to select a gown for Pilar that was exquisite without being gawdy, something that would accentuate her curvaceous physique without burying it beneath yards of unnecessary fabric and ruffles. Her shapely figure would fill out the dress in ways very few women's could.

Of course, what Grayson would've preferred most was to buy Pilar an ensemble to match the Emperor's New Clothes—the invisible kind that revealed all her lovely curves and swells to his hungry gaze. But considering the way his rocky courtship was progressing, he'd never see his wildest fantasies collide with reality. He was going to have to cease these stimulating hallucinations and return to the real world. Pilar didn't want him to be a part of her life, enjoying her affection and the warm circle of her family. Yet, he still felt compelled to offer her a special gift. She wanted a store-bought gown and by God she'd have one, even if it was the only thing she'd allow Grayson to give her—and maybe not even that! The gesture would probably offend her pride, of which she'd been blessed with a colossal supply.

"And I'll take that emerald green, off-the-shoulder silk gown too," Grayson insisted, indicating the dress that had caught his eye.

Laraine beamed in satisfaction. Grayson Hart's extensive purchases had awarded her scads of extra money. She forgave him for offending her with his remarks. Money in hand could cure her affronted dignity in one second flat.

When Grayson ambled out of the shop, laden down with

packages, his need to share his wealth with Pilar and her family still wasn't completely satisfied. Perhaps Pilar had refused to accept him into her life and let him share the pleasure of a close-knit family, but he wanted the Maguires to enjoy the kind of Christmas they'd long remember. Odd, thirty minutes earlier he'd been scowling at the holiday season and resenting the loneliness that surrounded him. But one look at greedy Laraine Barton had cured him for life. He was going to purchase gifts for every member of the Maguire clan, just as Virgil and Pilar planned to do. No one was going to spoil these feelings of generosity for him, not when it was all he had to put pleasure in his life!

Seeing the excited smiles on the faces of the young Maguires would partially fulfill the longing inside him. At least a few of his needs would be satisfied. The strongest of them, of course, would remain unappeased. It was becoming increasingly apparent that he'd been Pilar's first experiment with desire. She seemed to like the kissing part well enough, but she obviously wasn't all that enthusiastic about the man who'd done the kissing. She was going to let him starve to death after she'd whetted his appetite for her. That mischievous little imp! If she had a clue how many nights he'd wakened in a cold sweat because of her, she'd gloat herself sick. But he'd never give her the satisfaction of knowing!

"Grayson Hart is outside and he requests a moment of your time," Virgil informed Pilar as he ambled through the front door.

"I'm up to my elbows in dough," Pilar said without glancing up. "Can't you relay the message to me?"

Virgil stared thoughtfully at his granddaughter's rigid stance while she stood rolling out biscuits for supper. "A woman has to see to some matters herself. You've been avoiding Grayson . . . and don't bother denying it," he hastily added. "Grayson deserves your courtesy. Thanks to him, I've had dozens of orders to make extra money. You've treated him like a leper long enough."

Pilar considered telling Virgil why she'd avoided Grayson,

but she bit down on her tongue before the resentful words leaped out. While it was true that she thought of Grayson so many times a day that it exhausted her, she knew what he wanted from her. He wanted her to become another trinket on his chain of broken hearts—another source of physical satisfaction. She cared more for him than she should've, and the only way to protect herself was to avoid him. She couldn't trust herself alone with him, not when her traitorous body begged for his skillful touch.

"I'm extremely busy," Pilar muttered as she shoved the rolling pin over the dough.

Virgil snatched up a towel to wipe off her hands and shepherded her toward the door. "Consider this a test," he demanded. "If you can talk to him without feeling anything at all, then you've been ignoring him without reason. You'll have to convince me that the man means nothing to you. The way you've been behaving suggests you care more than you prefer. It's time to decide if it's the man himself you like or that house on the hill you're constantly staring at."

When Pilar's head swiveled on her shoulders and she turned to gape at Virgil, he grinned slyly. "Don't you think I know what's running through your head while you daydream? You envy what the man has—his wealth, his freedom. I'm aware of all the responsibility that's been dumped on you. It's only natural for you to want what you don't have, especially when you have so little. Now make up your mind how much or how little this man means to you. Go talk to him!"

When Virgil shuffled her out the door and slammed it behind her, Pilar had no choice but to confront her guest who leaned leisurely against the corral gate. The mere sight of Grayson's ruggedly masculine physique put her heart on a drumroll. Staring at him was visual torment. Curse it, why didn't he just go away and find some other woman to torture with his striking good looks, seductive voice, and arousing embraces? She was tired of wearing her heart out on him!

"Mrs. Barton asked me to drop this by on my way home," Grayson explained as Pilar moved hesitantly toward him.

Pilar glanced at him like a mouse approaching a starved lion. That wasn't like her, Grayson reminded himself. She was the epitome of feisty spirit and sass.

"Thank you for bringing the money by." Pilar accepted the pouch of coins he placed in her hand without meeting those entrancing green eyes that could destroy her defenses.

"Pilar?" His quiet voice wavered with a wanton desire he couldn't conceal. Just seeing her inspired memories of the intimate moments they'd shared.

"What?" She studied the toes of her shoes, as if something there demanded her undivided attention.

Gently, he cupped her chin, forcing her to meet his probing gaze. "I want you," he said simply and directly. "I've missed you."

His touch seared her flesh like fire. "I've—" She licked her bone-dry lips.

The gesture caused a knot of longing to coil in Grayson's loins. God, how he yearned to moisten her heart-shaped mouth with famished kisses!

"I'm going to kiss you, here and now, in broad daylight, despite all the curious eyes that might be watching," he forewarned her in a voice that rustled with unmistakable longing. "If you don't want me to, you'd better say so—and quickly. I'm a mite short on patience, and long on need."

Pilar followed the whispers of her heart and ignored the logic of her mind. Her lips instinctively parted in invitation as she drank in the sight and scent of him. It had been weeks since she'd allowed herself the pleasures of his embrace, the torment of wanting the only man who'd awakened her slumbering passion and left her aching for more than she dared to give. The instant his sensuous mouth captured hers, a moan bubbled in her throat and fire coursed her veins. Despite her floured hands, Pilar looped her arms around his neck and kissed him back with all the pent-up emotion that boiled inside her.

When his fingertips pressed into her spine, bringing her into intimate contact with the aroused contours of his flesh, she swore the skin had melted off her bones. Kissing this

105

raven-haired rake was like gulping water after being stranded on a barren desert. Pleasure expanded inside her like a rubber band that was about to snap. He inspired such an incurable hunger to touch and be touched, to absorb and savor the tantalizing sensations that rumbled like an erupting volcano. Was this simply a physical reaction to needs that had lain dormant far too long? Pilar wasn't experienced enough to know exactly what lured her to this muscular giant, but she sensed one thing for certain. She'd been too long deprived and all too aware of desire—the kind that could blaze like a bonfire.

Grayson's body pulsated with wild heat. He could feel the fullness of Pilar's breasts brushing against his chest and it drove him mad with wanting. He could feel her thighs meshed to the columns of his legs and it pushed him to the crumbling edge of self-restraint. It was broad daylight, for crying out loud! And he suspected Amity, Clay, and Rory were in the barn, tending their after-school chores and snickering in devilish amusement while he kissed the breath out of their sister. But damnit, a man could only stand so much before his self-control shattered like eggshells.

"Have dinner with me," Grayson rasped as his pounding heart forced out his breath in ragged spurts. "Or better yet, come home with me. I need to be alone with you. I need—"

Pilar retreated a pace and battled for hard-won composure. "I can't," she chirped, her voice one octave higher than normal.

"You mean you won't," Grayson scowled. "You want me and I want you. Why must you fight it?"

Blue eyes sparked with irritation. "Because if *I* don't *you* won't! You have everything to gain and I have everything to lose if I give in to you. I don't want to be your *challenge conquered* or the reason for your *triumphant smile!*"

"Did I say you were?" he muttered in irritation.

"Did you say I *wasn't?*" she questioned his question. "What do you want from me that you can't get from any other woman? And what can you give me that I couldn't find with another man?"

What did she expect? Love? Total devotion? Hell, he didn't even know if he had the capacity for those emotions since he'd never had a family to teach him their meaning. Why did women always have to look for some deep meaning in everything? Why did they analyze relationships to death? Why couldn't they just roll with the flow and accept whatever happiness they could find along the way?

Curse it, why were men such shallow, unfeeling creatures? Pilar wondered as she met Grayson's annoyed glare. *He, who had everything, didn't know what it was like to want something special and meaningful. He, with his dashing appearance, his fine home and money to hire others to provide services for him. He, who could wander up to his property to enjoy solitude when it met his whim or find companionship when he desired.*

Virgil had ordered Pilar to decide how she felt and to live with her decision. She was making her decision now and she was going to live with it, despite the intense longings of passion Grayson so easily evoked from her. This star-crossed attraction was over and done, now and forevermore!

Composing herself as best she could, Pilar stepped back another pace and raised a proud chin. "I want us to be friends, neighbors, and casual acquaintances," she insisted, though her betraying body protested anything of the kind! "You're welcome to visit my family when you please, but don't expect more than I intend to give."

Grayson could have cheerfully choked her for being so damned practical and sensible when he was feeling everything but! "Fine, if that's the way you want it," he bit out. Grayson got on his horse and left. Simple as that.

But his empty house echoed with loneliness and he cursed the impossible female who lived down the hill. She'd shut him out of her life for good. He ought to take her gift back. He ought to . . . he didn't know what! All he knew was that he felt bruised inside and out — as if he'd been used as a human punching bag. And the worst of it was that Pilar hadn't even laid a hand on him!

* * *

Pilar failed to be lured into the Christmas spirit after her last encounter with Grayson two weeks past. Although her family had tramped off on their traditional hunt for just the right tree and boughs of mistletoe, her heart hadn't been in it. Even though the stockings were hung and the handmade ornaments dangled from the pine branches, Pilar felt none of the bubbling excitement which tempted her brothers and sister to prematurely tear into their gifts. Although Pilar had purchased a frilly store-bought gown for Amity, a black felt hat for Rory, an ivory-handled pocketknife for Clay, and a new pipe for Virgil, her mood was still as dreary as the soupy fog that settled on the countryside. The Christmas Eve fog had turned out to be exactly like the one which had hampered General Jackson during the Battle of New Orleans a half century earlier. Old Hickory had attempted to fortify his barricade to battle the British. Fifty years later, Pilar was fighting an impossible war against the lingering image of spellbinding green eyes, raven hair, and a bronzed face that haunted her dreams.

Even after reciting to herself all the consoling platitudes, Pilar didn't feel a bit better. Grayson Hart hadn't stopped at the cottage in a fortnight, though he'd often been seen coming and going to Alexandria. Her family never failed to report his activities, and then they demanded to know why he hadn't paid them a visit. Weeks earlier, the children had resented Grayson's presence and his interest in her. Now that Grayson had made himself scarce, they missed him! They didn't know what they wanted from Grayson any more than she did!

Feigning weariness as an excuse to lie down and rest, Pilar climbed the steps to the one-size-fits-all bedroom. She retrieved the gift from under her pillow that she'd impulsively purchased for Grayson. To this day, she didn't know why she'd fussed over what to give a man who had everything, and purchased him a gift after she'd told him she wanted no more than friendship. Well, it *was* Christmas, she rationalized. It was a time for giving and sharing with friends. Grayson had seen to it that Virgil had plenty of orders to ease their financial burdens. That's why she'd bought Grayson the collapsible brass spyglass. Now he could view all the world from his lofty perch on the hill.

Tucking the gift in the pocket of her worn cloak, Pilar glanced from the steps to the window. She didn't want to explain where she was going to her nosy family. She would simply make her exit via the window and into the outstretched arms of a nearby tree. She would take Grayson his gift and return before her family missed her.

Pilar raised the window and grasped the limb. Despite the hampering skirts, she negotiated the tree and hopped to the ground. The fog was so dense that she was forced to navigate toward familiar landmarks to find her way to the path. Employing the fence posts as her guide, Pilar propelled herself up the hill toward the beam of light that led her — like a shining star — to the top of the hill.

Pilar's rap at the door was met with silence. It was better this way, she decided as she pressed her face against the window pane to survey the inside of the house. She could look to her heart's content without fretting over an encounter with Grayson. In her vulnerable mood, she'd probably surrender to this nagging ache of loneliness that had hounded her for weeks on end. If she had to stare into those emerald eyes for even a second her resolve would crack and she'd succumb to the impossible demands of her body — the only thing Grayson Hart wanted from her or any woman . . .

Pilar's thoughts trailed off when lantern light reflected off the freshly waxed floor and the enormity of the house swallowed her. She found herself peeking in one window and then another to view the monstrous mansion she'd coveted from afar. The high, ornate ceilings were engulfed in looming shadows. Dark, heavy furniture, which looked as if it had rarely been used, lined the walls of the many rooms that opened off the front hall. Plush sofas with plump gold velvet seats, framed by polished rosewood graced the parlor into which she peered. Despite the elegant furnishings and luxurious drapes, the house held so little invitation and warmth that she pulled her cloak close to ward off the chill. No fire flickered in the hearth and no sound reached Pilar's ears. This house, which she'd long envied and wished herself in, was like a sepulchre of shadowed silence, void of joyous voices or holiday cheer. It left her feeling incredibly alone and unwelcome. The plantation resembled a museum, so different from the lived-in cottage she called home . . .

An audible sigh escaped Pilar's lips when she spied the wilted sprig of evergreen — the meager symbol of the holiday season — which lay on Grayson's coffee table. The pathetic little branch couldn't compare to the decorated tree and surrounding gifts that filled half the space in the Maguires' parlor. A mist of tears clouded Pilar's eyes when she realized that the dream she'd harbored for this grand mansion was only an illusion.

It hadn't been this house that she wanted at all! It wasn't peace and quiet that she needed! This place was so quiet that it almost begged for the activity of rowdy youngsters and boisterous laughter. But what stunned Pilar to the bone was the knowledge that this house held no lure because the man who owned it wasn't here. Grayson was the one who made this house seem a forbidden dream. It was the man inside those elegant clothes who truly impressed and aroused her. It wasn't his material wealth that interested her. She didn't envy what he had — the loneliness and the silence. She wanted the man *himself.* He'd been kind and caring to her family. He'd offered her affection, limited though she'd ensured that it had been. The real reason she'd sent Grayson away was because . . . because . . . she'd wanted all of him, not just his passion, the pleasures of his touch or the riches he might be able to offer her in generous trinkets. She wanted to share her innermost thoughts with him, her hopes, her fears . . . and her love . . .

Now Pilar had nothing of Grayson except the cold, harsh realization that he'd been lonely in his gigantic house. He'd been silently reaching out for companionship and affection, longing to be a part of her family's circle of love. Ah, what a dreary Christmas he'd spend in this gloomy fog with his single sprig of evergreen. No wonder he'd once insisted he could cope with her brothers' blunt questions and ornery pranks, Amity's prissy ways, and the free advice Virgil offered anyone who took time to listen. No wonder Grayson hadn't blinked an eyelash at coming to dinner, even if it meant having peas spilled in the crotch of his fashionable breeches. Grayson Hart had wanted what *she* had. Imagine that! The man with everything had nothing but empty space, unshatterable silence, and tormenting solitude!

Without Grayson, this monstrous house was a foreboding prison. Her own home was cramped, but it was teeming with a warmth she'd never realized existed until she compared this tomb of loneliness to her cottage. *She didn't envy Grayson; she pitied him!* She resided in a household where she was wanted, needed, and loved. Grayson couldn't buy those precious emotions with all his wealth. The poor dear man! How had he survived so long in this suffocating vacuum? No wonder he made so many trips to town to relieve his boredom.

On that depressing thought, Pilar laid her gift beside the front door and disappeared into the curtain of fog that was growing thicker by the minute. Along the way, she thanked God that He'd shown her the error of her thinking. She was rich beyond measure . . . except for the love of that special man who'd tried to reach out to her without her fully understanding why.

Well, next time Grayson came around with some flimsy excuse to invite himself into her family, she was going to welcome him with open arms and an adoring smile. She loved him! That's why his heart-stopping kisses and bone-melting caresses lit inextinguishable fires inside her. That's why she'd become so moody, depressed, and resentful. She'd missed the velvety sound of his voice, his bright ringing laughter. And someday, she'd work up enough nerve to tell him so, even if he told her to take a hike. It was what she deserved after the way she'd treated him, all in the name of protecting her cautious heart. Her heart couldn't bleed anymore than it was bleeding now, and that was a fact! Grayson Hart needed to be loved and loved well—without restrictions or concession. She may never have a chance to win his affection, but at least she could include him in her family and provide the warmth and security of friendship.

What a shame she'd been too blind to realize how much she had to offer a man like Grayson! He appeared to have the world in the palm of his hands, but in actuality, he'd been deprived of those precious blessings in life that were more priceless than gold!

Reining his steed to a halt, Grayson peered at the beckoning lights that blazed from the Maguire cottage. Absently, he tethered the lead rope to the palomino pony he'd brought as St. Nicholas's special gift to the Maguire children. He stared longingly at the cottage—again. His jaunt into town on Christmas Eve had been a waste of time. Most folks had been home with their families, enjoying the festive season. He was still wandering around like a lost soul in search of paradise, unable to find contentment anywhere.

Grayson glanced down at the bulging sack that was strapped behind his saddle. Okay, so he was being obvious. All right, so he was using the gifts he'd purchased for the Maguires to invite himself into the golden halo of love that surrounded this family on this cold foggy night. He admitted it. But a lonely man grasped at excuses to relieve the unbearable longing for friendship, companionship, and affection on such a night as this. Even if he had to ignore Pilar's why-don't-you-go-home glares, he was going to give his gifts of clothes and toys and accept a hot cup of coffee if it was offered.

Swallowing his pride, Grayson nudged his steed toward the house and dismounted. His rap at the door rattled the hinges and hammered with an eagerness to be accepted and included. Damn, he *was* obvious! Virgil would see through him in a minute. The old geezer knew what had brought Grayson out on such a dreary night—desperation.

"It's Mr. Hart," Rory announced after he swung open the door. "And he's got lots of presents!" His voice rang with irrepressible excitement.

Grayson found himself surrounded by three bouncing children. They were pawing at the pouch that was slung over his shoulder to such extremes that he stumbled off balance and slammed into the door jamb. Finally, he gave up and handed the sack to Clay, smiling in amusement as the boy dragged the packages into the house to shake them before placing them beneath the tree.

With envious eyes, Grayson stared at the decorations that brought life to the oversized tree which graced the corner of the room. Red and gold satin ribbons had been tied in bows and hung on the branches beside the hand-carved ornaments Virgil had designed. Boughs of mistletoe and clumps of holly lined the doorways and mantel. The room was teeming with Christmas spirit and activity and Grayson ached to be a part of it, if only for a few minutes.

"Come join us, Grayson," Virgil invited while he rocked in his chair and puffed on his pipe. "I wondered how long you could hold out."

The sly grin that crinkled Virgil's aging features provoked Grayson to shift awkwardly from one foot to the other.

"A man needn't be ashamed when he goes where his heart leads him," Virgil continued as he indicated the vacant chair beside the hearth. "It's Christmas and this particular Christmas has been a long time in coming—for all of us."

Grayson sank into the crude chair to absorb the warmth of the fireplace and the flurry of activity beside the tree. His gaze sought out Pilar but she was nowhere to be seen. The pleasure that had greeted him at the sight of the children's anxious faces dwindled. This was all he'd wanted, wasn't it? To be included in the festivities of this family? To watch the children open his gifts and to share their joy and the vibrant enthusiasm of youth? Now he'd been accepted and included and *still* there was something missing. Again his eyes searched the darkened hall, hoping to catch sight of her . . .

As if he'd read Grayson's mind, Virgil smiled. "Pilar is up-stairs resting. She's been scurrying around all day, preparing the Christmas goose, mincemeat pies, plum pudding, and tending her usual chores. Rory, why don't you go tell Pilar we have company."

With visible effort, Rory tore himself away from the colorfully wrapped packages with his name on them. He bounded up as if propelled by a spring and dashed from the room. His feet pelted against the steps as he hurried upstairs. In less than a minute, his footsteps hammered on the steps, heralding his hasty return.

"Pilar's gone!" he reported to the room at large. "She flew out the window!"

A muddled frown furrowed Virgil's brow. "Are you sure?"

Clay pivoted in his squatting position beside the tree and grinned. "She probably sneaked off to take her gift to Grayson," he speculated.

"What gift?" Virgil questioned.

"The one she hid under her pillow. It had Grayson's name on it," Amity piped up as she possessively clutched her gifts to her chest. "Clay opened it to see what it was and then wrapped it back up—"

"Tattletale!" Clay growled at his big-mouthed sister. "Can't you keep a secret!"

Amity tilted her chin in a manner that reminded Grayson of Pilar in one of her mulish moods. "You tried to bribe me to silence and that isn't nice. Pilar says so!"

Grayson glanced around the cozy room which was filled to capacity. He had wedged his way into this household, bearing gifts, eager to enjoy the feeling of belonging to a family at Christmas. But without Pilar, there was an emptiness in the room. Without Pilar he was still a discontented outsider. It was more than physical desire that he felt for that blond-haired hellion, he realized. He wanted the woman herself, with all her saving graces and her flaws, with all her responsibilities and her caring family. Grayson suddenly understood what he'd wanted from Pilar: Her respect and acceptance, but above all, her love.

Yes, he'd hungered for her to obsession, ached to introduce her to the fiery passion she'd only begun to realize existed. But he'd wanted far more than that. The complexity of his feelings for Pilar was what kept drawing him back like metal to a powerful magnet. He liked the way she stood up to him, the way she argued with him out of pure contrariness. He adored the way dimples cut into her creamy cheeks when her face blossomed into a smile. He cherished the way her naïve body responded to his exploring caresses, the way she breathed new life into him when she returned his hungry kiss. He'd missed the sight of her, the sultry sound of her voice, the defiant tilt of her chin—everything!

"I'll see if I can find her." Grayson deputized himself as the sole member of a rescue brigade. "I wouldn't want Pilar to get lost in this dense fog."

"She's been lost in a fog for now onto two months, the way I see it." Virgil rocked calmly in his chair and puffed on his pipe. His graying brows lifted in amusement. "The same fog, I suspect, that has clouded your thinking, Grayson."

That perceptive old codger! He'd been amusing himself by watching Grayson and Pilar flounder through their on-again, off-again courtship, searching for answers to their befuddling questions. Virgil had known all along what Grayson had refused to see for himself. Grayson had fallen in love.

"Don't tarry too long," Virgil requested as his twinkling gaze shifted to the anxious young faces that surrounded him. "It will be difficult to keep these children from clawing open their long-awaited gifts. Christmas comes once a year, you know. And if Pilar is searching for you for the same reason you're about to search for her, the two of you will have all the tomorrows together that you desire. But for tonight, I want us all to be together. That, after all, is what the spirit of Christmas is all about."

Grayson was out the door and gone the instant Virgil stopped speaking. This was a night for special feelings all right, Grayson reminded himself as he swung into the saddle. No longer would he sidestep around his true emotions! When he found Pilar he was going to be open and honest with her, even though he'd never before shared his private thoughts with another living soul. If there was even a remote

115

possibility that Pilar cared for him, he was going to grasp at his chance at happiness. He could give her all the things she'd done without, and provide for her beloved family. And in return, he could have what he desired — that unique, intriguing woman. It was Pilar who'd burned brands on his mind and made him crave fulfillment in her arms. It was Pilar whom he needed and wanted, not because of the warmth of her family, but for herself. She was the one who satisfied the loneliness inside him. He wanted to care for her, to ease her burden, to share her sorrow, her joy, and her life . . . And he was going to tell her the first chance he got! And if she didn't love him yet, then she could learn to love him later, because he wasn't going to give her any reason *not* to love him!

Grayson urged his steed into a faster clip, despite the blinding fog that made it impossible to see five feet in front of him. He was halfway up the hill when he heard a thud and a muffled yelp, leaving him to wonder if he'd just trampled Pilar in his haste to find her. Egad! He'd been so anxious to locate this lost nymph that he'd literally run her down! His clumsiness certainly wasn't going to win him favor. He'd started out on the wrong foot — again!

In a single bound, Grayson leaped from his horse to search the foggy shadows for the fallen body who'd made no further sounds. "Pilar?" He groped like a blind man on his hands and knees. "Pilar, is that you? Where the devil are you?"

Pilar levered upon a wobbly elbow and tried to focus her fuzzy gaze on the blob that hovered a short distance away in the dense fog. The horse and rider had come upon her so quickly that she hadn't had time to react. Because of the clump of trees beside the path, she hadn't been able to leap sideways to avoid collision. The momentum of the powerful steed had knocked her off balance, catapulting her into an unyielding tree, forcing the air out of her. As of yet, she couldn't breathe properly.

"Grayson?" Pilar croaked when her vocal chords began to function.

Scrambling noises indicated his hurried approach. Inquiring hands flooded over her, checking for broken bones.

"Are you all right?" he questioned as he ran inspecting fingertips over her shapely form.

"I don't know," she admitted as Grayson propped her against his shoulder for support. "Give me a moment to gather my wits and check for missing appendages. I think one or two of them got knocked to kingdom come."

His relieved laughter echoed around her and she smiled contentedly at the sound. It had been an eternity since she'd heard his voice or felt his virile body pressed familiarly to hers. When his lips grazed her forehead, sensitizing her with his moist breath, Pilar melted. She'd been miserable for two weeks. Now the agonizing days seemed to evaporate as if they'd never existed. For here was the pulse of her very existence—the man to whom she longed to offer unconditional love. It had come to the point that she was prepared to settle for whatever scraps of affection Grayson would toss to her. Maybe she shouldn't have been so compromising, but even her pride couldn't battle the multitude of emotions this man aroused in her.

"Can you stand up, love?" he murmured in question.

"Do I have to?" Pilar whispered, perfectly content where she was in the circle of his protective arms.

"Not if you don't feel up to it, you don't," Grayson assured her. His lips grazed her forehead again, savoring her scent, the delicious feel of her body cuddled against his.

"I took your Christmas present to you but you weren't home," she informed him as she snuggled closer to his masculine warmth.

An unseen smile played on Grayson's lips. "I stopped by your house to give *you* a present but you weren't home, either."

Pilar jerked herself upright to peer into Grayson's handsome face. "My family knows I sneaked out? Sweet mercy! We've got to get home!"

When she tried to gain her feet, Grayson held her effortlessly in place. "We need to talk."

"Grayson, please!" Pilar squirmed, but to no avail.

"Pilar, please! This is important." Grayson expelled a

heavy sigh and formulated his thoughts, but he didn't know where to start. He had no experience at this sort of thing.

"Whatever you have to say will have to wait," Pilar insisted. "Don't you realize the razzing I'll face when I get home, and on Christmas Eve of all days! My family will hold this over my head for the rest of my life. They don't have a clue where I am or why I left."

"Yes they do. Clay found my gift under your pillow," Grayson informed her.

"That little sneak! I have no privacy whatsoever," Pilar muttered bitterly. "Now let me up. They'll laugh themselves silly before I get back."

When she squirmed free, Grayson's shoulders sagged. For a man who'd been so confident and sure of himself, he felt damned awkward when it came to baring his soul. The words stuck to his tongue like glue. But if he didn't say something, and quickly, Pilar would be long gone and he might not have the chance to speak from his heart for hours!

"Pilar Maguire, I love you and that's the truth. I want you to love me back. I need you to share my life and fill the emptiness. I want to be a part of your family, but most of all, I want you any way I can get you. I think you might come to love me too if you'd give yourself half a chance." Once the words sprang loose, they bubbled like a spring. "I even went to your house tonight to find a place for myself in the circle of your family. But without you there, the meaning of Christmas wasn't complete. You were the special feeling that eluded me. I couldn't find the peace I sought with your family because I didn't have you."

Pilar froze in midstep and wheeled back to gape at the coiled figure who sat on the damp path, oblivious to the damage to his expensive breeches. Her mouth opened and shut like a drawer, but no sound came out. She was thunderstruck. He loved her? Truly? *Her?*

The silence was killing Grayson. It was even worse than the silence that clouded the halls of his house. "Say something, for heaven's sake," he demanded.

Pilar moved gracefully forward to sink down in front of

him. Her hands framed his face, uplifting it to her adoring smile. "I already love you, Grayson," she confessed in a voice that quivered with emotion. "I didn't know how much until I peered through the windows of your house, thinking I would relish the solitude of its grand space and fine furnishings. But without you there, the mansion on the hill held no appeal, only silent emptiness. I realized that all the things I desired were meaningless without you. I thought you wanted me for the pleasure a woman could provide and I sent you away because I wanted more than a kiss to satisfy a temporary need. I wanted to mean as much to you as you've come to mean to me —"

Her words were muffled by his kiss — a kiss that rippled with hungry impatience and long-harbored needs, one that spoke of more than physical desire. Pilar found herself engulfed in sinewy arms and held so closely that she wondered if Grayson realized he'd practically squeezed her in two. Bullet-like sensations riveted her as his kiss deepened, stealing every ounce of breath and then generously giving it back. His hands roamed everywhere at once, cherishing the feel of her responsive body beneath his exploring fingertips. Pilar let go with her heart, body, and soul when Grayson whispered love words against her exposed flesh. He made her feel whole and alive and needed in ways she'd never believed possible.

The gift she'd purchased for him seemed unworthy of expressing the wondrous feelings that channeled through her. Only her gift of love, shared promises, and dreams of a future could compare to the emotions Grayson conveyed with his worshipping caresses and adoring kisses. It wasn't his wealth or his fashionable clothes that had attracted her to him. Indeed, those things had placed obstacles between them. It was this lonely, generous man who was willing to accept her for what she was and longed to be included in her family that mattered most. What a pity she hadn't realized that weeks ago!

Pilar swore she'd remember this Christmas Eve as she remembered no other. This was the time when she learned the true meaning of life and the sharing of the gift of love — a love so powerful that it couldn't be bought, sold, or given away. This handsome midnight-haired man who'd lived in his empty house on the hill had taught her to appreciate what she had . . . and to reach out for the love she wanted.

With extreme effort, Grayson broke his ravishing kiss and pushed himself to his feet. "I suppose you're right. We better go back," he said huskily. "Your brothers and sister are so eager to open their gifts that they can't sit still. And knowing them, they'll try to convince Virgil to form a rescue party to help me find you."

"When we have the time—" Pilar traced the sensuous curve of his lips with her forefinger. She couldn't keep her hands off him. She wanted to know everything about the man she loved, to feel his whipcord muscles beneath her inquiring fingertips, to convey her affection in ways that needed no words. "I want to give you the gift I've offered no other man . . ."

Grayson stepped away to stare at her in mock disbelief. "Without a wedding? I should say not, my dear lady! What kind of man do you think I am?"

Pilar peered up into his playful grin, loving him all the more—if that were possible. "Are you proposing, Grayson Hart?"

"Are you accepting, Pilar Maguire?" he countered.

"You only had to ask," she assured him softly.

"How does tomorrow afternoon sound?" Grayson chuckled, feeling the kind of elation he couldn't begin to express.

"Tomorrow sounds like an eternity away." Her throaty laughter filled the foggy space between them. "It seems I've no more patience than my youngest brother."

Grayson curbed his ravenous desires, knowing he didn't have to grasp at fleeting moments of pleasure, knowing he had a lifetime of love ahead of him. Gently, he drew Pilar into the possessive circle of his arms and bestowed the tenderest of kisses on her waiting lips.

"I want to fill your life, and your family's, with all the things you've done without," he assured her. "I want the halls of my house to ring with love and laughter. I want to see the same flush of excitement on the faces of our children, and our children's children, that I saw on your brothers' and sister's faces tonight. There are some wondrous holiday traditions that are of life itself. They're meant to last forever and ever, just like these mystifying feelings I have for you. They transcend all physical bounds and they bind the world together in common bond, securing it, despite the ravages of war. These feelings are heaven-sent, Pilar, and I want to share them and all my tomorrows with you . . ."

When his lips slanted over hers in another soul-shattering kiss, Pilar began to believe in miracles. The love this once-lonely man offered her had filled her world to overflowing. For the two of them, this was only the beginning of a legacy of love that would be handed down through generations.

Pilar peered up into Grayson's expressive features. She could see forever in his smile, eternity in his sparkling green eyes. Within the arms of this warm, caring man she had discovered paradise. "I love you with all my heart," she whispered before she kissed him with all the love and passion her body and soul possessed.

Grayson's massive body shuddered, as if besieged by an earthquake, freeing the emotions that had been bottled up in his soul. When Pilar murmured those soft words and gave herself up to him, Grayson fully understood the splendrous powers of love. And like the anxious young Maguire children he, too, couldn't wait to unwrap his special Christmas gift!

Texas Magic
by Emma Merritt

1

December 1872
Mistletoe, Texas

"Afternoon, Widow Driscoll." Standing in the street beside his buckboard, Bill Murphy nodded at Hannah, who was walking out of Driscoll Mercantile with a shopping basket over one arm.

"Her name is *Mrs. Carmichael,* not *Widow Driscoll,*" Blade grated as he moved up the boardwalk to join his wife.

Murphy's ruddy face turned an even darker shade of red and he pulled his hat lower on his forehead. "Sorry, Marshall, ma'am. I keep forgetting."

"Don't worry about it, Murphy." Hannah spoke gently and laid a gloved hand on her friend's shoulder. "Everyone in Mistletoe is having the same problem. All of you have been calling me Widow Driscoll for over three years; it's going to take more than three months for you to break the habit."

She smiled at the older man. A beautiful smile that had fascinated Blade the first time he'd ever seen it. That still fascinated him and absolutely drove him to distraction. His hand tightened on her elbow. They needed to be moving along.

"I guess we'll see you at the shindig tonight," Murphy said.

"Of course," Hannah answered. "You know I enjoy dancing."

Murphy chuckled and his eyes glimmered. "Always was the belle of the ball, you was, Hannah Dris—" The rancher stopped, his eyes darting to Blade as his cheeks reddened again. He brushed his hands down the front of his shirt. "I mean, Mrs. Carmichael. Guess I'd better get in the store and get my supplies. Got a lot of work to be doing. Good day to you."

The man bolted into the building, soon to be lost among the stacks of dry goods.

"You were awfully hard on him," Hannah said quietly. "You embarrassed him."

"I simply corrected the man," Blade pointed out in the same quiet tone. As his gaze lazily swung up and down the main street of Mistletoe, Texas, he adjusted the brim of his black John B.

"It's not what you said, but the way you said it. And it's the way you dress. You could wear another color besides black. It makes you look dark and brooding and unapproachable."

"That wasn't one of the stipulations when I was hired to be marshall." Blade laughed at her, his hand running down the soft leather vest he wore before it brushed past his six-guns to his Levis. He said nothing but his gaze clearly defied her to say the denim was any color other than an indigo blue that was slightly faded from washing—hardly dark and brooding. "Do you honestly believe people around here are frightened of my clothes that are similar to what nearly every man out here wears?"

"No."

He was glad Hannah never allowed herself to be intimidated. He had never appreciated coy females. He liked the way she threw back her head and glared at him.

"But yours are different; they . . . they add to your air of superiority and mystery. People are more frightened by the way you look at them."

126

This revelation fascinated him. "How do I look at a person, Hannah?"

She was a tall woman, but even so, she had to tilt her head slightly to look into Blade's face. An autumn breeze dislodged a strand of hair from her hat and blew it across her cheek.

"Hard and cold," she replied. "Your eyes turn the color of gunmetal and look as lethal. One look from your gray eyes can make an innocent person feel guilty, and a guilty person wish he were anywhere but close to you. Hell would be a safer, more desirable place."

"The very qualities you were looking for in a man," he said, realizing that Hannah's assessment rankled him.

"In a *marshall,*" she corrected, "but I'm stronger and perhaps more realistic than most. Please, Blade, be kinder to the townsfolk. They're frightened of you, and they shouldn't be. You're supposed to be the man who protects them."

Blade's hands curled around each of Hannah's shoulder. He didn't bring her any nearer to him. He just held her and stared fully into her eyes. "Let's get something straight, Hannah Carmichael. The town hired me to be marshall, not to be their nursemaid. I don't do nightly feedings or change diapers. Just to save a man embarrassment, I'm not going to tell him it's all right for him to address my wife by the name of her previous husband because it's not. You're my wife, and it's about time people around here recognized it."

It's about time you recognized it!

Blade enjoyed looking at Hannah; she was a beautiful woman. At the moment the afternoon sun made the tendrils of hair around her face glisten like burnished copper. He caught the curl and moved it from her face, the tips of his fingers brushing against her soft flesh.

Long, dark lashes framed eyes that were an unusual color, a blend of gold and green, at the same time neither gold nor green. They were like the sun when it first rises in the morning, a haze of glorious brightness defying any of

127

man's attempt to label them a particular color. Blade had seen them warm and friendly; he had seen them frosty like a nippy December morning. Mostly when she looked at him, he saw no expression in them at all. It was as if she closed herself to him.

He was married to her; yet she was still Widow Driscoll.

"Maybe they can't accept that we're married because I can't." She gazed straight into his eyes, her directness a trait he enjoyed and admired. Gladly he would incinerate himself in the fiery beauty of her eyes.

"Get used to it Hannah," Blade said, "It's a fact. We were married by the commanding officer at Ft. Stockton."

"It's a marriage on paper only, not a real one."

Hannah was telling the truth. While they had recited marriage vows, their marriage was not real in an intimate sense; it had never been consummated and if Hannah had her way about it, it never would be. Her relationship with him, her need for him and the marriage was strictly pecuniary.

Owner of the Driscoll Mercantile and Freight Company and the Mistletoe Hotel, in addition to vast personal property, Hannah was the wealthiest person in Mistletoe. When she had seen the Kipling Gang extending their daring raids farther and farther into West Texas, she had set out to find the community — and her holdings — a protector. She found him. Blade Carmichael.

Finding a husband had not been one of her goals. That was a condition Blade had insisted upon in exchange for his coming to Mistletoe to become the marshall, in exchange for his laying his life on the line to hunt down and bring to justice Arnold Kipling — a mutual enemy shared by both Hannah and him.

"If you're hinting that you want the terms of our agreement changed," he said his words slow and measured, "I could arrange it . . . much to your satisfaction."

"I'm sure you would like to think so." The sarcasm was soft but measured.

"No, Hannah Carmichael, I know so."

Her lips curled into a smile; lashes dipped for a mere second to lie as a dark crescent on her creamy cheeks, then they lifted to expose those brilliant eyes. "I'm not hinting for a change in the terms. I like them exactly as they are."

"Do you?" he murmured. "I wonder if you're truly as unaffected by me as you say."

"I am."

There had been times during the past three months that Blade had wanted to find out, especially at night when he heard her bathing in the adjoining room behind closed doors or early in the morning when clad only in her wrapper, a soft green material that clung to her body in all the right places and accented her slender height, she would open the door between the rooms.

Silence hung between them, heavy like an early morning fog in the mountains; it shrouded them in intimacy.

"Well then, Mrs. Carmichael"—he dropped his hands and stepped back—"that's the end of that. I'll devote all my energy to chasing and catching Arnold Kipling and his gang. I'll make sure they don't venture this far into Texas and touch any of your precious holdings. I'll protect you, Hannah. I promise."

Blade smiled, but his tone told her it was only the beginning. And if this was the first skirmish, she was well on her way to losing the war.

"Now let's go home and get some rest before the shindig tonight," he said. "If you love to dance so much, I have a feeling that I'm going to be on my feet all night."

Although Hannah had seen the crooked quirk of his mouth many times during the three months they had been married, her breath caught in her throat anew each time she saw it. She continued to look into that ruggedly handsome face, her gaze held by the smoldering intensity in his deep-set gray eyes. The air around her seemed suddenly charged with electricity. He seemed to emanate a magnetism that was unadulterated energy and power.

Almost she forgot his words, but by sheer will power she remembered. "You don't have to spend the evening dancing with me."

"If you dance, Mrs. Carmichael" — the low, seductive voice as well as dark, velvet-gray eyes caressed her — "it will be with me. And only me."

Something stirred inside Hannah, a feeling so sensuous, so intoxicating, that it frightened her. She was consumed by an exciting expectancy and couldn't take her eyes from his smile. Just watching it sent a warm glow through her.

Hannah tilted her head defiantly. "You're getting all too proprietary, Marshall."

"Not by the half." His eyes narrowed, dark lashes brushing momentarily against sun-browned cheeks. His voice when he spoke was as velvety sounding as his eyes had looked only seconds ago. Yet now there was a dangerous glint of resolve in both eyes and voice. "You and I, Widow Driscoll, made a deal. I'll stick to my end of the bargain, and you'll stick to yours. As long as we're married, the people of Mistletoe will think we're a *very happy* couple."

Hannah was quiet as she and Blade walked down Main Street to the large three-story house, a mansion in comparison to most of the houses in Mistletoe. In fact, the people of the town fondly called it the Driscoll Mansion. It had been Phillip's wedding gift to her. Now she was sharing it with another man.

She was sharing it with a man who was the antithesis of her gentle husband — a man who never owned a gun and couldn't have shot a person had his life depended on it. Who would have guessed that three years after his death — after the brutal death of Phillip and their seven-year-old son James by the Kipling Gang — she would be married to a man who earned his living by the gun, that she had searched him out in particular and that she had contracted a marriage of convenience to a stranger for the purpose of getting him to come to Mistletoe as marshall?

Blade opened the entrance door for her, and as they moved into the hallway, a room itself, Hannah stopped in front of the settee that stood against the wall and set down the shopping basket. Looking into the large cheval mirror

130

that was framed by an oak hat-rack and that formed the back of the settee, she removed her hat, then her gloves.

In the reflection of the mirror she watched Blade take off the black John B. to reveal thick wavy hair that was as dark as the shirt and vest he wore. He tagged the hat onto the nearest brass hook. Hanging her hat next to his, Hannah's gaze swept past the Colt .44s strapped around his waist to the Levis he wore. Low-waisted, snug in the hips, with slim legs, the denim hugged his lower body like a second skin.

"Uncle Blade!" A little girl's voice sounded through the house, the cumbersome wooden chair rolling across the floor as she proficiently angled around the various potted green plants that decorated the hallway. "You're home early."

Blade turned and smiled at his nine-year-old niece. "For a change. Hannah and I thought it would be a good idea if we spruced up a bit for the shindig tonight."

He turned to look at Hannah. As always, the gentling of his face when he looked at Allie touched a tender cord in Hannah's heart.

"Didn't we, Hannah?"

"We did." Hannah picked up her shopping basket from the settee and sat down. "Come see what we brought you."

"Me?" Allie asked, her little face brightening. She rolled closer.

"Well," Hannah said, "we can't have you going to the shindig tonight in just any old dress, can we?"

"You got my dress!" Allie exclaimed. "You stopped by Mrs. Peepers and picked up my dress."

Hannah pulled out the blue cambric dress, white pantalettes and stockings, and black patent shoes. "The dress just matches your eyes."

Allie's eyes, the exact color of the West Texas sky, almost the same color as the dress Hannah held up, reflected her excitement. "This is mine to wear tonight?" she murmured more than asked. She ran her hands over the fabric of the dress and pantalettes. Then she touched the shoes. Happiness fled from her face to be replaced by bitterness. "I don't

131

need any new shoes."

"Not tonight," Hannah replied lightly, "but you will as soon as you start walking again."

"You and Uncle Blade always say I'm going to walk again, but I heard the doctor when he told you that I wouldn't be able to." Her lips trembled; her eyes filled with tears. "He said the bullet came too near my spine. There was nothing he could do to help me."

Hannah caught Allie's little hands in hers. "You can walk again if you want to."

The child pulled away from her and wheeled to the door. Her back to them, she said, her voice rising with each word she spoke. "I want to! I really do, but I can't! I'm never going to walk again!"

Long strides carried Blade to the child. He knelt and pulled her into his arms, his hand cradling the back of her head as she cried into his shoulder.

"You'll walk again, baby," he promised. He also promised himself again, as he had so many times since the tragic accident, that he would see Arnold Kipling dead.

"I miss Mama and Papa." Allie sobbed against him. "I wish those outlaws hadn't killed them, Uncle Blade. I wish they were alive."

"Me, too."

God, how Blade missed his brother and sister-in-law, the only family he had left after the War Between the States. At the war's end eight years ago and with no family remaining but his younger brother, Blade had begun his journey to California and a new life. He traveled slow, working along the way as a hired gun—the only talent he could capitalize on to make quick and big money since the war had destroyed everything he owned.

En route he stopped to visit with his brother and sister-in-law at their ranch out of Bradburn, Texas. Blade could not believe what he found. His brother was almost destitute; their land was no good for beast or man. Blade had remained with his brother, using his savings to finance the endeavor.

After five years they finally found water and sunk a well that supplied them with irrigation; they could raise their food and cattle. Times were looking good, and Blade was thinking about moving on. The four of them, Ryan, Megan, Allie, and Blade, had ridden into Bradburn to get the month's supplies and a loan for improvements on the ranch. Ryan and his family were in the mercantile company when the Kipling Gang struck; Blade was across the street loading supplies into the wagon. He managed to kill two of the outlaws before the gang fled. Among the carnage that remained behind were Ryan and Megan. They left Allie for dead, a bullet in her back.

A local doctor told Blade there was nothing he could do for her; the best he could suggest was to take her to Ft. Stockton. Blade had, and the army surgeon had operated, removing the bullet that had lodged next to her spine.

Allie nestled closer to Blade, and his grip around her frail shoulders tightened. He remembered the doctor's prognosis. He had not accepted it then. He did not accept it now.

The sobbing turned into sniffs, and Allie pushed away from Blade. "I'm sorry, Uncle Blade."

"There's no need to be." He pulled his bandanna from his neck and wiped the tears from her face. "We all need to get angry and cry sometime."

"Do you?"

"Sometime."

Lena Murdock, the live-in housekeeper, walked into the hallway, planting her hands on her ample hips. Her white hair was pulled into a tight chignon on the back of her head. "It does me good, Marshall, to see you with Allie. When you choose, you can be a gentle man."

Blade chuckled and glanced at Hannah. Winking at her, he said to Lena, "Don't say that too loudly or to too many people, Lena, or my career as marshall will be short-lived."

Lena snorted, then said, "Supper's on the table. Y'all eat, so I can clean up the kitchen. Then I figure after I get this young lady bathed and in her clean clothes for the

133

shindig, I'll get myself ready for tonight."

Having folded and returned Allie's new clothes to the shopping basket, Hannah handed it to the older woman.

"Now, young lady," Lena said, "let's head that chair to the kitchen. Then we'll have that bath, and I'm going to crimp your hair so that you'll be the belle of the ball. You're going to want to dazzle all them young bucks with your beauty."

Wheeling away, Allie giggled.

"I had Claude take the tub up to your bedroom, Hannah," Lena called over her shoulder, referring to her husband. "The cold water's been carried up. You'll just need to add the hot. Kettles are full and ready to be heated. I'll put them on the stove, so they'll be boiling by the time you're through with supper."

2

Supper was a lively occasion. Hannah regaled Allie with the latest gossip in town, and Blade sat back silently watching them. Hannah was a woman who inspired pride in him; at the death of her husband, she inherited considerable wealth. Along with it came responsibilities as a civic leader and the business head of a financial empire, both of which Hannah shouldered well.

When Hannah heard of Blade's exploits as a shootist, she set out to meet and to hire him, making no bones about her reasons why. Although his condition that they marry gave her pause, it did not deter her. She simply issued a counter condition: theirs would be a marriage of convenience only.

At the time, he hadn't cared about any of the stipulations. While he had been attracted to Widow Driscoll from the first moment he laid eyes on her, his primary concern had been Allison Diane Carmichael. Pushing his wants aside, he had made Allie's welfare a part of the marriage contract. She was now Hannah's and his legal ward. If anything happened to Blade, Allie would have a home and a guardian. Hannah's attorney had already drawn the papers, and she and Blade had signed them. They were on file in Austin.

After three months of living with Hannah, Blade had gotten to know her well. Rich as Midas; tough as steel; and gentle as a lamb. During this time, the widow had not only gotten under his skin, as the old saying went, she was quickly burrowing her way into his heart. He wished she would burrow her way into his bed.

Every so often Lena would throw in a dry comment that caused all of them to laugh. When the meal was over, no one seemed inclined to be the first to leave. They continued to linger until Lena announced that it was time to get dressed if they intended to celebrate tonight.

Blade pushed back his chair and rose. "I'll carry the kettles of hot water, Hannah. You go ahead and make sure the door to our bedroom is open."

Hannah, moving more slowly than he, stood. She didn't like the way he was looking at her, the mocking glint in those gray eyes, the teasing laughter lines at the corner of his mouth. She had no idea what he had in mind, and she definitely did not appreciate his casual reference to her bedroom as theirs. Of course, that was part of their marriage agreement—a written contract signed by both of them. He wouldn't claim his conjugal rights, but it must appear that he and Hannah shared the master suite in her home.

"Be gone, woman, before my hands burn!" he commanded softly, a large steaming kettle of water in each hand.

Hannah walked ahead of him, up the stairs to the large suite of rooms that she and Phillip had once shared. She opened the door into her bedroom—into their bedroom. The copper tub stood regally in the center of the room in the last splash of afternoon sunlight; two large white towels and washcloths lay on the floor. The soap dish, fragrance water, and scrubbing brush sat nearby. How often she had witnessed this same scene when she was married to Phillip, she couldn't count. But with Phillip the room had not taken on the intimacy it did when Blade entered.

She stood at the door while he poured the water, then carried the empty kettles over to the fireplace and set them on the tile. "I'll take them down later," he said. "Who's going to bathe first?" The gray eyes mocked; the sensuous lips taunted.

"It—it doesn't matter." She moistened her lips.

Blade walked to where she stood and gently removed the door from her hands and closed it. He shoved the bolt in place, the grating metal echoing through the room louder than a gunshot.

For the first time in years, Hannah felt at a disadvantage. Gauche, awkward, naive, all these words aptly described her. Yet she said in what she hoped was a calm voice, "Please leave. I'll call you when I'm through."

"Where shall I go?" he asked, his eyes locking to hers. "Lena is bound to suspect something if I leave the suite. She's downstairs helping Allie dress, you know."

"You can go into your bedroom," Hannah said and broke the stare.

When she first met Blade at Ft. Stockton when she was returning from a buying trip in San Antonio, she had been unprepared for the impact of his physical presence. Unprepared for her own vibrant response—a warm exhilarating anticipation had stirred within her. So intent had she been to enlist his help in finding the Kipling Gang and bringing them to justice that she had dismissed the sensations; she had promised herself they would go away. But they hadn't. Then she had argued with herself that she could control the emotions, but the longer she was around Blade the more she discovered she didn't want to control them. She had not felt this way since Phillip.

No, Hannah, Phillip never evoked this kind of response from you. You were always in control, and so was he.

But Hannah had sworn when she buried the mangled and unrecognizable bodies of her husband and child that she would never care that much again. She would never open herself to such hurt and continuing pain—grief and anguish she would suffer the remainder of her life, that would always underline her happiness.

"It doesn't matter which room I'm in, Hannah," Blade said softly, breaking into her troubled thoughts, "as long as you're in it."

Hannah looked into Blade's fathomless gray eyes that

were suddenly warm . . . that were suddenly hot . . . and she felt strangely shaken, disoriented. As if he were a magnet, he drew her to him. She had a compelling desire to be with him, to really know him. It was unnerving and contradicted her firm resolve not to become intimately involved with the man.

During the past three months Hannah had come to realize that while she had loved gentle, dependable Phillip, there was room in her life and heart for a second love — possibly a love that was more passionate than her first one, one that transcended the first. Often she had wanted to take the moment's pleasure Blade extended to her, but was afraid.

Yes, she Hannah Driscoll . . . Carmichael, the woman who had taken over the running of her husband's varied businesses without a word of demur and who had taken her place in a man's world and had made good, was frightened of her own emotions.

"Even if I were in hell — and you were there with me — I'd be content." Blade's voice, like a sultry summer breeze, whispered seductively over Hannah.

What if she really cared about him? What if she fell in love with him? Blade had made no secret of his desire to ride off into the sunset when he had gotten Arnold Kipling. He had been heading that way when his family had been killed. His departure would leave her alone again, and she could not bear the thought of such devastating loneliness. She had borne it the first time; she didn't think she could a second. She had to stick to her guns; she had to keep Blade away from her heart, and that meant keeping him away from her body.

"Blade, you can . . . you can go into your room and do some of your paperwork," Hannah suggested.

"I could." He leaned his back against the wall and folded his arms over his chest. Amusement lurked in his eyes.

"Or you — or you could see if there's enough firewood for tomorrow."

"I could."

"Or you—"

"I could stay up here like the husband I am and help my wife." He pushed away from the wall and walked closer to her, close enough that his warm breath lightly blew against her face and neck. His voice was low and suggestive. "Help her undress. Help her bathe. Then help dry her off."

Hannah had to admit the suggestion was tantalizing. Her heart was hammering in her chest; breathing was difficult. "That's not a part of our contract."

"No, it isn't." His pronunciation was pointed. "I should never have agreed to a marriage in name only. Marriage of convenience is what you called it. Hell, I've found it to be nothing but a damned inconvenience. I'm giving you fair warning, Hannah, celibacy isn't for me and neither is adultery. Mark my words, with each passing day I'm becoming more and more frustrated and less and less patient."

Despite herself Hannah smiled and sweetly said, "That's your problem, Marshall."

"Yes, it is." Blade smiled, too, only his gesture wasn't nearly as sweet.

Before Hannah knew what he was doing, he bent to kiss her. The touch of his lips on hers was light and surprisingly soft, making no demands. But much to Hannah's alarm, it sent a tremor of desire pulsing through her, so strong that she wanted to throw her arms around him and cling. She forced herself to pull away. She drew in a deep breath of air.

"That's a breach of our contract, but I'm willing to overlook it this time. Don't let it happen again," Hannah said calmly, the twining of her hands the only indication of her discomfort. She was losing control, and that bothered her. Her sanity, her future happiness depended on her remaining strong; it depended on her denying Blade access to her emotions.

"Hannah Driscoll Carmichael," Blade said, and the husky tones tenderly raked over Hannah's exposed nerve endings, "you always act so prim and proper. I've never seen you passionate about anything. You're never angry or jealous or—"

139

"I get extremely emotional," Hannah confessed, voicing her truest fear, "I've just learned to control my base feelings. But I assure you, Blade, I don't feel any passion where you're concerned. Our marriage is strictly a written contract, nothing more."

He laughed softly, mockingly. "Hannah, you don't fool me one iota. I believe you're a love-starved woman who has never had proper loving."

"I remind you I was a married woman for seven years before I met you."

The gray eyes, though gentle, continued to laugh at her. "I remind you I said proper loving, not a proper marriage. And there is a difference."

Oh, yes, Hannah was acutely aware of the difference and had been ever since she and Blade had begun to share their lives together, to share the master suite.

"Please leave," she ordered quietly.

Strange, she thought, in annihilating one fear—in hiring Blade to get Arnold Kipling—she had created another one that was in a way far greater, far more devastating—her attraction to Blade.

Her back to the door, she heard the firm tread of Blade's boots on the floor, then the harsh grate of the bolt on the door. The door opened and closed. She was alone. She didn't have to turn around to know; she felt him when he was in the room; she felt the emptiness when he left.

He had touched her hardly at all; yet he had branded her his in that breathless touch. His lips had merely brushed hers ever so lightly and for only one brief second. Yet the soft caress seared her heart as surely as if it had been a red hot brand. Hannah had been shaken to the roots, ready to throw herself into his arms.

Maybe she was starved for love. It had been so long since she'd been kissed, since she had been loved.

Hannah Driscoll Carmichael—strange even her conscience was beginning to sound like Blade—*Phillip's kisses, his caresses never affected you the same way Blade's do.*

Blade was leaning against the column on the back porch,

drinking a cup of coffee, when he saw one of his deputies, an old army buddy, ride up. Lang Hopkins slid off the horse and ambled to where Blade stood. The deputy was dusty, evidence he had been in the saddle a long time.

"That Mexican priest is on his way, and he's bringing trouble with him."

Blade nodded and asked, "Want some coffee and something to eat?"

"Could do with both." Hopkins followed him into the kitchen, stripping his gloves from his hands and tucking them into his belt. "He's got a fortune in them gold and silver religious artifacts, Colonel. Just the kind of loot the Kipling Gang would be interested in having."

Blade set the cup on the table, then turned to the stove where Mrs. Murdock had stored the leftovers. He dished Hopkins a plate of food and set it in front of him.

"I have a feeling, Lang," Blade said, "that we aren't going to have to go after Kipling. He may just come to us. Stop by the newspaper office, and make sure Jenkins runs a big story on this treasure that Father Corriano is returning to the cathedral in San Antonio. Tell Jenkins to make sure it gets in all the newspapers for miles, especially in San Antonio and El Paso."

The deputy studied Blade for a long while before he said, "So Arnold Kipling is bound to see it?"

Blade nodded.

Lang leaned back in the chair and took several swallows of coffee; then he set the cup down and began to eat. "You and the little missus really hate Arnold Kipling, don't you, Colonel?"

"Yeah," Blade admitted, "we do."

And that's about all we have in common, except a damned marriage and our love for Allie. Blade had done all he could for his niece. Now he could concentrate on Arnold Kipling. After all, he reminded himself as he had done a thousand times before, this was his reason for being in Mistletoe. After all this was the sole reason why Widow Hannah Driscoll had married him.

"Marshall," Lena Murdock called out, "Claude and I will be in our rooms. Allie's had her bath and is in her room reading right now. I'll see you and Hannah later tonight."

"All right, Lena," Blade answered.

After Lang left, Blade checked on Allie, who was still reading. He climbed the stairs and knocked on the bedroom door.

"Come in," Hannah called.

He opened the door and saw her sitting in front of her dressing table. In the reflection of the mirror, he saw the soft green material of her wrapper draped over her breasts and knew she wore nothing underneath. The material was slightly parted to reveal a portion of her breasts. His hand, aching to caress the creamy, soft flesh, tightened around the knob. What did Hannah think he was made of? Steel?

His gazed lifted, and their eyes met in the mirror. Running her tongue around her lips, she smiled at him. She was taunting him, repaying him for what he had done to her earlier.

She stood and walked across the room to the chest of drawers. She held her head high, her shoulders straight, and she swung along on long, slender legs. She moved quickly and lightly with a natural unstudied grace, the material of the wrapper pulling across her buttocks. Blade thoroughly enjoyed the display.

Blade knew Hannah was only retaliating for what he had initiated, but he liked the way she teased him. He enjoyed the sensations that coursed through his body. He knew he should let the matter go, let her have her day, but something compelled him to push farther . . . to see how far she would go . . . to see if he could push her over the edge of propriety.

He walked into the small room where he slept. Here he took off his guns and laid them on the dresser. Sitting down he shucked off boots and socks before he returned to the big bedroom. His back to Hannah, he casually unbuttoned his shirt, slipped out of it and dropped it to the floor. As quickly he slipped out of the Levis; they, too, fell to the floor.

Hannah could not believe Blade Carmichael was undressing before her. She stood absolutely still; she wasn't sure that she was even breathing. His knit undershirt and drawers tightly hugged his huge frame, revealing taut buttocks and long, sinewy legs. He turned around and she saw the bulge of his manhood. She felt heat rush to her face, through her entire body, to start a burning in her lower stomach. She could hardly swallow.

His tanned hands rose, and she visually followed his every movement. How quickly his fingers worked the buttons through the opening of the undershirt. In the opened slit of material she saw a muscular chest covered with hair as black as that on his head.

When his hands dropped to the buttons of his underdrawers, Hannah caught her breath. Yet she couldn't—she wouldn't—take her eyes from him as he unfastened them.

And he didn't turn from her either.

The soft knit material parted. But Hannah saw no more. With a soft moan, she turned and raced from the room as if chased by the hounds of hell themselves, not stopping until she was in the kitchen. She braced her hands against the table and breathed deeply, drawing much needed oxygen into her lungs. For ten or fifteen minutes she sat there.

Finally she poured herself a cup of coffee, moved to the cabinet and removed a whiskey bottle, tipping in a liberal amount. She gratefully swallowed the liquid, welcoming the warmth as it spread through her body and calmed her nerves.

"Hannah," Allie called, "is that you?"

"It's me. I'm in the kitchen drinking a cup of coffee. Are you ready for me to help you dress?"

"Yes, I am," Blade said.

Hannah whirled around to see him standing in the kitchen door, a towel draped around his midsection.

As quickly Hannah turned from him. "You dress yourself." She wished she had a cup of whiskey with a little bit

143

of coffee. "I'll help Allie."

Drawing a deep breath she hoped was full of pure grit and resolve, she walked past him, her shoulder brushing against his chest, the clean smell of him filling her nostrils. If things continued the way they were going now, she'd either be sleeping with Blade Carmichael or be an alcoholic by the time they dissolved their marriage. She had the uneasy feeling she'd be sleeping with him because the alcohol surely wasn't dousing the desire he had ignited in her body.

3

"I do declare, we're sure sleeping better since Blade Carmichael arrived here in Mistletoe," Alberta Tierly said.

Maybe you're sleeping better, Alberta, but I'm surely not! Hannah hadn't had a sound night's sleep since she and Blade rode in from Ft. Stockton.

"You're a mighty brave woman to marry yourself to a man like him," the woman continued, shaking her head. "At times the marshall can be a fearsome being."

"Oh, yes!" Patricia Delaney, as petite as Alberta was tall and angular, nodded her head so vigorously that several curls tumbled out of the coiffure to flop across her forehead.

"All of us in Mistletoe are eternally grateful that you did marry him," Alberta added.

But am I? Hannah asked herself, and looked across the gaily decorated carriage barn, part of the livery stable, that doubled as a recreation hall for special events. As Blade had pointed out earlier, what had begun as a contractual agreement, a marriage of convenience, was turning into the greatest inconvenience Hannah had ever experienced.

Patricia gazed in rapture at the marshall of Mistletoe. "Blade Carmichael is truly an answer to prayer, an angel of God . . . albeit, an avenging one, you might say."

"I doubt I would say that," Hannah said dryly.

Before long the folks of Mistletoe would venerate her husband, not that Hannah totally disagreed with them. He was closely akin to deity . . . of some sort. To Hannah their ambitions for him were just a tad lofty; she felt that if any of the gods had given immortality to Blade Carmichael it was Hades—the god of darkness and the underworld. A frisson slid through her body. Hadn't he said that if she were with him in hell, he'd be content?

How resplendent he looked in his black suit and the brilliantly white shirt that acted as a foil for his sun-bronzed skin. Wavy black hair framed a face that reflected boldness, assurance, and no little amount of arrogance. Above the head of the man to whom he was talking, Blade glanced at her.

He winked, and for a brief moment his lashes rested darkly, even against suntanned cheeks, before they lifted. Behind the gentle mockery that seemed to always reside in those eyes there was also resolve. Although she had seen the color turn from gunmetal to downy softness, she had never seen them bereft of grim determination.

Fortitude and perseverance were traits that aptly described Blade Carmichael, traits that drew her to him and made her agree to marry him. She had felt that he and only he would be the man to find Arnold Kipling and to bring him to justice.

"You're so lucky to find a man like him, Hannah." Patricia sighed the praise more than spoke. "Why, the other day I saw him watching you as you walked away from his office toward the mercantile store. I declare, I believe the man treasures the ground you walk on."

"How fortunate can a soul be?" Hannah murmured dryly.

Then a serious thought registered: What would it be like for this man to treasure her, for his lustful gaze to turn to one of love? The mental voicing of the question sent weakness through Hannah's body.

Warmth seeped into her face as she remembered the magnetic pull she had felt when he brushed the tendril of hair from her face, when he kissed her. She remembered the awakening of her body and her passionate response. Even now she felt a hunger deep within her body for the touch of Blade Carmichael. Hannah's hand tightly gripped the punch cup she was holding. She wanted Blade Carmichael to treasure her.

"Yes," Alberta mused, "I believe Patricia's right. Why, Lewis told me Blade really sat down on Murphy today and told him not to call you Widow Driscoll again. Lordy mercy, I'll never make that mistake if Marshall Carmichael is close by."

As if he knew the women were talking about him, Blade turned his head a second time in Hannah's direction. This time his gaze caught and held hers. His smile set her heart afire and lifted her to a world that consisted only of the two of them.

Hannah set the cup down and braced her hands on the table to stay their trembling. She did not release Blade's gaze, but neither did she return the smile. Rather she stared pensively at him and wondered what kind of man he was— her husband. What kind of secrets did he hide behind those gray eyes and that rugged visage? What was he going to do when he had captured Arnold Kipling and brought him to justice? Strange, the idea of Blade's not being a part of her life left Hannah feeling bereft.

One of the men spoke to Blade, and he returned his attention to the group. The tension broken, Hannah lowered her head and gazed at her hands, still pressed to the table.

"I can hardly wait for the Mistletoe Ball," Patricia said and picked over the delicacies spread up and down the table. "Why, Hannah, when you and Blade stood up there together tonight, holding hands and announcing the ball, I felt tears moisten my eyes. I could see the two of you together beneath the mistletoe."

Hannah shivered with anticipation at the thought of standing in the grand music room beneath the mistletoe with Blade. She fantasized him taking her into his arms and kissing her fully, warmly. Her grandmother promised that any wish made beneath the magical twig would come true. What was her wish going to be this year?

147

"You and Blade certainly do make a handsome couple," Alberta agreed, "and y'all are gonna look grand hosting the Mistletoe Ball."

Patricia clasped her hands together and giggled like a young girl. "I can hardly wait to stand under the mistletoe with Dudley and make my wish."

Alberta rolled her eyes teasingly and said, "Can you imagine what kind of wish Blade and Hannah are gonna make?"

When Hannah gave them a tight smile, both of the women laughed good-naturedly and continued their prattle.

"Mrs. Peepers finished my dress today," Patricia said, "and it's one of the most beautiful I've ever owned. I had it made from one of those Butterick patterns out of black and yellow taffeta."

Hannah paid scant attention to what Patricia was saying. She was remembering, remembering Blade's touches, remembering his near nudity. She lifted her head at the same time that Blade turned his; again, as if by divine injunction, their gazes collided and held. The smile on his lips slowly faded; his eyes became intense and smoldering as if he read her mind and knew what she was thinking. Hannah couldn't pull her gaze, much less her thoughts from her husband. Without another word to the men with whom he had been talking, Blade moved through the crowd, walking toward her, his gaze never wavering from hers.

"Well," Alberta announced, "I also have a new dress. I had Lewis buy me one when we made our trip to San Antonio this year. How about you, Hannah?"

"How about me what?" Hannah asked, never looking at her friend.

Blade drew nearer; his strength like an aura embraced her protectively.

"Your dress," Alberta prompted. "Surely you're not going to wear the same gown you've worn for the past three years. The time for mourning is over. Seeing as how this is your first Christmas with Blade, and this is his first

148

Mistletoe Ball, you're gonna want to be beautiful."

"She's beautiful no matter what she wears," Blade said.

Alberta and Patricia gave each other a sly look and exchanged equally sly smiles.

Blade extended his hand; with no thought to do otherwise, Hannah laid hers in it. He closed his fingers, and she loved the feel of his warm, callused flesh against hers. The small ensemble played a waltz, the strains of music made romantic by the soft light from the Oriental lanterns that hung from the ceiling and by the smoldering deep in those gray eyes.

Hannah had known the first second she laid eyes on Blade Carmichael that he was a dangerous man. How many hearts had he conquered in the past? How many more would he conquer after he left her? The idea of Blade with another woman jolted Hannah. She often imagined the day he would ride off and leave her, but this was the first time she had imagined him with another woman.

Both thoughts distressed her, but the idea of his being with another woman distressed her the most and made her want to cling all the more to him. But she knew she would never voice her questions or her fears aloud and really wouldn't ponder them because the only thing that mattered to her was what happened between them now.

The overhead light played across his face, smoothing out the roughness, softening it with gentle color. He raised her hand, his lips brushing lightly across her flesh. The pleasure of his touch gently coursed throughout Hannah's body, leaving her with a breathlessness that was untypical of her, yet was definitely exhilarating . . . at this moment.

"Mrs. Carmichael," he said, the crooked, devastating smile touching his lips, "I believe this is our dance."

"Yes, it is, Mr. Carmichael," she murmured, wondering how long she had been walking on air, wondering how long she would continue to do so.

"Waltzes are a favorite of mine," he said.

His arm slid down her back as he drew her close to him, indecently close to him, more closely than others were dancing, but Hannah went without a word. He felt good and she seemed to fit against his body perfectly — as if they had been created for each other . . . and, after all, he was her husband.

The music floated around them, and somehow she managed to make her feet follow Blade's. But all the while Hannah was conscious only of the man holding her.

"Some songs are too fast," he said, "and you get hot and sweaty, your only reward the pleasure of music and exercise. With a waltz, you have music, exercise, and the full pleasure of holding the woman, of feeling her soft body in your arms, of smelling the scent of her hair and her perfume."

Like the clean water of Mistletoe Creek, Blade's words were a smooth, sweet caress that washed over Hannah; again they aroused desire in her . . . for him.

"You've a way with words, Mr. Carmichael." She smiled up at him, pretending a coyness she had never felt in her entire life. It had been a long time since she courted, and she was enjoying the fantasy Blade seemed to be weaving about them.

He bent his head lower, so that his mouth was even with her ear, and whispered, "I have an even better way with my body."

Suffused with passionate warmth and imbued with a daring she had not displayed for the man she had so recently taken as husband, Hannah laughed and didn't care that her cheeks were burning, didn't care if he could feel her heart pounding within her chest. "I'll have to take your word for that."

Amusement swirling in those beautiful gray eyes, Blade pulled his head back and gazed into her upturned face. "Why? You haven't taken my word for anything else since we've been married. I'd like for you to prove this for yourself."

"Perhaps I'm not interested," she parried.

"Perhaps you're telling a little fib."

"Perhaps you'll never know."

"Probably I will," he said softly with an assuredness that caused Hannah to quake.

His hand braced against her back, pressed her even closer to his body, and he swung her around several times. With his lean body so close to hers, with his whispering such evocative things into her ears, old longings returned with undue force. As she breathed in the rich scent of him and felt the smooth fabric of his jacket against her cheek, it was all she could do to stop herself from lifting her head and finding his mouth with her own.

She closed her eyes and let herself be guided across the carriage barn floor by Blade. She had never known that simply dancing with a man could elicit such a feeling of utter contentment. It felt so right to be in his arms, as if somehow a part of her had been missing and now for the first time she felt whole. What was happening to her? What was this overwhelming emotion that was permeating her body, curling around her heart and capturing her soul?

Lost in thought, she drifted to the music and was not aware that anyone had approached them until she heard Mayor Charlie Rogers speak.

"I'm cutting in, Marshall."

Her peace and contentment shattered, Hannah's eyes flew open. Blade tensed; his embrace tightened, but he never broke the rhythm of their dancing. He smiled at the city official, but his eyes were serious as was his voice when he spoke.

"Sorry, Mr. Mayor, I can't allow you to do that. Mistletoe has had Hannah Driscoll all her life. Now she's mine, and she's promised me every dance. Maybe . . . just maybe" — Blade looked into Hannah's eyes and smiled, the gesture tender and warm, emanating from his eyes, hopefully from his heart — "she'll save you a dance at the Mistletoe Ball."

Charlie chuckled soft. "Well, now, Marshall, put that way, I can't argue with you. No, siree, can't argue with a man who wants to dance with his wife — especially when she's a prize like Wid — I mean Hannah."

When the mayor walked off, Blade caught her to him

and held her. Neither spoke, rather they gave themselves to the night and the music and to each other.

Being held by him, absorbing his nearness, his chin against her temple, his hand gently caressing her back was wonderful. Absolutely wonderful. After three years of feeling as if she were the living dead, Hannah was truly alive. It was wonderful to be dancing again, moving in rhythm to the music, in rhythm to Blade.

This moment with this man was hers; it was wonderful, and she was fully enjoying it.

4

Hannah spent the rest of her evening in a euphoric haze, hardly aware of what she ate or drank — and she was aware that she had several glasses of wine too many — or what was said. She was vaguely aware of the conversation that centered on the Mistletoe Ball and the magical sprig of mistletoe that would be hung in the Driscoll Mansion on Christmas Eve. She was acutely aware of the magic of tonight, of an exhilarating enchantment created by Blade Carmichael. A feeling, sweet and sensual, pulsated between them to draw them closer together.

Vaguely she recalled Lena telling her that she and Claude were taking Allie home and putting her to bed. All too soon came time for her and Blade to leave, and she was afraid that in leaving they would break the magical spell. But they didn't; it was as if Blade created it himself and carried it with him. As they drove back to the house in the buckboard, she sat close to him, her head on his shoulder. He drove with one hand, so that he could put an arm around her and hold her close. She felt comfortable here, as if this was where she belonged.

Picking up the lamp Lena had left burning in the parlor, Blade carried it in one hand and in the other held Hannah's. The magic of the evening intact, he led her up the stairs, the light flickering shadows on the wall and on his powerful physique as he moved ahead of her. He opened the door to the master suite, and :hey entered.

He set the lamp on the small lamp shelf on the dresser and turned to face her, to watch as she slipped her gloves off and laid them on the marble-topped night stand. Only now as the light danced dimly over the furniture in the room did Hannah remember who she was, who this man standing in front of her was. His eyes were swirling with mockery, as if he were saying "it's time to pay the piper." The euphoria was dashed and reality settled upon her. The consequences of her flirtatious behavior pressed in on her.

Blade completely dwarfed the massive Renaissance-style bedroom suite that was carved from walnut and walnut burl. She backed up a step; he took a step forward. Hannah, for one of the few times in her life that she could remember, was frightened . . . not of him but of her own perfidious emotions.

Light flickered over his face, a face so handsome that when Hannah looked at him, she ached in her lower abdomen, an ache that increased in intensity the longer she was around Blade Carmichael. It was unfair that one man should possess so much appeal and that all of it should be concentrated on her.

"Good night," she murmured.

"Not yet." The low, husky tones rushed warmly over her, bringing pleasure, at the same time reminding her that she was a victim of the magical spell he had woven about her. She stared into his languid eyes and felt as if she were tumbling off a cliff. He pulled her into his arms. Although the kiss was gentle, tentative, it revived the fiery desire in her that he had ignited earlier; it abated all her arguments and doubts. She pressed closer, opening her lips to his and winding her arms around him. In immediate response, his mouth took complete possession of hers, the kiss slowly, sweetly deepening.

Pressing herself against the length of his body, she melted into his embrace with heedless abandon. Her fingers caressed his face and tangled in his hair. Unlike Phillip, who had been a soft, delicate man, Blade

154

Carmichael was a study in pure steel, and she loved it.

"Oh, Hannah." It was a hoarse whisper, as if his emotions were as fragmented, as unmanageable as hers. He placed kisses on her eyelids, her temple, the tip of her nose, and finally on her lips. When he buried his mouth in the hollow of her throat, a lethargic yielding overwhelmed her. She clung to him and turned her face into his shoulders.

His hands moved up her back to her shoulders where he kneaded the tender flesh as though she were a fragile butterfly poised for flight. "You've bewitched me, Hannah Driscoll Carmichael," he murmured. "Totally, completely bewitched me."

"No," she said, "it is you who have bewitched me. I should put you away from me, but I can't."

"You can't?" he questioned.

She lifted her head from his chest to gaze into his face.

"I don't want to," she whispered.

"It'll be good, Hannah." The softly spoken words, although expressed as a statement, were really a question.

"I have no doubt," she murmured, "but will it be right, Blade?"

"How can it be wrong?" He touched her hair. "You and I are married. This is one of the reasons why people marry; this is one of the things married people ordinarily do."

"But it isn't one of the reasons why you and I married."

"It's not too late to include it," he said.

One by one he freed the pins from her chignon and dropped them to the floor until her hair fell in a coppery mass about her shoulders. He brushed his fingers through it. "Your hair is beautiful, Hannah, as I knew it would be. For the past three months I've dreamed of seeing it hang like this."

She felt his hands on the buttons of her dress. The brush of his fingers over her breasts was Hannah's undoing. She moved away from him. "No, Blade," she said. "You promised me you wouldn't—"

"I've taken no more than you've given," he said, his voice still soft and cajoling.

She raised her head to his and opened her mouth to deny his words, but the denial would not come.

"I'll never take more than you give." His words were softly spoken. "I promise."

His head lowered; his lips hovered above hers for a fraction of a second. His lips touched hers, and his arms closed around her in an infinitely welcome embrace.

She would have stilled the hammering blows of her heart; she would have dammed the fiery flow of blood through her veins; she would have released the coiled desire that threatened to ensnare her, but she could not. She had been too long without these sensations. She had been too lonely for the past three years. Dear Lord, she had been lonely for her entire life, and Blade's embrace felt right and good. It was as if she had returned home after a long, long journey.

Like the earlier kiss, his lips were incredibly warm against hers. Unlike the other kiss, this one held no tentative gentleness; it was firm and moist and demanded a response from her. Without equivocation, question, or guilt, Hannah complied.

He eased his embrace but did not let her go. "Hannah?"

Her head down, her cheek lying against his chest, she breathed in deeply several times and said raggedly, weakly, "You promised me, Blade." She did not look into his face because she knew he would see the wanting in her eyes.

He caught her chin with his hand and tilted it upward. He made her look into his eyes. "Yes, I did promise." He removed his hand and stepped back. "I'll stop, Hannah . . . if that's really what you want."

She said nothing but took a step to close the distance between them. Without him she was cold and lonely.

"But I don't think you want me to stop. We've gone too far, haven't we, Hannah?"

Still she said nothing.

"I'll give you pleasure, Hannah. I promise."

In the lamplight Hannah gazed at this man who was her husband, who wanted to be her lover, yet who was a stranger to her. A man who would share only a few months of her life before he strapped two Colt .44's around his waist and rode off into the sunset, leaving her behind with nothing more than memories. She had enough memories to last a lifetime. She did not need or want any more. Yet she wanted—desperately wanted—the intimacy, the passion that this man proposed, the intimacy and passion that would forever change their relationship.

She contemplated the lips, the cheeks that were already shadowed with beard stubble, the tousled black hair, and at last those gray eyes that were so close to hers.

"Do you realize what you're asking of me?"

"Do you realize what you're denying yourself?"

"I'm no maiden. I've known the touch of a man before."

"And I would never attempt to erase that man's touches from your memories. I would not attempt to replace him in your life or affections," Blade said softly. "You loved him, and I'm sorry you lost him. But I'm glad there is no one in your life now, Hannah, because I want to give to you. I want to love and adore your body as none other but I can."

"Is this arrogance speaking?" she asked.

"No, a man making a simple request from a woman who has set his body afire with wanting."

Blade's lips covered hers and she forgot her denials; she knew only the power of his stroking, seeking hands and the fervor of his mouth as it moved over her face. As if he were giving her no chance to be shy or to protest, he swiftly moved to undress her, his hands sure and determined.

When she was naked, he leisurely looked his fill of her body, and she could see pleasure written on his face. Then before she became chilled in the brisk December evening, he carried her to the bed and gently placed her beneath the covers. He pressed his lips to her forehead, then stepped back to undress.

His clothes fell to the floor at his feet, and Hannah gazed unashamedly at what she had denied herself earlier in the evening. His form was magnificent, but she had known that. Even in clothes that was evident. As he had done to her, she allowed her gaze to thoroughly move down the entire length of his muscular frame. Her attention finally rested on his manhood.

Fear accompanied the anticipation that shot through her. It had been so long since she had made love, three years since Phillip's death, and a year prior to that when he had been gone on his trips. Even before, Phillip had never been a demanding lover. Blade Carmichael would be. Hannah was sure of that.

In a moment her body would receive him, and she wondered if she would disappoint him. As if she were a maiden, she was burdened with fears and doubts. When he slid into the bed next to her, she felt the heat of his body, she felt the pressure of his hardness against her thighs. That moment she knew a hunger so powerful she wondered if she would ever be satisfied.

Lingeringly, thoroughly as if time were suspended, he touched her; he kissed her; he worshipped her body with his hands and his mouth. He whispered endearments into her ears until her body was moistly warm and ready for him. He levered himself on top of her, and she received him. She gasped and her body pulled away involuntarily from the hard fullness of his intrusion.

"Hannah, my sweet." Holding her tightly, he breathed the words against her lips. "I didn't mean to hurt you. I wanted this to be so good for you."

"It is," she whispered. "It's just been so long. Too long." With a sigh of pure pleasure, her hands cupped his buttocks; she arched her hips and pressured their bodies together.

He thrust deeper, and Hannah knew a mounting bliss when she began to move in harmony with him. Her excitement and anticipation grew as she matched his drive with one of her own. She had not known lovemaking was a paradoxical blend of harmony and contradiction. It was feral and frenzied on the one hand, tender and leisurely on the other. Softness tempered the harshness; giving balanced the

158

demanding. Surely lovemaking had not been so with Phillip.

Then she could not think or reason at all; she didn't care to. Clinging to him, she felt her passion coming in thick, velvety soft waves, washing over her, cleansing away for the moment her doubts and fears. When it reached its zenith, she moaned softly and allowed her head to roll against the pillows. Blade's breathing heightened; he tensed, then convulsed with a groan, joining her in total satisfaction.

Neither spoke as he gently rolled to his side, his arms holding her close to his body. Hannah waited for her heart to cease its pounding; she waited for her breathing to normalize.

"Thank you, Hannah," he murmured, his voice husky from the passion they had shared. He bent to brush a kiss across her lips, a tender gesture, almost a loving touch.

Hannah did not know what to do next. Again feeling gauche, she began to pull away from him.

"No," he murmured, his embrace tightening sweetly about her, "tonight is ours, Hannah. Let's spend it together."

She relaxed and whispered, "Yes, the night *is* ours."

While the thought thrilled her, it also saddened her. Now that he had made love to her she didn't want to be alone . . . not ever again. Could she accept one night? Would she always be wondering if this would be the last? She had to protect herself; she had to. She was the only one who could.

"Blade—"

He pushed up on an elbow and with his other hand brushed the tangled hair from her face. "Don't, Hannah." He spoke softly but firmly. "Not tonight. No regrets. No talking. We'll do that tomorrow."

"Yes," Hannah murmured, taking refuge in the promise of tomorrow, taking consolation in the actuality of the moment, "we'll do that tomorrow."

She nuzzled her cheek against his chest and pressed quick kisses on his nipples. He sighed his pleasure, then be-

159

gan to give pleasure to her. Many breathtaking caresses later, she allowed him to make love to her again. Again she gave her love to him.

Tonight was hers—it was theirs—and she was going to enjoy it fully.

5

"Good morning, Mrs. Carmichael." Blade's voice was normally husky, but sleep made it even deeper and more husky; sleep imbued it with additional provocativeness. His mouth at her ear, his breath warmly blew against her skin. Although his body was curved around hers, he moved and he was closer to her still, legs against legs, his abdomen nestled to her buttocks, naked chest against naked back. One hand curled around her shoulder.

"Good morning," she murmured, having already surrendered to the devastating effect he had on her.

"You felt good last night," he murmured, nuzzling his cheek against her back, "and you feel good this morning. I have a feeling, Hannah Carmichael, that you'll feel good to me any time, and with time you'll only feel better and better."

It had been a long while since she awakened to the promise of such a wonderful day. She had not wanted daylight to come, fearing the magic would be gone. But it wasn't. The man and the magic were one, and presently they were hers.

"Since the contract is rather archaic now, what do you say we do away with it?" he suggested.

Still plagued by doubts, Hannah did not immediately answer. She and Blade did not have a future together. She was a woman with deep roots in Mistletoe; he had no roots at all; he was a man who wanted to be free to move on when he felt the urge. He had made that clear when he suggested the marriage—it was to be one of convenience for him, to provide a legal guardian for Allie in case he should be killed while hunting the Kiplings.

"Let's not be hasty," Hannah said softly. "I'll agree it's been compromised, but—"

"Compromised, hell." Blade chuckled. "We've totally broken it. I'd say it's null and void."

His fingers trailed over the swell of her breast, and Hannah sucked in her breath as pleasure winged through her.

"I like the feel of this. How about you, Mrs. Carmichael?"

Every time he referred to her as his wife by name, he reinforced the change in their relationship; he underscored the intimacy they had established, the rightness and the legality of it.

"I've known from the beginning you have a way with words," Hannah said, a slight catch in her voice. "Now I know you have a way with your body . . . as you assured me."

"You have quite a way with your body, Hannah Carmichael." Blade laughed softly and pressed kisses across her shoulders and down the indentation of her back. "Since we give each other so much pleasure, I call for a compromise. For the past three months we've had a marriage in name only, and that wasn't bad for either of us. But what we shared last night was better, Hannah, far better, wasn't it?

Hannah couldn't speak, but he didn't seem to need her answer.

He continued, "Why not have a marriage in fact as well as name?"

Hannah wanted this more than anything in the world, but knew it could not be. Even now she could have conceived his child. While the idea was warm and comforting to her, she didn't know how Blade would react if it proved a reality. Knowing how much he loved Allie, Hannah could only imagine his devotion to his own child. But she also feared that in the end, when he felt the inclination to move on, her carrying a child or the child itself would tie him to her—not love.

Hannah also knew that if Blade came to her again, she would receive him. Her sexual urges were healthy and Blade was a consummate lover.

"What about it, Hannah?" A tender note crept into his voice.

"I don't know," she murmured.

His tone grew more thoughtful. "Do you regret what happened last night?"

His hands curled over her shoulders, and he turned her over so that she was lying on her back. She looked up into his face, wisps of hair teasing her cheeks. A hand moved from her shoulders, and gentle fingers brushed the hair from her face.

"It's just going to take time for me to get used to." Time in which she had to steel herself to his leaving when his mission was completed, when his desire for her waned.

"Are you afraid to make another emotional commitment?" he asked, then as an afterthought said, "Or are you still in love with Phillip?"

Hannah wanted to ignore his questions; she wanted to throw caution to the wind and take what the moment offered, but that was not her nature. Honesty and directness were too much a part of her; however, she had also learned the value of discretion. Easing off the bed, she slipped into her wrapper and held it together by crossing her arms over her breasts.

"I'll always love Phillip," she confessed, moving to the fireplace to build a fire to ward off the chill. "And while I enjoyed what we shared last night, I'm—not ready for another emotional involvement, nor all the ramifications it entails."

"Such as?" he asked softly.

"Children," she answered, and for a second her thoughts centered on the months she had carried her son. He had been christened James Phillip, but she had called him Jimmy. "I could already be . . . with child."

"Which you wouldn't find pleasing?" Blade said.

"More you than me," Hannah replied and before she quite knew it, she was voicing her earlier concern, "You're touched with wanderlust, and one of these days you'll be wanting to move on. When that time comes, I don't want you to feel tied to me because of a child."

Blade stared at her for what seemed like a full minute. The features on his face sharpened; his eyes hardened. He threw the covers back, slid off the bed, and walked toward the room where he slept. "Maybe that's what you'd like to think, Hannah, but it's not that. You're life is full of ghosts, and that's the way you want it. It's easier to deal with them than with real live people."

His comment was abrupt, lacking in the gentleness that had characterized his behavior last night and earlier this morning. The warmth was fast dying; reality coming back. Already Hannah could feel the distance between them growing.

He disappeared into the smaller room. Never moving from the spot, Hannah heard doors and drawers open and shut. She heard water splash as he did his morning toilet. Finally she dressed. Hardly thinking about what she was doing, she put on her drawers, camisole, and slip. She was standing in front of the dresser holding her stockings and garters in her hand when she heard sharp knocks on the bedroom door.

"Marshall," Lena called, "Deputy Hopkins is here. Said it was important for him to see you. Deputies Dougald and Morgan have returned with some news about the Kipling Gang."

A towel in his hand, Blade appeared in the inner door and called out, "Tell Lang I'll be right down, Lena. Give him some breakfast while he's waiting." Wiping his face, he ducked back into his room.

Hannah dropped her stockings on the dresser and followed him. At the door she said, "I suppose you're going after the Kiplings."

Without looking at her, he fastened his gun belt around his waist. "That's the reason I'm in Mistletoe, Hannah, to keep Kipling away from the community and your assets and to bring the man to justice. That's what you're paying me for, isn't it."

To have her own words thrown back in her face stung.

"To think, I almost didn't stop at Ft. Stockton my way home from San Antonio," Hannah said bitterly. "I wish to God I hadn't. Then I wouldn't have heard you had recently killed two of the Kipling Gang when they robbed the Bradburn Mercantile Company. I wouldn't have known that you hired out for the highest dollar and that you had a personal interest in getting the Kiplings."

Blade stood in front of the dresser tying the bandanna around his neck. He laughed dryly and glanced at the bed, then back to her. "Think of all the fun you would have missed out on."

"That was cruel."

He turned, the gray eyes locking with hers. "Yes, it was."

They stared at each other; silence like an elastic cord drawing them closer and closer, each moving toward the other.

"You say you don't want another emotional involvement, Hannah," Blade said, "but it sounds to me as if you care about me. Or maybe, I'm reading too much into this."

"No, I care about you," Hannah confessed.

They were only inches apart now. Blade's eyes, filled with a deep, vital hunger that swept through Hannah like the rush of a flame through a drought-dead forest, caught and held hers.

"I wish it were more than care, Hannah, but I can live with it. It's a start."

Hannah cupped his beard-toughened cheek with her hand. "I want Arnold Kipling brought to justice, but I don't want you killed."

Blade pressed one hand over Hannah's, the other he laid over her stomach. "I'm not going to get killed, Hannah, because you and I have unfinished business to take care of."

Pressing a light kiss to her forehead, he turned and walked through the adjoining door. She heard his firm steps as he crossed her bedroom. She rushed after him, and when his hand closed over the door knob, she spoke.

"Blade, have you—has there been another woman in your life? Seriously, I mean?"

He paused only fractionally before he answered, "Yes, but while I was fighting in the war, she married another man."

"Do you still love her?"

"No. My ego was hurt for a while, but I soon realized as she had done that she married the right man."

Disappointment pierced Hannah's heart. She had been prepared for the many who meant nothing to him, whose faces were lost in the blur of one another, but not for the one who had touched his heart, whose face stood out in his memories as well as in some locket he had secreted away.

"But she's dead now. Killed by Arnold Kipling."

Hannah's gaze riveted to Blade's.

"She was my brother's wife."

Hannah's breath caught in her throat; an eternity passed as she and Blade stared at each other.

"I'll see you later," he said and closed the door.

After Hannah had put on her stockings and shoes, she moved out of the bedroom and descended the stairs. Blade had set her emotions into chaotic disarray; now he had jumbled her thoughts.

If he had meant his confession to put her mind at ease, he had not succeeded. To the contrary, it had very much unsettled her. Because the Kiplings had killed Blade's brother and sister-in-law, Hannah knew he had a personal reason for hunting down the outlaws. But she had not reckoned on his having once loved his sister-in-law. Did that give him additional incentive to want Arnold Kipling?

Troubled by her thoughts, Hannah stepped into the parlor to find it empty. Lena walked out of the kitchen into the adjoining dining room and opened one of the doors to the large buffet. "Blade and Lang left," the housekeeper announced. "Blade said he'd meet you over at the store later."

Hannah nodded and moved into the hallway. Stopping in front of the settee, she pulled a heavy stole from the rack and slung it over her shoulders. She quickly walked the distance to the mercantile company and unlocked the door. Across the street in front of the Mistletoe Hotel, she saw a Mexican military escort. Evidently Father Corriano had arrived.

Upon entering the building, she lit the lamps and built a fire in the wood stove. Later the door opened, and an elderly man, a stranger to Mistletoe, entered the store. Blade, moving from the other direction, came in behind the stranger. Her hand extended, Hannah walked toward the visitor.

"You must be Father Corriano. I'm Hannah Driscoll, owner of Driscoll Mercantile Company. I'm so glad to make your acquaintance and to be of service to you." She waved her hand toward Blade. "And this is my husband and the marshall, Blade Carmichael."

Confused, the priest looked from one to the other.

A tight smile touched Blade's lips. "We've been married for only three months, Father," he explained, an edge to his voice. "She's not accustomed to referring to herself as Mrs. Carmichael."

The priest smiled and nodded.

Hannah gasped and looked at Blade guiltily, but he averted his gaze. Their night together had evidently been nothing more to Hannah than sex.

"Blade—" Hannah said.

Blade ignored the apologetic tone and stepped around her. "Well, Padre, I guess we better get your treasures in here, so we can catalog and lock them in the safe. Do you need me to help bring them in?"

"No," the priest answered and walked to the window. He

167

knocked on the pane several times and motioned for his men to come into the store. Turning, he grimaced and pressed the tips of his fingers to the side of his head.

"Is something the matter, Father?" Hannah asked.

"A headache." He smiled wearily. "We traveled a long time yesterday before we were set upon by bandits. We outran them, then hid until nightfall. We have been moving ever since, and I'm extremely exhausted."

"Can I get you something for the pain?" Hannah asked. "Some aspirin powder perhaps?"

Father Corriano shook his head. "No, I'll feel much better after I rest."

"My deputy talked to one of your men, Father," Blade said, "who told us about the attack. We believe these men may have belonged to the Kipling Gang. Can you give me a description of them? Anything at all?"

"No," the priest answered. "I must say, Marshall, I was too frightened. All I could think about was saving these precious treasures that belong to God."

"Do you know if they were Mexicans or Americans?"

"They were not wearing Mexican clothing," the priest replied, "but we are so close to the border, señor, that it would be difficult to know if they were Mexican or American. Certainly one cannot make such a judgment by the clothing they wore, nor for that matter by the language, since many in this area speak both languages fluently."

Blade nodded his acknowledgement and walked to the window to watch the military escort as they brought the bags of religious artifacts into the store; he heard Hannah as she checked aloud item by item off the inventory list. But his mind wasn't on the treasure.

His mind was on Hannah. Widow Driscoll, so prim and proper, had never seen him as a man. He was simply a shootist, who from the minute she heard about him had determined to hire him to find and bring in Arnold Kipling. With no thought of Blade himself, she had coolly accepted his offer of a marriage of convenience as an incentive to

168

perform the task she required. In accepting the position of marshall of Mistletoe, he had legal protection to hunt down the outlaw who had killed his family in cold blood.

Blade had cared about this woman from the first moment he had laid eyes on her. Why else would he have insisted on marriage at all? Because he had determined right then and there, that he would not lose Hannah Driscoll. She would be his.

But she wasn't. She was still Widow Driscoll, and would probably be Widow Driscoll to her dying day. Certainly she didn't want to be his wife. She didn't even want his child!

Blade wanted a child—his and Hannah's child.

He was tired of drifting around by himself, looking and dreaming about what other men had. He wanted a marriage, a wife and a home; he wanted Hannah Driscoll, in truth as well as in fact, to become Hannah Carmichael.

"That's it, Señora Carmichael," Father Corriano said and sighed. Folding the inventory sheet that both of them had signed, he slipped it into his pocket. "I'm very tired. I think I'll go to the hotel and rest. I must be ready to travel in the morning. I want to get to San Antonio before Christmas."

"Would you like to come to the house for breakfast before you retire?" Hannah asked.

He shook his head. "Thank you, Señora, but I am much too weary. My body longs for rest more than for food."

When the priest walked away, Hannah turned to Blade and smiled. "Are you ready for breakfast?"

"You go ahead," Blade said. "I'll be in later. I want to check by the office and make sure one of the boys is here at the store at all times—day and night."

"You haven't forgotten we promised to take Allie into the mountains to get a Christmas tree today, have you?" Hannah asked.

"To tell you the truth, I had," Blade said, his gaze running across the jagged mountain range to the south of town. "I don't feel easy about leaving town with your safe

169

loaded up with those religious treasures. It could have been and probably was the Kipling Gang who attacked Father Corriano."

"You have five deputies," Hannah reminded him, none too gently. "And you can't let Allie down. This is the one excursion she's really looked forward to, Blade."

Hannah was right. He couldn't let Allie down. They had just pulled her out of deep depression, and he couldn't afford to let her sink that low again. Only Hannah with her exuberance, her love for Christmas, and her resolve that Allie would walk again had kept the child's spirits as high as they were now.

"Go on to the house and get Allie ready," he said. "I'll meet with the boys and work out a schedule, so that we don't leave the store unguarded."

"How long will you be?" Hannah asked.

"Give me a couple of hours." He pulled his timepiece from the vest pocket and looked at it.

Fleetingly Hannah saw the photograph of the young woman and she looked up at him. Was that Megan? she wondered.

"My sister," he replied. "She died during the war."

"I'm sorry for her death and for your loss," Hannah murmured, "but I'm happy the photograph is of her."

And not of another woman. The unspoken words hovered between them to fill Blade with unbelievable happiness. Hannah did care.

6

Gently nudging her gelding, Hannah led the way through the narrow mountain pass. Following her was Allie, secured on the gray mare in a specially made saddle. Her long brown braids hanging down her back, the child laughed and held her face up to the December sunshine. Blade rode behind.

"This is going to be the best Christmas ever," Allie shouted to Hannah. "We—I haven't had a Christmas tree in a long time."

In the clearing Hannah halted her horse and allowed Allie to ride beside her. She reached out and brushed tendrils of hair from the child's face, and tucked them beneath the hat she wore.

"This is going to be a very special Christmas for me, too," Hannah said. "I've always managed to have a tree, but for the past three years—" Tears stopped her words.

Allie caught Hannah's hand in hers and squeezed.

Regaining her composure, Hannah said, "Since Jimmy died, I didn't really have an interest in the holiday season."

"Now you do?" Allie asked as Blade pulled up beside them.

"Yes," Hannah answered, "now I do."

"Because you have me and Uncle Blade with you?" Allie said.

Hannah turned to look into those familiar gray eyes that were shadowed by the brim of the black John B. Still, through the shadows she could see that he asked the same question as the child.

"Yes," Hannah whispered, her gaze never leaving that of her husband, "because I have you and Blade."

The moment she uttered the words, Hannah knew them for the truth. She had released the ghosts of her past life and had fully embraced the living. This was going to be a very special Christmas for her. She had a family again, someone to love, someone to love her. She saw a flutter of emotion in the depth of Blade's eyes—hope, laughter, something that was altogether wonderful and awe inspiring. It was as if he read her mind. The corners of his mouth moved into a slight smile. He winked.

He nudged his horse forward. "I guess in a roundabout way you ladies are letting me know that this is the time for me to find and cut down that special tree for this special Christmas."

"Oh, yes, Uncle Blade." Allie clapped her hands together. "We want a pretty one and a big one, don't we, Hannah?"

"We sure do." Hannah laughed.

"One that we can put lots of candles on," Allie continued. "And decorations, too."

Hannah and Allie kept up the happy chatter as the three of them slowly made their way through the squat southwestern mountain range, finally arriving at a coppice of cedars. Carefully they rode through the trees, scrutinizing each.

Finally Allie pointed a finger and shouted, "That one, Uncle Blade!"

"Yes," Hannah agreed, moving closer to the tree the child had singled out, "this is a good one. It's tall and the branches aren't so thick that we can't burn candles on Christmas Eve at the Mistletoe Ball."

"Can I light some of the candles?" Allie asked.

"Most certainly," Hannah answered. "When I was a little girl, my mother always let me light the lower ones, and I did the same with Jimmy. After we lit the candles on the tree, we doused out all other lights in the room."

172

"And did you always have the Mistletoe Ball?" Allie asked.

"All my life," Hannah answered. "My grandmother is the one who gave me the mistletoe that we hang up on Christmas Eve, and it was my mother who started the Mistletoe Ball."

Looking over his shoulder, Blade asked, "Would I be guessing wrong if I said it was from this . . . er . . . magical plant that this illustrious town derived its name?"

Hannah nodded. "My father was in the military and served in the War with Mexico. After he was discharged from the army, he and Mother remained in Texas, moving farther and farther west. When Papa and several other freighters, one of them Ralph Driscoll, found the creek, they decided this was a good place for the town. Although Papa and Ralph were the founders of the town, my mother put her foot down when it came to naming it. Later they also named the creek Mistletoe."

"Can I see the mistletoe before Christmas Eve?" Allie asked.

"You surely can," Hannah answered. "I'll show it to you when we get home."

They returned to town late that afternoon as the sun was setting. Hannah and Allie went immediately into the house to locate the decorations while Blade deposited the tree on the back veranda and instructed Claude to build a stand for it. Afterward he rode over to the marshall's office to check on his deputies.

He was concerned about the Kipling Gang. Deputies Hoight Dougald and Jay Morgan, recently returned from El Paso, reported that some members of the gang had been seen there and in drunken ramblings had talked about Father Corriano's treasures. Blade had gone out of his way to make sure the story of the priest's stopover in Mistletoe reached all the newspapers in the vicinity.

He was sure — not by any tangible means but by an intuitive sense that had seldom proved wrong — that Arnold Kipling and his gang would soon be paying a visit to Mistletoe. Blade hoped the good father and his religious anti-quaries would be long gone before the gang arrived.

Blade opened the door and walked into the hallway, set-tling his hat on the rack before he entered the music room where Hannah and Allie sat in front of the tree, Hannah on the floor, Allie in her wheelchair. The room, warmed by laughter and happiness, was filled with the aroma of hot chocolate and popped corn. Popcorn chains—colored with vegetable dyes prepared by Lena—hung on the tree as did other decorations. Some of them were homemade; others Hannah had bought in San Antonio.

At the moment Hannah, holding a sprig of mistletoe in her hand and gazing up at Allie, said, "My grandmother brought this with her when she immigrated to America as a young bride. She hung it up in the parlor every Christmas Eve and promised me that any wish made under the mistletoe must come true."

"Always?" Blade asked, and Hannah turned to look at him. Wisps of hair curled around her face, and her eyes were shining. He had always thought her beautiful. Now she was more than beautiful. She was lovely. Her eyes sparkled, and her mouth curved into a warm, friendly smile.

"Always. I've never known it to fail."

Blade unfastened his gun belt and laid his six-guns on the sofa. He moved to sit on the floor beside Hannah. Gently removing the sprig of mistletoe from her hand, he looked at it.

"It doesn't look like much," he said. "It certainly doesn't appear to be magical."

"You can't always tell if something's magic by simply looking," Hannah answered.

"No," Blade murmured, his gaze centering on her rather than the mistletoe, "you can't, can you?" He smiled when her cheeks flushed.

"Well, well!" Lena drawled as she walked into the room. "Look at this, will you, Claude? Allie's got the tree all gussied up and ready for the ball."

174

"And I get to light the lower candles," Allie announced, then she turned to Hannah. "Who hangs the mistletoe?"

Hannah's eyes went to the door frame and to the nail that Phillip had sunk and left there permanently. Her grandfather, her father, then Phillip had hung it. Her gaze swung back to Blade.

"To keep up the tradition and the magic," she said, picking up a faded red box, "your Uncle Blade will have to do it. But until Christmas Eve, we'll return the mistletoe to the drawer for safekeeping."

After they ate dinner that evening, Hannah tucked Allie into bed, discussing the coming holidays with the child. When she finally entered the bedroom, lamplight dimly flickered in the room. A somber expression on his face, Blade sat in the rocker in front of the window . . . fully dressed even to his six-guns. The warmth they had shared earlier in the day as they hunted the tree, as he had held the mistletoe in his hands, faded. Dread like a bitter north wind blew over Hannah.

"What's wrong?" she asked.

He rose and walked to where she stood. "Morgan returned this evening while I was at the office. He's located the Kipling Gang's hideout. We're going to ride out and get them."

Hannah's gaze was compelling as if she were reading his soul. "Don't, Blade." She hadn't meant to beg, but the words were out before she knew it. She threw herself against him and brushed her palms up his chest to lock them about his neck. "Don't go, Blade," she murmured. "Please don't go."

"Hannah—"

"I know I hired you to get the Kiplings. At that time I was living for revenge, but not now. This morning you wanted us to have a real marriage. I want that, too, Blade, and we can't have it if you're . . . dead."

Blade held her close to him, wishing they could melt together and become one. But then he didn't wish it because he wouldn't be able to hold her supple body in his arms and feel her warmth against his. Her softness would forever be denied to him.

"I'm not going to die," he promised, laying kisses on the top of her head. "But I have to go after Kipling, or he'll come here to Mistletoe."

"We don't know that," Hannah countered. "Father Corriano will be gone by morning, and we'll—"

"Father won't be gone by morning." Blade sighed. "Dr. Fulbright dropped by the office and said he won't be traveling for several days at the least. He's in bed with pneumonia."

"I'm sorry," Hannah murmured. "I'll take him some soup." After a moment's pause, she said, "Maybe you're jumping to conclusions, Blade. We still don't know that the Kiplings will come to Mistletoe."

"They'll be coming," he answered. "I made sure of that." As he explained what he had done with the newspapers, dismay colored Hannah's facial features. "So you see, I have to go."

"When will you be back?" Her voice was drained of life.

"When I've captured or killed Arnold Kipling and his brother."

To Hannah the words were a death sentence for one or the other, perhaps both. They were final and brooked no argument. She tightened her arms about his body and pressed her cheek against his chest.

"Be home by Christmas," she said softly.

"So I can keep up the tradition by hanging the mistletoe?" Blade teased.

"So you can keep up the tradition," she agreed, then added, "so you and I can make our wish beneath the mistletoe and seal it with a kiss. So Allie and I can have the magic of Christmas. So we can have our miracle."

His face lowering to hers, he whispered, "I'll be back to hang the mistletoe and to claim my kiss, my wife, but I can't guarantee a miracle for you or Allie."

7

With Blade gone time passed slowly for Hannah. By night she shed her tears into her pillow and by day she hid her concern behind a mask of happiness. She had to think of Allie. Since the child had arrived in Mistletoe, her mental health had greatly improved. Her periods of depression occurred less frequently and were not as deep and traumatic. Hannah would not allow her own feelings to impede the child's progress.

After school was out each afternoon, one of the children would push Allie to the store where she would sit behind Hannah's desk doing her lessons while Hannah ran the store. On a calendar both of them marked off the days that Blade had been gone. Now that school was out for the holidays, Allie spent the entire day at the store. Laying her pencil down after having marked an *x* through the day's date, Allie pushed back in her chair and gazed at Hannah who straightened bolts of material on a nearby shelf.

"It's the twenty-third," the child said. "Do you think Uncle Blade will be back by tomorrow?"

"Yes," Hannah said with more certainty than she felt, "he promised, and in the four months I've known your uncle I've learned that he always keeps his word." She smiled at Allie. "He's got to be back. He's the only one who can hang the mistletoe."

"Are you going to wear the dress I saw you looking at this morning?" Allie asked.

177

Hannah reshelved the bolt of material. She had been un-aware Allie had seen her when she took the hunter green satin and velvet gown out and examined the alterations Mrs. Peepers had recently made. Alterations Hannah had asked for so that she would have a new gown for the Mistle-toe Ball. A new gown to wear for Blade. A color that the seamstress had assured her enhanced her eyes and her hair.

"Yes, I am."

"Is it new?"

"You might say it is," Hannah replied and began to straighten another shelf of dry goods. "I—I bought it the year that my—my first husband and son died. It was to have been my Mistletoe Ball gown."

"You never wore it?"

"No," Hannah answered. "Somehow, Allie, after Phillip and Jimmy were killed, I didn't think I could allow myself to live and be happy because they were dead. I missed them so much."

"Me, too." Tears ran down Allie's cheeks. "I miss Mama and Papa so much. I wish they could be here with us, Han-nah."

Hannah moved to the child, kneeling down to take her into her arms and to hug her. "I know, darling. Believe me. I know how you feel. But they aren't here. They're in heaven with God, and they want you to be happy."

"Like Jimmy and Phillip want you to be happy."

"Yes," Hannah murmured, amazed at the child's simple logic, a logic Hannah had never internalized for herself.

"I miss Uncle Blade," Allie said. "I hope he doesn't die."

"He's not going to die," Hannah assured her; yet she, too, had the same fears as the child.

Since Blade had been gone, she had closed her mind to recurring images of his being killed or injured. She forced herself to think only of the warmth and happiness they had shared, that they would share again. The thought jolted her; it surprised and elated her.

She loved Blade Carmichael!

She had loved two men in her life; she had lost the first one to Arnold Kipling, and was now in the process of losing the second one to the same man. If only she had not been set on revenge. If only . . . But she could not go back and change things now. She had found Blade; she had hired him to hunt down Arnold Kipling. She had agreed to a marriage of convenience, and she had fallen in love with him.

Smiling brightly, Hannah said, "You know, Allie Carmichael, you and I are going to be two of the best dressed women at the ball. Both of us will have new frocks."

"Yes," Allie said, "and I'm going to need some new ribbons for my hair."

"Why don't we look for some right now?" Hannah suggested.

"Marshall's back!" someone shouted from the street.

"Uncle Blade's back!" Allie shouted, pushing away from Hannah and wheeling the chair to the front of the store. "He kept his promise, Hannah."

Rising, Hannah hurried to the front of the store, opened the door, and wheeled Allie down the boardwalk. All the time her eyes were pinned to the four riders who made their way up the street. She didn't have to search for Blade. Without seeing his face she recognized him, the way he sat on the horse, his carriage, and the black hat and vest.

When they were close enough, Allie called, "Uncle Blade!"

By the time Hannah and Allie were in front of the marshall's office, Blade and the three deputies were tying their horses to the hitching post.

"I thought you might not get home in time for the Mistletoe Ball!" Allie shouted.

"I always keep my promises. I certainly wouldn't want to be the first one to break with the mistletoe tradition," he said, smiling at the child before he raised his head and looked at Hannah. Reaching up with a gloved hand, he pushed the brim of the John B. back on his head.

Her gaze hurried over his entire body as she assured herself that he was uninjured, that he was all right. Her head lifted, and she anxiously searched the face that was streaked with dust and lined with exhaustion.

"I'm fine," he assured her, his steps bringing him closer to Hannah and Allie. He knelt and hugged the child tightly; then he straightened, his gaze locked to Hannah's.

"Hello, Hannah," he murmured. "I've missed you."

Regardless of the dust, Hannah threw herself against him, marveling when she felt the two steel bands of flesh close about her, when she knew with absolutely certainty that he was fine. "Oh, Blade, you don't know how worried I've been." She buried her face against his chest, loving the masculine smell of him. "I'm so glad you're home."

His hand touched her chin to lift her face, his head lowering, his lips touching hers in a wonderfully warm kiss. A kiss that was endlessly sweet. A kiss Hannah wanted never to end. It deepened into a kiss that set her entire body on fire, that made memories obsolete and fantasies inadequate.

"I've missed this," he murmured, barely lifting his mouth from hers.

"Oh, yes." She sighed and snuggled closer to him.

"Well, Marshall" — the mayor's voice boomed from across the street where he stood with several other townsfolk — "what's the news?"

Sighing her regret, Hannah pulled away from Blade, but he kept her close to his side, his arm protectively — possessively — resting on her shoulder.

"Well, Mayor," Blade said, "the news is good, isn't it, boys?"

The three deputies looked at Blade and nodded their heads. Hoight Dougald tipped his head and spat tobacco juice into the street. "I'd say so, Colonel," he drawled.

"We dealt the gang a death blow," Blade announced. "Right now the majority of them are incarcerated at Ft. Stockton awaiting transport to San Antonio."

180

"Well, sir," Charlie Rogers drawled, "now that's some mighty good news. Mighty good."

Proudly Hannah gazed at her husband. The townsfolk had a new respect for their marshall. A respect born out of admiration, not out of fear.

Folding his arms over his chest and rocking back on the heels of his boots, Lang Hopkins said, "We did such a good job, we was invited to join the Texas Rangers."

"Blade told 'em we just might do that if things got too quiet around Mistletoe," Hoight said.

"You got the Kipling brothers?" Hannah asked.

Blade shook his head. "No, they escaped."

"And they swore to get the colonel," Hopkins added softly.

Hannah said nothing; she couldn't; she wouldn't. But fear in the greatest proportions she had ever known raced through her body, rendering her helpless. She was glad she was leaning against Blade, that he was supporting her. She was responsible for this happening to him. Had she not been insistent in his coming to Mistletoe? Had she not made it easy for him to go chasing after the Kiplings by becoming Allie's legal guardian, she could have perhaps saved his life.

"Well, Miss Allie and Miss Hannah"—Blade's smile included both Hannah and Allie—"what do you say we get to the house. I'm in need of a bath, food, and some rest."

Miss Hannah, not Mrs. Carmichael! Numbness, heavy, stifling, settled over her. Blade had called her Miss Hannah, not Mrs. Carmichael. Until that moment she did not realize how accustomed she had grown to his calling her that. To her it had become an endearment.

His hands on the back of Allie's chair, he began to push her down the boardwalk. "Uncle Blade, you've got to see the new dresses that Hannah and I are going to wear to the ball. They're beautiful, aren't they, Hannah?"

"Yes," Hannah murmured.

"I'm sure they must be," Blade remarked noncommittally.

"Mine's red and Hannah's a dark green."

He and Hannah listened to Allie's endless prattle as they walked home, smiling and speaking to the people whom they passed on the street. When they arrived at the house, Allie wheeled into her bedroom. She had things she wanted to do now that she was sure Blade was going to be with them for Christmas.

"Lena," Hannah called, "Blade's home and would like to take a bath."

"I'll have Claude bring the water and tub up," the housekeeper answered. Pushing through the kitchen door, she grinned at Blade. "Good to have you home, Marshall. This place has been mighty lonesome without you."

"Thanks, Lena." He hooked his hat on the rack. "I'll be upstairs waiting."

Hannah followed him up the stairs into their bedroom. Strange, she thought, how quickly the room had become theirs, not hers, and not hers and Phillip's. But hers and Blade's. He walked to the adjoining door.

"While you were gone," Hannah said, feeling slightly nervous, wondering why Blade was so withdrawn, "I moved your clothes in here."

Blade turned, and his expression was as troubled and dark as the beard on his face. A large callused hand clutched the door frame. "Hannah, I'm not staying."

"Not staying!" Hannah didn't trust her hearing.

Long strides brought Blade to Hannah. His hands curled around her shoulders. "I can't stay," he said. "To do so will endanger you and Allie. Arnold Kipling swore to hunt me down, and he will."

"You can't go," Hannah said. "I won't let you."

"As long as I'm here in Mistletoe, you and Allie are in danger. Kipling's fight is with me, not with Mistletoe."

She clung to him, biting back the tears. She could not bear to lose a second man whom she loved to Arnold

182

Kipling, but she was. Never had she loved or hated or feared so much in her life. Pushing pride aside, she pleaded with him to stay. But he was resolute.

"I'm going to take Hoight with me. Of the four remaining, I'll have the council appoint one of them marshall, and the others will be deputies."

Hannah listened as Blade talked, but her mind wasn't on the deputies; it wasn't on the protection of the town. All her thoughts were centered on her and Blade, on their future . . . or their lack of one. Perhaps, she deliberated, Blade was ready to move on, and this offered him the excuse he needed. She pushed out of his embrace and straightened up. She was through with her begging; she would not cry.

"I have one last request to make," she said. "I want you to remain through the holidays for Allie's sake. That's only three more days, if you count the remainder of today."

Blade contemplated Hannah for a second before he curtly nodded his head, then asked, "How's the padre?"

"He's recovered, but weak. Dr. Fulbright thinks he'll be able to travel in a few days."

Blade nodded. "I've already talked with the military at Ft. Stockton about Father Corriano. They said once he arrived at the fort, they would provide an escort on to San Antonio. Hoight and I are going to travel with him. I sent Hoight over to the hotel with the news."

Dully Hannah moved around the room, watching as Blade unfastened his gun belt and laid it on the dresser. He shed his boots and socks, but made no effort to undress further. Then Hannah realized Blade was as disconcerted as she.

"I'll go down and check on Allie," she said. "We were going to finish our decorations tonight."

He didn't ask her to stay. Standing at the window, looking out, he nodded.

Hannah closed the door and leaned back against it, her

eyes closed, her lids feeling the weight of unshed tears. She loved Blade. She loved him! She had to tell him.

She turned and flung open the door, rushing into the room. As if Blade divined her purpose, he turned from the window and they moved toward each other, their arms opened.

"I can't let you go. I can't lose you." The tears streaked down Hannah's cheeks. "Blade, I love you."

He gazed into her face for a second, a small smile tugging the corners of his mouth. His eyes twinkling, he said, "You picked a mighty fine time to tell me, Mrs. Carmichael."

Then his arms clamped around her and he hugged her tightly; his arms gripped into her flesh, hurting her but also reassuring her of his love. His face burrowed into the curve of her shoulder and throat. "Hannah, my darling! My darling wife. Because I return your love, I must leave. I must protect you and Allie."

"If you won't stay here, Blade, Allie and I will go with you. It's our right to be with you." She pulled back and gazed into his face. "After all, I am Mrs. Carmichael."

Blade smiled slowly, sadly. He reached out and brushed tendrils of hair from her cheeks and temples. "If I thought we could run away from Arnold Kipling, I'd take you up on your offer," he said. "But that's no kind of life for you and Allie. If we start running now, we'll be running the rest of our lives. I'll stay with you and Allie through Christmas. Then I must finish what I began. When I've done that, I'll be back."

Hot tears stung Hannah's cheeks. She recognized the determination in his voice; she acknowledged the wisdom of his words. She would argue no more. She would love him because she knew that his love for her would bring him back to her.

The knock on the door thundered through the quiet room. Claude's voice followed.

"Marshall, I got the tub and water for your bath."

"Mr. Carmichael," Hannah whispered, "you're going to get a bath such as you've never experienced before."

Blade laughed softly, the sound an alluring caress to Hannah's tattered nerves. "I like the sound of this, Mrs. Carmichael."

And so did Mrs. Carmichael!

8

It was Christmas Eve. Dusk had settled on the town, and candles flared brightly in the chandeliers through the house.

"Is it time yet?" Allie asked for an uncounted number of times. The wheelchair rolled behind the housekeeper as she laid out the buffet.

"Not yet," Lena replied.

Walking into the grand music room, the faded red box in her hand, Hannah surveyed the decorations. Brightly colored chains looped the walls, and oriental lanterns—the same that had been used at the shindig—were suspended from the ceiling to provide a spectrum of soft pastel colors. The band, Mistletoe's own, were dressed in their Sunday best and were sitting on the small stage at the front of the room.

Blade descended the stairs, hoping he looked as "resplendent" in the new gray suit that Hannah had bought for him as she had insisted that he look. Less formidable, she had told him when she tied the small tie about his neck. She had given him several quick kisses, before he had captured her for one long and thorough one.

He ran his fingers over the gold chain and withdrew his timepiece. When he returned it to the vest pocket, he lowered his hand, letting it rest on the butt of his six-gun. He regretted having to wear them, but if a situation should arise where he needed them, he would regret even more not having them.

Moving to stand by Hannah, he put his arm about her shoulder, his gaze going to the opened box in her hand. "I suppose it's time for us to hang the mistletoe."

"The mistletoe!" Allie squealed, heading her chair toward them. Her eyes were round and bright with excitement. "Oh, yes, Uncle Blade! And don't forget we must stand beneath it and make one wish. A wish that *must* come true."

"A wish that must come true." Blade wondered if Allie had been set up for another great disappointment in her short life.

"A wish that must come true," Hannah reaffirmed.

"Yes, sir," Claude said and brought in a small ladder which he leaned against the wall. "Any wish made under this mistletoe has got to come true."

"Yeah," Blade murmured.

With Claude anchoring the ladder, Blade climbed several rungs to loop the mistletoe over the nail.

"There," he said. "The mistletoe is in place."

"Well, Marshall, now I reckon you'd better be a'thinking serious like about your wish. Remember, it's gonna come true." Saying no more, Claude removed the ladder from the room.

"Well, Hannah, I'm finished in here," Lena said, following Claude out of the room. "We'll be getting dressed now."

Blade and Hannah looked at Allie, who in awe stared up at the mistletoe.

"Who's going to be first?" she asked.

Hannah smiled. "You. My grandmother said the youngest always gets to make the first wish because that's when the mistletoe has the most magic." Blade caught her hand in his.

Smiling tremulously, breathing in deeply, Allie rolled herself into the doorway beneath the mistletoe. She looked up for a long time before she closed her eyes and squinted in concentration, her lips moving slightly as she made her wish.

Blade felt Hannah's fingers tighten around his hand and knew she was as concerned about Allie's wish coming true as he was. If only she hadn't built up the child's hope in that damned twig. Even as he thought this, a strange sensation pervaded his body. A gentle breeze wafted through the room, a delicate forest fragrance filling the room. The mistletoe seemed to come to life, and its leaves turned a deep green.

Not a man to fantasize, Blade was a little uncomfortable with his thoughts. He glanced around the room. While nothing had changed, the atmosphere in the room was different, warmer, friendlier, more jovial. Along with the aroma of popcorn and chocolate, he could smell the outdoor freshness in the room. He looked at the mistletoe again. It definitely had changed. He lowered his head to look at Allie. Her rapt expression as she murmured her wish caught his attention.

Her eyes popped open and she laughed. "Now, Uncle Blade and Hannah, it's time for you to make your wishes."

Looking at Hannah, his eyes twinkling, he asked, "Can we make our wish together? Perhaps that way we'll conserve on the magic of the mistletoe."

Hannah nodded. "We could really conserve on its energy if our wish were the same."

Facing her, he caught both her hands in his and tugged her close to him. "I think perhaps our wish is the same, Mrs. Carmichael. I'm wishing that we would have a long, happy, and prosperous life together."

"Me, too," Hannah said, "with a large family so Allie will have some brothers and sisters to run and play with."

"Agreed," Blade said, his head lowering to hers. When his lips were almost on hers, he said, "Back in Louisiana, we have a rather old-fashioned custom connected with the mistletoe. You might say in its way it's magical, too."

"And what's that?" Hannah asked.

"When a lady stands beneath the mistletoe, she's asking to be kissed."

"For sure the lady is standing beneath the mistletoe. What's the magic?" she asked.

"This." He caught the drift of perfume—a delicate flower scent—on her skin; he caught the scent of her hair. His pulse accelerated, and he covered her lips with his, soft as a whisper. But the taste of her was not enough— and had never been.

During his life Blade had learned that a man could deprive himself of many things. He could live without fire; he could toughen himself against cold; he could live in darkness if he had to; he could talk himself out of need. He could do all that for a long time. But not forever.

Blade could not live without Hannah.

His mouth pressured against hers, opened, his tongue touching hers in an intimate dance of passion—and of something more—something deeper that gave sex meaning.

The magic of this kiss was that without uttering a word, without the rhetoric of lovemaking, Blade and Hannah became one. Through the touch of their mouths they communicated their soul's needs and desires. Each took the other's loneliness; they shared their fears. They promised each other that they were here, now and forever. They understood.

They released each other spiritually, but Blade's arms tightened securely around Hannah. He wanted her to know that he loved her; he would always be with her no matter what happened. He smelled the mountain laurel and heard the whisper of the night wind. He kissed her forehead.

"I love you," he whispered against her ear.

"I love you."

No matter what the future held, this one moment was

eternal. Both had shared the magic of the mistletoe.

"Now, what do we do, Hannah?" Allie asked.

Rather than shattering the fragile spell that bound Hannah and Blade together, the child's happiness enhanced the magic.

"Since the evening is pleasant, why don't we wait outside for our guests?" Hannah suggested, curling her hand around Blade's arm.

Blade pushed the chair and the three of them moved to the front veranda. The night gently settled around them, but Blade felt apprehensive. He felt danger. As always he gave credence to his intuitions.

"Hannah," he said quietly, "the wind is blowing a little strong out here. Why don't you and Allie go into the house?"

"Uncle Blade!" Allie swiveled her head toward her uncle, but he caught her shoulder and gently squeezed. She hushed.

"You're right," Hannah said, her gaze colliding with Blade's. In the look that passed between them, she silently acknowledged her own sense of danger. "It is chilly out here, Allie. We'll go in and get our wraps."

"We'll come back after we get them?" Allie demanded.

"Of course, we will," Hannah replied.

At the same time that Hannah began to pull the wheelchair backwards, Blade stepped away from Hannah and Allie. His eyes strained into the darkness. He thought he heard a twig break; he thought he heard a noise on the other side of the porch. He drew a deep breath and hoped that Hannah and Allie were in the house before something happened. Before the Kiplings came.

He heard a scraping noise in the shrub to his right, and out of the corner of his eye he saw the movement. A figure materialized, and shots blazed through the darkened sky.

"I figure killing you, Blade Carmichael, will be my Christmas gift to myself." Maniacal laughter filled the air.

"In case you don't know who this is, it's Arnold Kipling."

Blade cleared his six-gun from the holster and shot. He heard a gasp of pain and a string of curses. He stood there, his guns drawn, his eyes once more straining through the darkness to see, to find his other enemy. He didn't doubt there was another because wherever Arnold was his younger brother was.

"Uncle Blade!" Allie shouted.

Before Blade knew what had happened, the child's weight hit him, knocking him to the floor of the porch as shots from the other direction sang over his head.

In the midst of gunfire, Lena called out, "Marshall! Hannah! Allie! Are you all right?"

Protecting Allie with his body, Blade rolled over and shot. A scream. A thud. Angry curses told him he had hit his second target.

"We're fine," Blade gasped.

The housekeeper opened the door and rushed to Hannah's side.

"We're okay," Hannah said.

Claude rounded the house into the front yard. He carried a shotgun in one hand, a lantern in the other. Spotting the men who had tried to kill Blade, he said, "Don't move, you thieving bushwhackers unless you want to say goodbye to this world forever."

"Uncle Blade." Her arms around Blade's neck, Allie cried into her uncle's vest. "Oh, Uncle Blade, I thought they were going to kill you just like they did Mama and Papa."

"You threw yourself at me, didn't you, little girl? That was a brave thing to do." Blade's voice broke. "With you around those Kipling boys didn't stand a chance."

Allie nodded her head against him, and he held her closely and securely.

Horses galloped toward the house. The gate opened. Several pairs of boots clipped over the boardwalk. The deputies had arrived.

MORE PASSION AND ADVENTURE AWAIT... YOUR TRIP TO A BIG ADVENTUROUS WORLD BEGINS WHEN YOU ACCEPT YOUR FIRST 4 NOVELS ABSOLUTELY *FREE* (AN $18.00 VALUE)

Accept your Free gift and start to experience more of the passion and adventure you like in a historical romance novel. Each Zebra novel is filled with proud men, spirited women and tempestuous love that you'll remember long after you turn the last page.

Zebra Historical Romances are the finest novels of their kind. They are written by authors who really know how to weave tales of romance and adventure in the historical settings you love. You'll feel like you've actually gone back in time with the thrilling stories that each Zebra novel offers.

GET YOUR FREE GIFT WITH THE START OF YOUR HOME SUBSCRIPTION

Our readers tell us that these books sell out very fast in book stores and often they miss the newest titles. So Zebra has made arrangements for you to receive the four newest novels published each month.

You'll be guaranteed that you'll never miss a title, and home delivery is so convenient. And to show you just how easy it is to get Zebra Historical Romances, we'll send you your first 4 books absolutely FREE! Our gift to you just for trying our home subscription service.

BIG SAVINGS AND FREE HOME DELIVERY

Each month, you'll receive the four newest titles as soon as they are published. You'll probably receive them even before the bookstores do. What's more, you may preview these exciting novels free for 10 days. If you like them as much as we think you will, just pay the low preferred subscriber's price of just $3.75 each. *You'll save $3.00 each month off the publisher's price.* AND, your savings are even greater because there are never any shipping, handling or other hidden charges—FREE Home Delivery. Of course you can return any shipment within 10 days for full credit, no questions asked. There is no minimum number of books you must buy.

4 FREE BOOKS

TO GET YOUR 4 FREE BOOKS WORTH $18.00 — MAIL IN THE FREE BOOK CERTIFICATE T O D A Y

Fill in the Free Book Certificate below, and we'll send your FREE BOOKS to you as soon as we receive it.

If the certificate is missing below, write to: Zebra Home Subscription Service, Inc., P.O. Box 5214, 120 Brighton Road, Clifton, New Jersey 07015-5214.

FREE BOOK CERTIFICATE

4 FREE BOOKS

ZEBRA HOME SUBSCRIPTION SERVICE, INC.

YES! Please start my subscription to Zebra Historical Romances and send me my first 4 books absolutely FREE. I understand that each month I may preview four new Zebra Historical Romances free for 10 days. If I'm not satisfied with them, I may return the four books within 10 days and owe nothing. Otherwise, I will pay the low preferred subscriber's price of just $3.75 each; a total of $15.00, *a savings off the publisher's price of $3.00.* I may return any shipment and I may cancel this subscription at any time. There is no obligation to buy any shipment and there are no shipping, handling or other hidden charges. Regardless of what I decide, the four free books are mine to keep.

NAME

ADDRESS _____ APT

CITY _____ STATE _____ ZIP

TELEPHONE ( )

SIGNATURE _____ (if under 18, parent or guardian must sign)

Terms, offer and prices subject to change without notice. Subscription subject to acceptance by Zebra Books. Zebra Books reserves the right to reject any order or cancel any subscription.

"Colone., are you all right?" Hoight Dougald called.

"Fine," Blade answered.

"Over here, Hoight," Claude said. "I reckon it's them Kipling brothers."

"Be careful, Claude!" Lena hurried to her husband.

Standing over the two men, Lang Hopkins nodded. "Yep, it's them all right. Reckon they'll live to stand trial. Looks like both of them have minor wounds."

"We'll take them over to the calaboose, Colonel," Hoight announced. "We'll see y'all a little later."

Lena took the lantern from Claude and the two of them walked around the house, leaving the Carmichaels alone. Hannah knelt beside Blade and Allie.

"It's over," she murmured.

"Yes," Blade answered and caught Allie's shoulders and pushed her away so he could look into her face. Then he looked up at Hannah. "If it hadn't been for Allie, I might not be all right. Do you realize she saved my life?"

Crying and nodding her head, Hannah slipped to the floor beside him and Allie.

Allie, beaming through her tears, gazed at the vacant wheelchair, then she looked at the floor. She patted the planks anc said in an awestruck voice, "I sort of walked, didn't I?"

"You did," Blade agreed, looking over the child's head at Hannah. "And that means you'll be really walking soon."

"Oh, Hannah!" Allie shouted. "Oh, Hannah, I'm gonna walk again. I know I am. Let me try, Uncle Blade. Let me see if I can."

Rising, Blade first helped Hannah to her feet. Then he lifted Allie and assisted as she made her first dragging and faltering steps to the wheelchair.

"Oh, Uncle Blade," Allie exclaimed, "I can't really walk."

"Yes, you are," Blade said, resettling her in the chair. "You're just going to have to take it a step at a time.

193

You'll get better the more you practice. Right now, I'm going to take you to the music room where you can greet the guests. I think Hannah and I have some business to finish."

Wondering what Blade was going to do, Hannah followed him through the hallway and up the stairs to their room. He opened one of the dresser drawers and extracted a small leather pouch which he opened. He unfastened the strings and withdrew a sheet of paper. Tearing it to shreds, he unfastened the badge from his shirt and placed it on top of the dresser.

"The contract is over, Hannah," he said, "as is the marriage of convenience. From now on it's a marriage in every sense of the word."

"Yes," she murmured and went into his arms.

Several long and fully satisfying kisses later, the two of them walked downstairs to find the guests already milling in the music room. Greetings were exchanged; stories swapped about the capture of the Kiplings. Excitement rippled through the room.

"Hannah! Marshall!" Alberta Tierly's gusty voice carried across the room over the drone of conversation. "You're standing beneath the mistletoe!"

Blade glanced up, then down at his wife and smiled. "So we are." He looked at Alberta with a decided twinkle in his eyes. "What do you suggest we do about it, Mrs. Tierly?"

Nodding her head and grinning, Alberta clamped both hands on her hips. "Marshall, I took you for a smart man. If you don't know what to do underneath the mistletoe, then I ain't gonna tell you."

"I know," Allie called out, and all eyes turned to the child who rolled her chair and positioned it in front of them. "Uncle Blade showed Hannah earlier. He kissed her."

Blade chuckled softly when he saw the flush quickly rising on Hannah's cheeks.

"Well, Marshall," Alberta teased, "we only have Allie's word that you know what to do. I guess you're gonna have to prove it to us."

"Gladly, Alberta," Blade murmured. "Gladly."

Blade had never tasted a woman as sweet as Hannah. Each time he kissed her, it was like kissing her for the first time. He was reluctant to let such sweetness go, but from the applause he figured they had entertained the crowd enough. Also he felt Allie tugging at his jacket.

"Uncle Blade. Hannah."

Moving apart, both of them looked at her.

"Is it time to light the candles on the Christmas tree?"

"Yes," Hannah answered, moving with Allie toward the tree, "it's time. Lena, will you see that the other lights in the house are doused."

Hannah and Blade lit the upper candles and stepped back to allow Allie access to the lower ones. When they stood in the mellow light of the Christmas candles, the band began to play and the people to sing "O Tannenbaum."

Her eyes shining as brightly as the candles on the tree, Allie looked at Hannah. "This is the very best Christmas of my life," she said. "The mistletoe is magic. I wished I could walk again, and I will. I know I will."

Blade felt the bite of tears in his eyes.

"And I have an announcement to make," Hannah said. "Blade and I were married in a civil ceremony at Ft. Stockton and none of you were there to witness it. So I've asked Father Corriano if he would bless our marriage, and he consented."

Smiling, the priest slowly made his way to the couple.

The Christmas celebration lasted to the wee hours of the morning. Finally Blade and Hannah were tucking Allie into bed.

Sitting on the edge of the bed, looking down at Allie, Hannah said, "Your uncle and I know we can never take the place of your parents, and we won't try. But we want to adopt you, Allie, so you'll be our daughter also."

Tears glistened in Allie's eyes and she raised up on the bed and hugged Hannah. "I want you to adopt me." She looked from Hannah to her uncle. "I want you to be my mama and papa. My wish has already come true. I *can* walk again, and I'll have a real mama and papa again. The mistletoe is truly magical, isn't it, Hannah?"

"Yes, it is," Hannah agreed.

"It's even more than magical," Blade said, his hands settling on his wife's shoulders. "It's miraculous."

And they all believed it.

Cheyenne Mistletoe
by Georgina Gentry

Prologue

1889. A landmark year in the history of the old West. Colonel Ranald Mackenzie, greatest of the Indian fighters, dies insane and forgotten in New York. Belle Starr, fabled bandit queen, is ambushed and killed in eastern Indian Territory. Butch Cassidy and his gang rob their first bank in Colorado, and outlaw Bob Younger dies in a Minnesota prison. North Dakota, South Dakota, Montana, and Washington become states this year.

Most important to our story, the central section of Indian Territory, known as the "Unassigned Lands," is the prize as eager settlers race to win free homesteads. However, for some of the winners death, hunger, and trouble lie only months ahead in the bitter cold of winter . . .

1

Late Monday afternoon, December 23, 1889
The town of Edmond, Indian Territory

If she weren't desperate, she would never consider doing what she was about to do.

Genevieve Malone tied her sorrel mare to the hitching rail, patted the velvet muzzle, and picked up her burlap sack. "There, Blaze, you just wait here. If I can sell all this mistletoe, there'll be oats for you tonight."

And maybe something else besides turnips for Christmas dinner, she thought, *but then she had much worse problems than that to deal with.*

Ginny pulled her frayed coat collar around her blond hair and looked up and down rowdy Two Street. Indian Territory couldn't legally have saloons, but some were winking at the law, knowing liquor would be allowed once this area became Oklahoma Territory.

Never in her eighteen years had she even been in a saloon. Papa would never have allowed it. Now she seemed to have no alternative and the kids were hungry. Maybe some of the cowboys and soldiers in town to celebrate the holidays would buy from her. Ginny glanced down at her mother's wedding ring on her finger. If men thought she was a married woman, she might be safe walking into this tough saloon—or would she?

As she hesitated in the cold, a big half-breed wearing a pistol strapped low and tied down, crossed the street, brushed past her. He stopped, looked over her horse critically. "That's a good mare. You should be ashamed to take such poor care of her."

Ginny felt the blood rush to her face at his chiding. She started to tell him she was doing the best she could, that there was no money for oats, then pride held her back. She lifted her chin proudly, looked up at him. He was a little too rugged to be handsome, especially with that jagged scar at the corner of his grim mouth. "Since when does a gunfighter shame honest citizens?"

His bronzed face darkened with anger and his lip curled into a sneer. "A sodbuster! I should have known!" He turned and swaggered into the saloon, spurs jingling.

Ginny stared after him, both angry, and humiliated. There were more just like him inside. Ginny half-turned away, the icy wind cutting through her ragged clothes. She hadn't felt so alone and frightened since she and the kids had managed to dig that grave two weeks ago.

Maybe she could sell her mistletoe somewhere else. No, Ginny shook her head, she'd already tried all the stores along Broad Street with no luck. Times were hard this first winter after the land run, and anyway, those who really wanted holiday mistletoe had already ridden out to the Cross Timbers and cut it from the straggly trees themselves.

The wind picked up, the smell of snow in the air. She needed to get home before the weather worsened and night fell. However, even worse than entering this saloon and dealing with the rough men inside, she dreaded going home empty-handed to face three disappointed little children.

Ginny took a deep breath for courage and holding her sack like a shield, marched inside. The interior smelled of tobacco smoke, cheap perfume, and stale beer. Faded red garlands hung around the dreary walls. A table of men played cards and in a corner, a piano banged out Jingle Bells.

She felt all eyes turn to look her over. Talk gradually died and the piano stopped playing. The half-breed lounged against the bar, his jacket open, revealing a bright red shirt. His dark eyes swept up and down her slight frame. He frowned and pushed his Stetson back as he sipped his drink.

The bartender stopped wiping the bar, the dim light reflecting off his greasy hair. "What you want, girlie? This ain't no place for you."

What Ginny wanted was to turn and run out, but she thought of three tow-headed children and they were more important than her fear. Reaching into her bag, she held up a little green sprig. "I'm selling mistletoe, gentlemen, ten cents a bunch. Get in the holiday spirit!"

Some of the men smiled and a frowzy red-haired saloon girl in a green satin dress snickered. The bartender made a shooing motion. "The stuff grows wild everywhere, girlie, the trees to the east are full of it. Now get outa here!"

She was a Malone and stubborn to the core. Ginny stood her ground. "Think about it, fellas, a dime isn't much for a holiday decoration."

The red-haired girl sauntered over. "I'll take a bunch, farm girl." She threw the dime on the floor at Ginny's feet, jerked the mistletoe from her hand.

The coin made a ringing sound before it stopped against Ginny's worn shoe. Ginny hesitated. What she really wanted to do was slap the painted, insolent smile off the woman's face, but she forced herself to take a deep breath, bent to pick up the money.

The other laughed, turned, and walked back, hips swinging in the tight green satin. She held the mistletoe over the half-breed's head. "Merry Christmas, stranger; welcome to Edmond." She reached up and kissed him.

The men set up a whoop at her daring, but the gun-tough only slipped his muscular arm around her waist, lifting her off the floor and kissed her thoroughly while the others hooted and called out ribald encouragement.

Ginny felt the blood rush to her face. The half-breed set the saloon girl down and slapped her across the rump. "Sorry, baby, no sale."

The red-head winked at him. "Maybe I can change your mind, handsome. Where you from and what's your handle?"

The men hooted again. The gun-tough looked at Ginny, his hard mouth smeared with red lip rouge, his spurs jingling as he put one boot up on the brass rail. "I just drifted in from Tascosa this morning. They call me Hawk."

It suited him, Ginny thought with a shiver; a dark, lean predator if she ever saw one, and he radiated raw sexuality like a mustang stallion.

He looked at Ginny with his brooding eyes. The scar at the corner of his mouth seemed white against his dark face. "Get out of here, little sodbuster girl; this is no place for your kind."

"I'll be the judge of that." She tried to keep her voice haughty although her hand trembled as she held up another green sprig. "All right, gentlemen, who else wants to buy some mistletoe? Only ten cents."

"How about you, sir?" Ginny held out a sprig to a slightly drunken sergeant who stood at the bar.

The burly man grinned and handed her a silver dollar. Ginny looked at it a long moment. "Do you want ten bunches, sir? I might have trouble making change—"

"No, I'll take it out in trade," he hiccoughed. "Don't kisses always go with mistletoe?"

Before she could react, the sergeant grabbed her, pulled her to him, bruising her mouth with his while she struggled. He tasted of whiskey and his hands felt hot and sweaty as they slipped under her coat.

Hawk leaned against the bar, sipping his drink and watching the girl struggle in the arms of the drunk. Hell, she deserved it. The wedding ring on her hand reflected the light. Where was her man that he'd let her come in a saloon?

The blonde was slight and small, the man big and plenty drunk. She wasn't Hawk's problem. He had lived a long time by not mixing in things that didn't concern him. Hawk glanced around at the others. They looked uneasy and ashamed, but no one made any attempt to help her.

The redhead laughed. "Serves her right! Teach her to come in where she don't belong."

The girl's coat fell to the floor. The sergeant had his hand on the girl's breast now, fondling her while she struggled. Hell, she was a sodbuster and if there was one thing Hawk hated, worse than white soldiers, it was settlers determined to plow up and fence the Indians' land.

She fought to pull away, and when she did, the faded blue calico dress tore at the shoulder, revealing skin as pale as moonlight on snow. She looked right into Hawk's eyes, pleading with hers.

Almost thirty years ago, a Cheyenne girl had been raped by a soldier. Had his mother begged with her eyes and men had watched without helping her?

Without realizing he had crossed the floor between them, Hawk grabbed the man's arm. "That's enough. You've had your fun."

The soldier brushed Hawk's hand away. "I want more than a kiss, I want—"

"She isn't that kind; anyone can see that," Hawk said. "Let her go." Hawk caught the girl's shoulder, very aware of the feel of her bare, soft flesh as he tried to move her to one side.

"Why, you lousy Injun bastard!" The drunk swung, but Hawk had survived many a saloon brawl. He spun the man around, bringing his Colt up to slam him against the side of the head with the barrel.

The frightened girl scrambled out of the way. The bluecoat slumped to the floor. Hawk dropped his pistol back in his holster and glared at her. She was smaller and even younger than he had first thought, and as fragile as a flower. Tears glistened in the wide, blue eyes and her soft lips half parted as she looked up at him. He had a crazy impulse to grab her, pull her to him, kiss that full, soft mouth, tangle his hard hands in her yellow mane of hair. Instead he leaned over, picked up her worn coat, handed it to her. "What's your name?"

"Genevieve. Genevieve Malone." Innocently, the tip of her pink tongue ran across her lips. "I—I'm much obliged."

Hawk shrugged. "He's wearing Fifth Cavalry insignia. The Fifth killed a lot of my friends at Summit Springs." He looked at the gold band she wore. Hawk

206

had fought for her; as the victor, he should get to bed her. Instead, some sweaty white man would lie between her thighs tonight; some dirt farmer who didn't deserve such a desirable woman because he couldn't or wouldn't protect her. If this was Hawk's woman—but of course she wasn't.

The thought annoyed him and he realized suddenly that everyone was watching him. "Take your money, Mrs. Malone, and get the hell out of here! Your man must be *loco* to let you come in a saloon."

She gathered up her things and fled out the door while Hawk leaned against the bar with a sigh, pulled a *cigarillo* from his jacket, signaled for another drink. The bartender motioned for two cowboys to carry the fallen sergeant out. The piano played again and the redhead sidled up to Hawk, pressed close against his arm. "Hey, handsome, that was really something. You make love as well as you fight?"

He grinned ever so slightly as he lit a match with his thumbnail. "I've had no complaints."

"I'll bet you haven't." She almost purred as she took the match from his hand, lit his smoke for him. "Hope you're gonna be stayin', not much excitement in this sleepy burg."

"With you around, baby? That's hard to believe."

She pressed her breasts against his arm and the scent of cheap perfume drifted to him. He felt the heat of her, urgent, wanting. This redhead was his kind; no responsibilities, no questions asked and he liked his freedom. "Maybe later, Red." He took a puff of his cigar.

She looked at the well-used Colt on his hip. "You won't find much call for a hired gun around here."

Or almost any place in the West, Hawk thought. He didn't feel at home among the vanquished Cheyenne, and he'd never really been at ease among the whites, except for the outlaws who had befriended him young. Civilization was taming even the tough towns like Tascosa and Tombstone. The big ranchers didn't need his kind anymore; men were settling their differences in law courts instead of shoot-outs. He thought about his days in the Lincoln County war. Billy the Kid was dead now, and maybe Nevada, too, for all Hawk knew.

He felt the heat of her press against him, but saw the small blonde in his mind. "Any action up at Guthrie?"

She shook her head. "Not your kind—unless you handle a deck of cards as well. One of the train crews said that gambler, Flint, arrived there yesterday."

The Flint? I always wanted to play against him." Hawk studied the glowing tip of his cigar, sipped his whiskey. It was cheap stuff, but it tasted good and warming. The wind picked up a little outside. Snowflakes blew past the saloon's dirty window. Hawk only had a few dollars in his poke; not enough for a high-stakes card game against a big-timer like the mysterious gambler.

A bearded soldier gestured from the card table. "Hey, Mister, you lookin' for a little action?"

Hawk nodded, fingering the scar by his mouth. Picking up his drink, he dismissed the girl with a gesture. She'd be around when he had time for her. Right now, he needed to build his stake and there were three soldiers at that card table. Hawk had a double reason to hate bluecoats.

He crossed the dingy saloon, spurs jingling, and took a chair at the poker table with his back against a wall out of old habit. "What's the ante?"

"A dollar." A fat shopkeeper shuffled the cards.

In truth, Hawk was almost broke, which was the only reason he'd stopped in this sleepy town. He handled a deck of cards almost as well as a gun. His mind was on Flint. "How far to Guthrie?"

A scrawny private looked up from his cards. "About fifteen miles north."

"The weather seems to be gettin' worse," the fat man said, "No tellin' how bad it'll be by tomorrow."

Hawk looked out the front window. It was snowing steadily now and getting dark outside. Occasionally, the cold wind shook the flimsy building. His fine stallion, Concho, was warm and well-fed at the nearest stable. "Is there a train?"

"Yep. Tomorrow—if the weather don't cancel it."

The redhaired girl laughed. "Train crew said Flint's supposed to move on tomorrow. Why don't you forget about him, handsome? It's cold out there, but warm at my place."

The men guffawed, but Hawk turned his attention back to his cards. There'd be women in Guthrie; there were always easy women for him with no strings, no obligations attached. He thought about the famous gambler. If he waited until tomorrow, Flint might be gone and, besides, the cost of the ticket would dip into Hawk's meager poke. Fifteen miles wouldn't be so far to ride a horse.

It was still early. He'd clean these men's pockets and move on. There might even be an all-night game going on in the bigger town.

Hawk drained his whiskey, signaled for another as the players bet. The piano banged out a popular song from the old days: *O, Genevieve, sweet Genevieve, the days may come, the days may go, but still the hands of mem'ry weave the blissful dreams of long ago . . .*

Sweet Genevieve. By now, that little blonde was probably just walking through the door at some ragged soddie and into the arms of a farmer. Her face would be all cold from the wind, but her body would be soft and warm as the man picked her up and began to undress her, carry her naked to a featherbed.

The image annoyed him, but Hawk wasn't sure why. He took a deep puff of his *cigarillo* and raised the bet, took the hand. None of the white men could play worth a damn. In the hours that followed, Hawk won most of their money so the game broke up. He drank a lot more than he usually did, thinking about spending yet another holiday alone and among strangers. His old *compadres* all seemed to be dead and he never stayed long enough anywhere to form any new friendships. The wind rattled the building again and the men who blew in now had big snowflakes clinging to their coats.

Guthrie. Maybe some excitement there over the holidays. A man wouldn't feel so lonely in the midst of all those people. It was a big town, likely to become the capitol if this area became Oklahoma Territory. Hawk moved a little unsteadily toward the door.

The redhead caught up with him, grabbed his arm, pouting. "I thought you was stayin' with me?"

Somehow, she wasn't what he wanted in a woman tonight. He shrugged her hand off. "I don't like being fenced in or answerin' to anyone. I'm going to Guthrie." Hawk lurched through the door, spurs jingling, and into the cold night.

Later as he rode north, it occurred to Hawk that he had to be more than a little drunk to start out in weather like this. Even his fine bay quarter horse snorted in protest, the fancy silver on his bridle jangling.

"Okay, Concho, so we should have stayed in that hick town and ridden over in the morning," Hawk conceded and pulled his Stetson low, turned his coat collar up, "but we're on our way now, and it won't be so far."

Snow blew like needles against his face as if to mock him. There was no moon or stars tonight, only the light reflecting off the frozen crust that crunched beneath Concho's hooves. Hawk was a solitary man caught between two cultures, feeling completely at home in neither. Yet tonight, he felt doubly alone as if he and his horse were the only two things alive in this silent, frozen world.

O, Genevieve, sweet Genevieve, the days may come, the days may go . . . Genevieve . . . Genevieve. . . .

The refrain seemed to run through his mind over and over. He had been too long without a woman, Hawk thought, that was all. He'd find himself a blond whore in Guthrie to take care of his need.

To the east in the Cross Timbers, a coyote howled and the sound echoed and reechoed. *How far had Hawk come?* Uncertainly, he reined in, looked around. As a small boy, he might have hunted this area with his mother's people, but nothing looked familiar. Then in 1868, Custer and his Seventh Cavalry had hit that sleeping Indian village on the Washita southwest of here and changed Hawk's life forever.

It had been cold that November dawn, also, mistletoe clinging to the bare trees along the river. Wincing at the memory, he touched the jagged scar on his face where the officer had slashed Hawk with his saber. His Cheyenne mother had thrown herself across her little bastard boy to protect him when the saber slashed again. She screamed and her warm blood ran all over him. She had whispered: *Ne-mehotatse. I love you,* as she died. A Dog Soldier warrior named Iron Knife had rescued the bloody child from certain death. Yes,

211

Hawk had good reason to hate white soldiers.

If he had ever been in this area before, the blowing snow had wiped out any familiar landmarks. Civilization and the damned plows and fences had changed things so much, he might not have recognized anything anyhow.

All he had to do was keep riding north and he'd see the lights of Guthrie eventually. Hawk cursed himself for a drunken fool. He had no idea how far he'd come or how long he'd been riding. He stood up in his stirrups, the saddle creaking beneath his weight as he looked behind him. No lights from Edmond. Either the town was finally asleep or far enough behind him to be lost in the swirling blizzard.

He'd follow the railroad tracks north. Hawk nudged his horse forward, looking around. Nothing. Maybe the blowing snow had obliterated the tracks. Hell, he knew which way was north, he'd just keep riding.

Suppose he swung too wide and rode right past Guthrie? The thought scared him a little because he wasn't sure how many miles it was to the next town after that.

The coyote howled again and Concho snorted. Automatically, Hawk reached out and patted the stallion's neck. "It's okay, boy, in an hour we'll probably be riding down Guthrie's main street. They'll have a fine livery stable and a hotel with a warm bed and some hot coffee."

The wind blasted against his face and he tried to pull his coat up around his ears, shivering now. If he didn't find shelter soon, he might be in serious trouble. He cursed himself for a damn, drunken fool.

Was that a light off to his right? Maybe it had been a star or just ice shimmering in the darkness. God, he was cold! Concho shook his big head and the silver on his bridle jingled almost like bells.

"It's all right, boy; sorry I got you out in this weather. If I hadn't been a little bit drunk . . ."

Concho snorted.

"Okay; a *lot* drunk," Hawk conceded. It was that naive mistletoe girl. He had been so preoccupied with her memory that he drank a lot more than usual. He remembered her naked flesh against his dark hand; soft, fragile. She wasn't his kind of woman at all. Her kind wanted roots; wanted to stop a man from roaming; tie him down with kids and land.

Hawk knew a lot about horses, a little about cattle, but he didn't want to know about farming. He wasn't meant to live like some white sodbuster, breaking his back over a plow, putting blisters on his hands with gut-wrenching, sweating labor. The Cheyenne were hunters and had nothing but scorn for farmers. Their worst enemies, the Pawnees, were tillers of the soil.

The coyote howled again almost as if it were mocking him. Hawk looked around. *Was that a light or only his imagination?* Now he didn't even see that. Nothing. Not a town, nor a house, nor even a wind break unless he turned and rode east toward the Cross Timbers. *Just which way was east?* The chill cut through him, making him shiver as Hawk realized he was no longer certain. Drunk. Freezing. And lost.

2

Even though home was only a few miles northeast of Edmond, Genevieve had been afraid that she and Blaze might get caught out in the coming storm as she returned in the twilight. With a sigh of relief she rode into the yard, saw three small faces pressed against the cabin's window.

"We made it, old girl." She patted the mare's scrawny neck as she dismounted. "Sorry, you'll just get hay and turnips again. I'd hoped to sell enough mistletoe to buy you some grain."

What would Paddy do in this situation? Ginny blinked away a tear as she looked off toward the fresh mound covered with bunches of mistletoe out under the blackjack oaks. Would he tell her to try to hang onto the claim even though she wasn't at all sure she could work it, or give up, move into town, maybe find a husband or get a job clerking at the general store? Owning a piece of land had meant everything to the Malones. If anyone in town found out Papa was dead, would they take the homestead away from her because she wasn't twenty-one? She didn't know who to ask or who to trust. One thing was certain, Ginny wouldn't give up this hundred and sixty acres without a fight.

"That's not today's problem," she said to the mare as she led Blaze into the lean-to, and fed her. "After Christmas, I'll decide what to do next."

Some Christmas! She took her pitiful little bag of items bought with the dollar and a dime, and went into the cabin with a forced smile. "Well, here I am back with all sorts of good things!"

Little Mike, Rachel, and baby Beth, clustered around her. "What'd you bring? Did you see Santa Claus?"

Genevieve looked down into Mike's serious big eyes. Six years old, she thought, and already carrying the burdens of a full grown man. "Well, no, Santa Claus isn't coming this year because there's other children who need things worse than we do."

Five-year-old Rachel chewed on the end of her blond pigtail. "Nobody's worse off than we are with Daddy dead."

"That's not true," Ginny patted her head, hugged the toddler, Beth, who clung to Ginny's skirt. Ginny looked up at the small photo on the rough-hewn mantel. The five of them had posed for the photographer just before the land run last spring. How proud and handsome Paddy had looked; only a touch of gray in his reddish hair. All four children were blonde like their dead mother.

"That's not true," Ginny said again as if to convince herself. "We've got a Christmas tree." She sniffed the pleasing scent of the small cedar in the corner with its ragged paper chains and star on top. "And we've got enough to eat and each other."

"Turnips," Mike said, "I got a pot of turnips boiling like you told me. What did you bring from town?"

"Oh, lots of good things!" Ginny tried to say it brightly, "Some salt pork and some cornmeal and even a little coffee, and some surprises for Christmas Day."

Baby Beth took her thumb out of her mouth. "Doll?"

At that point, Ginny almost wept. "No, no doll."

216

Oh. God, why wasn't there enough for even one gift each for her little sisters and brother? What she had was three small apples and a candy stick to be divided between them.

"We'll make out," Ginny said with more spirit than she felt and rumpled Mike's yellow hair. "The Malones are proud folk and someday, we'll laugh about all this. Now how about me making a pan of corn bread to go with those nice turnips?"

Rachel chewed her pigtail. "There's no butter or milk."

"Maybe if we can get a crop in this spring, we can buy a cow. Remember Papa talked about owning a herd of cattle and some fine colts from Blaze? Maybe someone will even start a school for the children close by and you can go." Ginny busied herself before the hearth, thinking in another couple of weeks, all the turnips would be gone. She had to decide what to do soon.

They ate turnips, weak coffee, and some corn pone with no butter. Then they sat before their straggly Christmas tree and sang carols. Even with her arms around the children, Ginny felt lonely and afraid. With Papa gone, this family was now her responsibility and she wasn't sure she was capable, but she would do the best she could.

Her thoughts went to the big half-breed in the saloon who had rescued her. He looked like he could deal with anything the world threw at him. When she remembered the way he had looked at her, the warmth of his hard hand on her bare shoulder, she shivered a little. Wild as a mustang stallion and rootless as a tumbleweed blowing aimlessly across the prairie. No, not the responsible husband she needed to help keep this place going.

217

Had Papa ever been that kind of man? Paddy Malone had come to this country looking for his brother, Mike, who had immigrated earlier. He never found him. Instead he had fought in the Civil War on the Union side, then later, rode with the Seventh Cavalry for a couple of years before marrying her mother. There was little chance for poor Irish to prosper back East. Mama had died giving birth to Beth and Papa had brought the family here for the land run last April. Now he was dead and Ginny had to make the decisions.

As the big Irishman had lay dying of pneumonia, he had whispered, "Hang onto our homestead, Ginny girl, when I'm gone. The Malones have always been shanty Irish, but we've land now and that was always our dream."

She blinked back the hot tears and squeezed his rough, work-worn hand. "Papa, don't talk like that! You'll be here in the spring to plow and plant—"

"Naw, I'm done," he whispered and reached out to touch her face, "You look just like her; you know that? And you're named for her. Don't give up her dream, daughter."

She couldn't hold back the tears. "Yes, I'll hold on for the little ones, no matter what I have to do."

"It's not quite fair," Paddy whispered and a frown crossed his ruddy face, "we took it from the Indians, you know, not quite fair."

" 'Twas not our doin'," Ginny protested, "the government did it! You only made the run on Blaze and claimed a piece for your own."

His voice came faintly now. "I was at the Washita with Custer, did I tell you that?"

"You told me. Rest now."

"I've lit candles and said Hail Marys over that day.

Twenty-one years . . . still on quiet, cold nights, I hear the gunshots and the screams . . . Saw an officer kill an Indian girl with his saber as she threw herself across her little boy to save him . . ."

"Go to sleep, Papa, don't think about it."

"Ginny, me love," he whispered, and when she looked into his fevered eyes, she realized he saw not her, but her mother. "Ah, Ginny, me fine wife," he said ever so faintly, "I'm comin', me darlin', wait for me . . . wait for me now . . ."

Ginny came back to the present with a start, staring at the small Christmas tree and turning her mother's wedding ring over and over on her finger. Two weeks ago, she and the children had managed to dig Paddy's grave and cover it with mistletoe. It seemed like two years. If the authorities found out, they might take the land, or worse yet, put the little ones in an orphanage. How in the name of God were the Malones going to manage now?

The toddler had gone to sleep in Ginny's lap and the other two were yawning.

"We ought to go to bed." She gathered them up, put them in the crude bunks in the corner with the curtain across it.

"Ginny, you comin'?" Rachel asked sleepily.

"In a minute. I want to sit up a while longer." Ginny twisted her mother's ring, thinking about her beloved parents marriage. Someday she hoped she found a man who was big and strong and protective. She wouldn't mind if he had a few rough edges. However, there weren't many men who would marry a girl with a ready-made family.

She poured a cup of coffee, settled herself back in

the old rocker before the fireplace. At least living in the Cross Timbers, they had enough wood. Farther out on the plains, the settlers had to rely on "prairie coal," dried cattle, and buffalo manure for heat and cooking. Ginny had tried to fix the plank and sod cabin up as best she could, but to an outsider, it probably looked as pathetic as their straggly little Christmas tree.

The wind rattled the windows and somewhere in the distance, a coyote howled. Papa's old rifle hung over the mantel to keep it out of the children's reach, but Ginny wasn't much of a shot. However, Blaze was safe enough in the lean-to. Ginny wished she felt safe and secure. For just a moment, she remembered again the half-breed tough in the saloon and the way he had looked at her, the heat of his hand on her shoulder, the size and the power of the man.

He was just the opposite of the responsible farmer she needed for a husband. He had stared at her with a hot intensity that had scared her, with no mistaking what he wanted. She felt a deep, unaccustomed stirring as she thought about him.

What was that sound? Ginny strained to hear, then decided it was only the wind rattling around the sod and log cabin. It came again, a little louder now. Ginny felt the hair raise up on the back of her neck at the rhythmic jangle, stood up, looked toward the old rifle. Was that coyote nosing around outside? A coyote was a cowardly beast, it would run if she threw a hunk of wood at it.

The rhythmic jingle drifted on the wind. It sounded almost like bells. *What on earth?*

Mike came up out of bed, followed by the others. "What's that noise?"

Ginny could only shake her head at him.

But Rachel hit the floor running. "Sleigh!" She

shrieked, "Santa's sleigh bells!"

"Now, wait—" Ginny began, but the three children were already swinging open the door.

"Santa! Santa!"

A big man stepped inside, spurs jangling. He took off his Stetson, slapped it against his leg, shook the snowflakes from his wide shoulders. "I saw your light. Be much obliged for shelter for the night."

The half-breed. He started with surprise as he seemed to recognize her for the first time. "Well, I'll be damned; the mistletoe girl."

Little Mike protested manfully. "It ain't fitten to swear in front of women."

The man's dark gaze never left Ginny's face. For a moment, she thought he would laugh, but then he seemed to reconsider. "You got grit, boy. I beg the ladies' pardon."

Ginny managed to find her voice. "What—what are you doing out here, Mister Hawk?" Hawk. Yes, that fit him all right; a dark, dangerous predator. Her worst nightmare. Alone with three little children, no man to protect her, the rifle out of reach, and here was that half-breed gun-tough walking in out of the night. Ginny looked up at the rifle hanging over the fireplace, then at the pistol strapped to his hip. "Mister Malone isn't home right now, but he's due right back. He's gone over to the neighbors—"

"Ginny," Rachel looked at her with a frown. "Why do you say that? You know Daddy's—"

"Be quiet, Rachel," Ginny snapped. The family's only refuge might be if this gun-tough thought Paddy was due back any moment and decided to ride on.

Beth toddled over, took her thumb out of her mouth, and looked up at the big man with his red shirt visible in the collar of his coat. "Santa Claus?"

"Sorry," the man said, but he smiled at the child, "anyway, he'll be here tomorrow night."

All three small faces grew sad and Rachel sighed.

Hawk threw Ginny a questioning look and she felt ashamed that he might guess at their poverty.

"Kids, don't bother the man. Come over by the fire and I—I'll get you some coffee, Mister Hawk."

"Not 'mister,' just Hawk." He strode over, spurs jingling, and stood before the fire, the snow still clinging to his broad shoulders. "It's colder than a wh—" he glanced at the big-eyed children, "colder than a *lady's* heart," he said. "I took the liberty of putting my stallion in your stable. That's a good mare you've got."

Little Mike grinned. "Daddy spent all our money on Blaze. She's fine blooded, ran fast enough to get us this claim before anyone else got here."

Ginny handed Hawk one of her mother's china cups. Their hands brushed as she did so and she pulled back. He looked a little awkward holding the dainty cup in his big hand. She felt acutely aware of the size and strength of him. "I—are you hungry? We've some turnips and cornbread."

He frowned as he sat down at the table before the fire. "With all this game out there, you're eatin' turnips? If you were my woman, you'd be better fed than that."

"It suits us!" Ginny snapped and dished it up with jerky, angry gestures. "We—we love turnips!"

"Ginny's not a very good shot," Rachel said gravely, standing before the big man as he picked up his fork. "Papa was trying to teach her before—"

"Rachel!" Ginny said, "you know he's a good shot and he's due back from the neighbors any minute now!"

Hawk paused, looked around at the three children.

"Hellava night to be out. Must have been pretty important to take a man away from his warm bed." He looked at Ginny, then at the bed.

She licked her lips nervously, following his gaze. There was no mistaking what he was thinking about. She looked up at the rifle again. She didn't have a chance of getting it before he could stop her. What could she do to protect the children?

Rachel chewed her pigtail and looked him over. "We heard the bells, thought it was Santa."

Hawk glanced down at his spurs, then smiled. "Sorry about that. Reckon Santa'll be along tomorrow night."

"No," Mike shook his head and leaned on the table, "he's not coming at all this year; got poorer kids to see about."

Hawk looked around at the squalid room and she felt him assessing her frayed dress, the children's thin faces. His disapproving frown deepened. "Poorer than this?"

She forgot her fear, squared her shoulders proudly. "The Malones are beholden to no one! I was just cutting that mistletoe on our own land to sell and make a little extra, that's all."

He snorted. "This is *Indian* land, no matter what the white government says, and *Indian* mistletoe, *Cheyenne* mistletoe. I hunted this area once as a kid."

"Have you got kids?" Rachel twisted a pigtail and looked up at him.

"Nope. It's just me and Concho, that's all. Got nothing that ties me down from drifting."

"Mister Hawk is opposed to progress and civilization," Ginny snapped, not even knowing why she was angry with him.

"Progress, is that what you call stringing barbed wire

223

and plowing up good buffalo country?" Hawk said as he ate. "Or is it that white women just can't bear to see a man running free without trying to put a bit between his teeth and break him to harness? Sodbusters!"

"Before he was a farmer, our daddy was a soldier," Mike volunteered. "He rode with General Custer at the Washita."

"Did he now?" Something cold and hard crossed the man's face and the scar at the corner of his mouth twitched.

Ginny didn't like the way this conversation was heading. For the first time, she wondered about Hawk's past. "Children, don't bother Hawk; let him finish eating."

"They aren't bothering me; I like kids," he said almost gently and pushed his plate back, turned his chair toward the fire. Beth promptly climbed upon his knee.

Ginny reached for her. "I'm sorry, she's little and—"

"It's all right." He waved her outreaching hands away and then patted the small blond head. "Too bad Ginny ain't as friendly as you are."

Ginny felt her face flame. She scooped the toddler up off his lap, held her against her chest. "Mister Hawk, maybe you'd better be on your way now that you've had some food."

"In this weather?" He looked stricken and the wind rattled the hut as if to accent his words.

"It's less than a half-dozen miles north to Guthrie," she said, "I reckon that's where you were headed."

"As a matter of fact I was," Hawk grinned up at her as he reached in his pocket, produced a thin *cigarillo*. "But if you don't mind, ma'am, I'll wait until dawn. I mean to pay for the supper."

"That won't be necessary." If he stayed, how long

224

would it take him to figure out she and the kids were without a man to protect them?

"Oh, but I insist." He got up, went over to the fireplace, spurs jangling, bent to light his cigar from a glowing branch, came back to his chair. "You can put that baby down; you're in no danger from me."

Ginny hadn't realized she had been holding Beth against her breasts protectively as if to shield them from his hot gaze. "I—I wasn't worried about that."

"You don't act like it." His dark gaze swept over her boldly as if assessing what she'd look like undressed, then he stared into the fire.

Ginny stood the toddler on the floor. There was no sound save the wind whimpering outside and the crackle of the flames. She took a deep breath and besides the fire, the air smelled of cedar and his tobacco. She had forgotten how empty the cabin seemed without a man around.

Beth yawned. Hawk looked at the little girl and then around at the others. "You kids need to go to bed."

"They're not sleepy," Ginny said quickly. She was more than a little afraid to be alone with him.

"What're you talkin' about?" Hawk glanced around. "They're almost asleep where they sit."

Rachel began her usual whining. "I don't want to go to bed. I don't want—"

"Mike," Hawk said, and he spoke with male authority, "take your sisters to bed."

"Yes sir," the boy had a grudging admiration in his voice as he took the girls' hands, led them off to the bunks in the corner.

It was reassuring to have a man take charge. Ginny hadn't realized what a burden she had been carrying these past two weeks and how bone tired she was from the struggle of just keeping everyone from starving.

Hawk smoked his cigar and looked after the children a long minute. "What kind of a bastard lets his kids go hungry?" His voice was full of anger as he looked up at her. "A man with a woman like you ought to do better by her—"

"We're doing just fine," Ginny said, "and coming from a trail bum with no roots or responsibilities, you're a fine one to question another man's motives." She had stung him. She saw it in his face.

"A frail little thing like you doesn't belong out here; you'll never make it; you'll work yourself into an early grave and you're too pretty to be wasted like that."

She clinched her work-worn hands into fists in her lap. "Oh, but I will make it! This is my land to hang onto!"

He stared at the smoke trailing from his cigar. "Why do you homesteaders come, sweeping like a great white tide across my people's buffalo plains?"

Ginny shrugged and smoothed her frayed dress. "We come because we have nothing and no place else to go."

"It's *our* land." His dark eyes challenged her.

"It was *your* land," she said softly, "but the time of the buffalo and the wild days of roaming are gone as the warriors are almost gone. I don't know how history will remember the white settlers; maybe our grandchildren and our great-grandchildren will be ashamed of us, even apologize for us. But they will never know what poverty, what hunger and despair we faced."

"I hear they're giving food and things to the poor in town." Hawk said, "All you have to do is ask."

"*We* earn our own bread. The Malones are proud."

"On *Indian* land, you earn it."

"If it must be, yes!" She almost shouted, but she

couldn't hate him, she could only sympathize with him. Ginny sighed. "Times change, Hawk, and people must change, too."

He looked down at the gun on his hip and she saw in his expression what he was thinking. Soon there would be no more room for gunfighters and drifters. Those who would not tame would go the way of the buffalo.

"It will last my lifetime," he said, but he sounded uncertain. "I—I can't change."

She didn't fear him anymore, not the way his shoulders slumped and the way he stared into the fire, morose and sad. She wondered what ghosts he saw there in those flames?

They sat in silence a long time.

"I could use a drink," he looked up at her slowly.

"I've only got some peach brandy I was saving for fruitcake."

"What happened to the fruitcake?" He smiled slightly, and his sullen face was abruptly handsome.

She was past pretense as she shrugged. "I didn't sell enough mistletoe to buy the ingredients."

The wind rattled around outside but inside, it was warm and cozy. She got up, went to the crude cupboard for the brandy, looked up at the rifle over the fireplace.

"I'm not going to hurt you, Ginny," he said it so softly that for a moment, she wasn't sure of his words.

"I wasn't afraid of you," she lied.

"Then stop looking at that rifle. Here." He stood up, unstrapped his pistol, laid it on the table, pushed it toward her. "Now let's have a little of that peach brandy."

She felt both relieved and a little embarrassed. Of course she was behaving like a silly ninny. He wouldn't be interested in her when he was used to worldly, experienced women. She'd seen the hungry way that saloon girl had looked at him. No doubt before he'd left Edmond, that redhead had exhausted him. Ginny flushed at the thought.

"What's the matter?"

"Nothing." She saw an image of his big, muscular body lying between that woman's thighs and it both embarrassed Ginny and annoyed her. She had been a little fool to mistake the way he had stared at her. Probably he was used to prettier, experienced women who knew how to pleasure a man.

Ginny got the bottle and two glasses, poured them each some. She sat down in the rocker, staring self-consciously into the fire as she sipped hers. The taste made her a little giddy. Ginny never drank. From behind the curtain, she heard the children snoring. She glanced over at Papa's bed in the opposite corner. She could give that to the drifter. "I guess I can offer you a bed for the night."

"Much obliged. I wouldn't want to be any trouble."

"No trouble." She sipped her brandy and took another look at the pistol laying by her hand for reassurance. What a fool she had been to think he might have ever desired her.

He smoked, sipped his brandy, bent over, and took off his boots. "No point in waking the kids. Can't help but feel sorry for them since they were expecting Santa."

The brandy tasted good on her tongue. "Mike's shoes are worn out and Beth cries for a doll," Ginny admitted. "Rachel dreams of being a schoolteacher, and wanted a slate."

Hawk picked up one of Mike's little shoes off the floor, turned it over in his hands. "Sodbuster shoes. A

228

rancher's son would have boots. So where did you get them?"

"Enough," she said defensively and ignored his probing look as she drank her brandy.

"I'll bet." He got up, threw his cigar in the fireplace, looked at the photo on the mantel a long moment, came back, and poured them each another drink. "Nice-looking couple you make; but he's kinda old for you."

She started to correct his assumption, decided it didn't matter. The liquor felt warm all the way to her stomach.

"Cheers!" Hawk said. "Drink up!"

She touched her glass to his and took a big swallow. Nothing seemed as scary and bleak as it had an hour ago. With the brandy in her hand and sitting next to Hawk before the cheery fire, she didn't feel afraid and lonely anymore. For just a few minutes, she could pretend it was going to be a good Christmas and not think about the future.

Hawk watched the girl. She wasn't used to liquor; he could tell by the flush on her fair skin. There was something terribly wrong here, but he couldn't quite put a finger on it. Just why would a man be off at night leaving a woman and kids helpless against any range bum who rode in? Maybe like a lot of ex-soldiers, he drank. Maybe he was off at Guthrie or over at the neighbors helping them finish off a bottle for the holiday. One thing was certain, if Hawk had a woman like this one, he wouldn't leave her alone at night; he'd be curled up in that bed with her in his arms. Genevieve Malone was the most fragile, innocent-looking woman Hawk had ever seen, and that made her even more desirable.

Malone. A soldier turned homesteader. This family represented fences and plows, encroaching civilization. Worse yet, Malone had ridden with Custer and had been at the Washita that cold winter dawn in 1868. Hawk glanced at Ginny. Her husband must be almost twice his wife's age. She didn't really look old enough to be the mother of three children, but she must be older than she looked.

Hawk drained his glass. With a smile, he poured another for the two of them. Ginny looked a little unsteady as she drank it. Women were such fools. With his pistol by her hand, she felt safe. However, she wasn't safe from her own feelings and emotions. Hawk knew a lot about women. This one was vulnerable and naive. He wouldn't have to force her; she was going to come into his arms willingly with a little more brandy and sweet talk. With the weather like it was, her husband couldn't get back tonight and Hawk would be finished with the woman and gone by dawn.

He reached up and touched the scar on his face, remembering the pain, the way his beautiful mother had screamed . . . Could Ginny's husband have been that officer? Maybe not, but Malone had been there, so he wasn't innocent.

The little half-breed boy would finally extract his vengeance. Hawk would seduce Malone's woman and maybe leave a brown baby in her belly for the ex-soldier to raise. It was a revenge Hawk looked forward to when he got enough brandy in the sodbuster's wife.

3

Ginny sipped her brandy, stared into the fire, and felt the warmth of both spread slowly through her. She never drank, but after all, it was almost Christmas and there was no use saving the brandy when she lacked the other ingredients for the fruitcake. She hadn't realized until now how lonely she had been. It was cozy and warm sitting here by the fireplace while the snow fell and the wind blew outside. With his pistol laying next to her hand, the big man didn't seem so threatening.

"It was lucky for me I saw your light," Hawk said, and took a puff of his *cigarillo*. "I could have frozen to death out there."

"So where were you headed that was so important it couldn't wait for tomorrow?" She sipped her drink.

"Funny, it doesn't seem so important now," he shrugged and leaned back in his chair with a satisfied sigh. "I'm headed up to Guthrie to play a little poker; have some laughs and good times."

"Doesn't seem like much of a way to spend the holiday," Ginny said before she thought.

"It's the way I been spending it for a long time."

Ginny watched him smoke and stare into the crackling flames. "You don't have a wife? No family?"

"Mistletoe girl, you ask a great many personal questions. There ain't no one who gives a damn whether I come or go, and that's just the way I like it!" He glared at her with defiance, got up, walked over to the fire, threw his cigar in it, came back to the table, poured them each another drink. "Here's to the holiday!"

"Here's to the holiday." Ginny lifted her glass almost in a befuddled daze and gulped her brandy.

He stood looking down at her. "What a Christmas," he said softly. "Your man will be here with you and I'll be sipping a drink alone in Guthrie tomorrow night."

She felt a little giddy with the warmth of the brandy. "And Christmas Day?"

He shrugged and smiled. "For me? Oh, I don't know; maybe on to Wichita or St. Joe. I'll tell you one thing, Ginny, if I were your man, I'd treat you better, and I wouldn't leave a woman like you alone at night, no matter what the neighbors needed."

He was handsome when he smiled, even with the jagged scar at the corner of his mouth. "Hawk, about Paddy—"

"You work too hard, Ginny, your hands show it." Before she realized his intent, he caught one of her small hands in his, turned it over, frowned at her calluses and blisters. "A frail little thing like you shouldn't be doin' such hard work. A man ought to protect you, look after you."

Ginny jerked her hand out of his. "It takes hard work to carve a farm out of one hundred sixty acres of wild country. Anyway, that's mighty righteous talk, coming from a man who takes no responsibility for anyone but himself. It probably takes more guts and grit to work a place like this than you've got, Mister Hawk."

"Guts, grit—or stupidity?" His dark eyes were cold.

Hawk picked up his drink, sipped it. "I get cold chills just thinking about sweating over a plow. Ranching I might could handle; but not grubbing in the dirt."

"No one asked you to!" She flung at him. "When you leave here, you can go right on living your shiftless life of easy women, cards; hiring your gun to the highest bidder."

"You're right; no one asked." He looked down at her a long moment. "I was out of line. Can't we both be civil enough, maybe, to share a drink and a few kind words on such a bad night?"

"I suppose." She felt a little dizzy and warm with the brandy. When she looked up at him, he seemed thoughtful and a little sad.

"Do you dance, Ginny?"

"We've no music."

"It doesn't matter." He reached out, caught her hand, pulled her slowly to her feet. With his other hand, he took her glass from her, set it on the table. "There's music and good times in Guthrie and Wichita and St. Louis."

He had both her hands in his now. She looked down at his hands holding hers, up into his face. "What are you asking?"

"You know what I'm askin, Ginny," his voice was almost a whisper. "You're too pretty to waste yourself out here, working like a field hand and sleeping with some sweaty, clod of a farmer. You were meant for a man who appreciates a beautiful girl and who would take care of her."

"I—I couldn't," Ginny said, looking deep into his dark, brooding eyes, but in her mind, she saw herself dressed in silk and on the arm of this fast living gunfighter.

His face was close to hers and she studied the sensuous curve of his mouth, inhaled the masculine scent of his skin, brandy, and tobacco. "I want you, Ginny, come with me."

"No, I couldn't." She shook her head, a little unsteady on her feet. He let go of her hands, caught her arms, and ran his fingers up and down them very gently. No man had ever touched her like that. "I—I couldn't," she said again. "There's the children and the land."

"Damn the land! I like kids, but they don't fit into my life-style. I want you, Ginny, but I don't fancy being tied down." His hands went to her shoulders, pulled her close.

He hadn't said that he loved her; only that he wanted her. It was all moving too fast for her befuddled mind. "The man who gets me gets three children," she murmured, looking up at him, seeing only his mouth near hers, "and I can't give up our land, it's my only chance—"

"Take a chance on me, Ginny." Before she could react, he kissed her. For just a moment, she swayed against him as his big hands cupped her shoulders and pulled her against his virile body. His brandy-sweet mouth seemed hot as glowing embers on hers. While she clung to him, his tongue brushed against her lips, willing them, no, demanding that they open to his insistent caress.

All her senses seemed on fire and she arched her body, pressing against him. His arms went around her as his hands went to the small of her back. He held her against him so tightly, she felt his heart pounding against her breast, the hard maleness of him pulsating against her body.

The brandy inflamed her—or was it the taste and the scent and the feel of this virile male? Ginny took a deep breath and pressed her breasts against him, knowing he could feel the outline of her swollen nipples through his shirt as she rubbed against his chest.

One of his hands went to cup her small hips, lifting and guiding her to his pelvis, rubbing against her there. "Ginny, oh, sweet . . ."

She ran her fingers into the neck of his shirt, marveling at the hard muscle of his wide chest, feeling his heart pound with urgency against her palms. His hands seemed hot on her back as he fumbled with the buttons there.

She ought to pull away; she knew that, but his palms slipped under the faded calico now and stroked her bare back, warm and intense. She felt him caress her skin as his touch moved down her back to her hips. "You shouldn't —" she whispered, but his tongue was in her mouth again, stilling her protests.

She wasn't sure she could stop him now if she wanted to, and she wasn't sure she wanted to. For such big hands, they were gentle and experienced, she thought in a warm haze of emotion. Trembling chills raced up and down her nerves where he touched.

"Ginny, girl," he whispered, "sweet Ginny, I want you as bad as you want me. It can't be wrong if it's what we both want." He swung her up in his arms.

Did she want him? She barely understood what it was that men and women did to become man and wife. She hadn't realized it could make a woman feel on fire from her navel down to her knees. Heat seemed to radiate low in her belly and her breasts seemed heavy, the nipples swollen.

He carried her to the bed in the corner, lay her down on it, began to open her bodice.

"The children. The children will hear us —"

"They're asleep," he said urgently and pulled away

the fabric to bare her breasts in the firelight. Even though she'd never seen that look on a man's face, she knew what it meant and what he wanted.

She ought to protest and get up. He'd think she was a tramp. The way he looked at her set her afire even more than the brandy. "Hawk, I—I don't think—"

"Don't think, Ginny," he whispered. "Don't think; just relax and *feel*." His thumbs stroked circles around her nipples. "You know you want me to do this to you as much as I want to do it."

Before she could argue that she didn't, that she had never let a man touch her like this before, his dark head bent over her breasts as his hand slid down her bare belly.

"Ohhh . . ." She forgot everything then but the hot wetness of his mouth pulling at her nipple like a greedy child; his touch on her belly, lower, then lower still.

She didn't want him to stop, not now, not ever. Ginny caught his dark head between her hands, holding him against her breast, arching her body up to his caressing hand.

"God, you're beautiful!" he whispered and his breath felt hot against her fair skin as his tongue caressed first one nipple and then the other. "Love me, Ginny, there's no shame in it, you were meant to be loved like this . . ."

She couldn't think straight and she didn't know anymore about right and wrong or whether she was a fool for letting this stranger come in out of the night and put his hands and mouth all over her. Worse yet, she really didn't care if only this urgent need deep within her could be filled, this aching stopped.

She struggled to unbutton his shirt with trembling fingers, clawing at his back and chest as his hands

236

stroked her thighs until they shook.

"Easy, sweet girl," he whispered, "I'm going to please you like your man never pleased you, again and again."

"Hawk, about Paddy—"

"No, let's not talk." She felt him fumbling with the buttons of his pants. He took her hand in his, brought it down to clasp the hard, hot maleness of him. "There, sweet Ginny, I'm going to please you, love, give you what you want so bad."

If she hadn't been so drunk, Ginny realized dimly this would have scared her, but all she could think of now was how much she wanted him. She whimpered a little with her own urgent need. "Please, Hawk, please . . ."

Her dress was a tangle about her waist, but his hot, smoldering gaze told her he wasn't going to wait to take it off of her, or ever pause to get his clothes off. He was between her thighs, positioning her, both his big hands on her small waist, almost spanning it.

"Open for me, baby," he whispered, and his hands lifted her up off the bed, lifting her to him.

She was a little afraid, but her body wanted the maleness of him as he pressed against her. She reached up and caught his nipples between her fingers, causing him to gasp. "You surprise me, sodbuster girl," he murmured, "you're built so small."

Ginny opened her mouth to tell him she'd never done this before, but his mouth was sucking at hers, pulling the hot tip of her tongue between his lips. She felt the heat of him slide slowly into her body and it felt like being impaled on a fire hot saber. But she wanted it; oh, how she wanted it! She tilted herself up against him, put her small hands on his lean hips, and pulled him down on top of her. The sheer weight of

237

his big body broke through the silk of her virginity and just as she might have cried out, his mouth covered hers and his tongue went deep in her throat.

It seemed she could feel him plunging to the very center of her being, impaling her small body on the dark, hard sword of him. He seemed to be pulsating and throbbing deep within her, one of his hands under her, guiding her, the other tangled in her pale hair.

She was only dimly aware of the glow of the fireplace, the odor of the Christmas tree, and his masculine scent. The bed squeaked rhythmically under their straining, writhing forms as they meshed and mated. She felt the heat rising in her own body, the shimmering sheen of perspiration from his rippling muscles on her satin skin. Her insides seemed on fire, but her very being wanted to be consumed with this rising flame.

Then he gasped and hesitated, his powerful body straining and trembling. "Oh, Ginny, sweet Ginny . . ."

His body shuddered and began to give up its seed. She felt the hot surge of him deep in her velvet place, and suddenly her own body began to convulse, squeezing the very essence of Life out of his maleness into her womb. Darkness swept over her as she went into spasms that she couldn't control, and the bunk creaked as she pulled him deeper still. The last thing she remembered was his mouth on hers, her nails digging into the powerful, corded muscles of his back so he couldn't part from her until her body satisfied its need of him.

When she became conscious of her surroundings again, he lay on his side, still embracing her, but he hadn't disengaged from her body. His hand stroked a wisp of hair from her eyes ever so gently. "Love, you do surprise me!"

He had guessed she didn't know what she was doing. "Was I—was I not very good? I know with all those saloon girls you've known—"

"Good? I—I can't even describe it." He bent his head and kissed her so tenderly, so very tenderly. "I thought I'd been made love to before, but not like that; never like that." He pulled her very close against his chest while the wind rattled and blew outside, but she felt safe and secure in this man's arms. He loved her; he really loved her. She snuggled down against his wide chest and imagined how they would marry, farm this homestead, make it prosper, raise their own kids along with the three little Malones. At the end of a hard day's work, after he'd finished plowing and she'd put the kids to bed, they'd curl up and make love.

Her insides were hurting a little, but it didn't matter. She had loved Hawk from the first moment she had seen him, so dangerous to women, and yet so alone, so vulnerable. "Hawk, about tomorrow—"

He cut off her words with a kiss. "Tomorrow's not tonight's worry, sweet Ginny," he whispered. "Don't worry about tomorrow; let each day take care of itself. Tonight, let's just enjoy each other."

His maleness was growing hard again already, still in her body, Ginny realized. No doubt when they were married, he'd wanted to take her over and over every night. As virile as he was, she'd have a houseful of babies. The thought pleased her. She saw a sudden vision of herself with her belly swollen with his child, her breasts big with milk. His hands would be gentle as he stroked her belly, made love to her, his lips pulling at her swollen nipples.

Already he was rolling over on her again, not as urgent, but still wanting her, riding her deeply, thoroughly. She felt her body responding. "Kiss me, sweet Ginny, tell me you want me, too."

"Oh, Hawk, I do! I need to tell you about Paddy—"

"Sure, sweet, sure." His mouth cut off her words as he began to move within her, stroking her into a mounting excitement with his skillful hands. Then he poured himself into her again and she felt herself convulsing under him, biting his shoulders and digging her nails into his back as his hands went down to tilt her up to accept him.

She surrendered to his desire; let him merge his rising passion with her own. For a long moment, there were only spasms of overwhelming darkness and pleasure. "I love you, Hawk," she gasped, "I love you . . ."

Hawk looked down into her eyes. "I love you, too, sweet." He said it automatically, knowing it was expected of him. He'd said it to a thousand women. If a man didn't say it, the silly fools wouldn't let him between their thighs. Still, this girl was different; special. If she'd leave with him, he might seriously consider taking Ginny with him when he rode out. He'd enjoyed the farmer's hospitality in more ways than one, but it was all the man deserved if he'd been at the Washita with Custer.

And yet . . . Hawk looked down at the girl drifting off to sleep in the curve of his arm, her small, fair face against his dark, brawny chest. Without thinking, he reached down, touched the tip of her nose and she smiled ever so slightly in her sleep. She fitted into the hollow of his shoulder almost as if she belonged there; as if that place had been made for her blond head. She sighed and stirred in her sleep, threw her arm across him. On her left hand gleamed that gold ring. He felt almost a twinge of shame. Ginny had been so trusting, so easy to take. The hawk and a small song-bird as a victim; no contest. If this were his woman, he'd protect and cherish her.

Uneasily, Hawk thought about Paddy Malone. Just where the hell was he right now? Really at a neighbor's? Drunk in Guthrie? Already on his way home and about to ride into the place any minute and catch his woman asleep in the arms of another man? The children had tried to tell Hawk something and Ginny had hushed them. What difference did it make? Chalk up one more conquest. Hawk didn't feel triumphant, he felt a little ashamed as he lay there watching the fire die.

He sat up very slowly so as not to awaken Ginny, swung his legs off the side of the bed to the rough plank floor. *What time was it?* No way to tell but it must be near dawn. Hawk stood up, looked down. For only a moment, he looked at himself in the uncertain firelight. What the hell? Had he injured himself in some way?

The realization came to him. It had to be *her* blood. She was built smaller than he had thought, to tear her that way. Yet that seemed impossible for a wife and mother of three children. He went over to the fireplace, stared at the photo. *How could Malone's wife actually look like him?*

What the hell difference did it make? Hawk had desired Ginny and cold-bloodedly got her drunk and seduced her. White men used Indian girls all the time. So why did Hawk feel uneasy? He didn't want to think about it as he buttoned his shirt. When he remembered her hot and writhing in his embrace, he knew he'd never experienced such passion.

Hawk cleaned himself up as best he could without disturbing any of the other sleeping occupants of the crude cabin. He got his things together, picked up his boots and spurs, and carried them so the jingle wouldn't awaken anyone. But at the door, he couldn't resist tiptoeing back to the bed to look down at her. She lay like a sleeping angel, so soft, so innocent and vulnerable. Behind the curtain, he heard the children turn over restlessly like a litter of puppies.

Nice little kids, he thought, and then reminded himself that he didn't need kids; they were too much responsibility. Too bad Malone didn't take better care of them; but that wasn't Hawk's problem. He was a taker, not a giver. Ginny smiled in her sleep and he paused. *If you'd go with me, damned if I wouldn't take you,* he thought in surprise.

Of course she wouldn't go. The man who shared Ginny's bed permanently had to tie himself down to land and responsibility. Hawk was too wild a roamer to be broken to harness. He'd earned his bread with the speed of his gun and his skill with a hand of cards too long to give it all up for a back-breaking farm, even if a woman like Ginny and three cute kids went with it. He envied Paddy Malone even as he wondered about him.

He took a deep breath of the scent of the pitiful little cedar tree in the corner, looked around at the mistletoe hung over the door with a scrap of red ribbon in her brave attempt to decorate the squalid room. Cheyenne mistletoe. No, the hardy green plant was more typical of the gritty settlers who would endure and struggle to hang on and conquer this hostile land. Nothing could kill out or discourage mistletoe once it began to grow. And he was as rootless and drifting as the tumbleweed blown by the wind.

My mistletoe girl. He reached down ever so gently and pulled the ragged quilt up over her white breasts, remembering as he did so how warm she had felt in his arms. Hawk felt an unusual stirring of conscience and dug in his vest, counted his money. He had to have enough to get into that poker game and a little for a hotel room. In the end, he left twenty silver dollars on Ginny's pillow. It would at least buy the kids some gifts. The thought of their smiling faces pleased him.

Would she be angry when she awoke and saw the money? For the first time, it seemed important to him that she think well of him. *How can she, you bastard, when you used her and sneaked off into the night?* He chided himself as he tiptoed to the door, went outside into the cold, put on his boots and jacket. A gray dawn seemed to be just over the eastern horizon. Light snow fell and the wind blew against his face as he went to the lean-to. In the early light, he saw the outline of a plow in the corner.

"No, not for me," he promised himself as he saddled up. Then to Concho: "Sorry, old boy, I know you were beginning to like it here with that mare, but we've got to be movin' on." He led the stallion out and mounted, the saddle creaking under his tall frame. Hawk hesitated only a moment, looking back toward the cabin before he turned north and rode out.

On a rise under the post oaks, a small mound of dirt and mistletoe caught his eye. It looked like a grave.

Curiously, Hawk reined in, dismounted. A crude cross covered with icicles stuck in the ground at a crooked angle. The reflection off the snow barely illuminated the scrawled letters: R.I.P. PATRICK MALONE. BELOVED FATHER.

Patrick. Paddy. Good God. All the pieces of the puzzle fell into place. A virgin. Hawk had taken Paddy's innocent daughter. That made him no better than the long-ago soldier who had raped his mother. How did that feisty, foolish Ginny plan to manage now? A mere slip of a girl stranded out here on this prairie with no man to look after her and three little children. Hawk had a sudden urge to go back and . . . ? And do what?

It wasn't his worry. He'd only stumbled across the Malones, not created their problem. He thought about the naive girl. He sure as hell hadn't helped them, either.

Yes, he had, Hawk argued with himself. He'd left Ginny enough money to make it a few more days or maybe buy train tickets. All she had to do was give up this claim and leave. She wouldn't do that, not if she starved to death out here holding onto her homestead and her stubborn pride.

Damn it, in Edmond or the surrounding area, there must be some sodbuster who'd marry the girl, work the land. In his mind, Hawk saw some rednecked farmer making love to Ginny, shouting at the children, working them all in the field until they dropped.

There wasn't anything Hawk could do about all that. He swung into his saddle, rode out without looking back. These white sodbusters weren't his responsibility. Yet something gnawed at him like a field mouse in his gut as he rode north. The dawn came slowly as he left, snow still falling.

Ginny wouldn't be getting into Edmond today, Hawk thought as Concho snorted and steam drifted from his own breath on the cold morning air. This weather would keep her inside. So the Malones wouldn't have much of a Christmas. So what? Hawk shrugged. With the money he'd left, the girl could go in for supplies the day after Christmas. Maybe she'd think it over,

and take the kids with her, give up this silly dream.
Yeah, that would be the reasonable thing to do. He
had a feeling Ginny listened to her heart, not her
head. She was a scrappy little thing; just the kind of
woman he'd want as the mother of his own children—
if he was looking to get tied down, which of course,
he wasn't.

Hawk rode into Guthrie, put his horse in the stable,
got himself a hotel room, and went to bed. Christmas
Eve day, he thought as he dozed off. Tonight there'll
be plenty of celebrating and drinking and maybe a
chance to play against the well-known gambler, Flint.

Ginny awakened with a start in the cold gray light
of morning. She smiled as she remembered and
reached for him. "Hawk," she whispered, "Oh, it was
so wonderful and you won't regret staying and helping
turn this farm into a fine . . ."

He wasn't there. She sat up amid the rumpled quilts,
looked around. Of course it was past dawn so he'd
gone out to feed the horses or bring in some more
wood.

She glanced down at her mother's gold band. When
they were married, Hawk would get her her own ring.
Ginny smiled as she remembered the taste of his
mouth, the feel of his hard body. She didn't have to
be afraid or alone anymore; he would shoulder part of
these heavy burdens.

The light reflected off the coins on her pillow.
Money? She picked them up, furrowing her brow in
confusion. Twenty dollars. More than the Malones had
seen in a long time. A horrid thought crossed her
mind. Ginny jumped up, rearranging her clothing as
she ran for the door. "Hawk?"

She heard a faint stirring from the children's bunk,

but already Ginny's small bare feet raced across the cold planks. His boots and coat were gone. "Hawk?"

She struggled to open the door. Hawk would come in when she called, stomp the snow off his boots, take her in his arms. *I just stepped outside, Ginny. Why were you afraid?*

"Hawk?" She ran outside, the frozen snow like sharp knives against her bare feet as she headed into the lean-to. Blaze looked up, snorted a welcome. His horse was gone, too.

Ginny went out to look toward the north, the cold wind cutting through her worn dress. Hoof prints leading away were barely visible in the blowing snow. Maybe he had gone out hunting and would be back in a few minutes with a bunch of quail or a couple of rabbits. *Maybe—stop it, Ginny,* she told herself, *you know where he's gone.*

Money. He had left money on her pillow as if he were paying some whore for a night's pleasure. The hard realization cut into her more painfully than the cold. For a long moment more, she strained to look north, hoping against hope that she would see a big, broad-shouldered man riding toward her. All she saw was the snow whipping around her legs and the vast expanse of woods and land that lay between here and Guthrie. She had never felt so lost and alone. Ginny turned very slowly and went inside the cabin.

What a silly little drunken fool she had been to think the drifter had cared as much for her as she did for him. She had a terrible urge to saddle her mare, follow him into town, and throw the money in his face.

To what purpose? Ginny slumped down on the rumpled bed and stared at the silver. She had earned it; that was what he figured. What she had given in love,

Hawk had put a cash value on. Her virginity would pay for the Malone's Christmas—or maybe train tickets away from here. No, she gritted her teeth in stubborn determination, no matter what, she would fight to hang onto this land for the kids.

Little Mike crawled out of bed, rubbing his eyes. "Ginny? Are you all right? You're shiverin'."

She must not upset the children. Although her heart was breaking, she managed a weak smile. "I—everything's fine."

Rachel sat up, pulling at one pigtail. "Where's Hawk? Is he gonna stay?"

Little Beth pulled her thumb out of her mouth. "Hawk?"

Ginny took a deep breath to steady herself. Christmas Eve day. In her heart, she cursed him for what he'd done and herself for being such a blind, trusting fool. "Hawk had to ride on, kids. He—he never meant to stay."

Mike's little face saddened. "We thought he did."

"So did I," Ginny whispered and blinked back a tear, "So did I."

4

On Christmas Eve in the bustling town of Guthrie, Hawk stood outside the Reaves brothers' Casino on the corner of Second and Harrison streets in the darkness and looked around. The winter storm had ended, the stars were out, and snow lay white across the buildings and streets of the bustling town. Celebration was in full swing, people and carriages on the street, illegal saloons doing a landslide business, families coming in and out of stores. Laughter and shouts of "Merry Christmas!" drifted on the cold, crisp air. From across the street at the Blue Bell Saloon, Hawk heard a loud piano playing: *Jingle bells, jingle bells, jingle all the way, oh, what fun it is to ride . . .*

From another, drunken voices harmonized: "O, Genevieve, sweet Genevieve, the days may come, the days may go . . ."

Would he hear that damned song everywhere the rest of his life? With an angry gesture, Hawk tossed his *cigarillo* into the street and strode into the Casino. Ginny wasn't his responsibility. She was just such a naive and trusting little thing, she really did need someone to look out for her and those kids.

Sweet Genevieve. There weren't many girls like that one. Hawk felt angry with her because he couldn't get her off his mind. He had used her to get even with a dead soldier for being with Custer at the Washita and now Hawk's conscience bothered him. He hadn't even realized he had a conscience anymore. He pushed through the boisterous crowd, sat down at a poker table, and played grimly, winning hand after hand until he had a couple hundred dollars. Tonight he took no pleasure in the game.

Hawk gathered up his winnings, went to the bar. Over the mirror hung a prominent sign: *We, the citizens of Guthrie, are law-abiding people. But to anyone coming here looking for trouble, we always keep it in stock with a written guarantee that we will give you a decent burial. We will wash your face, comb your hair, polish your boots, place your sombrero on your grave, and erect a memento as a warning to others saying he tried and failed.*

He signaled for a drink, hoping to wipe Ginny out of his mind. Hawk was not one to start a saloon fight. Maybe what he needed to wipe out her memory was another woman. When he got through playing cards tonight, he'd pick out a pretty one. This year's holiday would be just like last year and the year before and the year before that for Hawk; a blur of drunken revelry that blocked out the loneliness until the holidays had ended.

An older brunette came up to the bar, spoke to the bartender. "Frank, I need five beers for that table in the corner."

Hawk looked at her curiously as the red-faced bartender moved to fill her order. Her Southern voice sounded too cultured and refined for a saloon, and under the thick makeup she had once been a great beauty.

The bartender slid the tray to her. "Hey, Kate, you hear that famous gambler, Flint, is in town? Heard he was at the Blue Bell earlier playing cards with Poker

Alice. Maybe he'll come in here tonight."

Hawk saw just a flicker of emotion cross her painted face before she shrugged and moved away with the tray.

He sipped his drink, lit a cigar, and waited. No one had to tell him when Flint came in. Heads began to turn and a murmur ran through the crowd. Hawk saw the tall man pause in the doorway a long moment, looking around. The fabled gambler might have been fifty, but was still handsome and lean. Only the lines in his face and the gray in his dark sideburns gave away his age. Flint walked toward a poker table, and men made room for him respectfully.

Hawk felt his heart beat faster with excitement as he studied the man. There was something courtly, yet tragic in the gambler's manner. Hawk felt himself drawn to the man as he elbowed his way through the crowd to the table. He grabbed a chair. "This a closed game or can anyone sit in?"

The others looked up at him; a rancher, a couple of prosperous shopkeepers—judging from their clothes—a cavalry officer, and Flint.

The gambler looked him up and down. "Sure, pull up a chair, son." He said in a cultured, Southern drawl, "I can take your money good as anyone's, I reckon."

Hawk grinned, pushed his hat back as he sat down. "Don't count on it. I'm pretty good myself."

So was Flint, Hawk found out over the next several hours. His respect for the man grew as the poker game continued and players began to drop out, until only four remained. It must be almost midnight, Hawk thought, glancing around the saloon. It was all but

251

empty now. Those who had a home to go to had gradually drifted away, with the exception of a small crowd gathered around the poker table to watch. Why had he never realized before how grimy and bleak saloons were? They all smelled like stale cigar smoke and spilled beer. Why did he remember the scent of a cedar tree?

Hawk noticed the woman called Kate had avoided this table, but now she watched from a distance. Several times, Flint glanced her way, but she seemed to be avoiding his gaze. Yet she didn't leave.

Looking from the hand of cards he held, to the pile of money in the center of the table, Hawk made his decision. "I raise."

At that point, the two shopkeepers both shook their heads, threw in their cards. "Too rich for me." They pushed their chairs back, grumbling as they stood up.

Flint hardly raised an eyebrow. He was easily the best poker hand Hawk had ever played. "I'll see you, son, and raise again."

Hawk began to sweat a little. Almost everything he owned except his horse and saddle had been bet. A lot of silver lay in the middle of the table. He had a good hand; full house. The chances the cool, unruffled gambler had anything better were slim—but the fabled Southerner hadn't built his reputation on losing. His dark eyes gave away no clues.

A cowboy came through the door and the wind blew in a fragment of music: "O, Genevieve, sweet Genevieve . . ."

Hawk swore softly. "I wish they'd stop singing that damned song; reminds me of a girl I want to forget."

Flint's gaze turned toward the older brunette who still ignored him. "Some women you can't forget, no matter what. With me, the song is 'Aura Lea.' "

The old Civil War favorite, Hawk thought, and looked curiously toward Kate who was now clearing a table. He studied his hand again, then said to Flint, "This girl would keep me from roaming, tie me down to a homestead."

"I understand better than you know." The Southerner stared at Kate again, sighed. "Sometimes a man learns too late what's really important. Don't let it happen to you." His gaze went from his cards to Hawk. "Well, kid?"

Hawk was certain he had the better hand; he could feel it in his bones. This Flint was good, but maybe not as good as Hawk had heard. Hawk hadn't expected to admire the man, much less like him. But winning gamblers couldn't be soft. Hawk decided to risk it all, pushing the last of his money into the pot. "I'll see you and raise you twenty."

Flint hesitated, looking at him long and hard as if trying to read Hawk's mind. He studied his cards and the pile of money on the table. There was more than a thousand dollars there, Hawk thought, but more than that, Flint's reputation was on the line.

From somewhere outside, a distant church choir drifted: *Silent night, holy night, all is calm, all is bright . . .*

Hell of a way to spend Christmas Eve, Hawk thought, watching Flint, waiting for his decision. The thought surprised him that where he'd rather be right now was sitting before the fire in that cabin with Ginny and three little kids. "Well?"

Flint looked at him a long moment, looked toward the woman again and she studiously ignored him. In the background, "Silent Night" mixed with "Sweet Genevieve" as someone opened the door again.

"Kid, I got to see 'em. I call." He matched the bet.

"Read 'em and weep," Hawk said with a triumphant grin, spreading his cards faceup on the table. *Three jacks, two sevens.* "Full house."

A murmur ran through the crowd and Hawk's heart almost skipped a beat because of the size of the pot. Only a straight flush or four of a kind could beat that hand. If Flint had either, he'd lay his cards out now, claim all that money, and leave Hawk flat broke.

Nothing changed in the gambler's handsome face. He looked from his own cards to Hawk's hand spread out for all to see. For a long moment, Hawk thought he heard the men around him breathing as they also waited. The Southerner seemed to be struggling with some inner turmoil. Finally, Flint tossed his cards facedown on the table, leaned back in his chair with a dismissing gesture and a tired sigh. "Reckon I can't win 'em all. The pot's yours."

An excited buzz ran through the crowd. "The kid's beat him with a full house! Never thought I'd be there to see Flint lose a big pot like that!"

For a long moment, Hawk only stared at the man across from him, the cards thrown facedown, the money in the center of the table. "Well, I'll be damned!"

He sighed with relief, reached out, raked the money into his Stetson. "That was some game, Flint. I swear I never played against anyone so good. Better luck next time."

The gambler shrugged, ran his hand through his graying hair. "You win a few, you lose a few. Kid, have you ever read a story by Dickens called *A Christmas Carol?*"

Hawk hesitated as he stood up. "Nope, can't say as I have. Why?"

The older man slumped in his chair, pulled out a

pipe. "This fellow can see his future if he doesn't change his ways, and it isn't good."

"So?" Hawk paused, a little puzzled.

"If you don't watch out, boy, *I* am your future." Flint stared into Hawk's eyes and lit his pipe. "Think about it."

Hawk took a good long look at the other man. Could this be himself in twenty or thirty years? He'd never thought that far ahead.

"Merry Christmas, Mister Flint," he said softly, "I'll consider what you've said."

"Think long and hard," the gambler blew a puff of smoke toward the ceiling. "Take your winnings and go back to that girl; make a home with her. If our paths ever cross at another card table, I promise you'll regret it."

Hawk didn't say anything, thinking it sounded almost like a threat. He looked around. The crowd was drifting away as the bartender made ready to close. Hawk nodded to the woman called Kate who hadn't moved. Then he went outside into the cold, crisp night.

A thousand dollars. Almost a year's wages for a soldier or a cowpuncher. He paused on the sidewalk, looking down at his hatful of cash. The Blue Bell on the northeast corner looked closed. Off to his right was a general store, closed now, its windows dark, with the owner's living quarters overhead. In the window were toys and clothes and trinkets. Farther down the street, another saloon and bawdy house still rocked with noise and laughter.

A thousand dollars. All Hawk's to spend. Enough for him to live a life of ease for a few weeks, or grubstake him as he drifted on to Wichita or down to Dallas, or even some glamorous place like New Orleans.

It was also enough to keep a small ranch or farm in supplies, seed, and food until the first crops came in—if a man was fool enough to do it. Laughter and loud music rolled from the bawdy house and he imagined the pretty women there, the whiskey and the good times.

Christmas future. Hawk considered his choices a long moment. No contest, really. No *hombre* with good sense would take on a run-down homestead, three kids, and responsibilities that weren't his. In his mind, he saw Ginny's blue eyes looking up at him just before he kissed her. *What a trusting little fool.* Hawk had never met a woman naive enough to put that kind of faith in him. She didn't seem to know the difference between a knight in shining armor and a jaded, used-up gunfighter. Or maybe she saw something in him that only a woman in love could see. How could she have been so blind not to realize what he really was?

Still clutching the Stetson full of money, Hawk made his decision, turned, and started down the sidewalk.

5

Kate stood off to the side, watching the man known as Flint still sitting at the poker table smoking his pipe and staring at the hand of cards facedown in the center. He didn't seem to be aware she was there. Around her, the customers drifted away as the bartenders, saloon girls, and waiters cleaned up and prepared to close for the night.

All evening, she had pointedly ignored him, now he looked so defeated; so alone. Pity overcame her pride and she crossed the floor. "Hello, Jim," she said very softly, trying to keep her voice cool, "long time no see."

He looked up abruptly and she saw the emotion in his eyes that he struggled to hide. He started to get up, but she waved him back down. "I've almost forgotten what it's like to be treated like a lady."

"'You will always be a lady to me, Kathryn. I heard you were in Guthrie, that's why I came."

"You shouldn't have come," she shrugged to keep from reaching out, touching his dear face. "We can't go back to what we were all those many years ago."

"That doesn't keep me from hoping." His love for her shone in his dark eyes for all the world to see.

She must change the subject. The past was too painful. "I think everyone was surprised that kid beat you,

Jim. Tomorrow they'll be saying the best gambler west of the Mississippi is slipping."

He took the pipe from his mouth. "Let them. It doesn't matter. Pride doesn't matter to me anymore."

"That doesn't sound like the man I once knew."

He smoked his pipe pensively. "Maybe I've changed. Even hell-raisers finally wear out—or die. What went wrong between us, Kathryn that two people from our background ended up like this?" He made a disparaging gesture to indicate their surroundings.

For only a moment, she closed her eyes and was a girl again, with all the wealth and ease of the old South, attending a gala ball, dancing to "Aura Lea" in the arms of young James Flinthurst. *Christmas Past.* "The war . . . among other things. I heard what you said to that kid about Christmas Future."

"It's true, isn't it?" he said wryly and sighed. "I didn't want him to end up like me. If only . . ."

"It isn't like you to be soft and sentimental." *If only,* she thought. *The saddest words in any language.*

"Maybe it was a foolish thought, but that's what crossed my mind on that final hand."

"It also isn't like you to lose." Before he could move, she reached out, turned his hand of cards over.

He caught her wrist too late. She blinked at the cards. "A straight flush! You had the boy beat!"

He took the cards from her hand, shuffled them quickly into the deck. "Now no one will believe you if you tell."

"I wasn't planning to tell anyone, Jim. But just for my own curiosity, why?"

He stood up, seemed to struggle for words, then shrugged. "I—I liked him. And maybe because he's just about the age our son might have been—if only . . . I can't bring back Christmas Past, although I

258

wish . . ."

She blinked back tears. "There's more, isn't there?"

Jim nodded. "He's got a girl, Kathryn. I wanted to give him the chance and the money to go back to her, do things differently than I did; not make the same terrible mistakes. I didn't want him to be still sitting at a card table a quarter of a century from now, spending his Christmas with a bunch of strangers."

She stared at him, seeing him differently than she had ever seen him before. "The boy'll blow the money on whiskey, fast women, and cards. He won't change, Jim."

"Maybe not, but I wanted to give him the chance; the chance to make things right that I passed up. Merry Christmas, Kathryn, I'm sorry I came to town. I know there's no chance you'd ever reconsider." He turned and started out.

She watched him walk away, thinking about everything that had happened in the past, all the bitter regrets, the time lost that could never be reclaimed, the children they might have had. Regrets. Bitter regrets for both of them.

He was almost to the door now and she knew that when he walked out, she would never see him again. "Jim, wait!"

He half turned at the door. "Don't feel sorry for me, dear. I brought us both to this, so I deserve no better."

She hurried across the floor, not sure of her own feelings. "What are your plans for the holiday?"

He puffed his pipe, shrugged. "I'm catching a train out tomorrow; not sure yet which way to go."

She caught his arm. "We—we might as well spend the holiday together."

He hesitated, as if afraid to hope. "Are you sure?"

259

She nodded, swallowed hard. "Christmas Eve; the night for miracles, Jim. If you can do what you just did, trust that young gunman to do the right thing, maybe it's not to late for us to pick up the shattered pieces of our lives."

"Oh, Kathryn! If you only knew how I've hoped!"

"Jim! Oh, my darling!" They were in each others' arms and she felt the hot tears on her face and wasn't sure whether they were hers or his.

Ginny lay on the bed staring into the darkness. Christmas Eve. No, by now it was almost Christmas Day. It had been so hard to keep up a cheery front all day for the children. They would have turnips again for dinner, but at least she had the three apples and the candy stick to divide. She also had the money Hawk had left.

Ginny made her decision. She must save the land for the children's sake. The money would buy food and a little time for the Malones. Maybe she could yet figure out a way to buy seed and supplies. If they only could survive until they got a crop in, they'd make it somehow.

Hawk. She closed her eyes, seeing his face before her. What a fool she had been to be taken in by the gun-tough and yet, she loved him still. "Where ever you are," she whispered, "I wish you a merry Christmas."

In the flickering firelight as she looked around the small cabin, she saw the mistletoe. *Cheyenne mistletoe,* he had called it. Whenever she saw a sprig of it, forever she would think of him, remember the taste of his mouth, the warmth of his powerful arms enfolding her as he loved her.

If there was ever a flower that embodied everything this territory stood for, it was the green plant growing wild in the scrubby trees. *I surmount all difficulties.* Surely the mistletoe would always hold a special place in the hearts of Oklahoma pioneer families.

For a moment, she thought she heard a familiar sound, a slight, musical jingle. The wind again; that's all. The sound grew louder. She got up.

Mike came out of bed, rubbing his eyes sleepily. "What's that? I thought I heard something."

"It's just the wind," Ginny assured him, "go back to sleep before you wake your sisters."

The jangling came again, louder now. Ginny was afraid to even guess what it might be.

The little girls bounded out of bed. "Sleigh bells! Santa! It must be Santa!"

Ginny wouldn't even let herself hope. Disappointment hurt too much. "Now, girls, I told you Santa isn't coming—"

"Or Hawk," little Mike's feet hit the floor. "Oh, Ginny, it might be Hawk!"

"No, it's just the wind." Ginny paused by the fireplace. "Hawk won't be coming back."

All three children tugged at the door and it swung open. A man stood there; a big, broad-shouldered man in a red shirt, a Stetson, and boots with noisy spurs.

"It's better than Santa!" Mike yelled, "It's Hawk!"

Only then as the children danced around his legs did Ginny notice he had a sack over each shoulder. He looked her straight in the eye. "Well, you might invite me in. I almost had to tear a general store's door down to get the owner to open up and sell me what I wanted."

"Come in, Hawk!" The children cavorted around him with delight, "Oh, we're so glad you came back!"

261

Ginny moved toward him slowly, unsure why he had returned. "Hawk, if you're having regrets, I don't want you to feel guilty and think you have to—"

"I don't *have* to do anything," Hawk said as he came into the cabin, spurs jingling. "I ran into Santa in Guthrie. He'd been trying to find the Malones and I said I knew where they lived, so he said he'd be much obliged if I'd help him with his deliveries before I move on."

The three children gathered around his legs as he set the sacks down on the floor, looked toward Ginny.

Tears welled up in Rachel's eyes. "You ain't stayin'?"

"That's Ginny's decision to make." Hawk waited.

She couldn't seem to move or speak. He had broken her heart yesterday and she couldn't bear to go through this again. "I—I thought I made it clear, Hawk, that I've got to have roots and that I come with a lot of responsibilities I can't just walk away from. You don't want that."

He reached in his coat, brought out a small box. "Ginny, I'm not much good. I don't deny I'll be a hard man to live with, and I don't know if you can turn a gun-tough saddle tramp into a farmer-rancher. What I want to know is, do you care enough about me to try?"

She stood there, so overcome with emotion that she couldn't speak as he fumbled awkwardly with the box. When he opened it, a gold band gleamed in the coming daylight.

"I reckon I'm doing this all wrong," he mumbled, "but then, I've never done it before. You'd have to settle for a bridal bouquet of mistletoe and a passing preacher."

The children set up a delighted dance. "Say yes, Ginny! Say yes! We want Hawk!"

He seemed to misread her silence. He shook his head, reached for the doorknob. "I reckon I got my answer."

"Hawk . . . wait." She managed to find her voice and ran across the room. "Oh, Hawk!"

She was sobbing as she went into his embrace and he held her so tightly that she almost couldn't breathe. His coat felt rough against her face and she took a deep breath of his masculine, tobacco scent.

His face felt cold against hers as he kissed her over and over. "Sweet Ginny! My sweet Ginny . . ."

In the refuge of his strong arms, she was safe; forever safe in his love. "I thought you were gone for good."

"I thought I was, too," he whispered, "but your song kept singing to my heart. Then I met my future and decided it wasn't what I wanted after all."

She nodded, not understanding, but it didn't matter. All that mattered was that he was here to stay.

She heard the children exclaiming over the packages and Hawk turned as Mike brought out a pair of shiny new boots. "Son, try those on and go put Concho in the barn, give Blaze a good feed, too."

Little Beth took her thumb out of her mouth and dug into the sack, held up a doll. "Mine?"

"You betcha!" Hawk said. "And a slate and chalk for Rachel. There's something in there for Ginny, too." He walked over, reached into the sack, brought out the most beautiful dress Ginny had ever seen. "Santa sent it all; he doesn't play good poker." Hawk paused thoughtfully, "But on the other hand, maybe he played better than I knew . . ."

Ginny took the dress, stroked the blue calico. It had been a long time since she had had a new dress. Then she kissed him again and it was as wonderful as she

263

remembered; laying her face against his shoulder; safe against the world, safe and warm in the security of his love. His lips brushed Ginny's cheek. *"Ne-mehotaste."*

"What does it mean?"

"It's Cheyenne," he said. "It means 'I love you.'"

"I love you, too, Hawk." She smiled, too happy to speak. "If you could shoot a wild turkey for dinner—"

"Cheyenne don't eat anything with feathers."

"But you can learn. It tastes good." She smiled.

"Sweet Ginny, you'll turn me into a homesteader yet."

She snuggled against him as if she couldn't get close enough to his big, hard frame.

"I brought a lot of food, too," Hawk said, "including stuff for a fruitcake—if there's any brandy left."

Ginny kissed him, wondering suddenly what miracle had brought him to their door when they had needed him so badly?

"No turnips," he chuckled, "as my wife, don't ever serve turnips around here again."

Ginny laughed, too, hugged him to her. "Don't worry!"

Outside, day dawned cold and clear on the Oklahoma prairie and the smoke curled up from the chimney into the pale blue sky. But inside the warm cabin, Hawk's family gathered around a straggly cedar tree, sang carols, and welcomed in the first of many happy holidays to come.

TO MY READERS

The 1889 Run was only the beginning of Oklahoma's land giveaways. For that first year, law and order was maintained by a few U.S. Deputy marshalls and the army. Captain Arthur MacArthur was sent from Fort Leavenworth, Kansas, to keep the peace in Guthrie. His son, General Douglas MacArthur, would make his own mark on history more than fifty years later.

Guthrie would become the territorial capital, but would lose out to Oklahoma City when the state capital was chosen. Both a lawless element and some of real life's colorful Western characters such as Poker Alice frequented Guthrie. Yes, the Reaves Brothers' Casino actually existed as did that warning sign over their bar. Although the Casino has been torn down, the Blue Bell Saloon still stands at the corner of Second and Harrison as a tourist attraction. Legend has it that in 1902, a handsome army deserter tended bar in the Blue Bell who would later become an early Hollywood Western movie star. His name was Tom Mix.

Of the thousands who made the run, only a few were lucky or rode fast enough to stake a claim. However, not all of those who got their one hundred sixty acres stayed on. Some starved out, gave up, or died in those first terrible years.

The straggly trees of central Oklahoma's Cross Timbers section are full of mistletoe. The new settlers used it for Christmas decorations, and even sadder, to spread over graves when there were no flowers in bloom. For that reason, mistletoe came to hold a very special place in their hearts and slowly became a white

man's symbol. "I surmount all difficulties," mistletoe'
language of flowers, surely described those determined
settlers. In 1903, Oklahoma would be the very first ter
ritory or state to choose a state flower, and there wa
no question what that popular choice would be. Mis
tletoe.

Yet while we admire the pioneers' gritty courage, re
member this land had been promised to the Indians
"for as long as grass grew and rivers flowed." In 1986
almost a hundred years after the first land run, repre-
sentatives of more than twenty of Oklahoma's Indian
tribes attended a special ceremony at the state capital.
Now mistletoe, the state's floral emblem, has to share
the limelight with the new official state wild flower:
Gaillardia pulchella. The bright orange-red blossom is
commonly called *Indian Blanket*. Hawk would say it
was only simple justice.

Tidewater Promise
by *Jo Goodman*

December 24, 1796

Everyone had an opinion. It was difficult to be a McClellan and not have an opinion. It was impossible to be a McClellan and not voice it. Sometimes there was unanimity, more often not. It was difficult to tell how the lines of the argument would be drawn, who would support whom. There were family ties to consider, parental and sibling affection. Then there were all the spousal ties. Marrying into the family made one a McClellan just as certainly as if one had been born to the name. Finally there were bonds of gender, with the men lining firmly on one side and the women just as committedly on the other.

They had come together, more than a score strong, to celebrate Christmas and a wedding. Christmas was coming as scheduled. The wedding was off.

Courtney McClellan stood on the edge of the flagstone veranda, leaning against one of the white columns. She hugged herself. It was cold enough now that she should have had a cape, but not cold enough to encourage her to go back inside the house to get one. The cold, she thought, was more inside her than outside. Her faint smile was self-mocking. It was because of the cold inside her that she had broken her engagement with George Monroe.

Most of the stunned family was still crowded in the drawing room arguing the merits of her last-minute announcement to cry off. Closing her eyes, Courtney could see her father standing at the fireplace, tapping a poker against the marble apron as he presided over the family meeting. She imagined she could still catch the scent of the pine garland, and the baskets of oranges, decorated with ribbons and pinned with cloves. She remembered thinking that the heady fragrances she associated with winter, with celebration, had little impact on her father's thinking or disposition once he heard her news.

Unbidden, the discussion echoed in her mind and she felt the disappointment and censure of her beloved grandparents, parents, and a host of aunts and uncles. She cringed inwardly as their voices came to her one after another.

Her mother's soft voice addressing her father, "Our daughter has a mind of her own. You helped raise her that way. I don't think we can force her hand."

Her grandfather's concerned reprimand, "When a man asks a woman to marry him and she says yes, then by God, he has every right to expect that she'll still mean yes come the wedding day."

Aunt Rae's practical interjection, "At least Courtney's not pregnant."

A chorus of male voices had been raised in unanimous disapproval of Rae's plain speaking. For all of a minute Courtney had ceased to be the center of attention and she loved her aunt for that. But then it started again.

"This is the third engagement she's broken," someone said. "The *third*."

"It's *her* future," it was pointed out.

"But it's a family scandal," came the objection.

"She's too stubborn by half."

The response had been quick. "That's a McClellan trait. You can't fault her for what she's seen all these years."

Courtney put her hands over her ears in an attempt to silence the voices. It was not enough. Her father's angry edict came to her clearly: "The next time she even thinks about marriage she should plan to present me with a *fait accompli*. I want to hear about her marriage *after* the fact."

It was then Courtney had come to her feet and made her

own opinion known. The drawing room had fallen silent as she stood. A pale wash of sunlight filtered in through tall, narrow windows, glancing off the powder blue walls and white woodwork. The curtains shifted slightly in the breeze coming up from the river. Shadows were scattered on the hardwood floor, across the walnut pie table, and on the back of the love seat. Someone rose to close the window. The shadows ceased to dance and the sunlight lay still, this time across the gentle slope of Courtney's shoulder.

She had her father's height and her mother's delicate features. Her silver-gray eyes were mirrors of Salem's own, but their provocative, mysterious slant was Ashley's. The shape of her generous mouth came from the Lynne side, the dimple at the corner was McClellan. From both parents she had inherited hair the color of midnight.

Courtney's hands were steady at her side, her shoulders straight. There was a touch of high color in her cheeks but her voice was calm.

"You're mistaken if you think I get engaged and break it with the lightness of feeling that one has for a schoolgirl prank," she said with quiet dignity. "I didn't set out to hurt anyone. I want to know the kind of love Mama has with Papa, that Aunt Rae has had with Jericho, that Uncle Noah and Jessa have shared these last eight years. Why should I settle for less than Grandpapa and Grandmama have had, or Uncle Gareth and Darlene, or Aunt Leah and Troy?"

She had looked at her father squarely then. "I'll never have that with George Monroe, Tom Broadwater, or John Rourke. I want to believe it's there, Papa, but it never is, not on my part."

Her fingers had begun to tremble. Her chin had come up a notch and she had hidden her hands in the folds of her hunter green gown. "But if I have become such an embarrassment to my family, I'll accept your decision." Tears had gathered in her eyes and spiked her lashes. The trembling in her hands had become part of her voice.

Courtney felt a rush of heat to her cheeks as she recalled the threat she had made then. Before she could call back the words she had swept from the room, ignoring her father's command for her return. McClellan pride and the ache in her own heart kept her from returning to the family fold now.

She pushed away from the veranda column and started down the path that led to the river. In her childhood the path had been beaten-down grass and dirt. She had loved the feel of it beneath her bare feet. Now it was laid with gravel and the stones jabbed at her even through her shoes.

The sateen skirt of her gown swirled around her as she turned and looked back at the house. McClellan's Landing was set among a grove of regal-looking willow oaks. They had been there, vying for their share of the sky with the Landing's four chimneys as long as Courtney could remember. White shutters framed all the windows. Sunlight winked at her as it was reflected off the panes of glass. The red brick and slate roof absorbed the warmth.

As a child, sailing with her father and mother on the *Clarion,* she had run to the taffrail with her brothers as their ship approached the James River from the Atlantic. It was their game to see who could spy the Landing first. There were a dozen stately residences in the Virginia Tidewater, but none save McClellan's Landing made Courtney's heart swell with such fierce love.

McClellan's Landing was a small community unto itself. Besides the outbuildings for the servants, the summer kitchen, and a stable for the draft animals, there were curing and storage sheds for the sweet tobacco crop, stables for the thoroughbreds, and a dock for shipping the plantation goods and livestock.

It was also largely a family enterprise. Some members were responsible for the farming, overseeing the plantings and harvesting, the crop rotation, the curing, and packing. Other members managed the raising of prime horseflesh. Her Uncle Noah, practicing law in Richmond, kept everyone apprised of the regulations that were thorns in the side of all McClellans, and it was Courtney's own father who was responsible for every aspect of the shipping.

The graveled path took Courtney to a knoll. She paused on its gently curving crest and breathed deeply. Even in winter there was a certain lushness to the Tidewater, a substance that could be felt in the salty air, heard in the rhythmic lapping of water against the shore. Loblolly and pond pines shaded her, bare black willow branches whipped at her as the wind swept off the river.

Courtney's skirt beat against her legs and her hair blew back from her face and shoulders. She stood there a long moment, staring at the blue-gray expanse of water, the bright white curve of the tidal waves, and knew in her heart that as much as she was drawn to the Landing, she was too much her father's daughter not to be drawn still more to the sea.

She started to walk toward the dock and halted again. A single-mast sloop was skimming the surface of the James like a water spider, her white, triangular sails full and curved as they cupped the air. She was expertly handled, gliding with such perfect ease that she seemed to be racing the wind rather than being guided by it.

The moment Courtney was certain of the sloop's destination she raised her skirt and petticoats and began running for the dock.

Cameron Prescott eased the sloop into its berth and tied it down. He moved with the grace of the sloop he had commanded, silent and deft, with an economy of motion borne of confidence and purpose. He raised his tricorn, touched his forearm to his brow, and adjusted his hat over his dark blond hair. He glanced over his shoulder at the dock, lines fanning out from the corners of his cool blue eyes, as he squinted in Courtney's direction. "Give me a hand, will you, Court? You weren't always so useless."

Courtney laughed. "You beast!" She jumped down beside him, careless of her skirts or her modesty. "Useless, am I?" She began helping him with the sails, her expert handling of the ropes and hoists equal to his own. "If you weren't my best friend, Cam, I'd . . . I'd . . ."

"Yes?" he asked, sidling up behind her.

She turned as his arms went around her waist. Her own encircled his neck and she raised herself on tiptoe, kissing him on each cheek, and finally hugging him hard. "I'd use you for fish bait."

"Fish wouldn't have me."

Stepping back, Courtney looked at him consideringly. He stared right back at her, giving as good as he got, his pale blue eyes amused. She liked Cam's straightforwardness, the way he dealt with her honestly and fairly, as he would any of his friends. She didn't have to watch what she said or did around him, he'd known her too long for decorum or strained politeness to be any part of their relationship. "You're right," she said finally, flashing her single-dimpled smile at him, "the fish wouldn't have you. You're too tall and too skinny." She reached under his navy jacket and tried to pinch him. He managed to elude her. "There! You see? Nothing to grab."

He chuckled. "Lean," he said. "I'm lean, not skinny."

Courtney's snort was more derisive than delicate. She pushed a lock of black hair from where it had fallen across her cheek. "Who told you that? Mavis Hamilton, I'll wager. Or Alice Parks. She's always interested in knowing when you're coming to the Landing. Someone's trying to flatter you, Cam."

He snatched her up, whipping an arm around her waist, and brought her flush to his body. He tweaked her nose with his thumb and forefinger, ignoring her when she yelped and holding her securely when she tried to wiggle out of his embrace. "Then it's a good thing I have you around to set me straight again, isn't it?"

Courtney's smile faded. She shook her head, her eyes darkening. "No, it's a good thing I have you to set me straight."

Cameron frowned and set Courtney away from him. "What is it, Court? What have you done now?"

She looked at him sharply. "Why does it have to be me who's done something? Why couldn't it be Papa or Mama or someone else who's done it to me?"

"Is it Monroe? Has George done something to you?" He cupped Courtney's chin and raised it, searching her face. "If he's hurt you . . ."

She placed her hand over Cameron's wrist and shook her head. "No, it's nothing like that. I'm afraid you were right the first time, Cam. It's me who's done it now. I've cried off again." She looked away too quickly, afraid of the censure in Cameron's eyes, and missed the shutter that had been drawn over his features. When she looked up again his only expression was one of concern. "There's not going to be any wedding tomorrow. I told George last night and I told my family today."

"I see," he said lowly. He touched her cheek, brushing away another lock of hair that slid across it. "Come on, let's get you out of this wind and up to the house where it's warmer. You can tell me all about it there."

Courtney hugged herself again. "No, I don't want to go back to the house. I just came from there. But if you want to go, I won't hold you back. I know you're looking forward to seeing everyone."

He was anxious to see the family. It had been three months since his business for the McClellans had brought him directly to the Landing and, before that, another three months. On that occasion he'd been given command of his own ship. It was still a stunning thing to him that these McClellans trusted and treated him as one of their own.

It had been Courtney's father who had first brought him into the fold, hiring him as a cabin boy for the *Clarion* when he had yet to reach his tenth year. Later, at the grand old age of thirteen, he'd proved himself helpful to Noah and Jessa McClellan when their child was abducted. They had thought him incredibly brave. That was ten years ago and Cameron knew now what he'd only suspected then: He'd been more foolish than courageous.

No McClellan since then had been interested in Cam's modest denial of his real contribution in that intrigue. Abandoned by his own family years before, he had been happy to make his own way to escape his father's brutal fist. Without ever knowing quite how it happened, Cameron became, for all intents and purposes, a McClellan. And Courtney, who had been his boon companion in the early days, who practically lived in his pockets when he was on shore, became as much sister as confidant.

At least from Courtney's perspective. It was a view Cameron had never shared.

He sighed now. "Of course I want to see everyone, but it can wait. I'm going to be here until the New Year. I'd rather hear about you first." He shrugged out of his jacket and slipped it around Courtney's shoulders. His white shirt billowed in the wind. He tucked the tails more securely in his buff breeches, then adjusted the collar of his jacket around Courtney's ears. "That's better."

"What about you?"

"I'll be fine. Where do you want to go?"

"The gazebo?"

"All right." He tossed the duffel bag containing his belongings back into his sleeping quarters in the hold. "Lead the way." His hand slipped around her waist and he lifted her easily onto the dock. When he would have climbed out himself he saw she had turned and was holding out a hand to him. Clasping it, Cameron pulled himself up. He did not let go as they followed the path halfway to the house, then deviated from it to go to the gazebo.

"What have you been doing these past months?" Courtney asked.

"I thought we were going to talk about you."

She hesitated. "Not just yet. It's so boring to cry on your shoulder all the time."

"They're broad enough."

Courtney glanced sideways. His shoulders were broad. She hadn't really noticed that about him before. It seemed odd to notice now when he'd probably filled out years ago. If she hadn't been so busy crying on them, she might have seen.

"Now what is it?" he asked. Cameron was too aware of

276

Courtney not to see when worry shaded every aspect of her features.

"What? Oh, it's just that I'm always realizing how selfish I am."

"Well, if that's all it is."

She smiled at the dry, indifferent tone he affected. He could always make her laugh. "You're very good for me, Cameron." She squeezed his hand. "Now tell me about you."

"If you're hoping to hear an adventure, you're sorely out of it there," he said. "I've spent most of these last months on the water. Oh, and a few weeks in Calais, then Paris."

"Paris," she said wistfully. "I've been there with Papa and Mama . . . but that was so long ago. Is it still so very beautiful?"

He nodded. "It rained hard one afternoon. I watched it from my room. When it stopped the sun came out and reflected off the rain-washed cobblestones. The street looked as if it were paved with gold. It's a sight I won't easily forget."

Other people would have told her about the cathedral of Notre Dame or the Royal Palace. They would have described the river traffic along the Seine, the crowded markets, perhaps the Sorbonne. Cameron told her about sun beating off water-glazed streets, and ribbons of gold winding through the city. Courtney rested her head against his shoulder as they walked.

Inside the house Courtney's Aunt Rae motioned to her sister-in-law to come to the window. She drew back the curtain a few more inches as Jessa approached.

"What is it you want me to see, Rae?" Jessa asked. "Oh, never mind. I see." And just to needle Rae a little she added, "That boy should have on a coat."

Rae let the curtain fall. "This is no time to be practical." When she saw Jessa was having fun with her, Rae's own smile turned rueful. "All right, laugh if you will, but you do see that he's been waylaid by Courtney. She's the only person who could keep him from coming here to see you first."

It was true, Jessa thought, taking another peek out the window. Cameron was but a decade younger yet Jessa had embraced him as a son. She had tutored him, helped him round off the rough edge to his manners, and encouraged him to attend William and Mary. He only stayed there two years, the sea's call was too strong, but Jessa didn't count it as a failure, not when she saw his cabin on the *Cristobel* was fairly lined with books.

Jessa looked at Rae curiously, a question in her clear gray eyes. "Did you know Cam was coming? You don't seem very surprised to see him."

Rae shrugged. "I know he likes to be here to celebrate Christmas."

"I know that, too. But that wasn't what I asked. Did you know he was coming?"

"And he would have wanted to be here for Courtney's wedding."

"I'm not so certain that's true."

Tossing a secretive smile over her shoulder, Rae left the dining room in search of Ashley. Courtney's mother would want know about Cameron's timely arrival.

Sighing, made both amused and anxious by Rae's penchant for scheming, Jessa followed in her wake.

"So then I had to pay their fines," Cameron was saying, "or they would have had to spend another night in the Paris jail and I would have had to find a way to set sail with only half my crew."

Courtney was laughing so hard tears had gathered at the corners of her eyes. She laughed harder when Cam gallantly offered his sleeve. She pushed his arm away and swiped at her luminous eyes with her fingertips. The single dimple at the corner of her mouth deepened. "Oh, Cam, and you say you don't have any adventures. I thought the French were rather blasé about their brothels."

"Not when they're taken over by American seamen and

the poor Frenchies can't even get in. I assure you, that was a matter of considerable concern."

She gave him a sidelong glance. "How was it that you weren't arrested?"

"I was at the ship, working out the details of the tobacco sale."

"Really?"

He nodded.

"Would you have gone to the brothel later?"

"What is it you want to know, Court?" He watched her squirm a moment before he took pity on her. "This particular brothel was filled with cabriolet chairs and marble cherubs. Drinks were served from a scarred cherry-wood sideboard and the women lounged in their chemises, smoking cigarettes and playing chess."

For all that she was fascinated, she was also suspicious. "You're making this up."

"I'm not. The bedrooms were—"

She held up her hand. "Just how many bedrooms were you in, Cam?"

His smile was enigmatic and a direct answer was not forthcoming. "The bedrooms were papered in lavender and rose. The canopies on the four-posters matched the paper. Above one bed, suspended on chains at each corner, there was a mirror."

"Now I know you're teasing me." When she saw his brows raise a fraction, she became a little less sure. "Aren't you?"

"The women weren't especially pretty, at least not as pretty as you might think," he said. "But they were friendly, even a little curious about us. They don't see all that many Americans."

Courtney snorted lightly in disbelief. "How could you answer their questions? You and your crew don't speak French so that anyone can understand it."

"I said they were curious. I didn't say they asked questions."

"Oh, you mean they—they—" Words failed her.

He nodded. "Their curiosity ran in the direction of mak-

279

ing comparisons. It wasn't something any of the men had to talk about." Now Cameron watched a becoming pale rose color flush her face. "I wondered when you were going to blush."

She gave him a playful jab in the side with her elbow, then slipping her fingers out of his, Courtney ran ahead to the gazebo. For a moment Cameron simply stood there, watching her go. His eyes, shaded by thick lashes much darker than his hair, passed over her flyaway ebony hair, her narrow shoulders, and the slim line of her back. The wind lifted the hem of her hunter green gown. He could see her lacy petticoats and the turn of her delicate ankles. Cameron's mouth flattened, his ice-blue eyes were remote, even pained. But when Courtney turned on the steps, waiting for him, she only saw his smile.

The gazebo was a white octagonal structure with latticework framing the lower half of each side. Benches were built along the inside walls. The roof was an ornately carved cupola. A black iron ship was perched at its crest, pointing out the direction of the wind.

"There's a bit of protection against the breeze in here," Courtney said. She sat down on one of the benches and indicated the space beside her.

"It would be warmer in the house," he said, sitting next to her. He leaned back and stretched his long legs, crossing them at the ankles.

"It's more crowded in the house, but you're welcome to go."

He didn't move. "They've all come to the Landing, then?"

She nodded. "There are children underfoot in every room. Grandmother keeps counting heads to make certain none of the little ones have wandered off. There are sixteen of us now. Seventeen, counting you. We'll all eat Christmas dinner in the kitchen, you know, while my grandparents, parents, and all the aunts and uncles eat in the main dining room."

Cameron said gravely, "I suggest a mutiny. We'll take over the dining room and force the first and second generations to feast in the kitchen."

"It's really not very amusing, Cam. You have a ship at your command. No one treats you as a child, at least not until you step foot at the Landing."

Cam said nothing. There was no reason to point out Courtney herself was the most guilty in that regard. He was surprised she mentioned his command. He thought there were times that she still thought of him as a cabin boy, taking orders instead of giving them, avoiding responsibilities instead of shouldering them.

"I can't seem to avoid being treated as if I have no more sense than my littlest cousins."

"Perhaps you should tell me about your broken engagement," he said. "I take it the news was not well-received."

One half of Courtney's full mouth lifted derisively. "Can you doubt it? I've embarrassed everyone. Mama took to the news better than Papa, of course, but I knew she was deeply disappointed." Courtney pulled Cameron's jacket more tightly around her shoulders. "I told everyone at once in the drawing room. It would have gone to a public hearing minutes after telling my parents anyway so I decided to do it myself. It was simply awful, Cam. Once I gave them the news they acted as if I weren't there any longer, or at least as if I were deaf."

Cameron felt the press of the latticework at his back. His arms were folded across his chest and his head was tilted to one side. He looked over at Courtney's bent head and said consideringly, "And after the rousing debate, how did the voters line up? All against you? Or was there some support among the ranks?"

She smiled and her darting look at Cam was appreciative. Trust him to understand how her family had discussed the matter. "It appears to be evenly split. All the men see it one way and the women the other. Even my grandparents are divided over it."

Cam's brows rose a fraction and he whistled softly. "It was a serious discussion then."

Nodding, Courtney slipped one hand under Cam's folded

281

arms and leaned against his shoulder. "I've ruined everyone's Christmas." Her short laugh was humorless. "The thing is, I planned the wedding for Christmas on purpose. I didn't want anyone going to the trouble they had with my first two engagements. There's always a feast here for the holidays so there wouldn't be a lot of extra preparation and Mama decorates the house so beautifully that nothing else is needed."

"How considerate of you."

She lifted her head and studied Cam's profile a moment, uncertain if she should take his words at face value. Finally she lowered her head again and said, "I thought so. I was trying to do the right thing by everyone this time."

"Did it never occur to you, Court, that by making the arrangements you did, you were really planning for just this end?"

Courtney moved away from him quickly, her back stiff. "That's a perfectly horrid thing to say! Of course I wasn't planning to cry off. I had every intention of marrying George Monroe when I became engaged else I would have told him no."

Cameron was not at all perturbed by her prickly anger. "Then why aren't you marrying him tomorrow?" he asked reasonably.

"Because I don't love him!"

"But you did."

"Of course I did!"

He was quiet, thinking it over. "So what happened to change your mind?"

Courtney stood up and went to the other side of the gazebo. Through the trees she could see the mast of Cam's sloop, bobbing and swaying on the James. "Nothing happened," she said quietly. "I woke up yesterday morning and knew absolutely that I didn't love him and that I couldn't marry him for any other reason."

"Then there's nothing wrong with George."

She shook her head. "Not a thing. He's generous, very thoughtful, and gets on well with my family. All of them.

You and I both know that's no mean feat. We share a number of the same interests and he's never been put off by the fact that I have my own opinions. In fact, he displayed a remarkable degree of deference."

"A paragon," Cam said dryly. The last thing Courtney needed was someone always giving in to her. "Who was it before George? Tom Broadwater?"

Courtney nodded. "There was nothing wrong with him either. He was quite handsome, very intelligent, and he played the spinet beautifully. He didn't seem to mind that I couldn't. He accepted me for precisely who I am. It never bothered him that I wasn't nearly as accomplished as he."

That's because he hadn't appreciated any aspect of Courtney save her beauty, Cameron thought. "I see," Cam said. "And before Tom? It was Peter Davies, wasn't it?"

Courtney turned suddenly. "Oh God, no. I never said I would marry Peter. That was the story he put out. Credit me with some good sense, Cam. Peter and I would have never suited. He didn't enjoying riding or sailing. He toured his plantation in a carriage! Can you imagine? He was much too old for my tastes."

"Too old? He was younger than either Tom or George. They're both in their thirties. Peter can't be more than twenty-eight."

"Well, he seemed older than my grandfather."

Cameron chuckled at that. "So you were never engaged to Peter. That leaves who? John somebody-or-other?"

Courtney was not amused. "You know very well it was John Rourke. I cried on your shoulder often about him."

"You thought he'd never love you."

"I was seventeen. I thought he'd never notice me."

"He did."

"That's because you helped me make him jealous." She sat on the bench opposite Cameron. "Do you ever regret doing that?"

"What? Pretending an interest in you?"

She nodded.

"I am interested in you."

"Oh, you know what I mean."

"Yes," he said after a moment, his pale blue eyes implacable. "I know what you mean, and no, I don't regret it."

"I just thought . . . since things didn't turn out quite as I had planned, well . . . I thought perhaps you were sorry for your part in it."

"I'm not the one who got engaged nor the one who broke it off. What was it you eventually found not to love about John?"

Courtney raised her hands in a helpless gesture, at a loss to explain. "There was nothing about him not to love. I just knew one day that I didn't." She had to raise her chin a notch, not in defiance but as a way of holding back the tears that welled in her eyes. "It's not them, Cameron. It never has been. It's me. There's something about me."

Cameron went to her then, lifting her by the elbows so that she stood in the circle of his loose embrace. Her cheek was warm against his chest and where her tears touched his shirt, he could feel the dampness on his skin.

"What am I going to do?" she asked plaintively.

His voice was gentle. "It's not the end of the world, Court."

It wasn't precisely what she wanted to hear. "I wish it were."

He found a handkerchief in one of his jacket pockets and gave it to her. "Here, wipe your eyes and blow." He smiled when she obeyed without hesitation. "No, I don't want it," he said when she tried to hand him the handkerchief. "Put it back in the pocket. Good. Now tell me why you're so sure it's you and not them."

She shook her head. "I don't want to talk about it."

He didn't press. "All right. Then tell me why you're so bent on avoiding your family right now. Surely the worst is over. You've already told them the news."

"Yes, I've done that," she said a shade reluctantly. Courtney lifted her face and drew back so that she could see Cameron better. "I threatened Papa."

Cameron's eyes narrowed. "What have you done,

Court?"

"It wasn't only me," she said defensively. "Papa did his share of rash speaking."

"I'm certain that's true." Because you could cause a saint to bargain with the devil, he thought. "But I care for what you said."

"Oh, very well," she said, pulling away from him. "I told Papa that he needed not worry about another engagement. I fully intend to marry the first man I lay eyes on and have done with it."

"You told your father that?"

"I did."

"And?" he prompted, his voice carefully cool.

"And what? I mean to do it. I've been very careful about my choices in the past and we see the pass I've come to as a result." Her smile was self-mocking. "This time I'm not going to advance cautiously at all. Actually I was trying to think how I might meet some man here at the Landing. It isn't likely we'll have many eligible guests for the holidays, not when word circulates about what I've done to poor George. I'll be a pariah. What about you, Cameron?"

He was silent a moment. His heart thudded loudly in his chest. Could she hear it? "Me?" he asked.

Courtney slipped into his coat. The cuffs touched her fingertips. She began rolling them up. "Yes, do you have any ideas how I might meet some man here?"

She wasn't looking at him and for that Cameron was grateful. He'd come as close to making a fool of himself as he ever had. Except for his slightly indrawn breath, the brief gasp when pain struck his soul, Cameron managed to keep his balance as the very ground seemed to shift beneath his feet. His heavy lashes shaded the frost blue color of his eyes.

"No, Court," he said, his tone neutral. "I don't have the least idea how you'd meet a man here." He thought the pain could only go so deep but the longer he stood there, watching her roll the cuffs on his jacket, indifferent to his hurt, indeed, indifferent to him, the more thoroughly the knife was driven. He stepped away. "If you'll excuse me, I should

285

be going up to the house now."

She paused at her task and looked up. "You're not going to leave me now, are you? I thought you'd help me arrive at some plan."

"Not this time, Court. I think you'd do better to work out of this scrape on your own." He turned and stepped lightly down the gazebo stairs. It was difficult not to run.

Courtney leaned against one of the supports, watching him go, miserably aware that she hadn't even her best friend to stand with her. When he turned toward the river she called out to him. "I thought you were going to the house."

"I have to get my duffel," he called back. Then he disappeared over a rise.

In her bedroom, Ashley's breath misted the window pane. She wiped the spot with her fingertips and glanced at Jessa. "Where do you suppose he's going?"

Jessa's eyes followed Cameron as he walked away from the gazebo. She had hoped he would turn toward the house. "I'm not sure. You don't think he's leaving, do you?"

Rae was peeking over the top of both their heads. "I want to know why Courtney isn't following him. That isn't like her. Do you suppose they've had an argument?"

Nodding, Ashley's eyes sought out her daughter standing on the steps of the gazebo. Courtney's head was bent. She was absently rubbing the sleeve of Cam's jacket with her palm. "Look at her. I've never seen her so alone. She's likely to break my heart."

"This is simply not to be borne," Rae said. "I'm of a mind to go out there and have a talk with both of them."

Jessa and Ashley spoke simultaneously. "Don't you dare!"

Rae blinked at their vehemence. "It was just a thought."

Neither Jessa nor Ashley were entirely convinced by Rae's sheepish defense. Exchanging a glance, they rolled their eyes. Be certain it remains just a thought," Jessa said. "It seems to me you've done quite enough simply getting Cameron here."

"Getting Cameron here?" asked Rae. "What do you mean? If you suspect me of something, Jessa, then you may as well say it outright."

Ashley placed her hand over Jessa's wrist. "Don't bother accusing her of anything. She'll deny it."

Rae smiled. "Would you expect me to admit to something I didn't do?"

Jessa's sigh was cut off as she saw Courtney start running toward the river. "Do you think she's going after him?"

"If she has any sense," Rae said firmly.

Watching Courtney go, Ashley felt the heaviness in her breast ease.

Cam was rising from the hold, the duffel bag slung over his shoulder, when Courtney came running across the dock. He looked up, his features carefully indifferent. "What is it?" he asked.

Courtney came to an abrupt stop and held up one hand as she tried to catch her breath. "Let me take out the sloop," she said.

"No."

She was so startled by Cam's answer that she could only blink stupidly. "No?"

Climbing out of the sloop, Cam stood on the dock. "No," he repeated. He made to walk around her but Courtney grabbed his forearm.

"Why not?" she asked.

"I don't need to give you a reason. It's my sloop. I don't want you taking it out."

Courtney's silver-gray eyes widened. She almost stamped her foot in frustration but held back, knowing what Cam would think of such a childish gesture. "Oh, all right," she said, not quite able to keep the sullenness out of her voice. She looked at the sloop then back at Cameron. "Go to the house if you must."

Releasing himself from her grip on his arm, Cameron took a few steps, stopped, looked back at her and said, "Aren't you coming?"

She shook her head. "Not yet." Courtney moved to the end of the dock and sat down, dangling her legs over the side. She leaned her shoulder against one of the pilings, pointedly avoiding Cameron. She could feel his eyes on her, boring holes in her back, and though she grew uncomfortable, Courtney refused to give in. Waiting him out, she was finally rewarded by the sound of his retreating footsteps.

When she was certain he was out of sight, Courtney's legs stopped their rhythmic, childlike swinging. How many times, she wondered, had she waited for Cameron's return with just that posture? And how often had her enthusiastic greeting left him no doubt he was welcome at the Landing? The memory of the picture they'd both made on those occasions brought a smile to her lips. Years ago she had fairly danced on the dock, whooping and yelling, laughing and jumping, when the ship he was on came into view. He'd lean over the edge of the taffrail, his hair bright yellow in the sunlight, and wave so hard that she feared he would drop overboard.

"If you were here right now I'd push you in," she mumbled to herself. "And it would serve you right. Do you think I can't handle your precious sloop?" She stood, hesitated only a few seconds while she glanced in the direction of the house, then jumped on the sloop's deck. With an efficiency born of long practice, Courtney made ready to set sail.

It was the duffel bag, tossed carelessly at her feet, that stopped her cold. Her posture was defiant, the set of her mouth mutinous, as she looked up at Cam. He was an imposing presence on the edge of the dock, towering over her, his body rigid with anger.

"You needn't have thrown your duffel at me," she said coolly, taking the offensive. "I might have been hurt."

Cameron's pale blue eyes were hard. He ignored her gambit. "What is it that you did not understand? Can you not comprehend the word 'no'?"

"I don't think I like your tone, Cameron."

"At this moment, Court, I don't think I like you." He saw her wince.

Being hit by the duffel would have hurt less. Some of Courtney's reckless bravado faded. Her fingers toyed with the rope they held. "I would not have damaged your precious sloop," she said, unable to look at him now.

He was quiet a moment, staring at her bent head. "I wasn't concerned about the sloop."

She raised her face. "Then why . . ."

Cameron climbed down and took the rope from her hands. His voice was carefully neutral, his chiseled features set impassively, but hard. "There's a storm coming."

Courtney looked to the west. Dark gray clouds had gathered in the distance. "I hadn't noticed."

"I know." He stood there, waiting for her to make some move toward the dock. When she didn't, he said, "Come back to the house with me, Court."

"No. Not yet."

His sigh was barely audible. "Very well," he said. "Then help me take her out. There's time enough before the storm gets here."

Courtney threw herself against him, laughing joyously, and kissed him on both cheeks. She repeated her thanks several times, as eager and grateful as a child. Her eyes shone. "You won't regret this."

He gently disengaged himself from her fierce hold. Turning his back on her he said under his breath, "I already do."

Some of Courtney's pleasure faded when Cameron turned away. She stared at his back. The wind pressed his white linen shirt against his skin. There was tension in every line of his body. "Cameron?" she said softly.

He glanced over his shoulder. His brows were arched in question. "What is it, Court?"

For a moment she didn't answer. Couldn't answer. There was an odd wrenching in the pit of her stomach, a missed beat of her heart. His tricorn rested slightly back on his head. There was a fringe of dark blond hair at his brow. She suddenly had an urge to touch his hair. She envied the breeze that caressed it.

"Court?"

She blinked. "Nothing," she said. "It was nothing." Looking away hurriedly, afraid he might see something in her eyes she did not understand herself, Courtney bent to her task.

Once they had the sloop out Cameron let Courtney take the sail. He sat against the side, his legs stretched out across the deck. His hands were idly busy with a rope, making a series of knots—sheepshank, bowline, figure eight—with no thought at all to what he was doing. His long fingers wove the rope, dismantled it, then wove it again.

Courtney watched his hands as she ran the sloop directly before the wind. Why had she never noticed what beautiful hands he had? His fingers curled around the rope, twisted it. How would they feel sifting through her hair?

Cameron felt her eyes on him and looked up, saw the direction of her gaze, and held up his hands, examining them critically and a little self-consciously. "Not as soft as George Monroe's, are they?"

"More capable though," she said. Her eyes wandered away, uncomfortable and uncertain with the direction of her thoughts. It was difficult to look at his hands and not think of them touching her. The calluses on the pads of his fingers would be pleasantly abrasive. His hands would chase a shiver across her skin, raising heat just below the surface.

"Are you feeling quite the thing?" Cameron asked. "You're flushed. Perhaps I should take the sail."

"No," she said quickly. "No, I'm fine." She concentrated on the sail, letting it all the way out. A sudden shift in wind or course would cause a jibe. The boom would come slamming hard to the other side and knock one of them senseless if they weren't careful. Her dark hair fluttered around her cheeks and shoulder. She pushed it back, tucking it into the raised collar of Cam's jacket. "Do you remember the first time we went sailing together?" she asked.

He grinned. "We had too many captains and not enough mates."

"There were only the two of us."

"My point exactly."

She laughed. "You thought you knew everything."

"I'd been working on your father's ship for three months."

"Yes, but you were the cabin boy, not the captain."

"It seemed all the same to me back then. Besides, you were only a—"

Courtney made a distasteful face, finishing his sentence for him. "A girl." She feigned a shudder. "How awful for you that you were bested by a girl."

"Odd . . . I don't recall being bested. We both took a swim that day. And you went in first."

"You threw me in."

"You disobeyed an order."

"You weren't in command. I was." Her eyes crinkled as her smile widened. The dimple appeared. "I got you in the water, didn't I?"

Cameron's own smile was playfully derisive. "That's because you lied. You said you couldn't swim."

"It was sweet of you to want to save my life."

"I was thinking of my own skin. Salem would have killed me if anything had happened to you."

Courtney's smile vanished. Her eyes were grave. "Is that really the reason you did it?" she asked. "Because of Papa?"

No, he thought. He had loved her even then. What he said was, "We were friends, Court."

She nodded. The sweet, wistful smile shaped her mouth. "We were, weren't we? The very best of friends." Courtney hauled in the sail as she changed course. The wind came abeam now. The leading edge of the sail fluttered. She drew it in a few inches for the perfect rim. The sloop skimmed the surface of the water effortlessly.

"Where are you taking us?"

"Norfolk. That's where your ship's anchored, isn't it?"

"That's where the *Cristobel* is. There was cargo to unload. But we're not going that far." He cut her off before she could question his decision. "I just came from there," he said. "I have no intention of going back. And I am the captain now."

"A despot and a tyrant." His easy smile, not a whit remorseful or apologetic, held Courtney still. The wind beat at the sail. She held it steady, glad Cameron could not know the vibration had started with her, with his smile, and not with the beating breeze. "Oh, very well," she said lightly. "We'll only go as far as Jamestown."

Having averted a mutiny, Cameron settled back. While his fingers worked and reworked the rope he watched Courtney's competent handling of the sloop. Her touch was sure. She raised her face to the wind and it blew color into her cheeks. "You'll have to go back to the Landing sometime," he said.

"But not yet."

"No," he said. "Not yet. Not if you're not ready."

She was silent. Courtney's eyes were the same gray of the clouds as her glance darted between the sky and the shore. There were breaks in the pines and white willows, places where the bare oaks opened up to landscaped gardens grown brown and tangled in the winter, places where graveled paths led to magnificent red-brick plantation homes. The tidal waters of the James lapped at the side of the sloop. Diamond droplets of water cascaded against the bow.

"I never meant to hurt George," she said. Tears were diamond drops in her eyes. "I would have married him if I thought I could."

Cameron's eyes were shaded by his lashes. The corner brim of his hat cut a shadow across his face. "Did you fall out of love?"

"I don't know." She looked at Cam helplessly. "How does one know something like that? I'm not certain I loved him ever. I know I wanted to. I know I should have."

"Should have? What makes you think that?"

"Because I went about it so carefully this time." Her smile was watery as she swiped impatiently at her eyes. "George was a proper age for me. Responsible. Respected. There was nothing about him that one could fail to admire. His proposal made me envied."

"And?"

"And . . . nothing," she said lowly. "I couldn't bear it when he touched me."

Cameron sat up a little straighter. His fingers stilled around the bowline. "Courtney."

She waved aside his concern. "It wasn't always like that. Not in the beginning anyway. I felt uneasy at first but then I told myself I shouldn't enjoy being kissed, not before the marriage, certainly not before the engagement."

"That's absurd."

"Is it? I don't think so. It's happened every time. I like the idea of being in love I think, but I've no interest in what must accompany it. There's no passion in me, Cam. I'm not like the rest of my family."

He snorted. "How do you come by these notions?"

She heard the laughter in his voice and it angered her. Courtney turned away, set her mouth tightly, and refused to respond.

Cameron moved beside her, laying his hand over hers on the rudder. "I didn't mean to laugh, Court, not when it distresses you so. It's simply that, well, it's laughable."

She removed her hand from under his and let him take control of the sloop. "I shouldn't have told you. I'm sorry I did."

"No, Court, I'm sorry. I swear I'm sor—" Cameron saw tears gathering in her eyes again. "Oh, hell . . . it's just that . . . oh, hell." Slipping his free arm around her waist, taking her completely by surprise, Cameron kissed her full on the mouth. Hard. And long. And deep.

The sloop shuddered as the wind came over the port bow. Cameron broke the kiss, steered the sloop into the wind, filling the sail from the other side. "I'm sorry." He said it because he thought he should, not because he meant it. Courtney hadn't been cold in his arms. Quite the contrary. After the first moment her response had been as full and promising as he'd known it would be. "There's passion in you, Court," he said lowly. "I'd be no kind of friend to let you think otherwise."

Slightly dazed, Courtney nodded slowly. Unconsciously her hand was lifted to her lips. Her fingers lightly touched the swollen curve of her mouth. She had been kissed before

293

but no one had ever curled her toes. She told him that.

Cameron concentrated on the sloop, tacking first to starboard, then to port, and pretended not to hear. Overhead the sky was darkening. The sloop raced against the onset of the storm. He glanced upward. Grimaced.

He could still taste her against his mouth. That kiss had been a stupid thing to do. He would never forget the taste of her, the scent of her hair, the color in her cheeks as he drew away, color the wind hadn't put there. He would never forget. The memory would be torture.

Courtney stared down at her hands. "You taught me how to bait a hook. Do you remember? Papa always let me fish with him but you were the one who let me bait the hook. You taught me about bowlines and sheepshanks, how to make a reef knot or splice a line. We have been good friends, haven't we?"

Cameron didn't look at her, not certain he liked where she was heading. "We've been good friends," he said.

"You taught me how to climb into the sails of my father's ship. You taught me how to whittle."

"Jericho taught you that."

"You taught me better."

He shrugged.

"We were up to every trick together. To this day no one knows we're the ones who finished off that keg of beer in the cellar. Remember that woman Uncle Noah was going to marry?"

"I'm not likely to forget Hilary."

"Remember how she flogged Big Billy with her whip for being slow? We cared for him without anyone's help afterwards, and when he begged us not to say anything we didn't."

"He was afraid it would have gone the worse for him."

She nodded. "And we kept the secret. Over the years we've kept a lot of secrets and promises between us, crossed our hearts and spit. I suppose that's the sort of things friends do."

"Sometimes," he said, a cautious note in his voice and in

294

his eyes.

Courtney brushed a strand of hair from her cheek as she turned toward him. In profile his face was hard, the line of his jaw clean and taut. A muscle worked in his cheek. "Teach me about kissing, Cameron."

The muscle ticked faster. "No."

Before she lost her nerve she said, "Teach me how it is between lovers."

His hand tightened on the boom. "NO!"

"It will be our secret. No one has to know."

"No."

"It's not as if you'd have to marry me. I wouldn't expect that."

His eyes rolled upward. "Thank God for small favors."

"That wasn't a very nice thing to say, Cam."

If both his hands hadn't been occupied just then, Cameron Prescott would have throttled her. With a sidelong glance he managed to convey the thought nonetheless. "Stop it, Court. I've said no. There are boundaries to friendship, at least to my way of thinking there are. I shouldn't have kissed you like that. I'm sorry if it put ideas in your head."

She paled. "You didn't like the kiss. I didn't do it right, did I?"

Was she serious? "Don't play the fool. You know perfectly well I—" Then he looked at her, really looked, and saw the anxiousness and uncertainty. He told himself to leave well enough alone, let her believe what she would and be done with her latest cork-brained scheming. Even as he was thinking it he heard himself saying, "I liked the kiss, Court. You did it fine."

"Oh."

"You don't need any lessons. You need the right—"

"Man," she said. "I know. But can't you help me until I find him?"

It only got worse, Cameron thought. Like an expert marksman her aim was always true. Somehow he managed to speak. "I—don't think so." She looked as if she might object. Cameron was thankful for the skies opening up just then. A fat drop of rain splattered on Courtney's shoulder. Another one hit the back of his hand. "Get below."

"I can help."

He shook his head. "I can manage. There's no need for both of us to get wet. We've almost reached Jamestown. I'll take her to shore myself."

Courtney stood and began to slip out of the jacket he'd loaned her. "Take this at least. It will help."

The rain was already coming harder and faster. "Below, Courtney. Now."

There was no brooking him when he used that tone. She kept the jacket on and hurried below deck. The sloop's hold was utilitarian. Besides the duffel bag there was nothing in it that belonged to Cameron. In spite of maintaining the sloop was his, he had merely borrowed it from the McClellan armada at Norfolk. The single bunk was unmade. Chipped cups swayed on their hooks above the small Franklin stove. Wood was neatly stacked beside the stove, held securely in a canvas sling. There was a cupboard with clean linens, a washstand with basin and pitcher inside, fresh water in a cask, and another cupboard with a few staples. She found tea and coffee, sugar and salt, raspberry preserves and jerky. In the spring and summer when the sloop was used to make regular pleasure runs between Norfolk and the Landing the larder would be filled. Courtney wished that was the way of it now.

With skillful tacking Cameron reached the dock. The sloop stopped when he headed it directly into the wind. Lashing it to the pilings, he hauled in the sails so the boat wouldn't be battered against the dock. By the time he climbed down the ladder into the hold, his shirt was soaked. When he tipped his head water rushed from the curled corners of his tricorn as if it were a downspout. He tossed the hat in the direction of Courtney's laughter, spattering her with water.

"That was very bad of you," she said, placing the hat on the stove where it could dry. "I've made some tea. Would you like some?"

"Put a little whiskey in it and I'll accept." He plucked at his wet shirt. It clung to him like skin he needed to shed. "Below the bunk," he told her. "In one of the storage drawers. I think there's a bottle there."

Courtney knelt in front of the bunk. The sheets she'd placed over it were clean but slightly musty. She smoothed a corner before she opened one of the drawers. "Here it is." She held the bottle up and looked over her shoulder for Cameron's approval. Her breath caught in her throat.

He was simply beautiful. Droplets of water glistened on his naked shoulders and clear beads clung to spiky strands of hair at his nape. The muscies in his arms bunched as he rolled up his soaked shirt and tossed it in a corner. The buff breeches molded his thighs, clinging to the long, hard length of his legs. He may as well have not had them on.

She changed her mind about that when Cameron started to take them off. "What are you doing?" she asked. Her voice was pitched a notch too high. She pretended not to notice.

Cameron was not so polite. He laughed out loud. His thumbs hooked in the waistband of his breeches. "I'm going to take off my breeches. I'd be pleased if you'd get out a dry pair from my bag."

Putting down the bottle of whiskey, Courtney rooted through the duffel, found a pair of soft leather hunting breeches, and threw them over her shoulder at Cameron.

"I need a pair of dry drawers," he told her.

Heat flushed her cheeks. Biting back a small groan, Courtney found the drawers and tossed them to Cameron as well. She could hardly understand what was wrong with her. She'd been swimming in the James with Cam since she was eleven. She'd grown up in a home with brothers and uncles, lived on a ship for months at time in almost the exclusive company of males, had nearly married on three separate occasions, and now with Cameron, she was hot and cold in the same moment, fevered and shivering in the same heartbeat.

She didn't turn around until he reached over her shoulder

to get the whiskey.

"What about you?" he asked. "Whiskey in your tea?"

Courtney nodded. Definitely, she thought, whiskey was important right now. The roll of distant thunder brought her to her feet. She found some candles, lit them, and closed the hatch just as lightning seared the sky.

Cameron saw her jerk at the sight of the lightning. He handed her a mug of tea. "Not quite the Christmas Eve you expected, is it?"

Her smile was rueful. "You know I'd forgotten. About it being Christmas Eve, I mean. I haven't the right spirit for the season." She sipped her tea. Over the chipped rim of the cup she found herself staring at Cameron's naked chest. The bent of her thoughts gave her a guilty start. A droplet of tea fell on her chin. Before she could brush it away Cameron's finger was there, touching her gently. The sloop's hold suddenly seemed very, very close quarters.

Cameron saw her shiver. "That jacket's wet. You'd do better to exchange it for a dry blanket. There must be some where you found the sheets." The first thing he'd noticed when he entered the cabin was that she had made up the bunk. He had been trying to rein in his thoughts ever since. He set his tea down. "I have to get a shirt." Turning away, he missed the expression of relief in Courtney's eyes.

Courtney hung the jacket, wrapped herself in a faded quilt, and sat down cross-legged on the bunk. The mug warmed her hands and the tea and whiskey warmed her throat. There was a small ball of heat in her stomach that had no reason to exist save for Cameron. "How long do you think we'll be here?"

He finished tucking in the tails of his dropped shoulder shirt. The button at his throat was left unfastened. "I'm not sure. It doesn't seem the rain's going to let up any time soon."

"I suppose I should have thought of that before I insisted we take out the sloop."

"I'm the one responsible, not you. You could have insisted all you wanted and I could have still said no." He picked up his tea and joined her on the bunk. "The pity is, I don't tell you no often enough."

Courtney thought of their conversation on deck before the storm broke. He'd told her no then. Several times.

He searched her face and plucked the thoughts out of her mind as if they were his own. "Forget about that kiss and everything else you want from me. Your family trusts me to take care of you, Court."

She leaned forward until her mouth was a moment from his. Her breath was sweet, her voice soft. "Then take care of me." Her lips settled over his.

Salem McClellan stamped his feet as he entered the house from the side door. Water dripped from the fringed sleeves of his leather coat. He took off his hat, gave it to Ashley, and spoke to the other family members huddled in the large kitchen. The warm, inviting aroma of freshly baked bread and sugar tarts could not soothe the expectant faces. They waited to hear from Salem.

"The sloop's gone," he told them. "There's no sign of Courtney nor Cameron anywhere. They must have taken it out."

"What could Cam have been thinking?" Jessa asked. "He would have seen the storm coming, wouldn't he?"

Ashley sighed. "I doubt when all's said and done that the blame for this will fall at Cameron's feet. He'll accept more than his share of the responsibility — he always has — but this is Courtney's doing."

Salem was torn between fear for his daughter and guilt that he had forced her to this pass. He sought out Ashley but there was no accusation in her eyes. She helped him out of his sodden coat. "Cameron will take care of her, Salem. He loves her as well as any of us."

"That does not assuage all my fears, wife."

Rae laughed at her brother's dry pronouncement. "I wondered if you knew," she said.

"Knew that Cameron loves my daughter? I'm not so blind as you might think, Rae. The only person at the Landing who doesn't seem to understand is Courtney herself." His eyes darted to the other members of his family. "I suppose everyone here has been thinking Cameron's timely arrival is Rae's doing. If I know my sister, she's been careful not to take the credit but somehow manages to make everyone think it just the same."

Ashley poked her husband in the chest. "You!"

"I'm not certain your surprise flatters me. Cannot a man further the interests of true love, or is that strictly a woman's province?"

One of his brother's laughed. "I think Cupid was a man."

Another sniggered. "Cupid was a baby. It ain't the same."

Ruddy color touched Salem's complexion but Ashley was hugging him hard and he liked having her with him again. He slipped his arms around her and spoke over the crown of her soft ebony hair. "Whatever I might have wished for Courtney and Cameron, this bit of business was not part of it. The weather's right for fog. It won't be long before the entire river's shrouded with it."

Ashley lifted her face. "Then there's nothing we can do."

"Not now. Cameron will know what to do." Salem had to believe that. He couldn't have lived with himself otherwise.

Her lips were soft. They tasted faintly of tea and whiskey. The tips of Cameron's fingers pressed whitely against the mug he held. He did not move. He did not encourage.

Courtney drew back. She searched his face, her own eyes pained. "Why won't you teach me this?"

"I've told you why." The rain beat a steady tattoo against the upper deck. Cameron concentrated on that and not on the unsteady beat of his heart.

"I don't believe those reasons. There is something wrong with me."

"Only that you can't see past your own nose."

"What does that mean?"

"Leave it, Court," he said sharply. He rose from the bed and leaned against the ladder. He wanted to go topside and stand in the cold, driving rain. His jaw ached from clenching it so hard.

"You're angry with me," she said.

"I'm angry with myself."

"Why?"

Cameron bent, picked up the whiskey bottle and poured two fingers worth into what was left of his tea. He swirled the contents before he took a long swallow. "It's nothing you would understand," he said finally. "Nothing I can share."

Courtney sat up straighter. "Stop treating me like a child! I'm a woman!"

"Then act like one! Act as if you know I'm a man!"

For a long time there was only the sound of the rain and the drumming of thunder.

"I'm sorry," he said. "I shouldn't have—"

The blanket slipped from Courtney's shoulders as she shook her head. "No, it's true, isn't it? I've not been seeing things very clearly. That's what you meant about not being able to see past my nose."

He shrugged. "It's not important."

"But it is." Every time she'd noticed something about Cameron today the prickle of heat had been accompanied by a twinge of guilt. She hadn't understood it then. She did now. He was her best friend and she wanted him in a way that had very little to do with friendship.

Unfortunately he didn't want her in the same way. He'd told her no often enough. He was a man and she had been insensitive to his feelings. She'd called on their friendship to get him to teach her about passion. He'd been right to say no when there was no passion or love in his heart.

'I'm the one who's sorry," she said, unable to meet his gaze directly. "I didn't take your feelings into account. Only my own." Her faint smile was filled with self-mockery. "I told you I was selfish."

Cameron wished he had not given himself away. Loving Courtney was never meant to burden her, yet she seemed to be weighed down by the revelation. Her head was bowed, her shoulders sloped. Her smile had mocked but her eyes were sad. He finished off his whiskey. "It's not as if there's blame to be attached. Neither of us can help the way we feel. Not about this."

She nodded slowly, raising her eyes to him. "Friends?"

"Friends."

There was an uncomfortable silence, then Courtney grinned. "I feel as if I should cross my heart and spit."

He laughed. It had been that sort of solemn vow. Their shared laughter pushed aside the awkward moment. "I have a deck of cards in my duffel. Do you want to play a few hands while we wait out the rain?"

The diversion was a welcome one. They sat on opposite ends of the bed, tossing their cards between them. Cameron was a methodical, thoughtful player. Courtney appeared to pick up and discard on whim but she won two out of every three hands played.

Courtney gathered up the cards to shuffle them. One of them had slipped under Cameron's knee. Her fingers brushed his leg as she reached for it. A frisson of awareness touched her and she glanced at Cam to see if he noticed. His pale blue eyes were distant, his features stoic.

She snapped up the card and started shuffling. Suddenly she was aware of the silence. "Listen!"

Cameron cocked his head to one side and looked at her inquiringly. What he heard was the cards passing through her hands.

"The rain," she said. "It's stopped."

He stared at the ceiling. "So it has." He honestly didn't know whether he felt relief or disappointment. Swinging his legs over the side of the bunk, Cam went to the ladder and climbed topside. In less than a minute he was back. "It's no good, Court," he told her. "We're not going anywhere to-night. The fog's as thick as cotton batting. I can't get the sloop upriver in this. We'll have to wait 'til morning."

"But it's Christmas Eve."

"And tomorrow will be Christmas. There's really nothing I can do about that. You can't spend the holiday with your family *and* run away from them."

"I wasn't running away."

His look was patently skeptical. "Oh no?"

"No. I had every intention of returning tonight."

"With a husband on your arm."

"What? Oh, you mean that threat I made to Papa. I've had time enough to think on it. I've changed my mind. I'm never going to marry."

Cameron blinked. His fingers raked his damp hair. "You're never going to marry," he repeated, shaking his head. "When did you decide this?"

When I realized the first man I met wouldn't have me as a gift. "Does it matter?" she asked. "I've made up my mind."

"You really are a piece of work, Court."

"Courtney," she said. "My name's Courtney. You make me feel all of twelve when you call me Court."

He blinked again, startled by her tone.

She saw his reaction. She could not bring herself to apologize. She was unaccountably angry with him for reasons she couldn't even name. Courtney dealt the cards. "We may as well play. There's nothing else to do."

"We have to sleep sometime, Courtney," he said gently.

And that was the very thing she was trying to avoid, the thing that had fired her anger. Was she always so transparent to him? "We don't have to sleep now," she said. She picked up her cards and fanned them open. "I'm not the least tired."

Cameron returned to the bed. "Let me know when you are," he said calmly. "You can have the bunk and I'll take the floor."

She chose a three of hearts to discard. "We'll argue later," she said. "It's your turn."

In the end it wasn't much of an argument. They played cards until Courtney could not keep her eyes open. She made a few tired protests about taking the floor in his stead but they were ignored. Cameron helped her with her gown, unfastening the buttons then politely turning his back while she slipped out of it and into the bunk. He hung the gown on a peg and made up a bed on the floor.

Courtney came wide awake the moment his boots

thumped to the floor. By the time he snuffed the candles and stripped down to his drawers, she was one exposed nerve.

Cameron listened to her breathing and knew the even cadence was forced. He knew because he was guilty of much the same thing.

"You're not sleeping," he said.

"No." She stared at the darkened ceiling. The sloop rolled in its berth, rocking the bunk like a baby's cradle. "I'm not tired any more. Are you?"

"No." He hesitated. "Are you afraid I'm going to attack you?"

"Not at all," she said quietly. "I'm afraid you won't."

Cameron sighed. "I thought this was settled. Why are you so nervous?"

"I just told you why." She turned on her side and leaned over the edge of the bunk. "Only you don't believe me."

"What is it you want from me?"

"You," she said. "I want you."

It seemed he'd waited forever to hear those words and now they meant so little. "I'm not tutoring you."

"I don't want you like that. I just want you."

Cameron sat up. His head was level with hers. His voice was husky, resigned. "I don't say no to you nearly enough." He found her mouth in the darkness.

Courtney's lips parted beneath his. She felt his tongue trace the soft inner side of her lip. It was the most exquisite sensation she'd ever known.

Rising to his knees, Cameron cupped her face. He held her steady while his mouth explored hers, nudging and nibbling. Her response was tentative at first, then eager, every movement mirroring his. He kissed her closed lids, her brow, the curve of her cheek. Courtney's hands slipped over his. The feel of his work-roughened hands beneath hers seemed so very right, the touch of his fingertips on her face, adoring.

He raised himself to the edge of the narrow bunk. It was too dark to see her clearly. "I want to light a candle." His thumb brushed her lower lip. He felt her nod her assent but

304

it wasn't enough. "Courtney?"

"All right," she said softly. "Light a candle."

Cameron lit two. Shadows chased light across the bunk and then across Courtney's face as she sat up. Her eyes were wide and luminous, and as Cameron approached she moved to the far side to make room for him.

"You haven't changed your mind?" he asked.

Now she understood about the candles. It wasn't merely about seeing her. It was about giving her a chance to think. "I know what I want, Cameron." She raised the sheet and blanket. "I finally know what I want."

He stared at her upturned face for a long moment. Slipping in beside her, he kissed her. They fell back on the bunk together. His fingers threaded in her hair. He sifted through it, let the soft strands curl around his fingers, cross his palm like the whisper of silk. She touched his shoulder. Stroked his arm. Her darkening eyes never left his face. She raised her hand and brushed his cheek, caressed his temple. She thought she knew him so well, but now, touching him, she knew him differently.

Her mouth parted beneath his. She reveled in the taste of him, the weight of him as he moved over her. The wide straps of her cotton chemise slipped over her shoulders. Cameron traced her collarbone, first with his finger, then with his mouth. The edge of his tongue was warm and damp. There were tiny, tasting kisses on her neck and at the hollow of her throat. He nuzzled her, blowing gently against her skin just below her ear.

"That tickles."

"Hmmm."

The vibration of his voice had the same effect. "That tickles too," she whispered. She turned her face into his neck and kissed him.

"I like it," he said.

"So do I." Her teeth caught his ear lobe and tugged.

He kissed her hard. Courtney's chemise was pushed lower. His hands covered her breasts, and when she gasped at the sensation he tasted the sound of pleasure against her lips. His thumbs brushed her nipples. They stiffened at his touch.

Courtney caressed his shoulders, his arms, his back. Her neck arched as his mouth covered her nipple. His lips were gentle but the suck of his mouth was hot. Fire traveled on a taut thread just below the surface of her skin. Heat coiled at the very center of her, resting heavily between her thighs. She twisted under Cameron, arching, reaching, pressing herself against him in a way that relieved the ache. She felt the length of him, hot and hard against her abdomen.

She said the first thing that came to her mind. "Can I touch it?"

Cameron had imagined making love to Courtney any number of times. It was the stuff of daydreams and nighttime fantasies. He had thought he might be tender, loving her slowly, delicately sipping her flesh, making her want him with caresses that were so pleasuring she would cry. He had thought he might love her with urgency, as if there could be no waiting or holding any touch in reserve, needing and desiring so essential that she would cry out.

But this was Courtney McClellan, his best friend, his secret sharer, and he knew now he should have imagined loving her with laughter.

"God, yes," he said, burying his smile against the curve of her throat. "You can touch it."

Courtney's fingers slipped below the edge of his drawers. She felt him suck in his breath; his skin rippled in the wake of her touch. Shyness was simply overwhelmed by curiosity. Her hand closed around him. There was a soft murmur of pleasure that could have belonged to either of them.

Cameron stripped off his drawers. Courtney squirmed out of her chemise. Both items sailed over the side of the bunk. They stared at each other, their eyes as eager as their hands. She caressed his back from shoulder to buttocks. His skin was taut and warm and smooth. The ridge of his spine fascinated her. She traced it with her thumb.

His kisses spiraled around her breast. Her flesh swelled under his attention. There was a small cry at the back of her throat as his tongue flicked across her nipple. Her fingers pressed in his back. She moved restlessly and his legs separated hers. She liked the sense of her body defined by the shape of his. She knew the curve of her breast by the cup of his palm, the indentation of her navel by the exploration of his tongue, the length of her legs by the strength of his.

"Courtney?" Cameron asked for assurance and reassurance.

In response Courtney's hand slipped between their bodies. Her thighs opened as her legs curved around him. She did not tell him she was ready; she showed him.

Caution was abandoned. Cameron pushed himself into her as Courtney rose to meet him. His mouth slanted across hers, swallowing the urgency of her sweet cry. He drew back slightly, his lips barely touching hers. "Have I hurt you?"

"No," she whispered. She held him tightly, her eyes wide and black as she searched his face. "That is . . . not overmuch . . . oh, Cameron . . . it's . . . it's splendid."

He groaned as she shifted under him, moving to accommodate his entry. A grin split his face. "Splendid?"

She nodded. Her own smile was serene. He started to ease out of her and her smile vanished. Courtney's legs tightened around his flanks. Her fingers curled around his arms. "Don't leave me."

Thrusting into her again, he kissed her hard. Loving her, not leaving her, was on his mind.

Pleasure was a pinwheel of heat at the center of their joining. Their bodies rocked in unison. He touched her; she held him. They were eager traders, bartering their kisses for comfort, their passion for pleasure. They shared desiring and selfishly clung to excitement.

Their bodies glistened in the candlelight. The gold threads in his hair mingled with the ebony of hers. When she shuddered in his arms he felt the vibration pass from her into him. His body tensed moments after Courtney's release. He whispered her name and without even realizing it, he whispered something else.

She rested in the curve of his arm as her breathing calmed.

She listened to the sound of his breathing, felt the beat of his heart just beneath her palm, and sensed the passing of tension from every line of his body.

"Did you mean it?" she asked after a moment, her voice soft, hesitant.

"Mean what?"

Courtney's face tilted toward his. She was afraid to hear his answer and afraid not to. "Did you mean it when you said you loved me?"

Ashley patted the space in bed beside her. "Come away from the window, Salem. It's no good watching for her. You said yourself the fog won't lift until morning."

He used the back of his hand to wipe where his breath had misted on the cold pane. Salem padded softly to the bed and slipped under the covers that Ashley held up for him. They both curled on the side, one body curving against the other. His arm slid around Ashley's waist just below her breasts. "I keep thinking I'll catch sight of the sloop returning. God, Ashley, I never meant to send her flying from the Landing."

"She's of an age," Ashley said quietly. "This is her time to use her wings."

Salem's breath fluttered strands of his wife's dark hair. "I wish she had more sense," he said. "How did we raise her not to have more sense?"

In the darkness of the bedroom they had shared for twenty-one years, Ashley smiled, laying her hand over her husband's. "We raised her just fine. Courtney has as much sense as she wants or needs to have right now. We should be very happy that she showed so much courage in breaking her engagements — all three. She wasn't suited to marriage with any of them. She was very wise to know it, even if it only occurs to her at the last moment."

"I'm glad we're not fighting. I didn't know if you'd ever speak to me again."

"You knew I'd speak to you," she said, correcting him. "It's other things you were worried about." Ashley's feet nudged Salem's as she warmed herself against him. "Tell me

308

something. If you had already invited Cameron here, why were you so angry with Court when she cried off with George?"

"I didn't know that Cam would come, or even if he did, that it would mean anything to either of them. We still don't know that. As the wedding approached I thought I'd been wrong about Courtney and George, that perhaps they were suited, and then she suddenly decides poor Monroe is not what she wants after all. I meant what I said today, Ashley, most of it anyway. Courtney cannot keep getting herself engaged and crying off."

"It was good of you to command Cameron back here."

Salem's low chuckle ruffled her hair. He kissed the back of her head. "I was not so demanding as that. I simply made certain he knew the wedding date was set for Christmas and that he might find it in his best interests to share the holiday with us at the Landing."

Ashley was silent a moment. "I know he loves her, Salem, but do you think she loves him?"

"Of course I love you," Cameron said.

Courtney did not care at all for the lightness in his voice, the way he dismissed the question as if it were of no account. She sat up, drawing the sheet to her breasts and stared down at him. "I see," she said softly. He hadn't meant it, not the way she hoped. Nothing had changed and she had been naive to suppose it might. She bent her head and kissed him lightly on the mouth. "Friends?" she asked.

"Friends," he repeated, whispering. He watched her straighten, his heart in his throat, and just as she was turning her head he glimpsed the gathering of tears in her eyes. He reached for her but when his hand touched her shoulder she jerked away. His fingers only grazed her skin. Cameron sat up, taking the quilt as Courtney drew off the sheet and wrapped it around her. She left the narrow bunk and went to the bottle of whiskey sitting on the floor. After pouring a small amount in her mug she stood by the stove, warming herself.

She held up the mug, composed now, her beautiful features shuttered and cool. "Would you like some?"

Cameron shook his head.

Courtney shrugged. "It must be after midnight," she said, glancing toward the hatch. "Christmas Day."

He studied her carefully. Behind her candlelight burnished the slope of her shoulder and bare arm.

"Mama likes to tell the story of her first Christmas Day at the Landing. Have you heard it?"

It wasn't what he wanted to hear now, but he didn't say so. It was almost as if Courtney were in shock, stunned by the enormity of what had occurred between them and needed to put it from her mind. "I don't think have," he said lowly.

"Mama was only weeks away from bearing me. You can imagine how she looked, so petite and delicate except for an enormous belly." Courtney laughed. "She always looks sideways at my father as she tells it, reminding him her condition had much to do with him."

Cameron blanched a little but Courtney didn't notice.

"It was not long after news of Bunker Hill had reached the Landing. All along the Tidewater people expected the British to invade their homes. My mother didn't know that plantation owners greeted Christmas morning with a cannon salute. When Grandfather's cannonade announced the day, Mama thought the Landing was under siege from the redcoats. She couldn't wake Papa so she determined to save the Landing herself. She found a pistol that wasn't even primed to protect everyone. When Papa finally roused himself he thought she was a most amusing sight.

"Actually he says she was plainly ridiculous, barefooted and wearing his nightshirt, waving a pistol about as if she meant to take on the army alone. He also says it was love for her, not fear, that put his heart in his throat just then." Her smile and her voice softened. "I think I should want someone to love me like that, love me at the moment I look most ridiculous."

Cameron's fingers tightened on the quilt. "What hap-

310

pened then?"

"What? Oh, you mean with Mama. Well, when she realized there was no danger, she took strong exception to my father's laughter. She thought to serve him a lesson and aimed her pistol and fired."

Cameron's brows arched. "Never say . . ."

Courtney nodded. "Mother didn't know it, but the pistol was primed. Papa ducked and the bullet went through the headboard and into the wall. Mama fainted. Aunt Rae was there, watching this last piece of business. She says that she decided then she wasn't suited to marriage."

His smile was faint. "She changed her mind," he said. "What about you, Courtney? Might you change your mind?"

Courtney ignored the question and sipped her whiskey instead. "It must have been quite a Christmas morning," she said wistfully.

"You may still have the adventure you crave, Court. I shouldn't be surprised if there are pistols aimed at both of us on the morrow."

"Why ever would you think that?" For a moment she was genuinely bewildered, then she saw his eyes drift pointedly to the bed and back to her. "Oh, you mean because we . . ." She finished her drink instead of her sentence. "No one's going to do anything, Cameron, because I'm not going to say anything."

"Perhaps not," he said, "but I am."

Courtney set her mug down hard. "I forbid it."

"I don't see that you can do anything about it."

"Why would you want to?" She approached the bunk but did not sit down. "Surely what happened here is no one's concern but our own."

Cameron's voice was quietly earnest. "What happened here, Courtney? No, perhaps that's not the right question. What did you want to happen?" He caught her wrist and pulled her down on the bunk. "No, stay here. Tell me what it is you wished? Or was it only about a lesson in loving for you?"

311

She could not meet his eyes. Courtney stared at his hand around her wrist instead. "It was a lesson in loving," she said, "but not the one you thought I wanted. You don't really want to hear this, Cam. The knowledge won't ease your mind."

"Let me decide," he said. His hand squeezed her wrist, not threateningly, but encouragingly.

I love you. She meant to say the words aloud but they remained caught in her heart. She lifted her eyes to his. "I love you, Cameron. It's what I knew before I lay with you and what I knew after. I wish I had known it forever, but I didn't. Perhaps I couldn't. Before today I wasn't ready." She saw the change in his features, the tension replaced by something she could only identify as shock. She tried to pull away but he held her fast. "Let me go, Cam. I told you you didn't want to hear. I knew you didn't feel the same for me. It wasn't fair to tell you."

"I want to hear," he said. "You tried to tell me before, didn't you? And I wasn't listening then."

"You aren't listening now. Let me go."

He did, but it was only to take her by the shoulders. "Do you mean it, Courtney? Do you really lo—" He stopped. Courtney wasn't paying him the least attention. Her nose was wrinkled and she was looking around, trying to find the source of the pungent aroma that was only now assailing him.

"Do you smell it?" she asked. "Something's burn—"

He saw it in the same moment as she. His tricorn was smoldering on top of the stove where Courtney had placed it hours ago to dry. "I think it's done," he said.

Courtney leaped from the bed, dragging her sheet and stumbling as she tripped over its ends in her hurried attempt to save his hat. She picked it up between two fingers, juggled it in her hands when it proved too hot, and blew on it. Her last effort only served to fan the smoke and spark the flames at the brim. She dropped it on the floor and tried stamping on it. It skittered out from beneath her feet. She chased it down and tramped on it again, this time with lightning quick steps.

Cameron watched her dance, smashing his hat with heel and toe as if it were a thing to be despised. His heart swelled. She looked plainly ridiculous, holding up her sheet with one arm, the other flung out to give her balance. Her hair swung across her cheek, slipped over her shoulder. Her face was a concentrated grimace. She stopped suddenly, surveyed her handiwork, then looked up at him and solemnly pronounced, "It's only fit for burial, I'm afraid."

He slid off the bed, hitching the quilt around his waist. He stopped when he stood directly in front of her. His eyes grazed every part of her face. Her lips were damp and slightly parted. Her cheeks were flushed. Her dark brows were arched in question and her silver-gray eyes were luminous. "Don't you know, Court? There's never been a time I haven't loved you." Then his arms circled her and over the smoldering, crushed remains of his hat, he kissed her breathless.

They did not make it even the few steps necessary to reach the bunk. The tricorn was kicked aside. The sheet and blanket tangled around them as they knelt on the floor. Their makeshift clothing was discarded as their arms and legs became the tangle. They loved furiously, hungrily, each knowing what had not been known before, that the love they bore was shared and returned measure for measure.

They only noticed the floor was cold and hard beneath them in the quiet aftermath. Holding hands, laughter reminiscent of the childhood conspirators they had been, they returned to the bunk and cuddled for warmth.

"You're going to marry me, aren't you?" she asked.

"I was the first man you laid eyes on."

Courtney's happy smile faded as she remembered the things she had said to him then. "I was horrible to you. You were right. I couldn't see past the nose on my face."

He placed a finger over her lips. "As long as you can now and as long as I'm the only man you see, little else matters."

She kissed the rough pad of his finger, then drew his hand to her heart and held it against her breast. "Why did you come to the Landing, Cameron? Was it because it's Christmas?"

Cameron smiled. "Do you want to hear that it was because of you?"

"Only if it's true."

"It was because of Christmas . . ." He heard her soft, disappointed sigh. "And you."

She punched him lightly and was pinned to the bunk for her efforts. She tried to evade his kisses but in the end she was happy to surrender.

"I came back," he told her, "because your father managed to get a letter to me in Paris. He wrote you had set a date with George Monroe and if I cared anything at all for you I'd be here for the wedding."

"Papa did that?"

"He did."

"What do you suppose he meant?"

"I don't know. Perhaps only that I should come as your friend."

"And perhaps something more."

"Something more is why I came. But you had already cancelled the wedding and there seemed no need to rescue you from your own folly. In any event, you didn't look on me as anyone who might save you."

"I should have. You've always been the one I measured the others against. George and Tom and John. I wanted to love them, I think. I tried to love them. But none of them were you and I didn't understand that then." She smoothed back a lock of hair across his brow. "I'm glad you waited for me to learn my own heart, Cameron."

He bent his head and kissed the tip of her nose. "And I'm glad you don't accept no for an answer."

A cannonade at McClellan's Landing celebrated the arrival of Christmas morn and the return of Courtney and Cameron. Like prodigal children they were taken back into the fold, surrounded and blessed, their happiness multiplied in the sharing of it.

Courtney eased herself from her father's fierce and loving embrace. "It's Cameron I'm going to marry, Papa. No engagement this time, just the wedding. Will we have your blessing?"

He did not have to ask if she knew her own mind this time. This was his daughter as he had never seen her before, radiant when she looked at Cameron. "It will be everything I could have wished," he said. As Courtney turned to Cam, he felt Ashley's hand slip in his and squeeze it gently.

There was a wedding that day after all and no one seemed to mind that every guest, save the minister and the servants, was a McClellan.

Salem gave his daughter over to the care of a man he admired. Ashley watched her first born take flight with a kindred spirit. A handkerchief was surreptitiously passed among the women. Noah's arm slipped around Jessa as they listened to Cameron speak his vows in a clear and steady voice. The entourage of Courtney's brothers and cousins were suitably impressed by the solemn affair, but anxious for it to be ended. There were pies and presents waiting and, being McClellans, they had opinions regarding the priority of events.

"I now pronounce you husband and wife."

The words were said with all the import and gravity the ceremony called for and yet when Courtney looked at Cameron there was a glint of mischief in his eyes. He lifted her veil and bent his head. His voice came soft and deeply to her ear. "What would they do if we crossed our hearts and spit?"

Laughing, Courtney threw her arms around him and raised herself on tiptoe. "Friends?" she whispered against his mouth.

"The best of friends."

Cactus and Thistle
by Evelyn Rogers

1

Hands on hips, Mattie Campbell ceased pacing in front of the fire and stared up at the redheaded brute of a man leaning against the mantle. Over six feet tall he was, and beneath his rough clothes every inch hard muscle covered by tight, ruddy skin. Or so she supposed, although it wasn't a matter she gave much thought.

"No Christmas tree," she said with a shake of her head. "That's impossible!"

Even as the words slipped out, she regretted them. She was a guest at Hawthorn and should not question the rules. Besides, open opposition was a poor method to use with Robert Campbell if she hoped to change his mind. She'd seen evidence of that often in the two weeks since she arrived.

Not that she'd found a *good* method. Not yet, at least.

"No tree, and no gathering in the Great Hall." Robert's craggy features settled into a scowl as he glared right back down at her, his brown eyes hard as nuts. "That's what I said, and that's what I meant."

Mattie shook her head, setting loose a blonde curl from the lightly pinned bun at her nape. It trailed against her neck. "But you surely don't mean—"

"Aye, I surely do."

The matter settled, he shifted his gaze from her and took up the pipe on the mantle, his broad hands working with ease as he filled the bowl from the brass humidor beside it.

He bent with grace to select a burning twig at the edge of the fire, and she could sense his muscles at work beneath the white linen shirt.

He puffed a time or two, then tossed the twig back into the fire. Smoke curling around his face made him look more forbidding than ever, and very much the laird of a vast estate.

Unable to look away, Mattie studied each movement and tried to understand this cousin of her late husband. James had been a kind and gentle man and, except where finances were concerned, a manageable one. Not so Robert, who could out-stubborn the meanest Texas mule.

As she watched, she tried even harder to understand her reaction to him. Countless times she'd dealt with difficult men on the ranch, beginning when she took charge after James's death five years ago. There had been some rip-roaring arguments during those early days, fights over breeding stock and feed and a hundred other details that came with raising cattle and sheep. She hadn't always got her way, but that was no problem since she hadn't always been right.

No matter the circumstances, none of those Texans had ever set her blood to boiling the way this Scot had, time and time again. There was something about him that kept her on edge.

She turned away, her foot tapping beneath the folds of her pink woolen gown. Right now she was very much on edge, and not just for herself. She thought of the thirteen-year-old girl waiting upstairs. It was for her and for the younger sister with her, as well as for herself, that Mattie had approached Robert on this rainy December afternoon. For them all, Mattie could not give up.

Standing beside him, she stared into the fire. "I talked to Janet last night about Christmas."

Robert grunted. " 'Tis no surprise. She's been home from school but two days, and already you're filling her head with women's foolishness."

Her eyes shot up to him. "In Texas, men celebrate Christmas, too."

"You're in Scotland now."

She most certainly was, Mattie thought as she fought her rising temper. Having planned her world tour with care, she was *purposefully* here at Christmastime.

Silently she counted to three. "Look, Robert," she said, her voice modulated, "I know we got off to a bad start. You didn't ask me here, and I thought you had, through your daughter's letter. It came at such a good time, right when I'd received a generous offer for the ranch."

"A Scot would never sell his land."

He would if he were dissatisfied enough. She swallowed the words. Robert wouldn't understand, and in truth neither did she. She had known only that with her parents and husband long dead, Texas no longer seemed home.

She tried again. "As soon as I got off the train and caught sight of you, I knew you were upset."

Something flickered in his eyes and then was gone. "Mayhap I should have brought the bagpipes to greet you."

Stubborn as a mule and sarcastic to boot, she thought as she threw back at him, "A smile would have been enough."

She forced one of her own, to show him how it was done. "I can understand how you felt. You got my letter and right away decided I was after something. Maybe you were a little too blunt in asking me what it was as soon as I got in the carriage, and maybe I was a little too blunt in my answer."

"I'll leave with nothing more than I brought is what you said. 'Twas not blunt. I took it for honest."

"It was completely honest." Did he doubt her word? Mattie felt her temper rise and she forgot the smile. What she'd like to do is tell him exactly how the scene in the carriage had hurt. She'd arrived in Inverary bubbling with excitement, but those bubbles had lasted about as long as biscuits at a roundup camp.

And then had come edicts against her roaming through this big old castle, most of it closed down, and against her riding about the countryside. Everything she'd suggested he turned down; after their first awkward meal together he'd even announced he would dine alone since it was then he

321

tended to the books.

Sheer luck had helped her catch him here in the library; usually he made use of it only when she was occupied elsewhere, hiking about the estate or preparing for bed. He was a stubborn man, all right, standing there puffing on his pipe and acting as though she had already gone. She itched to get her hands on that thick throat of his. If her hands would go around the muscled column.

But Janet and Amabelle awaited upstairs. She would have to resort to more peaceful ways of persuasion.

"You have a wonderful home here, Robert," she said in complete sincerity.

He looked at her in surprise. " 'Tis a drafty old castle, that's what it is. It cannot offer much pleasure for a woman."

"But it's got such character," she said. "That's why it would be so wonderful to open up the unused rooms and invite all the neighbors in."

He sighed in exasperation. "You've an obstinate streak in you, lass."

"So I've been told. The truth is, I crossed an ocean thinking I would have for the first and only time in my life a white Christmas. Silly, I suppose, but it was in my mind. And that meant all that goes with it. Tree, candles, ribbons—"

"A white Christmas, you say?" He pushed away from the hearth and settled into the straight-backed arm chair behind him, his long legs stretched out toward the warm bricks, one booted foot crossed over the other. Coarse black trousers, tucked into the boots, gave her an all-too-visible idea of just how well formed those legs were.

"Have you not noticed it's raining outside? Or do you not know the difference between rain and snow? From what I hear of Texas, there's little of either one."

Mattie ignored his taunt. She also ignored the picture he presented with his shirt open at the throat and his powerful legs seeming to reach forever. Standing as close as she could to the fire, she continued as though he hadn't interrupted.

"—holly, wassail, mistletoe—"

322

"You *are* a stubborn one, Matilda Campbell."

Angry as she was, she felt a pleasurable chill when she heard her name roll off his tongue in that Scottish burr he had. No one had called her Matilda since she was a child.

"And," she ended, her voice softer, "of course a yule log. Not just for me. It would be good for the girls, too."

He stiffened. "The bairns are content with our Scottish ways."

He spoke with such finality that a more timid woman would have sighed and excused herself. But Mattie had made promises, and she was not one to go back on her word.

Readying herself for further argument, she decided against looking down at him again. Not that he intimidated her, but he did have an unnerving manner that she'd never dealt with before. When she caught sight of him on her walks, his figure stark and strong against the hills, something caught inside of her. She'd observed the gentleness of him when he handled an injured lamb, and again something caught.

A few times she'd gone right up to him and asked about the stock, letting him know she, too, was knowledgeable. Admiration had flared in his eyes, but the look was always short-lived, and he'd always gone his separate way.

No shared meals, no rides, no opening of doors. In so many matters he got what he wanted, and she'd kept her arguments to a minimum. But not now. There was trouble in this house, an estrangement between father and daughters; she'd seen that as soon as the girls arrived two days ago. They'd come in as ladies, not as children home from boarding school, and they'd gone straight to their rooms. She'd seldom seen them with their father since.

In talking with them last night, she had spoken of Texas and what it was like this time of year. With no thought of stirring up trouble, she had mentioned Christmas; when they had shown interest, the details, the remembered good times had poured from her. It had seemed right and natural to suggest such a celebration here. As much as she wanted it for herself, she believed it might do wonders for this branch of the Campbell clan.

She stood close to Robert's chair; one small step and the skirt of her pink gown would brush against his trousers. He gave a toss of his head, as if he could shake the unruly wave of hair from his forehead, and she thought of a wild chestnut stallion jerking his proud head in much the same way.

"Please—" She had to clear her throat and start again. "Please, Robert, hear me out a little more."

"More?"

He stared up at her and their eyes held. There it was again, that little tremor in her midsection, only stronger than ever, and this time accompanied by the quickening of her pulse. Did he feel it, too? It was a question that even Mattie could not ask.

He brought the pipe to his mouth. She watched him bite on the stem, watched his lips tighten as he drew a deep puff, watched the smoke curl about his face. Suddenly she became aware of the rise and fall of his chest, of the crackle of fire at her back, of the faint sound of her own shallow breath. Most of all, she realized how much alone they were.

His eyes, normally so wide and deeply brown, narrowed and lightened at the same time. He blinked once, looked away, and the moment of tension passed. "It's quite a list you've got there, Matilda. Tree, wassail, mistletoe."

"A yule log, too," she said, letting out a deep breath.

"Anything else you've read about? Always thought it was a mistake to educate a woman. Gives 'em grand ideas."

She felt a flare of anger. *And what would you know about women?*

Biting back the question, she fingered the high lace collar at her throat. Like her, Robert had lost his mate a long time ago and, like her, had never remarried. He'd never spoken of the woman who had been his wife, although Mattie, long past grief, had been willing to talk about James.

Somehow she sensed that for all his land and wealth, this gruff man in front of her with his wide shoulders and powerful legs, his strong hands and muscular grace, this man had not fared so well. The woman in her made her think of consoling him, of touching him, of holding him in her arms.

All in the cause of familial consolation.

She brushed aside the thought. Holding Robert? What on earth had made her think of such a thing? She was better off thinking of getting her hands around his neck. He was seven years older than her twenty-eight years, not a child like his daughters, and he did not invite her sympathy or her affection.

Mattie brushed at the wisp of curl tickling her neck. "You're educating your girls," she said, then seeing his frown, added hastily, "which is a wonderful idea."

His eyes followed her hand, but his lips kept their resolve. "They're learning to be ladies, and to stay free of the mischief that might tempt them if they spent most of their time out here in the country."

The edge of bitterness in his voice shook her. "But they're such good girls."

He seemed to settle back. "Aye, good Scottish girls. I'm trying to tell you, Matilda—"

Again Mattie felt a ripple of pleasure.

"—we Scots don't look at Christmas the way you Americans do. It's sentimental nonsense, that's what it is."

"Nonsense!"

"Aye. Since Cromwell's times, we've held to that belief. New Year's, now that's a proper holiday."

James had told her something of the same, but he'd soon come around to celebrating Christmas the way she asked. Biding her time while she considered another approach, Mattie threw herself into a matching chair on the opposite side of the hearth and reached for the basket of knitting on the floor. She'd never been one for the finer domestic arts, riding and roping being more natural to her, and occasionally turning out a pan of biscuits that brought the ranch hands running, but here she'd needed something to pass the time.

Boldly sitting beside Robert on a rainy afternoon, knitting occupying her hands and the pipe occupying his, she half expected him to suggest she leave, but he did not and for a few minutes a feeling of contentment settled over her.

Her eyes trailed around the library with its dark paneled walls and shelves of well-worn books, its austere furniture and faded woolen rug covering the stone floor. Robert had made this the center of the house, with only the kitchen and a small dining room and the bedrooms upstairs also in use.

The library had a rough charm; all it needed were some simple touches, a lamp or two, a few pictures, maybe a vase of heather. In short, a woman's touch. She was certain Robert would not agree.

Her gaze settled on the stuffed boar's head over the fire. It was the symbol chosen centuries ago for the crest of the Campbell clan. Mattie thought it particularly apt.

" 'Tis the English you're thinking of." Robert's voice, rolling out of his wide chest, startled her and she dropped a stitch.

"What are you talking about?"

"The foolishness of lighted trees and ribbons."

So they were back to that, were they? Her feeling of comfort fled. "The English forgot Cromwell, why not the Scots? It's 1880, not 1680. Isn't it time you considered that the holiday just might be worth recognizing? More than the ribbons and the tree, it's a time for sharing, for thinking of others, for gathering loved ones around."

He looked at her with those hard brown eyes of his that masked his thoughts so well. For just an instant they warmed as they drifted across her face and slowly down to the knitting in her hands. "You come from a feisty clan, I'll give you that much. Not many around here will stand up to their laird."

"You're not *my* laird, Robert Campbell." Mattie felt an unaccustomed flush in her cheeks.

"Nay," he said, the warmth in his eyes gone, "that I am not."

The scowl returned, more formidable than ever. When he turned his attention to the fire, she concentrated on the rectangle of brown and blue wool in her hands. For the next few minutes she knitted and purled, then unraveled what she had done, all the while wondering why he was so upset, and in turn why his anger shook her so much.

She returned the knitting basket to the floor and sat on the edge of her chair. "When I decided to come here, Robert, I was hoping for a large celebration. I knew there weren't many Campbells nearby — James had told me you lived pretty much isolated from the rest of the clan — but all the same I pictured it, with workers and their wives and children crowded in the Great Hall. You didn't mention the holiday, and I kept quiet."

" 'Twas a wise decision."

"But when the girls and I were talking, they got as excited as I had been. They seemed like family, sprawled out on my bed in their nightgowns and their questions coming so fast. I know it was foolish of me to think such a thing. They're not blood relations, any more than you are."

In truth, the three of them were the closest people to family that she had in all the world, but she couldn't think of a way of telling him how she felt without sounding like a lonely, lost woman. And that, she most certainly was not.

She hurried on. "I promised them I would speak. It would have been a one-time thing, this party I was thinking of. Nothing more. No permanent change in your customs."

"I want no changes at all. After you're gone, the bairns might expect . . ." He broke off.

She waited for him to go on, but he did not. "I knew I had to speak or forever call myself a coward."

"I doubt if you could ever be considered that, Matilda."

The impish streak that surfaced at the most unexpected times did so right now. "I could put the tree in the barn. Kind of in memory of the first Christmas."

He glanced at the pipe, whose fire had gone out, and set it aside. "I said no tree."

"You don't have to see it—"

"No!" he bellowed.

"All right," she bellowed back, and her cheeks burned

with embarrassment. How could he have yelled out that way, and how could she have responded in kind? She pulled herself to her feet and tried to regain what little dignity she could muster. Swallowing, she said, "I'm sorry for bringing it up, and even more for not accepting your first no. You're absolutely right. This is not my home and it was not my place to suggest changes." She was startled to feel a lump in her throat. She was about to cry, she who had not cried in years.

She looked down at him and saw he read her distress. He, too, stood and she lifted her eyes to his. "What is there, Robert, that makes us unable to carry on a simple conversation? And I don't mean just today. I've admitted to being much too forward. But I've been here two weeks and except when we're talking about sheep, we've barely exchanged a civil word. I hear you talking with others while you work. You seem very much at ease, yet never with me. Do you dislike me so much?"

"I've taken no dislike to you."

"But then, what? Can't you feel this . . . thing between us?"

"Aye," he said huskily, "I can feel it." He hesitated, but the faraway look in his eye kept her from breaking the silence. "I did so as soon as you stepped from the train, your cloak blowing open in a gust of wind, and your hair falling free, yellow as the harvest moon just past. 'Twas a foolish little hat you wore to protect you from the cinders and smoke."

He spoke as if they were both back at the Inverary station and were about to start over again. She wished very much that they could.

"Robert —"

He seemed not to hear her. "I knew who you were right away. Like a shooting star in the early morning sky, that's what you looked like."

His voice was tender and confused her all the more. Whatever had brought about the change, she knew that she liked this new Robert. She liked him very much. In a rush of

328

warmth, she touched the sleeve of his shirt. He jerked as if she had hit him. She could see the tic in his stubbled cheek and fire flare in his eyes.

"I talk tomfoolery," he said, raking a hand through his hair. "You drive a man to distraction, that's what you do. You should never have come."

The sudden rejection cut deep, coming as it did so close to the tenderness. Aided by a sudden insight, she lashed back. "It's because I am a woman, isn't it, that you don't want me here? Well, Robert Campbell, maybe a woman's presence is just what you need."

She tried to back away, her only thought to edge around the chairs and flee his presence. He caught her wrist and yanked her hard against him. His arms imprisoned her against his chest, the neck she had wanted to strangle a few minutes ago on a level with her eyes, so close she could touch it with her lips. She could count the poundings of his pulse. And she could feel his heat.

"Maybe you're right." His voice was a husky growl, and she felt a shudder ripple through his massive frame. "Maybe it is a woman I need."

Her own pulse quickened and her blood absorbed his warmth. "Robert, no—"

His mouth took hers hungrily. At first she was too stunned to fight him, and then, trapped so tightly against him she could not move, she felt a sweet pain rush through her, filling vacuums of loneliness she had not realized existed and weakening her far too much for a fight.

His lips were rough and firm against hers, yet soft and smooth as he rubbed them back and forth, burning and cooling, arousing feelings she had thought forever dead. Dizzy from his assault, she could think of nothing except that she wanted very much for Robert to do everything that he did. With her own reckless urges overtaking her, she answered his kiss.

Her hands spread against his chest and she sighed into his parted lips. He answered with a groan. His tongue touched hers. At first she tasted only tobacco, but in an instant that

329

was masked by a far more provocative savor, the wildness of Scotland, the untamed heather, the rocky, windswept shores.

He shoved her away as suddenly as he had yanked her close. Looking up at him in astonishment, she struggled to catch her balance. A cold wind swept across her, though no window or door had blown open, and she felt an icy hand clutch her heart. She put her fingers to her burning cheeks and stared at the buttons on his shirt. His chest heaved with the same ragged breaths that dragged through her.

Nervously she smoothed her hair.

"That will not happen again," he said.

She lifted her gaze. For a moment she saw the imprint of her lips on his, but that was impossible. Perhaps it was because she still could taste him that her imagination had conjured up such an image. She forced herself to look into his eyes; they were as cold as the wind.

"Do you speak to yourself or to me?"

"I speak to us both. That will not happen again." And, as an afterthought, "You are a guest in my home, and I have not behaved with honor. Accept my apology, please."

She felt as though he'd slapped her. How could he face her with such calm and control when she could barely stand?

She tilted her chin high. "Apology accepted."

Hating the quaver of her voice, she pushed past him and hurried into the hall, slamming the door behind her. Her knees trembled, and she leaned against the wall for support. Shame washed over her as she remembered the way she had responded to him. She felt as though she had exposed some terrible raw wound deep inside her that she had not known existed, and he had poured salt on that wound.

What a terrible mistake she had made by coming here. All she had wanted was to meet him and his girls, to stay with them through the holidays, and then to leave, but he'd not cared to meet her. His kiss had taken her by surprise, she told herself as she touched her fingers to her lips. That was why she had weakened so readily.

She called herself a liar. She had responded because she

had been unable to do anything else.

But what had made him want to kiss her in the first place? Why had he spoken in such a . . . a poetic way about harvest moons and shooting stars? And then the sudden rejection. If she didn't know it was impossible, she would have thought she saw fear in his eyes when he shoved her away.

The more she was around him, the less she understood what drove him to behave as he did, and the less she understood herself. She needed to get away from this house for a while and do some serious thinking, but another one of her walks seemed inadequate to still the turmoil he had stirred.

What a stubborn, strange, provocative man he was. He had forbidden her to ride, either alone or accompanied. She who had ridden through the Texas brush country since she was five years old, and on mounts that had turned her father's hair gray. She'd done a lot of thinking on those rides, and she had a lot of thinking to do now.

She would simply have to disobey him. Before facing the girls, she would put on her new and unworn riding habit. If the weather was not too damp, she'd pick out a horse and saddle it herself, and she would ride until she had decided just what to say to them, and just what to say to Robert when next they met.

...from text a reason...
...ons understood not. But not...
...when he was in the same house with Martin...
...the made...of...made...under...

2

With the sound of the slamming door bouncing against the library walls, Robert picked up the pipe from the chair-side table. It rested, small and familiar, in his hand.

A simple thing, he thought, carved long ago by his old friend Angus. So often it had stilled his raging thoughts, focused his mind away from searing reflections, cooled his fires as its own blaze burned hot. But not today.

Not ever when he was in the same room with Matilda Campbell. She had the face of an angel with her smooth white skin and golden hair, but the devil's own conflagration lit her blue eyes.

Heaven help him, he'd wanted to get his hands in that hair and he'd wanted to stroke that skin. He'd known before he kissed her that the savor would be sweeter than honey newly gathered on a summer's eve.

The memory of what he had done and of the fool things he had said lashed at him. Shooting star, indeed. She must have thought him daft. His thoughts were a torment, just as each night was a torment, with him lying awake in his bed thinking of her sleeping in the next room.

His hand tightened around the pipe, snapping the stem, crushing the bowl until he could feel the warm ashes against his palm. He threw the pieces into the fire and with his head bent, he braced his elbows against the mantle, his eyes closed, the heat from the flames burning his face and neck. In vain he tried to still the matching flames that flared inside him.

Woman was the curse of man, and Matilda Campbell was as bad as any. Nay, worse, far worse. He hadn't wanted any of the others, the daughters of his neighbors, the widows come to call during the first weeks of his solitude. But God as his witness, he wanted her. He had done so the moment she got off that train, and today he'd been fool enough to tell her so.

He could have told her more . . . how he'd kept himself apart as he watched her standing on the Inverary platform. He'd seen happiness in her eyes as she scanned the waiting carriages, eagerness on her parted lips. What a beauty she was, and filled with life. He'd felt as though a horse had kicked him in the stomach. His greeting had been gruff and for two weeks he'd done his best to avoid her, but the ache had not gone away.

Today, when she'd stood there arguing with him, her fine chin raised, her eyes glinting, her breasts lifting and lowering with each angry breath, he had controlled himself. Then her voice had softened, and she had touched him. It was more than any man could stand, and today he was very much a man.

Another minute of holding her, of kissing her and feeling her soften in his arms, and he would have had her on the hearth. He would have taken her, hard and fast, and reveled in her response as she lay under him. He would have given in to a weakness that he believed long dead.

'Twould have been a cruel and stupid thing to do, cruel because he could make her no promises, stupid because he knew the one time would not be enough. He could be stupid on occasion, but he did not consider himself a cruel man. It was passion that drove him, and terrible hungers that could destroy his soul.

Ah, but he hungered for Matilda Campbell.

A mighty shudder went through him. He must not think such thoughts or his body would never cool. She was to be here two more weeks, past this cursed Christmas she so much wanted to celebrate and into the first day of the new year. Somehow he would have to regain control of himself.

He thought of the two lasses upstairs. With all his heart, he loved them, Janet with her hair and eyes so like his and a temper to match, and the dark-haired Amabelle, the gentle one who seemed wise beyond her years. Thirteen and eleven, they were, growing to womanhood.

He loved them, but he didn't know how to talk to them. He feared they would ask questions he did not want to consider, would demand answers that could bring them hurt.

He loved them, but they were better off at school and not on this lonely land. And the way he was behaving, he was better off becoming a Presbyterian monk. His mouth twitched at the idea. At least he hadn't lost the power to jest.

The door opened. "Papa, may I come in?"

Janet did not wait for him to reply. Back to the door, he listened as she crossed the floor, and he turned to look down at her. She came no higher than his chest, but she glared up at him as though their eyes were on a level and she his equal.

The Campbell temper was at work. Had Matilda so quickly reported what had taken place?

"I heard the argument in here."

"Do they teach you in school to listen at closed doors?"

"I could have heard you in the next county. As it was, I was walking down the hall."

Robert could well imagine the pace she had set as she moved past the library. A hobbled lamb would have made better time.

"I think you're wrong," she continued, unblinking.

A brave lass she was, to speak so, but unwise at the same time. "We've never recognized Christmas in this house, other than an exchange of gifts. 'Tis not the way with Scots."

"But just this once—"

"I'll not change my mind, Janet. We'll keep things the way they've always been." He could have added that it was

335

the safer, known way he wanted to keep, but she would not have understood.

Janet sighed in exasperation. "It would be wonderful. We might have a good time here, instead of —"

"You go too far, lass," he said, his voice rising with his anger. Never had she spoken to him in such a way.

"Don't you want to laugh? Don't you want to dance?"

"I'm not a man for laughter, nor for cavorting about. You know that, lass."

"But I don't know why."

Weariness overcame him, and a strong wish to be alone. "Janet, go to your room. This discussion is done."

"No, it is not."

Robert stared down at his daughter in amazement. What had come over everyone in this house? Matilda Campbell, that's what. Jamie had chosen a fiery woman when he immigrated to America. How had his meek cousin ever managed her?

"She's stirring at things she should leave alone."

"Who is it you speak of, Papa? Matilda?"

"And is it Matilda now? Better you show your respect and call her Mrs. Campbell. She's a woman grown, not a lass."

" 'Tis not a name I've heard spoken much. Mama was Mrs. Campbell."

Her words struck him. "Enough, Janet."

"Can't I even say the word mama? Is it forbidden in this house, too, along with laughter?"

"Enough!"

She swayed away from him, but he could see her eyes harden. She looked so small, so young, so filled with fury. He wanted to speak of his admiration for her courage in holding her ground, like a Highlands warrior, but not so much as he wanted to turn her over his knee. He'd never touched either of the girls in anger, but he wanted very much to do so now.

"No tree, you say. No Christmas."

"Aye, that's what I say."

"It's not fair."

"I will decide what is fair. Before you say more, lass, you'd best go to your room."

But Janet, as angry as he, ignored the order. "I know what else went on in here. You kissed her, didn't you?"

He stared at this stranger who was his daughter and said, "What happened is none of your concern."

"You kissed her all right. I heard it get all quiet. That's when I ran upstairs, but I'll bet she didn't like it."

"What do you know of such things?"

"I know. Girls talk. Besides, I'm almost a woman."

"You're thirteen. A bairn."

She shook her head obstinately, and she looked very much like a child, a very stubborn and angry child.

"A woman," she threw back, standing very much as Matilda had stood in front of him, hands on hips. How did they know to defy a man this way? Was it bred in them?

He stared down at her, not knowing what to say. But then he seldom knew how to speak to his two bairns; his spoken words always sounded much harsher than they had in his mind. Perhaps if he had had sons . . .

Nay, that wasn't the answer. He wouldn't trade the lasses for the whole of Scotland and he'd always assumed they knew it. Mayhap he had been wrong. Janet took his denial of the Christmas request as a denial of her, but that was not true at all.

He felt the wall grow strong between them and felt his own helplessness to bring it down. Far easier it was to confront her disobedience. Turning away, he strode to the door and yanked it open. "Leave, Janet. Go to your room and stay there until I send word you may come out."

"You can't treat me like a bairn forever, Papa." Tears trickled down her freckled cheeks. "I'll never get married," she said, her hands clinched at her sides. "Never. At least to a man like you. No wonder Mama—"

"Janet!" he roared.

She hurried toward him, stopping when she stood in the open doorway. Tears streamed down her cheeks, and she

337

brushed a sleeve against her runny nose. "I hate you, Papa. I hate you! I hate you as much as you hate me!"

With a sob, she ran from the room. Listening to her footsteps on the stairs, Robert stood in stunned silence, unable to believe his daughter could have said such a thing, pain cutting at his heart as he wondered if she had spoken the truth.

3

"I hate you!"

Janet's terrible words struck Mattie as she was hurrying down the stairs, her fingers working at the buttons of her riding jacket. She halted as the sobbing girl dashed past her, along the hallway, and into her room, slamming the door closed. Heart in her throat, Mattie hurried after her.

She pounded on the door, but the lock clicked just as she tried to turn the knob.

"Janet," she pleaded, "open up. We need to talk." The answer was muffled crying. "Please, Janet. Let me in."

"She won't do it."

Mattie turned to the younger sister Amabelle, who stood with rounded eyes at the bedroom doorway across the hall. In the dim light her young skin looked colorless against her smoothly combed dark hair and the collar of her brown dress.

"She has to," Mattie said. "She needs to talk to someone."

Amabelle shook her head. "She won't. She's like Papa." The girl blinked. "They argued, I'll bet, about Christmas."

"I . . . I suppose so. I wasn't there."

"You argued with him, too. I knew you would. He didn't want a tree or anything else."

"I'm sorry. I couldn't convince him." She glanced back toward Janet's room. Behind the door the sobs continued; Mattie needed no confirmation to know that her interference in the Campbell family was the cause.

"Has this happened before?" she asked with a heavy heart.

"Not as bad as this. We don't defy Papa."

Perhaps not, but Janet was getting older, Mattie thought, and was developing a mind of her own. The man who had argued with her downstairs, the private, unyielding giant of a man, would not readily accept such a change.

Did Janet really hate her father? Mattie could not tolerate the thought. She had loved her own father, and her mother, too, and missed them as much now as she had right after their death when she was little older than Janet.

She felt so helpless standing here between the two sisters, one crying her heart out behind a locked door, the other bravely blinking back tears in the drafty hall and discussing in her thin little voice the way things were.

With all the best intentions, Mattie had made a mess of things. Not even Robert could deny now that he was estranged from his girls.

But having brought the estrangement into the open, Mattie could no more turn her back on the Campbells than she could have ignored an injured child she passed on the road. Her own problems with Robert must be forgotten. The kiss must be forgotten. Most of all, whatever it was that simmered between them must be pushed from her mind. She would concentrate on his worries with the girls.

But what to do? She thought of Robert downstairs in the library. If he hadn't listened to her about a few ribbons and a party, he certainly wouldn't engage in any talk about the troubles in his home.

What was he doing now? Smoking his pipe and staring silently into the fire, no doubt, his legs stretched out and the smoke curling around his face. She could picture him very well. But she could not imagine his thoughts.

She smiled down at Amabelle. "Would you like something to eat? I could have cook bring you a tray. It wouldn't spoil your appetite for supper."

Amabelle shook her head. "We're not to eat between meals."

Robert had them well trained. She thought of Janet's outburst as she ran from the library. Perhaps not so well trained as he thought. He was such an enigma to her, a contradiction in so many ways. Considerate he was with his stock, yet stern with his daughters; forbidding when he spoke to Mattie, yet tender when she asked how he felt about her. There had been a fire in him when he pulled her into his arms, and a barely contained violence, yet his lips had been gentle on hers.

The memory of his lips and of his arms and of his warmth shivered through her. She must forget.

She glanced down at Amabelle, who looked at her with quiet, questioning eyes. "Maybe something can be done. I'll try."

Amabelle nodded, but it was not a gesture of confidence. She did not smile as she stepped backwards and closed the door.

Mattie knew of only one thing to do. Before changing her mind, she straightened the feathered riding hat that rested on the crown of her head and hurried down the stairs. Boldly she threw open the library door.

"Robert, we've got to—" She stopped. The room was empty. She made a quick tour of the downstairs. Cook, a matronly, curt-speaking woman, reported the laird had not come that way. The cobbled carriageway outside the front entrance to Hawthorn revealed only that the rain had stopped. Mattie sighed impatiently. Robert could be headed anywhere on the huge estate.

Securing the jacket of her wool habit tight at her throat, she hurried out to the stable. The garment was a forest green, one of several new costumes she had purchased in New York. It had looked fine hanging in the Fifth Avenue emporium, and she'd thought it gave her a dashing look. Right now she hoped it would keep her warm against the damp Scottish wind.

The stable hand, a boy little older than Janet, informed her that the laird had saddled one of the mounts and ridden out "like all the ghosts of the clan were after him."

"Could he have gone to see Angus MacGregor?" she asked, referring to the oldest of Hawthorn's workers. When they met on one of her walks, Angus told her he'd been at Hawthorn since Robert was a boy. He was the only one she knew to seek.

" 'Tisn't likely they're together. Mr. MacGregor be working a fence to the south, and the laird, he rode north."

Mattie came to a quick decision. "Where is this fence?"

The boy directed her. "But you'll not be getting there afore dark wi'out a horse."

"I don't intend to try. Don't help me. I know I'm not supposed to be riding and I wouldn't want to get you in trouble."

She looked over the stalls and quickly selected one of the Hawthorn mares. From the corner of her eye, she saw the boy nod his approval. The sidesaddle she found in the tack room. Within minutes she was mounted and riding into the gray day, her direction south. A half hour later the sound of hammering guided her to the man she sought. She topped a rise, gave a moment's glance to the rolling hills covered in wild heather and boulders, then urged the mare into the shallow valley where Angus worked, pounding away at a post, driving it into the damp ground.

She'd talked to the man only a few times during the past weeks, but each time she'd heard admiration and affection in his voice when he talked about his laird. "Robbie," he called him. Gruff though his old-man's voice had been, he'd spoken the name with love.

He glanced up briefly, a cap pulled low over his weathered face, his still-burly body covered in a heavy wool jacket. He must be seventy, she thought, but he'd retained his physical strength. Without a word, he returned to his pounding. The thud of the hammer striking the post echoed in the hills.

Mattie dismounted and watched in silence as he worked, knowing she must have better luck with him than she'd had with his laird.

Setting the hammer aside, he stomped the ground around the base of the post. She moved close and did the same.

"Ye will get your fine boots covered wi' mud."

"I've been dirty before. Are there more of these to do?"

"Nay."

"Then could we talk?"

"I've still got other chores. There be no time to waste."

"This won't be wasted time. I promise."

Something in her voice must have caught him, because he studied her face for a moment, then nodded his head toward a large, rounded boulder where they could sit well above the damp ground. She tethered the mare in a crop of grass and, joining him on the boulder, started right in.

"There was trouble at the house." Angus did not respond, but she was not daunted. "An argument between me and Robert, and then another between him and Janet."

"Why are ye telling me, lass?"

"I've no one else to tell," she said simply, "and I need your help."

He looked at her straight on. "Why are ye at Hawthorn? 'Tis something I've asked meself since ye arrived."

"I had the money for the journey, and the time, and Janet invited me."

"And?"

"And I wanted to see the land my husband loved. To see it covered in snow. James mentioned the holiday season here and I wanted to see it for myself. A white Christmas was to be a wonderful memory."

" 'Tis strange weather hereabouts, wi' all the rain. Ye should hae got your wish."

"More than anything, I wanted to meet the family that is as close to blood relation as I'm ever likely to have." She smiled at him, surprised that she found it so easy to speak these words from her heart. "I'm a Campbell, am I not? I could not ignore my clan."

"And wha' do ye think o' the Campbells now? A difficult lot, would ye nae say?"

"I most definitely would."

"At least ye don't put a soft name to things."

Mattie felt highly complimented. "It's not my way."

He fell to silence, and Mattie could see his mind was at work. She did not interrupt, but instead turned her attention to the sweep of the land, to the far high hills with their scattering of trees, to the gray and brown of sky and land. It should have been desolate, even oppressive, but she saw in it a bleak beauty that reminded her of Texas.

Oh, the terrain was different, and the temperature, and she wasn't likely to see heather growing beneath a mesquite. But both were hard countries that bred hard men and women. They demanded the best of their people before they yielded their rewards.

Angus began to speak again, slowly at first, then gradually quickening his pace.

"Wha' I say to ye this day I've told to nary a soul. And neither has the laird."

"I'll not repeat any of it."

"Do wi' it what ye think best, lass. I've known Robbie from the day he was born, the day his mither breathed her last as she gave him life. Worked for his father, I did, and after he died, stayed on. Robbie was always full o' mischief, leading wee Jamie into all sorts o' trouble. Your husband was raised here, ye know, his own branch o' the clan having passed on."

"He talked of those early years, but after I met Robert, I . . . I had a hard time believing he'd told me right."

"The two of 'em liked nothing better than t' hae a good time, but 'twas Robert who led the way. I couldna' see he had a serious thought in his head when he was a lad."

"Robert?"

"Aye. The lad he used t' be ain't the man he became, not by ha'f. Allus had a dog or two running alongside him, and a crowd, too, sometimes, waiting t' see wha' he was about."

"But he's always so alone now. And the only animals I've seen at Hawthorn are the stock. Certainly nothing like a pet dog, which was one of the things I noticed first. In Texas I always had a couple of hounds to keep me company."

"As did Robbie. He was eighteen when the old laird rode out in a storm. Struck by lightning, he was. The only bairn,

344

Robbie had t' take over the running o' the land. He changed overnight."

Mattie pictured a tall, broad-shouldered youth with laughing brown eyes and wild red hair, his long legs carrying him up the hills and down, his deep voice occasionally bursting into song. She saw him so clearly she could almost reach out and touch him. And she saw those eyes turn solemn and the songs die as he suddenly became a man. Her heart twisted, and she felt a moistness at the back of her eyes.

"Your laird and I have much in common," she said. "Except that when my parents died, there was an uncle to help me run the ranch, and when he was gone, James came along. It was only after I was widowed that I really learned to care for myself."

"Ye were nae one t' weep and wail, were ye, lass?"

"I didn't have the time."

" 'Tis as ye spoke. Robbie and ye have much in common. Taking over as laird was a great responsibility for a lad who wanted nothing more 'n t' court the girls. But he was a Campbell, and he knew his duty. A descendant of kings, he is, an' distant cousin to the ninth duke of Argyll, did ye know that, lass?"

"If I ever thought of it, I would have imagined descendants of kings as somehow, I don't know, maybe more dignified."

"Ye must be thinking o' the English kind."

Mattie grinned. "I must be."

Angus did not return the grin. "After Jamie left for America, Robbie went through a lonely time. Went to Edinburgh, he did, and brought back a wife."

"Was she pretty?" Mattie could not resist asking.

"Aye, bonnie enough if ye like the sort. Too frail, t' my way o' thinking. A rosebud in a land o' thistle. Ye wouldna' hae seen the likes o' her stomping in the mud. But Robbie seemed content enough. She gave birth t' the two bairns, and left."

"Left?" Mattie had not expected that.

Angus nodded. "At least she tried. Took off one night wi' another man, a stranger who'd been passing through, a dealer in wool who stayed at Hawthorn while he took care o' his business. Strange business, it was, that called for stealing another man's wife. The carriage they had taken overturned. Robbie went after them. He found them too late t' save their lives. I thought for a while we'd have t' bury him, too."

Mattie felt the young husband's heartbreak as if it were her own. She'd been right to want to hold him, to give him comfort.

"Her leaving changed him more than his father's death, didn't it, Angus?"

"I knew ye'd ken wha' I had t'say."

"But the girls—"

"He loved them as much as ever, but he never told them wha' had happened. Seven and five, they were, too wee t' hear the truth, and then it seemed too late. He never told anybody but me. We got them back t' the house and Robbie let everyone believe he'd been in the carriage, too. There were rumors, but no one said anything against the laird outright. They respected him too much for that."

"His people really do love him, don't they?"

"We're nae a people for speaking o' love."

"But you feel it."

He looked at her for a long time. "Aye, we do."

"And he could never forgive her, could he? Even though he's longed for her all these years." She felt a hurt that went beyond sympathy.

"That's nae the way it is. His grief was for the mitherless bairns. He forgave the woman, said he'd driven her t' leave. He'd wooed her and then spent his days and ha'f his nights away. She dinna understand. Or maybe it was that she saw the mistake in the marriage more'n Robbie."

"The rose and the thistle."

"Aye. It was himself he couldna' forgive. He sent the bairns away for most o' the year, although it like t' broke his heart. The two of 'em had each other, he told himself, and among them all they made a kind o' peace."

"Then I came along, prickly as a cactus, causing trouble."

"I dinna say 'twas a good peace."

"I guess you didn't, did you? He seldom speaks to his daughters, Angus. Why?"

"He dinna ken how. He's been lonely, and there's things that he forgot."

"Like how to talk, and how to laugh."

They looked at each other for a moment, then Angus looked away to the far hills. "Ye hae a zeal for the land. I've seen it in your eyes more'n once. There's not many foreign born who do." He looked back at her. "I've never seen this cactus you speak of. Is it anything like a rose?"

"Not in the least."

"I dinna think it was."

A gleam lit his rheumy old eyes, and on impulse Mattie gave his hand a squeeze. "Thank you, Angus, for giving me this time."

"I'm hoping I can return the thanks."

"What do you mean?"

"Think on it, lass. You'll ken soon enough wha' I mean." He rose slowly and stretched his legs. "Not much daylight left. You'd best be getting t' the house."

Mattie stood and gave him a hug. She took pleasure in seeing a blush steal across his weathered cheeks.

It was a pensive ride she took back to the stable. She thought about all the things she had said to Robert, and the things he had said to her.

The kiss they had shared took on a special meaning. How long had he denied himself such a show of passion? She suspected it had been since the death of his wife. A tremor came deep inside her. No longer did she feel distress because of what had happened between them; there was no shame because she had returned that kiss.

What she did feel was a foolish, impossible, overwhelming yearning to be back in his arms, to sense the beat of his heart, to feel the touch of his lips. He was lonely, that was true, and had been for many years. She saw that she was lonely, too.

But he had said that what had happened between them must not happen again. With a sense of loss, she admitted he was right. There were complications enough in his life. She must concentrate on the family and forget everything else.

Angus said he loved his daughters, and she believed him. How terrible it must have been, how hurtful when Janet flung out those words of hate. Mattie was responsible for the girl's rebellion since she was the one who had pursued the matter of Christmas; somehow she must heal the rift between Robert and his children.

Had she really been so wrong to insist upon the festivities? She had wanted all the trappings that went with the celebration, and the girls had wanted them, too. But trappings alone had not pushed her into that fight. Whether anyone else in the Highlands believed her, she knew the power of Christmas; she'd experienced it since she was a child.

By the time she reached the stable she had already formed a plan.

4

Mattie waited until after supper to put her plan into motion. With Robert sequestered in the library, where he'd ordered his meal, she began by seeking out a private talk in Janet's room.

This time, not bothering to knock, she barged through the unlocked door and came right to the point. "You have to apologize to your father, Janet."

The girl lay on the bed, her eyes trained on the ceiling. Slowly she turned toward Mattie. "After he apologizes to me."

Mattie recognized the look on her face as one worn often by the patriarch of the house. Mulishness, she called it, although father and daughter probably considered it pride.

"What's he going to apologize for?" she asked. "Denying your request?"

Janet returned to her study of the ceiling. "A small celebration wasn't an unfair thing to ask for."

"Of course it wasn't."

"Then why am I the one at fault?"

"Because you went too far. Because he's the father and you're the child."

"I'm not a child."

"You're acting like one."

"So is he."

"Why don't the both of you go out in the fields and

349

throw stones at each other? Last one standing wins."

"He's bigger than I am."

"And older and the bearer of more responsibility. Until you're of legal age, he gets to make the rules."

"That's unfair." She glanced at Mattie. "You sound just like him."

"And do you hate me, too?"

That one took Janet aback. "Of course not."

"You don't hate him, either."

Tears matted the girl's lashes. "Sometimes I don't like him."

Mattie softened her tone. "And that scares you, doesn't it? Because it makes you think that maybe you really do hate him and you know what a terrible thing that would be." She crossed the room and sat on the edge of the bed. Taking Janet's hand, she was relieved when the girl did not pull away.

Turned again to Mattie, Janet stifled a sob. "Why doesn't he love me? I'm his daughter. His firstborn."

Mattie pulled the girl into her arms, where she cried quietly for a minute. "You're going to have to take what I say on faith, dear. He does love you. He just doesn't know how to say it or how to show it."

"How do you know he does?" Janet asked with a sniffle.

"I said you had to have faith. And you prove it by going down to the library right now." The girl stiffened but Mattie kept on. "You walk right in and like the descendant of kings that you are, you stand straight and you have the courage to tell him you were wrong saying what you did."

"I can't."

"Oh yes you can. Kings, remember? Weren't they warriors, too? They had to be very brave and do what they knew was right."

Janet hiccuped, then held silent for a moment. "I'm a descendant of queens, too."

Mattie eased away and smiled down into a tear-streaked face. "How silly of me not to put it that way." She was rewarded with a tentative grin.

It took several more minutes of talk and a promise to accompany Janet downstairs, but at last Mattie got the yes she was after. After a quick splash of water on her face and a comb pulled hastily through her hair, Janet walked into the hall and down the stairs, Mattie close behind and Amabelle staring after them from the doorway of her room.

One brief knock and they entered the library. Robert was sitting at his desk facing the door, his hands folded over a stack of papers in front of him. The room was chilled, for he had allowed the fire to burn low, and Mattie had the impression he was getting little work done. He was wearing the same open-throated shirt from the afternoon, his hair more unruly than ever, and there was a pinched look to his mouth as he watched them enter.

His eyes drew her attention the most. Watchful and surprised and hurting — she read it all even though he would have denied the hurting with his last breath. Funny how she was beginning to understand this dour Scot. Her heart went out to him, and it wasn't in pity. In a curious way she found she admired that proud, stiff manner he had, even while she wished he would soften toward his girls.

All the breeding that was in Janet must have come to the fore, because she strode ahead of Mattie and stood before her father's desk. "I want to apologize, Papa, for this afternoon. I was wrong to say such things."

Standing aside, Mattie caught the flicker of pleasure in Robert's eyes and the twitch of his lips. "We were hard on each other, lass. Think no more on today. 'Tis best forgotten by us both."

"Thank you, Papa." She turned and started toward the door, then hesitated and looked back toward the desk. "I wasn't wrong to ask, Papa. 'Twas the way I did it that I apologize for. I don't hate you. Anger was talking then."

"And I don't hate you."

Mattie figured it was the closest the two of them could come to declaring love; she turned to follow Janet from the room.

"Stay, Matilda. I'd have a word with you."

"Of course," she said calmly, but it was hardly calm that she felt. Inserting her wishes into the Campbell clan was one thing when Robert was out of sight; facing him was something else, and Mattie knew it was her turn to call on the courage of her ancestors. Surely there was a warrior or two somewhere in her background, if not an actual queen.

She wasn't quite up to standing in front of the desk the way Janet had done, however, and with a nod of acquiescence, she took her place in a fireside chair. "Can we talk over here? The room is cold."

She rested her hands atop the skirt of her blue woolen gown, resisting the urge to fiddle with her hair or even to take up the knitting beside her. He strode to the fire, taking time to toss another log onto the dying flames, and turned to look down at her. Her gaze fell to his worn black boots and when he did not speak, slowly she lifted her eyes, trailing them up the long length of him, taking note of the strong legs beneath the coarsely woven trousers, the flat abdomen, the wide chest, and the hint of chestnut hair in the opening of his shirt. His face was stubbled, his lips set in a line, and when at last she reached his eyes, she saw a flash of the fire she'd seen this afternoon.

She jerked her gaze to the hearth, her stomach knotted, her heart beating like a tom-tom. Oh, there was definitely something between them. Something both of them had to ignore.

"What do you want?" she asked, then held her breath as she waited for his answer.

"You went for a ride today."

She wondered at her disappointment. "Yes, I did. I know that you instructed me not to—"

"Instructed. Aye, that I did, and it was wrong of me to have done so. I'm told you have a fine seat."

She looked back at him. "A what?" she asked, a blush stealing over her cheeks.

"You ride well.

"Oh. Thank you." She felt foolish, knowing he realized

352

her misinterpretation.

"Please ride whenever you choose."

Curiosity drove her to ask, "Why did you change your mind?"

"Just say it's my way of thanking you for getting Janet down here. She would not have come on her own."

"She meant what she said," Mattie assured him, adding hastily, "just then, of course. Not earlier this afternoon."

" 'Twas that earlier time which forced me to some difficult thoughts. If Janet had not come to me, I would have gone to her."

Mattie was tempted to ask what he would have said to his daughter, but he was being so agreeable, she did not want to push her luck. The idea of mentioning Christmas came to her, but she quickly suppressed it. Those difficult thoughts of Robert's could not have included a change of heart about the holiday.

"As you may have noticed," he went on, "I don't deal easily with the lasses."

"I notice you're not calling them bairns."

"They're growing into womanhood. Janet, at least, and Amabelle is not far behind. I pray my second lass will not be so willful as my first."

"Don't count on it. Women have an unfortunate habit of taking on minds of their own."

His face darkened. "Aye, that they do."

Mattie wanted to bite off her tongue. Too well she remembered all that Angus had told her. Had he been wrong? Had the laird cared for his lady more than anyone knew?

Silence descended, and the usually glib Mattie found herself at a loss for words. She had the sinking feeling that if she remained much longer alone with Robert she might start to console him, which would be presumptuous and wrong and humiliating if he, as seemed most likely, rejected her sympathy.

The undeniable truth was his presence unsettled every nerve in her body. With him standing so tall and handsome and so masculine, and worst of all, so very much *near*, she couldn't think straight, couldn't breathe right, couldn't keep her hands from twisting in her lap. Surely he could see her reaction. One kiss hours ago, and she was like a schoolgirl again, hopeful of catching a beau.

Her business here did not involve intimacy with Robert. She'd given herself to no man other than her husband — even though she'd had opportunities back on the ranch — and she wasn't about to throw herself at this one now.

Keeping that thought in mind, she stood and found herself dangerously close to him, so close his breath stirred her hair. She felt the tension between them stronger than ever; it shimmered like heat waves in the air. If he so much as touched her gown, she was lost and he'd have a hard time pushing her away, given the manner in which she would be clinging to him.

"Matilda," he said softly. Her name rolled on his tongue and was almost her undoing. The temptation he offered was like a forbidden fruit. How sweet he would taste, and how wonderful he would feel as they held each other tight. And what a hussy she was to think such things. Just as he was fighting this tension, so must she.

She stumbled away from him and around the fireside chairs, her eyes pinned to the rug, her mumbles along the lines of excuse-making about having to get back to the girls. She doubted he could understand a word. Compared to the stiff-backed Mattie who had entered the library a short time before, a far different woman fled.

Refusing to consider what he was thinking right now, she rushed up the stairs. In the hall she paused to catch her breath. This evening Robert had shown cracks in the solid, somber front he presented to the world, but he wasn't quite ready to let down his guard. For all his acceptance of his daughter's apology, he had remained aloof behind that desk. She wanted to see him gather both of the girls in his arms. And that's all she wanted. Or at least it was all she could allow herself to want.

Once Robert let the warmth of fatherly love openly

change the way he saw life, and the way he saw himself, then perhaps he could accept a far different kind of love. He needed a woman to ease his loneliness. A good Scottish woman, she told herself.

Summoning Amabelle, she invaded the privacy of Janet's bedroom once again. "I've an announcement to make and I need the cooperation of you both. I've figured out a way we can have a small Christmas celebration after all."

"How?" they asked at once.

"You exchange gifts, don't you? Well, you'll give your father a feast and a party. It will be your present to him."

"Papa won't like it," predicted Amabelle.

"Papa will go through the ceiling," Janet said.

Mattie wasn't exactly overwhelmed by their response, but rejecting the worry that they just might be right, she told herself desperate situations called for desperate cures. "It will be a secret. I've brought some shelled pecans from home to make a real Texas pie, and you can show me how to put together haggis and the rest of your Scottish dishes."

She went on with some more suggestions and questions and eventually the girls began to show the enthusiasm for the holiday that they'd shown the night before. At the same time Mattie's own confidence in her Grand Plan returned. All right, so she was interfering, but only because these Campbells were her family. She *needed* them to be.

The magic of the holiday must stay strong in her mind. If for some reason the magic didn't work on Robert, she would humble herself, take complete blame as the adult who had dreamed up the secret, and slink out of the country as soon as she could.

She had reason to doubt the wisdom of her scheme often during the next few days. At first Robert was no more available than he had ever been, but on the second night when he showed up at the table and said he decided to take his meals with them, she wondered if he might not come around all on his own. But it was too late to cancel everything. The girls were so excited, planning the food and arranging for the bagpipes to play, and asking Angus if he would help them invite the closest neighbors to attend the celebration.

Mattie had not really planned on the presence of anyone other than family, but by the time she learned of the expanded party, verbal invitations had already been extended. To keep her own mind away from worry, she turned her hand to cleaning the Great Hall. Cook got several of the women to help her during the day when Robert was far from the house; secrecy was further aided by the fact he never went into what he thought were closed-up rooms.

As she worked, Mattie began to appreciate the beauty of the old stone castle, even more than she had that first day when she'd seen it in the distance, rising like a fortress at the top of the hill. Had kings really walked these rough floors? What laughter, what political intrigues, what confidences had been exchanged here? She wished the walls could talk.

Three days before Christmas, she and the girls decided on a trip to the nearby town to purchase a few supplies—ribbons and scented candles, primarily, and a secret purchase or two that none of the three cared to reveal. The girls could spend the night with the friends they hadn't seen yet during the school holiday, and a cart could be sent for them the following day.

Mattie was surprised when Robert agreed to the plan. She approached him in the library after supper, saying she had volunteered to do the asking. He sat behind his desk while she explained how the girls wanted to visit their friends for one night. It wasn't a lie, but then neither was it the complete truth.

Listening to his deep, rolling *aye* and looking at his thoughtful face looking back at her, she felt the doubts return. Were they doing the right thing in keeping so many secrets from him? Would he forget the initial anger that was sure to come and let the spirit of the day overtake him? Or had she gone too far this time?

It was to the last question that she gave her own silent *aye*. This time she had gone too far. It wasn't something she could admit to the girls, however, not this far along in the planning, and early the next day under a cold, gray sky they set out in the carriage. At Robert's insistence, one of the Hawthorn men held the reins, although Mattie had assured him she was fully capable of handling the team.

After making a few purchases and depositing the girls with their friends, two sisters close to their own age who readily welcomed them for the night, she climbed back into the carriage for the return ride.

By the time she arrived, her mind was made up. Difficult though it might be, she would go directly to the library and tell Robert what was going on. If he wanted to cast her into the night, she wouldn't blame him, but she couldn't help but think that with the gentler manner he'd been exhibiting over the past few days, he wouldn't be too angry, especially since she was confessing everything of her own free will.

Tossing her cloak onto the bannister of the stairway, and her bonnet, gloves, and packages onto the bottom step, she smoothed her blue gown and pulled an unruly curl into place, then headed toward the closed library door. He wasn't inside and she went to the kitchen to ask Cook where he might be. The woman, tight-lipped and pale, gestured toward the Great Hall.

"He noticed the clean windows from outside."

"Oh, no." Before Mattie's courage could fail her, she hurried along the downstairs hallway and through the open door of the large room. The draperies were pulled open, allowing what little was left of the afternoon light to spill inside. His back to the door, Robert stood by the cold fireplace that Mattie had paid two workers to clean. He still wore his heavy black coat, and chestnut hair brushed against the collar.

Slowly he turned to face her. A dozen yards separated them, but she could feel his anger; it struck her much as a blow from his hand would have done.

"Is it Christmas you're planning in here?" he asked. His voice was as chill as the air. "Tell me it's not, Matilda."

There was no pleasure in the way he said her name.

"I was going to talk to you tonight."

"Were you now?"

Mattie swallowed. All her courage seemed to drain away and puddle at her feet.

"Yes, I was. I decided a secret was not such a good idea."

"So you say."

"It's the truth." Even with shadows falling across his features, she saw he did not believe her; she saw he felt betrayed. The distance between them became unbearable, and on shaky legs she hurried across the room, stopping in front of him, hands clinched at her sides. "It's the truth," she repeated, softer.

Cold brown eyes stared down and chilled her bones. "How far has it gone?" he asked.

"We've started the food—"

"Cook's in on it, too."

"And Angus has asked the neighbors."

"Angus? That surprises me."

"He didn't want to be a part of it, but the girls begged and he could not turn them down. Oh, Robert, it was all my idea. Nobody wanted to do any of this, but I talked them into it."

"You've a manner about you that turns things upside down, don't you, lass?"

Her heart broke at the bitterness in his voice. "I wanted to make things right with you and the girls. That's all."

"You've a strange way of going about it, talking them into lies."

Mattie hugged herself. "It was wrong. I freely admit it." She could not stand the way he looked at her, and in her nervous state she hurried to add, "It's just that when I heard about their mother—"

"What about their mother?" The words fell like stones from his lips.

Mattie felt a buzzing in her ears and thought she might faint. What had driven her to say such a thing? Was her brain not functioning at all? She felt like a man who was digging his own grave.

"I heard she died when they were young."

"You can do better than that. Angus told you the truth."

There was no way she could deny it. "I went out to him and asked questions. It was after you kissed me and after Janet said those terrible things. I was confused and worried. I wanted to talk to you, to understand how you felt and see if I could help, but you were no where to be found. I felt responsible—"

"Enough." No longer the proud, angry Scot, he sounded weary enough to be carrying the world on his shoulders. " 'Tis too late to cancel this celebration you've been so intent on. I'll play the host as best I can, but do not think there will be any pleasure in the doing. And I have one favor to ask of you, if you can find it in yourself to do what I ask."

"Whatever you say," she whispered.

"Leave the girls to me. I will deal with them when they return tomorrow. I am their father. Surely even you can see that is my right."

She nodded, her throat too tight for her to say another word. He took a wide path around her. She turned and watched him walk out the door. Unable to stand any longer, she sank to the floor, her skirt pooling up around her, and felt her heart turn to lead.

"I'm sorry," she whispered into the cold, empty silence of the vast room. Little he cared, nor should he. For all the best intentions—the usual excuse she made when trying to go around his wishes—she had hurt him, and the hurt returned to her a thousand fold.

She had known him little more than two weeks, this

proud, stubborn, vulnerable man who once had been an enigma to her. Now she knew his every thought. That was the way of a woman in love.

Oh yes, against all reason and most certainly against all hope, she had taken him into her heart and she knew that whether she ever saw him again after this disastrous visit, she would hold him there forever.

5

After a solitary supper that she did not eat and a restless evening spent pacing her room, Mattie fell into bed shortly after ten, hoping for the oblivion of sleep that did not come. Never had she felt so unhappy, not when her parents died because she had been too young to realize how permanent death really was, and not when James, too, passed away. She had loved him, but theirs had been a quiet kind of love that hadn't reached her soul.

Everything was different now. All that she thought or dreamed or felt was colored by Robert. A single kiss had stirred passions she never imagined before, but her caring went beyond a physical heat. She wanted to suffer his wounds, to free him from pain, and if her leaving quietly was what he wanted, then no matter the cost in happiness, she would do that, too. Huddled beneath a blanket, she realized the worst thing about going was that she would never know how he fared.

She lay still, too miserable to be restless. She estimated it was after midnight when Robert entered his adjoining room and slammed the door closed. Usually he didn't disturb her when he retired, but there was nothing usual about tonight. She heard his heavy footsteps pacing, heard the door to his wardrobe open and close, heard the pacing begin again.

Picturing his long stride as it took him back and forth

within the confines of the bedroom, she wanted to cry but the tears would not come. She'd asked once if he disliked her; he said no, but he certainly did now. She'd seen to that.

Was it the ultimate torture to lie here and listen to his anger? She could stand it no longer, and she got up from the bed. Her actions seemed directed by someone other than herself as she donned a white wrapper over her white cotton gown. Barefooted, she left her room and knocked at his door.

He flung it open so quickly, she wondered if he'd been about to come to her. Dressed in shirt and trousers, he made her feel foolish standing in his doorway in her night wear.

"I heard you in here," she said. He did not help her with a response. "I wanted to explain again. If you'll hear me out."

He stepped aside and motioned for her to enter. She did so slowly, cautiously, her heart pounding so loudly that she thought surely he could count the beats. She tried to concentrate on the room. She'd never been inside and she let her eyes trail over the drawn draperies on the opposite wall, the wardrobe on the wall backing against her room to the left and the banked coals in the small stone fireplace to her right. Most of all she saw the high, wide four-poster bed that occupied most of the room.

Behind her, Robert closed the door and she turned to face him. He stood straight and tall as ever, his nut-brown eyes masking whatever he felt. She wanted to smooth the shock of hair from his forehead and to kiss the frown lines around his mouth, and then tell him what she had to say. But she saw no sign of the man who had called her a shooting star, the one who compared her hair to the moon.

Mattie tried to imagine herself back on the ranch handling one of the hands who was sure he knew more about cattle than any woman ever could. She failed. This was Robert, tough and tender, unapproachable and vulnerable, and altogether endearing. In all the world he was unique, and so was this new-found feeling inside her. There was nothing for her to do but take a deep breath and begin.

"Whether you believe it or not, I did it for you." The words came easier than she had thought, and she hurried on. "It wasn't because I did not care what you wanted. It was because I cared so much. I thought that if you saw the lights and the laughter and saw the shared happiness . . . if you felt the true magic of the day, then you would want to have good times again."

"Listen to me, Matilda. I've no patience with these good times you speak of. There's enough to do running the lands and seeing that the people are adequately rewarded for their work without adding complications."

"But they're not complications. They're reasons for living. This work you speak of. I found myself doing nothing else but working. For five years I thought it was enough. And yet I must have always felt something was missing because when I was offered good money for my ranch, I took little time to decide to sell. I surprised myself as much as I did the hands."

She took a deep breath, waiting for him to say something, but when he did not she went on. "The idea for a journey to foreign places came to me right away, and I knew that journey had to begin here. Do you believe in fate, Robert? Maybe it was really fate that sent a wealthy rancher to my door. And maybe it was fate that made Janet write the letter inviting me here."

"What fanciful things are you saying, lass?"

"I don't know. I don't seem to know what I'm going to tell you until the words are already out, but I believe everything I've said. With all my heart. You speak of complications. I'm a complication, I know, but you're a complication to me. I care about what worries you and I regret more than you can ever know that I have become one of those worries."

"You're an interfering woman, Matilda."

"You didn't mind my interfering when it came to Janet's apology. But I'm not supposed to interfere with you."

"My worries are my own. I'll not have your pity."

"Good thing because you haven't got it." She wanted to tell him all that she felt, but there were some things she could not say. "You have my respect," she said instead, "and my good will."

His eyes warmed as he looked down at her wrapper, and she saw a softening of his lips. "And is that all I have?" He took a step toward her, and her breath caught. He moved close. "Tell the truth, Matilda. Have I nothing more?"

He brushed the back of his hand against her cheek. The hand was rough, a working man's hand, and she liked the way it dragged across her skin. She stared into his eyes and everything that had ever simmered between them returned, hotter than ever and more insistent.

"You know you do," she murmured.

"Tell me all that you want right now." What a demanding Scot he was, but he asked for no more than she was willing to reveal.

"I want you to kiss me again, only this time I don't want you to push me away." Slowly she undid the tie of her wrapper, and the garment slipped to the floor. She watched his eyes lower to her breasts. "I want you to make love to me, Robert. I've never wanted anything more in my life."

"Ah, lass," he said as he crushed her in his arms. "I've fought it long enough, God knows. I want the same." When his lips came down on hers, it seemed that all the hunger he'd kept pent up over the years was let loose. Enfolded in his commanding embrace, she felt small and delicate, yet strong enough to welcome all the passion he had to give. She was liquid fire.

With her arms wrapped around his neck, she felt the full size of his shoulders; when she touched her tongue to his, he shuddered and she felt the depth of his need. He broke the kiss, but he did not try to push her away. "It's been a long time, lass." His voice was a rasp.

She did what she had yearned to do when she first came into the room. She brushed the hair from his forehead, stealing a moment to wind the thick chestnut curls around her fingers, and she kissed the frown lines by his lips. "It's been a long time for me, too."

His mouth once again was on hers, and his powerful hands stroked her back, then moved lower to caress the curve of her buttocks. She was naked underneath the gown, and it seemed he was touching her skin.

He shifted her higher, holding her tight against him, and his swollen shaft pressed between her thighs. The sudden intimacy sent bolts of sensation shooting through her. This time it was she who shuddered.

"I'll not hurt you," he whispered into her parted lips. "I'll stop if I do."

"Oh, Robert, you'll not hurt me. My body was made for this." She kissed him. "I want you so much."

His ran his thumb along the outline of her mouth. "Don't think me daft, but I want to look at you without the gown. For a wee bit without the touching. If I touch you, it will be over too fast."

Mattie fought a wave of shyness. Robert wanted to see her, and she wanted to please him as much as she wanted to please herself. They had both waited a very long time, and everything must be right.

Freeing herself from his embrace, she undid the buttons of her gown and pulled first one side and then the other past her shoulders, revealed the fullness of her breasts and then the taut nubs. His intake of breath was as erotic as his touch.

The gown joined the wrapper on the floor, and she stood before him naked, her blond hair loose about her shoulders, one thick strand falling across her breast and curling around the tip. He took a long time to look at her, his eyes like the banked coals in the fire as they lingered on her breasts, on her long, slender legs, and at last on the triangle of pale pubic hair. Mattie thought her legs would buckle from the heat of his gaze.

"I want to see you, Robert," she managed, although she did not recognize her voice. "Call me daft."

His eyes moved to hers, and they both smiled. "I'm not near so beautiful," he said.

His huskiness pleased her. "I'll bet you are."

As he pulled the shirt from the waistline of his trousers, she watched his fingers at work, following them as they unfastened each button, saw the broad chest that was shaped by muscles just as she imagined it would be. Fine golden hair grew thick close to his throat and between the brown nipples, then thinned out at his waist.

He threw the shirt aside, and she studied his arms, taut skin pulled tight and corded with sinew, the lower parts covered by the same fine hair that dusted his chest. Everything about him gave testimony to the hard work he had put in through the years, and her fingers itched to explore what she saw.

He made short work of his boots and socks, and then came the rest of his clothing. Shy and eager at the same time, she concentrated on his legs, on the gloriously muscled calves and hard, strong thighs.

"You'd look good in kilts. Will I see you in them?"

" 'Tis the dress for Christmas day."

She hated to hear him mention the holiday, afraid he would be reminded of their troubles, and tonight she wanted nothing to go wrong.

Her eyes went to his manhood, and she could not breathe. His hair was darker there, and he was magnificent. "You were wrong, Robert. You are beautiful." Her eyes eased up to his. "Touch me. I cannot wait any—"

She was in his arms so quickly that she forgot the rest of her words. This time, skin to skin, she lost her hold on reason. With his lips pressed to her hair, he swept her up and carried her to the bed, resting her gently in the center as he lay down beside her. The counterpane was cool against her back, but every other part of her burned.

Words were lost as they stroked and caressed each other, Robert's powerful torso and long, strong legs covering her slender body, then shifting away, tantalizing her as much as his hands and his lips. His stubbled cheek scratched against her nakedness, and she loved the sensation. His rough palm brought even sharper delights as he rubbed it across her nipples, and then his tongue touched the tight buds as if to soothe them. Soft, steady cries came from her throat.

At first she kept her eyes closed and reveled in his love-making, but she found an even greater rapture when she looked at his face. His eyes were dark and deep with longing and admiration as he gazed upon her body, and his lips were swollen, as she knew hers must be.

When he slipped his hands between her thighs and felt the moist heat that told him she was ready, he looked into her eyes and without words his gaze told her it was time. Positioning himself between her parted legs, he slipped inside her, letting her tight, long-untouched body take the full length of him slowly. His thrusts were likewise slow at first, and then as her own hungers became more urgent, he quickened the pace. She reached rapture just before he did, and she rejoiced in the powerful shudders that coursed through him as she held him tight.

At last the shudders subsided, but they continued to cling together, their skin slick with sweat where they touched, Robert's fingers gently stroking the damp curls away from her face. She felt smaller than ever, enfolded in a tender embrace by a forceful, strong-willed man. And in her own right, she felt forceful, too, able to bring him to an unaccustomed tenderness.

With great care, as though she might break, he pulled away, shifted the covers from beneath them, and tugged them back up for warmth against the night air. As if Mattie would ever be cold again.

Lying beside her with his head propped on his hand, he surprised her with a boyish grin. She brushed the hair from his forehead. "I've made you laugh?"

"I'm laughing at myself, Matilda. I feared I had forgotten what to do."

She grinned back at him. "It was a foolish fear."

"Aye, that it was." Shifting her around so that she faced

the other way, he pulled her against him and their bodies curved together. Again he stroked her hair.

"We'll have the wedding after New Year's. 'Tis best if we wait."

"Wedding?" She could not keep the surprise from her voice.

"You did not think I'd take you to my bed, woman, unless I made you my wife."

He sounded hurt, as though she had offended him, but this time Mattie gave no thought to his feelings, wrapped up as she was in her own confusion. Somehow she had missed the proposal and more, she had missed the declaration of love.

"The lasses will be pleased," he said, then with a chuckle added, "Angus, too. And there's many a Campbell who'll be struck mute with shock."

Mattie could barely breathe. He made it all sound so definite. He bedded her, he wedded her, and that was the end of that. In truth, she would have given all that she had in the world to be his wife, but only if he let her through the shadows of his thoughts. He made love to her magnificently, but they had never had a real and honest talk.

She called herself a fool. Could she really turn him down? But he had never asked. He ordered, even told her when the ceremony would be, and she could see that before long he might easily slip back into the withdrawn, brusque man who had met her at the train. At night the passionate lover, by day the private man.

When he kissed her that first time, he spoke of his honor, and Angus had said he was a man who saw his duty and did what he must. Honor and duty were wonderful qualities, but they were no substitute for love.

Mattie stopped herself. Having lain with Robert, she was more than ever certain of her feelings, and she must not make the mistake of assuming his too soon. He might truly care for her, but could she ask him how he felt? She thought not; the words must come from his heart. Perhaps by Christmas, two short days away, he would have declared himself in ways that left no doubt how he felt. The magic of the day might give him the words.

She eased away from him and turned around. With her head on the pillow beside his, she asked that their plans remain a secret until after the holiday. "Let's have one celebration at a time," she said.

"I'd like to tell the lasses."

"Then you might as well tell the world. Do this for me, Robert. We've already enough to deal with if we want to make this holiday right. Remember, you Scots aren't used to this kind of celebration, and I'm going to have to show you how it's done."

For a moment she thought she had gone too far, bringing up her interfering manner that way, but he merely shrugged. "If you say so. You know my opinions all too well about this tomfoolery, but I'll go along as best I can."

Was love tomfoolery, too? And even marriage? Would he someday feel as though she had trapped him by coming to his room? Afraid he might see the fear in her eyes, she closed them and pretended to go to sleep but it was a long time before the questions would ease enough for her to rest.

6

Mattie greeted Robert's returning daughters at midmorning the next day with the announcement their father knew about Christmas and was willing to participate.

"Did you hold a gun to him?" asked Janet as she clambered down from the pony cart which had been sent to fetch them.

"Not exactly." A flush stole over Mattie as she remembered the exact moment Robert promised he'd "not be a burden on the day." Still in bed, they'd been holding each other as he growled the words against her neck.

"He saw the Great Hall was missing some dust and he figured out what was going on," she said.

Amabelle, her arms loaded with packages, accepted assistance from the Hawthorn stable hand who had been at the reins of the cart. Standing beside her sister in the carriageway, she smiled up at Mattie. "We bought gifts in town after you left."

"Hush." Janet poked her with an elbow. "They're supposed to be a secret."

"Your father's out in the fields gathering branches to decorate the hall," said Mattie. "I'll bet he would welcome your help."

In excited agreement the girls hurried inside to leave their purchases and Mattie turned her feet toward the kitchen, where the makings for pecan pies awaited. She found Cook devoting her energy to the scraping of a sheep's stomach.

As the two worked side by side, Cook explained how the stomach would be soaked in cold water overnight, stuffed with sheep's innards, oatmeal and onions, along with various seasonings, then boiled slowly.

"We'll serve it on Christmas Eve, along with neeps and nips."

Cautiously asking for a definition, Mattie was relieved to hear they were mashed turnips and whiskey.

" 'Tis a fine dish to set before the laird," Cook said.

Mattie did not admit she would prefer a thick slice of roasted beef or one of the more traditional parts of lamb.

She kept quiet for the rest of the day, devoting her energies to the food preparation and to the decorating of the hall after Robert and the girls returned with the branches of evergreen.

"I've got a lot on my mind," she explained over a late supper when Janet asked if she was worried about something. "I've done so much talking about the celebration, now I've got to see that everyone is satisfied."

"I've no doubt you will, Matilda," Robert said, a spark in his eyes. It was the only time he'd made even the slightest reference to their lovemaking since they scrambled out of bed shortly after dawn.

For the rest of the meal he devoted his attention to the girls. That was exactly the way it should be, Mattie told herself as she left the table early, explaining she still had much to do before retiring.

And indeed she did, most of it thinking as she put her knitting needles to work in the privacy of her room. Outside the winter wind howled, and she could not shake the feeling that if she awoke to a world of white, Robert would say the words she longed to hear before the holiday was done.

In case snow did not fall, she came up with another plan, this one involving only her. To her dismay, she pulled open the draperies the next morning and stared out at a gray sky and a stretch of brown rolling hills. Putting the girls to work with ribbons and candles in the Great Hall, she told Robert she needed to make a last-minute trip into town.

He stared at her wonderingly. Before he could see her heart in her eyes, she turned away, saying at Christmas it was best not to be inquisitive.

She returned less than three hours later, just as father and daughters strode in from the fields, a freshly cut tree in tow. Knowing how he felt about such "nonsense," she loved him all the more. To her surprise, Cook came up with gingerbread decorations baked the night before, and the tree took its place beside the hearth in the Great Hall.

As darkness settled over the cold land, the room was lit with a hundred candles and the blazing yule log that Angus and several of the workers had fetched at Mattie's request. The stone walls took on the glow Mattie had pictured in her mind.

"The wanderers will be arriving soon," Janet said as the Campbells gathered in front of the fire.

" 'Tis traditional," Robert explained, "although we've not recognized the custom in these parts for years. Bad luck it is to turn anyone away on this night."

"Like *Las Posadas* in South Texas," Mattie observed, then translated, "The Inns. A procession walks through town re-enacting the journey of Joseph and Mary in Bethlehem. When they are taken in, a celebration is held."

She went on to describe the *piñatas,* paper figures stuffed with candy and toys and broken open by blindfolded children wielding sticks.

"Seems a dangerous undertaking," Robert said. "I'd fear for our safety if Janet were so armed." He shot an affectionate glance toward his elder daughter, who pretended not to have heard.

"I think it sounds wonderful," said Amabelle. "I wish we could have one of those whatever you said."

"I suppose we could stuff a sheep's stomach with candy and hang it by the fire," Mattie said with a straight face.

The girls giggled and Robert shook his head, and Mattie felt like part of the family.

The moment was interrupted by Cook and two women who had volunteered to help with the food. They came in bearing trays and bowls, setting them on the tables which had been dragged into the room, and Mattie excused herself to help.

Haggis and shortbread, neeps and nips, this was a Scottish

feast, and Mattie found she liked it all. As Janet had predicted, the knocker on the carriageway door was soon banging, and the first of the wanderers appeared. The parade of visitors, most of them workers on the Campbell land, continued through the evening. All were served, with more than a few casting surreptitious looks of surprise at their laird as he moved among them, wishing them all a merry Christmas.

Angus and Robert spent some time together in friendly conversation, and Mattie was relieved to see no sign that Robert was angry over confidences revealed.

Long after midnight the last of the wanderers left, and as the family settled into chairs before the fire, the girls begged for the exchange of gifts.

"Amabelle won't rest," Janet explained, "unless it's done."

"Amabelle," Robert said. "Of course. And you wouldn't be hoping for a surprise or two yourself?"

"Papa, I'm much too old to get excited over such things."

"I'm not," Robert said, his brown eyes twinkling, and Mattie was filled with such warmth that she had to restrain herself from settling into his lap and kissing him smack on the lips. But he did not look her way, and the urge cooled.

Mattie and the girls excused themselves to hurry upstairs for their arm loads of packages, and within minutes they were all back in front of the fire. The girls tore into theirs first, Janet giving up on any attempt to be far too "old" to enjoy such an activity.

Mattie had brought them black lace *mantillas* to drape over their heads and Spanish combs for their hair, along with two cornhusk figures of young girls. It didn't take long for Janet to end up with both of the shawls and Amabelle to claim the dolls.

Robert presented them with new dresses and bound blank pages where they could record their thoughts. "Sometimes 'tis best to write down what pleases or displeases," he said with a look at Janet, "afore we speak what we feel."

"The point is well taken, Papa," she said.

And sometimes. Mattie thought, *it's imperative to speak what we feel.*

Maybe she should have gone ahead and said she loved him. But then, she thought with a heaviness of heart, if he had followed her declaration with one of his own, she would never know whether honor drove him to speak.

"It's our turn," said Janet as she and Amabelle pulled more presents from under the tree. A pipe and tobacco went to their father — "I noticed you've been without yours," Janet explained — and a book of Robert Burns poetry for Mattie.

"I hope you like it," Amabelle said shyly, and Mattie gave both girls a hug.

At last it was time for her to exchange gifts with Robert, and she handed him two packages, one containing the blue and brown Campbell tartan that had belonged to her late husband, and the second, the matching woolen scarf she had been knitting since she arrived.

"You can use it to polish your boots," she said.

"Nay, Matilda," said Robert. "I'll wear it with pride."

There and then she decided he wasn't always the honorable man since he had resorted to a lie, and she smiled her appreciation at his words. If the smile was a bit forced, Robert seemed not to notice.

And then it was time for his gift to her. Excusing himself, he left the room and she wondered if perhaps he might be going for something special. A ring? A silly thought. He had promised to keep their betrothal a secret. But sometimes a man carried away by love did crazy things.

Robert carried away? Never, she thought, and she should not expect it. But oh, how she wanted him to stride back into the hall, throw himself in front of her chair, and against all that she had asked of him, reach for her hand. Mattie knew she was being unreasonable, but she could not change how she felt. Her heart soared with love every time she saw him and ached with regret when she could detect no sign that he felt the same.

Robert returned within a few minutes, hands hidden at his back. The high-pitched bark she heard from behind him as he strode into the room told her he was not holding a ring. A dozen feet from the hearth, he came to a halt and kneeled.

"Angus told me of your love for pets," he said as he deposited a russet and white collie puppy on the floor. "I decided it was time we had one around here. You'll have to name her, but she's already trained to doing her business outside."

Mattie was touched and heartbroken at the same time. Chastising herself for being unreasonable, she knelt beside Robert and scooped up the puppy, who licked her cheek. "She's beautiful," Mattie said in all sincerity. "Thank you."

Janet and Amabelle joined her on the floor and as Robert backed away, the three took turns petting the frisky animal, who exhibited enough enthusiasm to take all that they gave.

Cook entered with a pot of chocolate. "If ye won't be wanting anything else, I'll bid good night. We've a busy day on the morrow."

Mattie poured, then cradling each of her gifts she excused herself to settle the collie for the night. Finding the right size box, along with woolen scraps for lining, took a while. As she placed the puppy and makeshift bed on the floor of her room, one soulful glance from a pair of soft brown eyes and she was on the rug, stroking the dog with one hand and turning the pages of her book with the other.

One poem caught her eye: "To a Louse on Seeing One on a Lady's Bonnet at Church." Only a Scot could pick such a topic, she thought, and was struck by a particular couplet:

O wad some Power the giftie gie us
To see oursels as ithers see us!

How should she see herself, she wondered as she returned to the Great Hall. Robert was sitting in front of the fire, both girls nestled in his broad lap. They did not hear her enter.

"She was a fair young lass. The bonniest in all of Edinburgh," he was saying, and Mattie realized with a start he was speaking of his wife. "From what you said, Janet, the other day in the library, you know something of what happened between us. I worked hard and she grew lonely. 'Twas a stormy night she decided to leave. Her death was an accident, a terrible thing for which I have grieved."

"Did you love her?" asked Janet.

"Aye. And I love both the bairns she gave me."

"I love you, Papa," both girls said in unison.

Mattie brushed a tear from her cheek. Here was what she had wanted—the bringing together of the Campbell clan—but she could not rejoice for at that moment she saw herself for what she was: a lonely woman who had intruded upon the home of a lonely man. She'd brought changes, and for that she felt good, but all those changes did not make her belong.

Quietly she exited the room and sought refuge in her room, but after the previous night spent in Robert's arms, she found the bed cold and lonely. Within five minutes she had the puppy beside her in the bed. Stroking the collie's soft hair, she decided her fact-finding trip into town that morning had been a good idea. As soon as Christmas was done, she would use her knowledge to alleviate what would become a painful situation for the laird of the Campbell clan.

Christmas morning was spent preparing the day's feast, roasted beef and pecan pie being the main features, and Robert made no attempt to speak to her alone. In the afternoon a huge bonfire was lit on the grounds near the house, and the crowds began to gather. Robert appeared in his kilts, and Mattie saw she had been right. With those fine, strong legs of his, he looked magnificent.

Which did not help to ease the ache that had become a part of her. Bagpipes played as the fire began to die, and the pipers entered the Great Hall, where the dancing began. By now Robert had the crowd warmed to his new demeanor, and he delighted them by demonstrating he was light on his feet. Included in one of the rounds, Mattie demonstrated that so was she.

After the feast, as the sun went down, Angus took her aside.

"Lass, ye have worked miracles, but it seems to these auld eyes ye dinna share in the pleasures o' the day."

"Whatever are you talking about?" she asked brightly.

" 'Tis ye and Robbie I'm speaking of."

"Everything is fine. You can see he's not upset that we planned this without telling him."

"Tha's not wha' I mean, lass."

She grew solemn. "Trust me, Angus. All will be made right." Afraid he would ask for particulars, she withdrew and avoided his company for the rest of the evening.

When the last guest had departed, she excused herself, claiming a headache, and Robert exclaimed with a frown that she had been working far too hard. She wanted to kiss those worry lines from his face, as she had often yearned to do; instead, she assured him she would be all right.

Asking Amabelle to take the puppy for the night, she hurried upstairs to write the letter she had been composing in her mind the past two days.

7

Robert lay still in the early morning hour and felt an ache for Matilda such as he had never felt before. His bed was a cold and lonely place without the woman who would be his wife. He had wanted to take her into his arms a thousand times during the past days, but she had asked that he refrain and he had done so. The sacrifice had come at great cost to his physical well-being.

A glance at his bedside clock told him the hour was seven, late indeed for a man used to rising well before dawn, but he'd stayed up late with his lasses talking and listening. It had been a time to treasure; the only thing to make it perfect would have been to have his future wife by his side.

He glanced again at the clock. The girls would be sleeping for hours yet. Matilda no doubt wished to sleep late herself after all her hard work, but it was a wish he was not prepared to grant. He'd waited until after Christmas, just as he promised. Now it was time to extract a few promises of his own—like a ceremony as soon as arrangements could be made.

Pulling on his trousers, he did not bother with a shirt as he stole from his room and knocked on Matilda's door. When she did not respond, he entered the room, his bare feet making no noise on the carpeted floor. The bedcovers were thrown back, but Mattie was not to be found. She must have arisen early, he told himself, and then he spied the folded paper on the bedside table. It bore his name.

Within a quarter hour he was dressed and riding like a man possessed along the road to town. Within another quarter hour he spied the Campbell pony cart far ahead, its pace brisk beneath the leaden sky, and he took off cross country to shorten the distance.

Matilda must have heard him as he rejoined the road directly behind her, for she applied a whip to the flanks of the horse. Robert spurred his mount beside her and with the wheel dangerously close to the stallion's pounding hoofs, he grabbed for the reins. She turned panicked eyes on him and did the work he had been trying to do, jerking back on the reins until the cart came to a halt.

She gasped for breath. "You could have been killed."

Astride the restless stallion, Robert pulled the letter from his coat. "What kind of foolishness is this?"

He watched her eyes grow stubborn and her chin tilt. He wanted to shake her and to kiss her at the same time, but he forbore doing either one.

"I said what I had to say, Robert. Now please let me get on my way. The coach for Inverary leaves before long, and I have to arrange for someone to return the cart."

"You've a mind for details. I'm to send your baggage to Edinburgh and that will be the end of that."

"It's for the best, Robert. If you let that temper of yours settle, you will agree."

She said the wrong thing. Robert bounded from horse to ground in a flash and before she could react, he was up in the cart beside her. " 'Twas not temper that brought me out on this cold morning, Matilda. I'm taking you home where you belong, and I'll not hear a nay."

He expected her to turn on him, to flay him with words that he was prepared to answer. What he did not expect was the rounding of her shoulders and the solemn face she lifted to him. Her hair was in a tangle beneath her bonnet, and there were shadows under her eyes. Robert felt such a tenderness for her that he thought his heart would break.

"I can't," she said softly. "It's time for me to leave."

"You didn't write why and I've yet to hear the words from your lips. Have you changed your mind about becoming my bride?"

"You never asked me."

"Nay, you're wrong. I held you in my arms and—"

"And announced we would be wed. I took it for a sign of your honor, Robert, since I had so brazenly come to your room and you had not ordered me away."

" 'Twould have taken a man of stone to close that door to you, and surely you remember I am very much a man of flesh."

She looked away. "Oh, yes, I remember. But you didn't ask me to be your wife; you informed me. And there were other words you did not say. I had the foolish notion that if the snow would fall, then I would hear what I needed to hear and all would be well." Her eyes went to the threatening skies. "But I got neither, and I knew what must be done."

She shifted her glance to him. "You are a man who knows his duty, but you do not owe me the rest of your life."

Robert ran a hand through his hair, and as though the action cleared his mind, he saw what she meant. Turning her to face him, his hands gripping her shoulders, he looked into those sad and beautiful blue eyes.

"I love you, Matilda Campbell, more than I've loved anyone and for more reasons than there are minutes in the day. You brought happiness to Hawthorn once again, and it's been an age since those walls have heard laughter and music and song. You've made the lasses look upon the old castle as their home, and you've made me a happy man. Up until this morning, when I confess to a wee bit of displeasure."

She opened her mouth to speak, but he stilled her words with a kiss. He felt no withdrawal on her part, but rather a softening against him and a yielding of her lips that brought him great satisfaction. It was a long while before he let her breathe, and when she did it was to whisper, "I love you."

"Will you be my bride? I could kneel beside the cart, but I'd have to let you go and I'm not of a mind for that just yet."

"You're doing everything just right. Except—" He saw the

381

worry lines between her eyes, and he brushed his lips against them.

"What bothers you, lass? I want your mind at rest."

"I can't help wondering if you're just telling me what you know I want to hear. I kept waiting for you to say something the past two days."

Robert decided then and there that he would never completely understand this woman, even though he would love her to the end of his days.

"You asked me to keep silent, and so I did." He grinned. " 'Tis a lesson in obedience you could learn."

Her lips twitched. "If I do say yes, I can't promise always to obey. What I do promise is to talk things out with you. If you will talk."

"I can't promise always to talk." He caught the return of the frown. "You ask much of a private man, but if anyone can change my ways, 'tis you." He kissed her again to seal the promise. "I need an answer, Matilda. Will you be my bride?"

"Oh, yes, Robert." This time she kissed him, and he was the one who came up for air.

"You'll make a fine Scot, lass. You're stubborn and outspoken, and you've the courage of a thousand Campbell warriors."

"They're words to warm a woman's heart."

"And you're the bonniest in the land." Which called for another kiss. Robert was getting decidedly uncomfortable with all this kissing that required him to remain seated and apart from her more than he wanted. She had indeed sparked in him the fires of passion, and the heat was fast becoming unbearable.

He hopped down to tie the stallion to the back of the cart. Something in the air caught his eye and he glanced around. "Look, Matilda. It's snowing."

He watched as she stared at the soft white crystals drifting around her. Leaning forward, she tried to catch them in her hand. "It disappears."

"Not for long. You didn't get your white Christmas, my

382

love, but you'll be having a white Hogmanay, there's no doubt."

"What did you say?" she said as she got down from the cart and stood beside him.

"Hogmanay? 'Tis our name for New Year's."

"Before."

"White Christmas?" He teased, knowing what she meant.

"In between, Robert. What did you call me?"

He took her in his arms. "My love."

She wrapped her arms about his neck. "I wanted to hear you say it again, my darling, darling Scot. You do love me, don't you? That's more important than any falling snow. It's the most important thing in the world."

FEEL THE FIRE IN CAROL FINCH'S ROMANCES!

BELOVED BETRAYAL (2346, $3.95)

Sabrina Spencer donned a gray wig and veiled hat before blackmailing rugged Ridge Tanner into guiding her to Fort Canby. But the costume soon became her prison—the beauty had fallen head over heels in love!

LOVE'S HIDDEN TREASURE (2980, $4.50)

Shandra d'Evereux felt her heart throb beneath the stolen map she'd hidden in her bodice when Nolan Elliot swept her out onto the veranda. It was hard to concentrate on her mission with that wily rogue around!

MONTANA MOONFIRE (3263, $4.95)

Just as debutante Victoria Flemming-Cassidy was about to marry an oh-so-suitable mate, the towering preacher, Dru Sullivan flung her over his shoulder and headed West! Suddenly, Tori realized she had been given the best present for a bride: a night of passion with a real man!

THUNDER'S TENDER TOUCH (2809, $4.50)

Refined Piper Malone needed bounty-hunter, Vince Logan to recover her swindled inheritance. She thought she could coolly dismiss him after he did the job, but she never counted on the hot flood of desire she felt whenever he was near!

Available wherever paperbacks are sold, or order direct from the Publisher. Send cover price plus 50¢ per copy for mailing and handling to Zebra Books, Dept. 3589, 475 Park Avenue South, New York, N.Y. 10016. Residents of New York, New Jersey and Pennsylvania must include sales tax. DO NOT SEND CASH.